SomeWhere SomeTime

GERALD B. KEANE

DESTINY PUBLISHING

New York• Sarasota •Tombstone

Disclaimer

SomeWhere SomeTime is a work of fiction. Everything within its covers, including parts of this disclaimer, is the product of the author's imagination and does not recount actual events. Any similarity to real events is purely coincidental.

Actual names of living persons have been used for some characters, utterly without permission or authorization. The actions, conduct, and motivations of the characters do not necessarily reflect those of the persons whose names have been used.

The Space-Time Research Project is not an existing entity. Nothing herein should be taken to reflect upon the actual government program that is diligently working to advance time travel. Their efforts and achievements to date deserve our full support.

Published by Destiny Publishing, Sarasota, Florida

First Destiny Publishing Edition October 2014

Manufactured in the United States of America

12 11 10 9 8 7 6 5 4 3

Cover Art & Design by *Creative Photogenics*

ISBN-10: 0615700071
ISBN-13: 978-0615700076

DEDICATION

This book is dedicated to the brave Americans
who pioneered and civilized the West
and to Wyatt Earp, a flawed hero who was
larger than his legend.

SomeWhere SomeTime

by Gerald B. Keane

May, 1876 - Dodge City

"These cow drives are going to change Dodge," the tall man said after some thought. "And maybe a lot more than that. These people, you and me, too, we're about to see the future."

"Wyatt, you think too much," said the smaller man. Although only twenty-two years old and five years Earp's junior, Bat Masterson was one of the few men who could speak that way to Wyatt Earp.

"And you talk too much," Earp said, leaving his words hanging before adding, "and you don't think near enough."

Earp and Masterson were sitting on the plank sidewalk on Front Street. After a drizzly spring, the warm day brought Dodge City's populace outside, and most of them were talking about the cattle approaching from Texas. It was May 1876 and the first cattle drives had already left Texas headed for Dodge City, Kansas. The drives were headed toward Dodge, because Kansas had banned Texas cattle from

1

the eastern part of the state. A tick carried by Texas cattle had infested Kansas herds with Texas Splenic the year before, causing the legislature to push the drives to the western part of the state.

"Guess the learned men in Topeka don't care if our cattle get the splenic," said Bat, taking no offense at Wyatt's barb. His tone betrayed his contempt for politicians.

"Neither does the mayor, it seems," added Earp.

"He wouldn't dare ban the cattle from Dodge," Masterson said. "He'd be run out of town if he tried."

Earp kept his thoughts to himself as he scanned the street. He was the recently appointed chief deputy marshal and given full rein over the police force. Almost immediately, Earp brought in Masterson, an old buffalo-hunting buddy, to give him a hand.

Earp's expectations had been dampened when Masterson hobbled into Earp's office a couple of weeks earlier. Bat was limping badly from a gunshot wound and needed a cane to get around. Earp shook his head and rolled his eyes. "Oh, great," he said in greeting Masterson, "you're gonna to be a big help."

But Wyatt could hardly send his friend away. Now, almost inseparable, they often spent their quiet time sitting together surveying their kingdom.

"Think this delectable burg will go the way of Abilene?" Bat asked.

"Could be," Earp said. "Could change everything," he added cryptically. "Could even change you and me."

Masterson shrugged. Yep, Earp thought too much.

They watched as most of Dodge's 800 citizens enjoyed the warmth and sunlight, men and women alike crowding the wooden sidewalk and dusty street. Earp's sharp eyes missed none of them, but, when two men hitched their horses directly in front of his chair, he gave a jerk of his head, signaling to Masterson it was time to find a place with a better view.

As they ambled down the sidewalk, nodding to the happy citizens they passed, Bat peered out across the Arkansas River a couple of hundred yards away. He seemed to be looking for the cattle herds, still out of sight, that were churning up the dusty plain just over the horizon..

Yep, Bat thought, Wyatt might just be right. The future is coming.

Chapter 1

I inhaled the Washington air of the twenty-first century, but exhaled it in nineteenth-century Kansas. With my next breath, I took in only clean, fresh air, smelling only grass and dust. If our plan had worked, I was in Dodge City, Kansas and the year was 1876. But something didn't look right. I'd been in the target field before. The last time, I was with a college professor, the field was full of ripening sorghum, and the year was 2010. Now, I was alone, and there was no sorghum. The absence of sorghum was the best evidence that I'd left the twenty-first century. I'm Will Barrett, the world's first time traveler. But I was lost and disoriented.

I was standing in a field of tawny rodents, thousands of them. If prairie dogs were aggressive, I'd be in trouble. But prairie dogs are passive creatures, and my biggest risk was that they'd chirp me to death. However, the turkey vultures circling overhead worried me. Vultures don't circle unless they see a meal on the ground. Did I look like nineteenth century road kill to them? Did they know that I was in the wrong place?

The air was fresh and clean, but it was also blowtorch hot,

and the wind scorched my face. The sun was so intense I could hardly keep my eyes open. My armpits dripped with sweat, and my mouth felt like sawdust. The temperature had to be over 100 degrees. I had no food or water, and no idea where or when I'd find them. The wonders of twenty-first century science had transported me 134 years back in time, only to deposit me who-knows-where to die from lack of the most basic of necessities.

Before I died, however, I took a moment to reflect on what we'd accomplished.

The *Space Time Research Project* (STRP for short), a black operation of NASA and DARPA, had sent me on my journey. Few people outside STRP knew of the program's existence. We operated from a small "campus" abutting Neil Armstrong University near Washington, D.C. As a cover, the university fallaciously listed our entire staff—all sixteen of us—as students and faculty members.

Time-travel is heavy on theory and light on hardware. Beyond computers, all our equipment could easily fit inside a large suitcase. Everyone who worked on the project, with one exception, was under thirty-five years of age. To outsiders, we were just another graduate program.

The sole exception, the new Project Director, John Dolan, was out of place in the program. We believed the impossible could become reality, but Dolan only believed in his government paycheck. He was a political appointee and, fortunately, had little authority over our work. His role was to lobby for funding with the two congressmen overseeing the project. He barely acknowledged our existence, and we ignored him. That is, except for me.

I gave Dolan a free pass his first week on the job. I thought he deserved a chance, and, sensing my deference, I was soon his fair-haired child.

Despite Dolan's marginal role, my fellow engineers treated

me with a wary respect because of my seeming relationship with him. For a short time, Dolan and I gave each other credibility. I liked the arrangement, but wasn't so naïve that I didn't see resentment growing. To battle it, I struggled to maintain a close relationship with each of my fellow engineers.

My precaution proved wise. One morning, as I approached Dolan's office, I heard unhappy voices from his office. I couldn't catch the words, but the tone of the conversation made me hesitate outside the door. I heard Dolan say, "Missy, don't bring your tears in here. We have a job to do."

A second later, a popular young secretary rushed out of the office and bumped into me. Startled, she looked up at me through reddened eyes. Tears streaked her makeup and reflected her despair. She ran on without a word.

When I entered Dolan's office, he looked up. I pointed in the direction of the departing secretary.

"Nothing important," Dolan said. "Nothing at all."

His face was as cold as a Wisconsin ice fisherman's.

Emboldened by our relationship, I said, "It seemed important to her."

Dolan glared at me and raised his index finger.

"Look, Barrett, don't you ever question me." He paused to regain his composure, before continuing in a quieter but even colder voice, "She's a throwaway. We can't let flotsam like her interfere with our aims. She can leave if she wants."

Neither of us spoke for a moment as Dolan stared briefly toward the door. When he looked back at me, his anger was gone, and he spoke as if the two confrontations never occurred.

"You needed something?" he asked.

I paused briefly before saying, "No." I left without a further word—I needed to think. I could speak with him later—if I still wanted to.

As I walked to my office, I mulled the thought that I, too, might become flotsam if it suited Dolan's fancy. As I thought, my respect for the man ebbed away.

Thereafter, I found myself viewing Dolan as if I'd learned he was a pedophile. Once you see under a man's skin, he never looks the same again.

A couple of days later, Dolan approached me in the hallway.

"Will," he whispered to me as we passed, "I need to speak with you." He nodded toward my office and hurried in. I followed him, and he closed the door behind me.

"Sit down," he said in a serious tone.

He scrutinized me as if he were appraising a horse. He made me uncomfortable, and I decided to sit down and get control of things.

"John, you seem upset about something."

"No, no, no," he coughed out a mirthless laugh, and brushed aside my concerns with his hand. "I'm not upset. I'm excited."

He pursed his lips and giving me a final appraisal, he said, "Will, you're the star here." He paused. "You'll likely be the first man to travel through time."

I hoped he was right, but shrugged noncommittally.

"You can probably choose the target for the first voyage."

He stopped again. Was he being theatrical or just nervous?

"We must reach agreement on the target and present a unified front to the boys." He looked at me for assent.

"Well," I said cautiously, "we need to do what's best for the project in the long run."

"Will," he said in an avuncular tone, "the project is going to be just fine—in the long run. But you and I won't be here for the long run. We're just minions in a huge episode that will go on for hundreds of years after we're gone."

I nodded. Once we overcame the technical issues, time travel would be a frequent occurrence.

"We have the chance to enrich the present in very material

ways."

I squinted at him, not liking what I thought I heard. Did he mean the current time when he said "present," or had I heard another meaning—"present" meaning "those currently in this room"? I widened my eyes to invite Dolan to explain himself.

"Will, what I'm saying is"—he paused again, annoyingly—"we can make museum curators the happiest people on earth, if you know what I'm saying."

"No, John, I don't mean to be dense, but . . ." I shrugged. I knew, and he knew that I knew, but he had to say it.

"Take, for example, if you pulled a discarded Michelangelo painting out of the garbage, and brought it back. Any art museum in the world would pay millions for it."

We stared at each other. I blinked first.

"John, we can't disturb history. I'll think about it, but can valuable items appearing with no provenance benefit the art world?"

I offered him a way out. "Are you suggesting we retrieve artifacts to make the project self-supporting?"

John shuddered at my question—he clearly didn't mean that.

"Will," he said, almost whining, "no project pays its way. And, besides, the possible rewards could never put a dent in the budget."

"A few million is lost in the rounding at OMB," he said. "But a couple of million to you and me, well now, that's a different story."

He sounded like a smarmy, snake-oil-salesman.

"John, I'm not sure we should do that."

He cut me off before I could say more.

"Will, think about your family"—I had no wife or kids—"and your responsibilities to them. Don't pass on this opportunity. And, don't forget, you can be a national hero." He waited for me to agree with him.

"I'd really like to support you for the first trip," he said, giving me a sharp look, "But, of course, I have to believe you're the best man."

He let that sink in.

"Let me sleep on it," I said.

When I stood up and came around my desk, he didn't move from his chair. He gave me a baleful stare while I waited for him to get up. After an awkward few moments, he stood and faced me.

"Think about it, Will. Think about it very hard."

He turned and left. As I watched him leave, my body and mind were heavy with fatigue.

I returned to my chair, reached down and turned my equipment off, picked up my briefcase, and left for the day. Yes, I would think about it.

Chapter 2

Joey was aghast. "Let me get this straight," he said, the strain evident in his voice, "Dolan offered to let you keep artifacts you bring back from your missions? And offered to help you market them? And you turned him down? What am I missing here?"

"It's not right," I said without conviction.

"It's right if he says it's right," Joey pleaded.

"Joey," I said, "he caught me off guard, and it didn't feel right."

"Okay, tell me what's wrong with it," Joey said. "Ever since Dad left, you always said you'd be rich and famous someday. You're certainly going to be famous. Now, Dolan's going to make you rich."

"You think I should get in bed with him? I'll get fleas if I do."

"Have I ever steered you wrong?" Joey asked.

That was the problem with this conversation. Joey was always looking out for me, and I trusted his judgment. He was two years older than me and, ever since Dad left, he'd been like a father to me. I followed his lead in everything, from Little League baseball to getting my Ph.D. The only differences between us were that I was theoretical smart and Joey was practical smart, and that he didn't burn with my ambition.

I thought back to the day our family collapsed.

It was 1984, and I was six years old. Even that young, I could tell something was wrong—Dad hadn't been around for several weeks. While it wasn't unusual, it was different this time. Maybe it was how Mom was acting. When I asked Joey what was happening, and he didn't answer, I knew for sure.

Come dinnertime, the other shoe started falling when, halfway through the meal, Mom cleared her throat. She'd been quiet as usual while we ate. This time, however, she'd looked especially grim when she sat down.

"Well, boys," she said, trying to sound light, which she didn't, "looks like we're on our own."

Joey kept his head down, looking at his plate. There was silence for a moment. Mom had a tear running down her cheek, and her lips were shaking. She had difficulty talking; she started to say something a couple of times before she got anything out.

"I don't think we're going to be seeing your father again," she said, barely swallowing a sob. "He's run off—for good this time."

I started crying quietly. When my crying got louder, Joey glanced at me. He didn't say anything, and I couldn't tell if he was miffed at me for making a scene or whether he felt sorry for me.

"We're going to do just fine," Mom said without conviction. "It's not your fault," she said as she blinked tears down her cheeks. "That's just your dad's way. I'm sure he loves you."

"You're both fine young men, and you're going to turn out just fine," Mom said. "We'll work together and make it through this."

I looked to Joey for reassurance, but he was back to looking at his plate. When Mom didn't say anything more—she didn't seem to know what to say—I got up from the table and walked slowly to my room. When I closed the door, I dove onto my bed and buried my head in my pillow. I cried for a long time—until I was cried out. When I finished, my only thought was that I was six years old and didn't have a father.

I decided then that I'd show him. And, since that day, Joey had been the only father I would have, or ever need. Now, for one of those rare times, my substitute father and I were at odds.

"Look, why don't we go see a lawyer," Joey said.

We met with Skylar Marlowe, a FISA-vetted attorney. At first, she was skeptical of our story about time travel, but she recognized me from the cover of *Time Magazine*, and decided to take us at face value.

"Hmmm," Marlowe said in that annoying way that lawyers act when they don't know the answer. "You have an interesting situation."

Joey interrupted her temporizing. "Forget the circumstances," he said. "The issue is whether Will could get in trouble for following the explicit directions of his director?"

Marlowe did what lawyers often do—she made the problem more complicated. "You have the law, you have an ethical issue, and, most importantly, you have a public relations problem."

"What's the ethical issue?" Joey said, a challenge in his voice.

"I did some brief research after you called," Marlowe said. "I found that a similar situation came up during the Apollo 15 mission. One of the astronauts secretly carried 400 stamped envelopes to the moon for a stamp dealer."

Joey almost jumped out of his seat. "And what happened?"

"The whole crew was disciplined," Marlowe said. "The good news was that the astronauts sued NASA for the return of the envelopes . . . and won."

Marlowe gave Joey a smile as she finished.

"Was there any rule against what he did?" I asked.

"Apparently not," Marlowe said. "That's where the ethical and public relations issues come in. Are you cheating your fellow engineers, and how will the public react when it comes out?"

"What do you recommend?" I asked.

"If you're only doing what the director told you to do," she said, "how could anyone criticize you?"

"Yeah, right," Joey said, the smile returning to his face. He turned toward me and shook his head in an 'I told you so' manner.

"If you're going to do it, get Dolan's directions in writing," Marlowe said. "Get it written into the mission plan if you can. Next, include your fellow engineers in the arrangement. If Dolan has his way, the artifacts from future missions, the ones you're not on, could be big, really big."

"And how would we handle the public relations issue?" I asked.

Marlowe shrugged. "Frankly, my reaction's the same as yours," she said. "It doesn't feel right, and I don't know how you'd ever justify it to the public."

"What about citing the Apollo incident?" Joey asked.

"The whole thing hurt NASA's reputation. It wasn't pretty."

"And the astronaut? What happened to him?"

"No one on the mission ever flew again. I do have a practical question—will the things you bring back have aged? Won't an expert think they're new, and brand them as fakes?"

Joey turned toward me.

"Oh, Dolan's plan is to have me stash the items somewhere and let them age. They arrive back at the same time anyway."

Neither Joey nor Marlow understood my explanation.

"If I came back on January 1 and brought the items back with me, or if I came back and we dug them up that day, we'd still have them on January 1."

Joey still seemed troubled. "But suppose Dolan, uh, didn't wait for you to come back? If he already knew the hiding place and dug up the items the day before you returned."

"He wouldn't . . ."

"Yes, he would," Joey said adamantly before pausing. "If you were to hide something while in the past . . ."

"Yeah, go on," I said.

"Why would Dolan have to wait for you to leave? He could retrieve it today, even before you left."

"Yeah, but what if I didn't hide it?" I asked, knowing it was a lame question.

"Dolan retrieves it today," Joey said, putting my question in context. "But then you decide not to hide it in the first place. A classic time-travel paradox."

Skylar intervened. "My guess is he wouldn't do it on this trip. However," she said with a dramatic flair, "when the stakes get higher, ..."

I had an idea. "All we'd have to do is make sure that it would take two to recover the artifacts."

"Why do you have to tell anyone where you're hiding them?" Joey said before turning to Marlowe. "Okay, what's the bottom line?"

"My guess is that you'd get away with it legally but . . ." She shrugged.

Joey looked at me. I shrugged, too. Although we didn't have any firm answers, I'd heard all I needed to hear.

Chapter 3

After that meeting, I avoided Dolan for several days, until he left me a voicemail asking to meet with me in the morning. I could hardly refuse.

I prepared for the meeting. I didn't want to be caught by surprise again, and I didn't want to end up in an argument about what we discussed.

I knocked on his door at 8:30 the next morning. He gestured me in with the same somber look I'd seen at the last meeting. He came around his desk and closed door behind me.

"Will, I want to follow up on our conversation," he said. "First, you do understand that these conversations are completely private. We can't have anyone thinking I'm favoring one candidate over another."

I nodded without agreement.

"I gather you're not inclined to go along with my plan?" he said. I gave him no response. "Let me be more specific."

I gave him no encouragement, but he went on anyway.

"The preservation of history is important to Western civilization. The more we know about the past, the better we are as a people. A world with thirty Rembrandts is richer than one with fifteen. A museum with many Egyptian artifacts is better than one with only a few. Okay, that's not disputable."

This was the salesman's tactic of getting you saying 'yes' as he leads you up the road to selling you the pig in a poke.

"I'm suggesting we join our own interests with those of the world for the betterment of both."

I stared at him. Dolan gestured with his eyeglasses and brushed some papers on his desk. He stuttered as he continued.

"If you went to ancient Egypt, you might see artifacts with a different eye if you were a partner rather than just a hired hand."

He tilted his head, seeking agreement. I stared back.

"That's all I'm suggesting. You deserve more than your government salary for the tremendous risks you'll be taking."

Dolan fidgeted in his chair. His sordid plan had a certain allure. Nevertheless, I was squirming in my seat, and perspiring despite the air conditioning. As I listened to this sleaze ball, my gut knotted and I felt my gorge rising into my throat.

I wanted to go along, if only to please Joey, but . . . If only Joey were here, and he could hear Dolan slobbering like the pig he was, maybe he'd understand my reaction. My distaste for Dolan, and the tension I felt in rejecting Joey's advice, was causing my stomach to burn. I wanted out and thought the best way to shut Dolan down was to shame him.

After letting him stew for a time, I broke the silence, "I don't mean to sound like a boy scout, but I knew my salary when I signed up, and I knew the risks. I don't expect anything else."

Dolan interrupted me.

"Very noble of you," he said. I didn't hear sarcasm in his voice, but, was sure it was intended, I felt my face flush. Apparently, my words only sharpened his cynicism. He began to speak again but, this time I interrupted him.

"No, John, that's not nobility," I said. He'd turned my words against me, ridiculing my values. "That's reality. I get paid for what I do."

Realizing I was speaking too loudly, I took a deep breath to regain control.

"You didn't let me finish," he said, cutting me off before I could continue. "We pay you for doing your job, but you could get a bonus for outstanding performance. No one is entitled to a bonus—an employer gives it to show appreciation. I'm your employer, and I could choose to reward you."

I just shook my head. This was a losing battle. In contrast to my angry retort, Dolan continued in a reasonable tone.

"The practical limits are our budget. I can't give you a cash bonus." He paused for effect here. "But," another pause, "I can let you benefit from your work."

He let that hang in the air. I felt like a third grader being chastised for not knowing how to spell 'cat.' After letting me simmer in my obvious naïveté, he went on in an even more pedantic manner.

"You couldn't remember the Mercury Program, but NASA let the astronauts sell their stories to *Life Magazine*. They profited from fame developed one hundred percent at taxpayers' expense. Your perk will be in not having to account for every object you bring back."

I was beaten, but I tried to save face with a few facts he glossed over.

"John, you're forgetting some of the facts. First, all of the astronauts got equal shares. John Glenn got the same as the lowest one on the totem pole. And, second, it was all above-board. And, finally," I was reluctant to throw the bomb, but I was hot, "none of the NASA administrators got a penny from *Life Magazine*."

Dolan gave a visible start at my last point, but he took his time before speaking, and then he spoke slowly.

"Will, there were hundreds of bureaucrats in the NASA

chain. I'm alone here. I'm a forty-year government employee. I've paid my dues, and I'd like to think of myself as one with you and the other candidates."

I didn't bite on that one.

"And, of course," he said, "everyone will share in the rewards. I hope you didn't think we'd keep it all to ourselves?"

"What about the publicity issue?" I asked. "Are we going to announce the bonus program to the press?" My tone was more biting than I'd intended.

He didn't answer at first. Of course, there'd be no press release. But Dolan didn't fold easily.

"Yes, certainly we'll disclose everything," he said with renewed enthusiasm. "But," he opened his palms before delivering the punch line, "we can't disclose anything as long as we're a secret project."

Dolan was dangerous, not only because he was dishonest and manipulative, but because he was also smart. Dishonest and smart are not a good combination.

"Well, we'll talk again," he said, ending the conversation.

"John," I said, "this is a very bad idea. Nothing good can come of it."

I spoke those words in a friendly manner, trying to soften the implied threat of the last words.

"Millions, Will," he muttered distractedly as he ushered me to the door, "literally millions, and no one loses a thing."

I felt drained as I walked back to my office. Dolan was crazy. How could we sell the plunder? Did he consider the effect of high-grade artifacts appearing on the market out of nowhere? Surely, the Dutch government would ask where unknown Rembrandts came from and how they'd left its country. The secrecy of our project would protect us for a while, but not forever.

No, the whole idea was too crazy to consider. Of course, my weighing the weaknesses in the plan belied my "nobility." Why bother looking for holes if my answer were a simple No?

Did Dolan's last comment, about the "millions," make an impression on me? I switched my conscience off and didn't answer my own question.

Chapter 4

Dolan's manner had changed by the time I ran into him. He paused next to me as we passed in the hall and spoke so only I could hear, "Word's out that maybe you're not the right man for an early mission."

I got the picture—although he'd been almost championing me, now he'd use that role to undermine me. Now, we'd test how successful I'd been in maintaining close ties with my colleagues.

"We have seven qualified men," I said to Jerry Knorr as we ate lunch. A fellow engineer, Jerry wanted to make the first trip, but he wasn't in serious contention. He glanced up from his sandwich.

"Who's going first?" I asked.

"Maybe you," he said.

"A lot of risk on the first one," I said.

"You getting cold feet?" he asked, giving me a surprised look.

"Orville took a big risk going first," I said, shaking my head, "but none of us would want to be Wilbur. The risk isn't going to scare anyone off. The device'll be safe before anyone jumps."

Jerry nodded.

"Would it be okay if it's me," I said.

"Are you qualified? Yeah."

"Suppose Dolan doesn't agree?" I asked.

"You having a problem with Dolan?" he asked.

I shrugged.

"We decide. Not Dolan."

"Is that an endorsement?" I said.

Jerry shook his head. "I'm keeping an open mind," he said with a smile. The smile was supposed to soften the comment, but I took it to be a rejection.

Each of the seven project engineers brought specialized knowledge to the program, but we all kept up with every aspect of the project. We'd solved the technical problems and prepared for the first launch by experimenting with animals. We started with white mice, sending them back a few minutes in time. We all laughed during the first experiment when the mouse arrived back from the future while we were preparing to send it. Eddie Fitzgerald, a short, powerful man with uncanny wisdom but no subtlety, highlighted the paradox of the incident.

He looked down at the newly arrived doppelganger and said, "Let's not send him and we'll have two mice. Then, we can plan to send both of them, and we'll have four."

Something was wrong with Fity's logic—we all called him Fity—but none of us, the world's experts on time travel, could immediately verbalize what it was. It was a variation on the Grandfather Paradox called the Bilker's Paradox, but with a typically Fity twist.

"Good idea," I said. "Then we can plan to send you but not do it, and we'll have two of you." I waited a couple of beats before adding, "That's all we need."

21

Despite Fity, we sent the mouse. As Fity might have put it, "A good finish deserves a good beginning."

We moved on to cats, then dogs, and, finally, a small cow. Each successful test brought us closer to confirming that the rig was man-safe. After a couple of dozen successful round trips, we certified the device as man-rated. It was time to select the jumper, and the target.

I turned my attention back to Dolan. If he were to torpedo me, he'd do it now. He called a meeting of the engineers. His presence at "our" meetings put me on edge.

Dolan was almost six inches shorter than me, and had a round face with "bureaucrat" all but printed on his forehead. At his best, he was a dedicated functionary who'd spent his adult life, almost forty years, in government service. At worst, he was a venal, self-serving political hack with no appreciation for scientific advancement. His only interest was John Dolan. He was director of STRP as a product of political exigency. The President ignored his near indictment for corruption in his last position where he monitored mining operations on government land in Montana. Our project's secret nature allowed the President to appoint Dolan without congressional approval or public scrutiny. The politics in this case victimized the American taxpayer, the project, and, if Dolan had his way, me.

The project was already in the late stages of development when Dolan took over. From the first day we'd gathered as a team, long before Dolan, we'd informally debated possible targets. He knew that we engineers, the 'Heisenbergs,' would select the targets and travelers, but he intended to influence the choice of the first target to spite me. Now, just two months after he arrived, he made his play.

He pointedly ignored me when he greeted the other six.

"Gentlemen," he announced, "our first target must be one of the following three destinations: Ancient Rome, Greece, or

Egypt."

He outlined his reasons for those three and hinted the missions could "enrich us beyond our dreams."

An uneasy silence followed his edict. Just two weeks before, we formed a committee to choose the target. Appointing the members was delicate, since no one on the selection committee would be considered for the first jump. Since Bill Reed, Mike Hanly, and I were the frontrunners, Jerry Knorr graciously nominated himself, Fity, Jim McDonnell, and Kevin Keane. He looked around for support and finally received it from Kevin. Jim and Fity climbed aboard, and we elected the four men unanimously. They elected Jerry chairman and, within days, they established protocols for the target.

Despite that arrangement, we were captives to Dolan's lecture. Since I hadn't joined in Dolan's plan, he played his hand without me. Some uneasy looks passed around the room as Dolan spoke—but not from everyone. Had Dolan already compromised some of them?

Citing security, Dolan said, "We need to speak candidly, so I don't want any of you to take notes or record this meeting."

I didn't like the secrecy and had a digital recorder in my pocket. I later learned I wasn't the only one.

"Gentlemen," Dolan continued, "we have an opportunity to serve our country and receive some, let's say, fringe benefits."

Some heads nodded. I hoped the nods signaled they were onto Dolan, not that they were supporting him.

"Our mission is to gather data and return it to this century," he said. "There's nothing in our mandate about retrieving artifacts. Nothing says we are to gather artifacts," here Dolan paused to get our attention, "and nothing says we can't."

Dolan couldn't miss the tension rising around the table, but he gave no chance for anyone to speak.

"We are completely within our mandate in bringing items back to enrich our society." He looked pointedly at each of us, challenging anyone to contest his assertion.

Raising his voice and quickening his tempo, he went on. "We'll go to ancient Greece, to Rome, and to Egypt. After the ancients, we'll go to Renaissance Italy and post-Renaissance Europe to secure DaVinci, Michelangelo, and Rembrandt paintings. They'll be worth millions."

He spoke with defiance of any opposition. "And, yes, we will benefit along with our culture."

I couldn't read everyone's reaction. Was Dolan on his own? Would anyone oppose him? Were some of them already on board with him? Was I alone?

I decided to raise a flag, and give my colleagues something to rally around.

"John," I said. "I respectfully suggest a more modest first mission."

I smiled at him, but he didn't smile back.

"We already have a committee that has met and established criteria for the first mission," I said. "Jerry, perhaps you could bring Mr. Dolan up to date."

Jerry Knorr's look made it clear he didn't want to be in this position.

"John," he started with a scratchy voice, "Will's right. We have met, and we're pretty far along. Fity, Jim, Kevin, and I have tentatively established criteria: (1) the target time must be relatively recent, (2) but not be so recent as to overlap people now living, (3) our traveler must be able to blend in easily, physically and culturally, (4) the time and place must be relatively safe, but, of course, (5) it must have historical significance."

Jerry looked at Kevin, Jim, and Fity for support. Kevin and Fity nodded.

Jim looked around nervously before speaking. "What Jerry said is, uh, right. But they're just guides. We could . . ." he stopped in mid-sentence and looked in vain to the others for help. "We could review them if we're heading in the wrong direction."

Jerry, Kevin, and Fity were visibly unhappy with what Jim said.

"What I mean," Jim added, his voice shaking, "is that we're keeping an open mind. No specific place has been decided on yet."

Dolan smiled at the opening Jim gave him. When Jerry, Kevin, and Fity only shook their heads in disgust but said nothing, I decided to stick my neck out further.

"Let the committee do its work and come back with a report," I said. "Then we can debate it."

Dolan he shuffled the papers in front of him. The tension was palpable now—no one spoke, no one coughed, no one moved.

Ignoring my suggestion, Dolan filled the void. "I've developed a list of items we should be able to locate at each of the targets," he said, pulling a sheet from his packet. "All of them can be safely transported back with our traveler."

He passed copies around the table.

"Each item has one or more asterisks next to it," he said, looking down his list. "The more asterisks, the higher the value."

When no one said anything, I accepted that Dolan had them all buffaloed. All eyes, except mine, focused on the list as if it were the Rosetta Stone.

"The proceeds from any recovery will be divided into ten portions," he continued. "Seven portions would be divided among the seven members of this Board, each of you receiving one-tenth."

The room was silent as Dolan went on. "If a Roman papyrus sold for $8,000, each of you would receive $800. That might not seem like much, but we could produce as much as two or three million dollars the first year—real money. When we start retrieving sixteenth- and seventeenth-century paintings, the yield will quadruple."

Dolan looked around the table, smiling like a car salesman. No one smiled back.

At this point, Fity, a staunch defender of The 7's authority, glanced toward me, and I caught his eye. He didn't look away fast enough, and my look dared him to speak up. After taking a deep breath, he did.

"Sir," he said. "What Jerry said is right. We believe we're on the right track. While Rome, Athens, and Egypt are excellent ideas, the language issue alone would make them impossible for now. We need to look at targets that fit our standards."

Bill Reed, the conciliator, jumped in. "There's no need to lock in anything now. Everything's possible—Rome, Athens, whatever. Let's keep an open mind."

Was Bill leaning toward Dolan? His comment cut both ways.

Kevin hadn't said anything yet, and his silence was deafening.

"Kevin?" I asked. "We haven't heard your thoughts."

When Kevin spoke, it was clear he'd been readying his words throughout the debate. "Bill's got a point—we're getting close to deciding, but nothing's been eliminated yet. We have set some preliminary standards. We'll keep looking at them while we consider everyone's ideas. This discussion's been helpful to us."

"And when might you finalize the standards?" I asked.

Kevin deferred to Jerry.

Jerry again squirmed. "Two weeks?"

"Good enough," I said and turned to Dolan.

"I hope we'll have a further opportunity to discuss this," he said, temporarily acquiescing to the developing consensus.

I watched the reactions: Jerry took a deep breath of relief while Jim looked chastened. Fity had defended the committee's work as Kevin and Bill avoided a confrontation. Mike Hanly hadn't expressed himself, and seemed content to stay out of it. Where did he stand?

Everyone else turned his eyes to Dolan, who, in turn, looked at Jim, apparently giving him one last chance to reiterate his support for Dolan's proposals. When Jim looked at his fingernails, Dolan's face reddened, and the veins in his neck stood out. He tried to keep his composure, but his hands betrayed him, as his fingers ripped at the edges of his papers. Finally, seeing the tide had ebbed, he turned reluctantly back to Jerry.

"Well, Mr. Knorr," he said through drawn lips, "perhaps we should hear you out. Any current ideas about targets?" He tented his fingers, as he stood ready to pounce on any flaws in Jerry's comments.

Jerry wanted none of the fight. "We haven't decided on anything yet." He looked toward me.

"Okay, Will," Dolan said, "it looks like it's you again."

"There are a lot of possibilities," I said, clearing my throat. "We should, perhaps, be looking at a pivotal period in American history—the expansion west in the nineteenth century. With cattle drives and colorful figures, the 1870's created the central myth about the United States."

"So," Dolan asked unkindly, "are we going to send one of our men onto the Oregon Trail?" I didn't bother pointing out that the Oregon Trail predated the massive migration west by more than a decade.

"No, John," I said. "I was thinking in terms of the cowtowns of Kansas. The cowboy typifies the independent American."

"And?" he asked feigning interest.

"Dodge City, 1876," I said.

Although I knew the committee would require formal presentations, several of my fellow engineers, not including Jim McDonnell, murmured their support.

I looked Dolan in the eye and saw a look I never want to see again. He took a few moments to calculate his best argument. Then, he spoke, trying to appear reasonable.

"I fear, Mr. Barrett," he said, "that Dodge City"—he didn't conceal his contempt as he said the town's name—"would present problems. As you said, our popular history of the period is anything but accurate and we'd need massive research before we could consider it. Now, let's move on to—"

I interrupted him. "The research is done. I'm something of an expert on the frontier period. I've reviewed every newspaper published in Kansas in the 1870's and read virtually every book on the time, the territories, and the major figures. I'll be submitting a manuscript to the University of Oklahoma within a year."

Dolan flinched, his eyes twitching. He opened his mouth to speak, but nothing came out. I saved him further embarrassment, I don't know why, by continuing.

"It's one of several possibilities that meet the committee's guidelines. Let's let the committee do its work and, when it's ready, we accept its decision."

Dolan harrumphed, crumpled his papers into his fist, and, without looking at anyone, stormed out of the room. This wasn't over.

I looked at Jim and Bill after he left. I still couldn't tell where they stood, but I knew we'd find out soon.

Chapter 5

I left the meeting uneasy about my future. Even though Dolan's proposal wasn't welcomed, neither were my fellow engineers hostile to it. If I'd had my way, they would have tossed Dolan from the room and required him to apologize before he could come back.

"You're upset about something," said Joey on the telephone.

"Dolan made his pitch to the team," I said with dejection in of my voice. I needed to hear that the situation hadn't gotten beyond fixing, but I wouldn't believe it if I heard it.

"Should I say 'I told you so' now?" he asked.

"Don't make it worse," I said.

"What'd you expect?" Joey said. "He's offering them the chance to make money."

"Is it too lame to say money isn't everything?"

"Okay, tell me what happened."

I summarized the meeting for him.

"Will, you're paranoid," Joey said. "You can't be upset? Dolan's the one who got stiffed."

"Only Fity stood up to him," I said. "Jerry, Bill, and Kevin were weasely, and Jim sold out completely."

"No, he didn't," Joey said with exasperation. "From what you told me, he brushed him off just like the others."

"You didn't see him," I said. "He acted like a lapdog."

Joey didn't speak for a few moments. I didn't expect much support but . . .

"Put yourself in Dolan's shoes," he said, speaking more calmly now. "He makes a dramatic offer to these underpaid government employees. He offered them riches they'd never see their entire lives—and what does he get?"

"Toadyism and capitulation."

"No," Joey almost shouted, "he got no rah-rahing, no

29

agreement, no one jumping on board. They left him hanging out there."

"That's how you see it?"

"Damn right I do. If they rallied behind anyone, it was you. You got to pitch your target, and you flattened Dolan when he tried to spike it. What more could you want?"

"I wanted someone to call Dolan a slug, and have him slink back into his hole."

"These are government employees," Joey said. "They're not going to alienate Dolan unnecessarily. Putting him off with 'we have a committee working on it' was the easy way out. Celebrate."

"Yeah," I said without conviction. "Maybe you're right."

"I am, I am," he said. "If you think Jim's weak, talk to him. Give him a pep talk. Thank the rest for their support. Co-opt them. Even if they didn't think they supported you, re-enforce the idea that they stood up to Dolan and put him in his place."

My mood brightened as he spoke. Joey wasn't my biggest supporter on this issue, but he gave me the tools to make the best of the meeting. I hoped he was starting to share my reservations about Dolan and his plan, but I didn't ask. He was co-opting himself by giving me the suggestions.

In seconds, I'd gone from being adrift in the current of other peoples' agendas to having a means to direct those agendas.

"You're always a big help, Joey," I said and hung up.

I sat down and thought out my plan. I'd leave Dolan to his own devices, and give my attention to my six fellow engineers. I analyzed each of their reactions, their seeming inclinations, and, most of all, their personalities. I knew instinctively that, engineers or not, their reactions, and their agendas, were the product of their basic personalities. Realizing that, I especially felt better about Jim McDonnell. I'd known him a long time and knew his basic decency. I became convinced that his comments to Dolan didn't mean he'd abandon his values.

I wasn't out of the woods yet, but at least I had a plan.

Chapter 6

"So what do we do if Dolan wants us to go to Egypt?" I asked Jim McDonnell.

"He's the director," Jim said.

"Have you read his authority?"

"No," he said, "but certainly 'director' means he sets the direction of the program."

"This is a DARPA project," I said. "You know DARPA's protocols."

Joey's suggestion that I read up on DARPA, the Defense Advanced Research Projects Agency, now came in handy.

Jim looked at me blankly. I guess he didn't know any more than I did before I did my research.

"DARPA funds a project for five years with a guarantee of no interference," I said. "That means Dolan has no say."

"That makes no sense," Jim said. "DARPA may keep their hands off, but someone's got to be in charge. Dolan's not DARPA, he's STRP."

"Read his job description," I said, my frustration showing. "Then, you decide what his role is."

I needed to get Jim over his title worship, and for him to see Dolan for what he is.

Apparently, Jim didn't like my tone. "If Dolan's not in charge, then who is? You?"

He had a point. I was acting like there was a power struggle, with me on one side and Dolan on the other.

"I don't want the job," I said. "We make the decisions as a team, Jim—you, me and the other five. We've done that so far, and it's worked."

"You think so?" he asked, a hint of a sneer in his voice. "Then why are you and I fighting?"

I wanted to say 'because you're acting like a horse's ass, and seem willing to turn us into Dolan puppets.' I didn't. Instead, I said, "I'm not fighting you—I'm fighting Dolan's attempt to take the program from you and me. I trust you and Jerry and the rest, but I don't trust Dolan."

"You don't think we need a referee?"

I looked at him sharply. "When have we needed a referee before?"

"Up until now, we haven't," he said. "It was easy for the team to work together to get ready, but the whole team can't make the first jump."

"We can all be part of the first mission if we stay a team," I said.

"Nah, I don't think so" Jim said. "This could fracture us beyond repair."

"It doesn't have to."

"We're all competitive," Jim said. "A blind vote for who should go would result in one vote for each of us."

"I hope not," I said. "We have to have more faith in each other than that.'

I saw where he was coming from. Maybe, he had the program's interests at heart, and didn't want jealousy to ruin the team effort.

"Doesn't Jerry's committee, and your willingness to serve on it, prove that we can set our ambitions aside?"

"I didn't see you set your ambition aside," he said. There, it was said.

"I wasn't asked to," I said with a shrug. "But if your committee picks someone else for the first jump, I'll back your decision all the way to the President."

That quieted him.

"I trust you guys will do what's best," I said. "Can't you give me, Bill, and Mike, the same benefit of the doubt?"

He nodded his head slightly, but I couldn't tell whether he was acknowledging my point or agreeing to trust us.

"If you think we need to choose a chief Heisenberg, or Stripper, or whatever, I'll back your motion," I said. "But, it won't be Dolan—it'll be one of us."

Jim didn't seem to want to argue further. It was time for me to leave. I stood up and offered my hand.

"I just want you to think about it."

Jim took my hand, and gave another ambiguous nod as I left.

"How'd it go with Jim?" Joey asked on the telephone.

I recounted our conversation. "How do you think it went?" I asked.

"You were there."

"I don't know," I said. "He heard me out, and I left when he ran out of arguments. That doesn't mean he agrees with blocking Dolan."

"You did what you could," he said. "What's next?"

"Jerry's committee's asked for presentations," I said. "He's accelerating the process but, if we don't stick together, Dolan will torpedo everything. He'll blow off the committee's decision, and do what he wants."

"Jerry can make that harder for him if he phrases the report right," Joey said.

"How?"

"Dolan will take a wishy-washy recommendation as an invitation. A clear and forceful decision would make that much harder."

"You want it to say 'It is the decision of the full committee that the target is Appomattox Courthouse, John Smith is the first jumper, and he will be sent on July 1st?"

"Exactly," Joey said. "No ambiguity, no hint that there's anything more to do."

"That still leaves the plundering-for-profit issue out there," I said.

"Get Jerry to address that in the decision," Joey said.

"I doubt Jerry's willing to take that on."

"Maybe you need another committee," he said. "Maybe, you, Bill, and Mike should do that."

"I don't know where Mike stands," I worried. "And Bill's a placator."

"Now you're trying to stack the committee," Joey said. "You just shamed Jim into trusting the team. You have to trust Bill and Mike to do the right thing."

His words made me sound like Dolan. But, yeah, I *do* want things done my way.

"Trust them," Joey said. "The fact that they're uncommitted is a plus. It'll make the others more willing to agree to let you three decide. And, Will . . ."

"What?"

"Don't play your hand in advance by talking to them," Joey said. "Have a clear conscience, and trust that they'll approach it with open minds."

"Okay," I said.

"Is that an 'Okay, I hear you, Joey,' or is it 'Okay, I won't talk to them'?"

"Okay, I won't talk to them."

I hung up with the increasing concern that everything, the target, the jumper, and the plundering, was out of my control. I felt I had no support.

Chapter 7

By May 1st, Knorr's committee narrowed the potential targets to three—the Civil War, the Revolutionary War, and Western expansion. The committee directed Bill to research the Civil War, Mike to do the Revolutionary, and I, of course, got the West.

Now, that the West was in contention, I had to make a compelling argument for a specific place and time. I'd liked Dodge City, but I also had my eye on 1881 Tombstone, Arizona. Both 1876 Dodge and 1881 Tombstone featured Wyatt Earp, the archetype Western hero.

Tombstone had the most famous event in Western history—the Gunfight at the O.K. Corral, but Dodge City presented the classic confrontation between cowboys and the law in a different context, through the theatre of cattle drives instead of the cattle-rustling of Tombstone. Earp was a deputy marshal in Dodge, but held no position in Tombstone, yet he ended up in the middle of everything in both places.

The common theme in both places was the resentments left over from the Civil War. As was usual in the West, both towns pitted the badge-wearing Yankees against the embittered Confederate cowboys.

The more I compared the places, the more their differences appeared. Tombstone had the more dramatic events, but Dodge presented the more complete experience of the cowboy West. The kid in me wanted to go to Tombstone, but the mature researcher preferred Dodge City. I had one chance to make a compelling argument, and I had to get it right.

The target committee directed each of Bill Reed, Mike Hanly, and me to prepare a thirty-minute presentation. So far, the committee took no position on the plundering.

After spending a couple of weeks preparing, I felt confident when my turn came. I'd settled on Dodge, and the committee listened attentively to my presentation and took notes. Then each of them but, especially, Jim McDonnell, grilled me on every possible detail. The interrogation convinced me that Dodge City was the right target, but I didn't know if I persuaded them. Since I didn't hear Bill or Mike's presentations, I couldn't know how they were received.

I ate dinner with Mike and Bill, and found they had the same experience I did. Neither of them came away with any inkling of what Jerry's committee might do. We'd wished each other well when we separated for the night. I'm sure that 'well' in this context meant second place. Since the committee promised a decision by ten the next morning, we'd know soon.

I called Joey before I retired. His support and encouragement only made me more anxious, and I slept uneasily. I, admitted to myself, for the first time how desperately I wanted the mission. I would have gotten more sleep if Joey hadn't encouraged me that I had a chance.

I awoke just after dawn and went to the gym to rid myself of my tension. After I lifted weights and ran, I showered and went to the cafeteria for an early breakfast. I hoped to see Jerry, Kevin, Fity, or Jim and get some indication what they'd do, but none of them was there, and I was left with my tasteless food and private concerns.

I returned to my room after breakfast and tried to kill time. The TV had only junk morning shows on, and I turned it off after fifteen minutes.

I picked up the novel I was reading. However, since it was about time travel, it gave me no respite from my worries. I put it down and watched the clock as it moved slowly, very slowly, toward ten o'clock. I couldn't tolerate being in my room any longer and I returned to the gym.

I took a half a dozen laps around the upper deck track

before returning to the weight area, where I repeated my usual routine of sit-ups, bench presses, curls, etc. I struggled with all the lifts since the anxiety sapped my strength.

Just after ten, I noticed a security guard push open the door to the weight room and look around. He was about to leave when he saw me.

"Hey Will," he said. "I almost didn't see you there."

"Just resting between sets," I said. "What's up?"

He shrugged. "Don't know, but they want you in the conference room."

"Uh-oh," I thought. "This is it."

I wasn't going to stand on ceremony by cleaning up. I went directly to the meeting and rushed into the conference room dressed in my shorts and a tee shirt. It was obvious I'd kept everyone waiting.

"Sorry," I said. "Working out."

Jerry Knorr pointed me toward an empty chair opposite the committee between Mike and Bill.

"I'm not going to drag this out," Jerry said. "Although we felt every one of the proposals had great merit, we unanimously decided that Will's proposal had the greatest potential. The first voyage will be to Dodge City, Kansas."

As I let out a deep breath, I could feel the deflation on both sides of me. I didn't look at Bill or Mike, but I'm sure my efforts to contain my exhilaration fooled no one.

"Frankly," Jerry continued, "we reached unanimous agreement on the nineteenth-century West, but we had some reservations about the actual target. Ultimately, we deferred to Will's choice of 1876 Dodge City."

Jerry's words were a triumph for me, but Jerry wasn't looking me in the eye, and his manner had my stomach churning. When he had difficulty clearing his throat, I sensed I was about to learn what caused my concern.

"We further decided that, with his expertise, Will should be the manager of the first mission. Bill will be supervisor. They will be entrusted with all details about how, and when, it occurs, but the first traveler will be Mike Hanly."

I sagged at the words. I'd gone from Mount Everest to Death Valley in two sentences. No one on the committee would look at me. Was Dolan behind this? Was this a fix?

Still not looking at me, Jerry went on. "Let me explain the committee's reasoning. We felt that each of these men developed an emotional attachment to his recommendation, and rightly so. We wanted them to be passionate. However, passion brings with it a certain narrowness of focus. Before we debated the target, we decided the target and its advocate should be separated. And, let me be address one possible concern—no outside agency influenced our decisions. This is what's best for STRP. Any questions?"

I was so dejected that I almost forgot to address my other issue. As we stood up to leave, I remembered and asked, "Did you make any decision about whether we should be retrieving artifacts?"

"No," Jerry said. "We discussed it, but couldn't reach agreement on whether that was our decision to make."

Clearly not wanting to debate the non-decision, Jerry said, "This meeting is adjourned. We'll deliver a written report of our decision to the director within the hour. Congratulations, Will, Bill, and Mike. Godspeed."

At that, the committee members broke into smiles and stood up, applauding as they focused on the three of us. I stood there awkwardly and did my best to accept their good wishes. Inside, I felt like crying. *My* baby turned over to Mike Hanly! As much as I respected him, it *was* my baby.

When the clapping stopped, I shook hands with Bill and actually hugged Mike. I approached Jerry to thank him and, in turn, thanked each member of the committee. When I reached Fity, he of such diplomacy, reminded me that Dolan could try to reject the decision. When I reacted to his comment, he smiled and added, "And, considering how he feels about you, he'll probably try to substitute the Civil War and appoint Bill to go."

"Thanks, Fity," I told him. "I'm going to suggest that you take the second trip, . . . as long as it's to Ireland during the potato famine. Maybe you'll lose some weight."

I called Joey as soon as I returned to my cell.

"We're going to Dodge City," I said.

"Absolutely fantastic," he gushed.

"Not really," I said. "Hanly's going, not me."

"No shit," he said. "They can't do that. Why would they do that?"

I related Jerry's explanation.

"Dolan?" he asked.

"Jerry made a point of denying Dolan influenced them but . . ."

"Want me to kill the son of a bitch?"

Chapter 8

Joey suggested we meet for dinner instead of taking revenge on Dolan. I reluctantly agreed.

I had a lot of time to fill before dinner. I disconnected the phone—the last thing I wanted was sympathy calls—and lay down to think, but my thoughts were too jumbled to focus.

My disappointment took over every cell of my body—I felt as if someone had beaten me up with a bat. How could I ever face the team again? I'd always be the man with the best idea for a mission but didn't have the right stuff to fly it. Hanly was the man and I was the . . . what was I? The also ran, the second man to invent the telephone?

I speculated on what was said during the committee meeting. Was I even considered for the mission? Was I the sacrifice in a compromise decision? Maybe someone said, "I like Will, but he's a screw-up. We can't risk sending him on the first mission."

I tried to rest but, despite overwhelming fatigue, I couldn't get any decent sleep. I felt even more tired after an hour of trying. I had to get out of the room. I hurried off campus, walked to the Metro stop, and took the train toward downtown.

After I got off a few blocks from the National Air & Space Museum, I walked to the Mall and paused to look at the museum. I'd always wanted to be honored there along with the Wrights, Lindbergh, and Glenn. I laughed to myself about my pathetic, futile ambition.

I entered the museum and was immediately taunted by *The Spirit of St. Louis* hanging above the *Wright Flyer* and, below them, Glenn's *Friendship 7*. I choked back a sob as I looked at those iconic craft.

A woman walking by dragged her little boy past me as he stared wide-eyed at me. I heard him say to his mother as he turned away, "Why does that man look so sad?"

I took a cab to Morton's for my dinner with Joey and arrived in a cold rain. Climbing out, I thought Why waste a great meal on a failure like me?

The hostess led me to a corner table where Joey already sat. He rose as I approached but, God bless him, he didn't put on a phony happy face. He embraced me without a word, and guided me into the booth.

When we were both seated, we looked at each other without saying anything. After a few labored breaths, I broke the ice.

"I'm not going to be good company," I said. Joey shrugged. "There's really nothing to say. I got rejected—big time."

Joey stared at me. He didn't even nod.

"I've decided to resign," I said.

Still, Joey said nothing.

"Come on, Joey, say something." Even then, he took his time.

"Resigning, huh?" he repeated, nodding as he spoke. He paused to think before adding, "Probably a good idea."

"I don't have any choice," I said. "I have no future with the program."

Joey continued his tight-lipped manner.

"I agree," he said, his voice flat. He asked a waiter for a pad of paper and a pen.

"Okay," he said. "Let's compose your resignation letter."

I grew uneasy. This wasn't like Joey.

"Mr. Dolan colon," he said as he wrote. "Although I have been honored to have been a member of the STRP team, I must resign my position. Good start?" he asked.

I studied his face, trying to read his mood. He seemed to take my silence as agreement, and went back to writing. "Since I was passed over for the first mission, and since I am not used to rejection, I will not remain in a program that does not appreciate my talents."

Joey re-read his words on the page before he shook his head. "No, that won't do at all," he said crossing out his sentence. "How about," he said slowly, and began writing again, "There could be no rational basis for selecting someone clearly less qualified than I to make the first jump. The target committee had no right to assign my mission to someone else, especially Mike Hanly."

He looked down at his words with a grimace. "No, no, that's weak," he said as he slashed through the words again. He studied his page for a few moments before exclaiming, "I've got it now. How about . . . This is all about me, and no one, especially my teammates, had the right to choose anyone, especially someone as unqualified as Mike Hanly, over me. I did not join STRP to be second to anyone. I quit. Take your program and shove it."

He dramatically dotted the last sentence and looked up at me with a look of satisfaction. "That should do it," he said.

As Joey played out his skit, I became increasingly light-headed and my stomach cramped. My heart thumped and I had trouble swallowing. I felt my shirt sticking to me as my whole body started sweating. I was ashamed. I'd always thought of myself as a team player, putting the interests of the program ahead of my considerable ambition. Joey's satire revealed the childish way I was handling the rejection.

"We can revise it if you like," he said.

"Enough," I said. "Point made," I said, holding my palm up in surrender. He gestured for me to speak, but I was getting nauseous—the day's disappointments coming to a head.

"What do you want me to say?" I asked. "I felt shitty when I walked in here. Now, I feel worse."

He said, "You think I'm going to encourage you to act like a two-year-old? You've disappointed me. I thought you were something special, but you're nothing but a spoiled baby. I'm supposed to . . ." He stopped with a disgusted shake of his head and looked away as if he couldn't stand the sight of me.

Joey's disappointment hit me harder than the committee's decision. My stomach clenched and my sweat turned cold. I got up and ran quickly to the men's room. I just made it to the nearest sink before I heaved. I supported myself on the sink until my legs stopped shaking and the cold sweat stopped. I ran some water into the bowl until I had cleansed it of my insides. I washed my face when my hands stopped tingling. As I was drying it, I looked into the mirror. I didn't like what I saw looking back.

Chapter 9

When I returned to the table, Joey was swizzling a straw in a Coke. He didn't look up until I'd slid back in to my seat. He studied my face as he continued to stir his drink.

"I'm sorry I let you down," I said. He pursed his lips and nodded, watching the spinning cola. I waited for him to speak.

"What do you do now?" he asked after a long, pained pause.

"Well," I said with a stiff smile, "I don't resign."

"No," he said. "You don't."

"I guess I go to Hanly, and commit myself to his mission," I said, not fully convinced of what I was saying.

"*His* mission?" Joey asked. "Did I hear that right?"

"*His* mission," I repeated. Joey nodded.

"You're not just on probation with me," he said without looking at me. "You're on probation with everyone in the program. You've been handed a setback, a humiliating one, and everyone will want to see how you handle it."

I thought about his words. He was right.

"I didn't screw up," I said. I wanted his affirmation that it wasn't my fault.

"You almost screwed up," he reminded me. "You'd never live it down if you abandoned Hanly and the program. The guys may not realize it, but they need you now more than ever."

"Do I need to talk to the rest of them?" I asked.

He shook his head. "They'll get the message from what you do. Let them form their own opinions."

I slept well that night. Joey had given me a reason to go forward and, while I'd never be mentioned with Glenn and Lindbergh, I could at least live with the reflection in the mirror.

I met with Mike Hanly the next day. He seemed jittery as I closed the door to his office.

"I just wanted to talk about what happened yesterday," I said. Mike watched me warily.

"You're a great choice for the mission," I said. He nodded noncommittally.

"In case you're worried," I said, smiling with an open heart, "you've got my complete support. I'll do everything I can to get you ready. When you succeed, and you will, I'll take it personally. I will be just as proud as if I went. Are you okay with that?"

Mike looked relieved, and he managed to reciprocate my smile when I offered my hand. As he stood up, he held onto my hand and said, "I'm sorry you didn't get it."

I squeezed his hand and firmly shook my head. "Don't be. I really, really wanted it," I said, "but I've accepted that I can probably contribute more supporting you than going myself."

Mike didn't seem to know what to say, so I added, "I'm even practicing not calling it *my* mission. Every night, I'm going to say 'Mike's mission' fifty times until it comes naturally."

"How about if we call it *our* mission?"

I turned and walked out, repeating all the way out: "Mike's mission, Mike's mission, Mike's mission, . . ."

I felt better. I felt like an adult, something I'm not used to. I returned to my office and gathered my research material. I needed to organize it into a course that would prepare Mike within a few weeks. In anticipation of getting selected, I'd developed a schedule for all the training and consultation I'd need, along with my historic research. Now, I needed to formalize it so I could make it work for Mike. As I was shuffling through my files, my phone rang.

"Mike here. I know you're supposed to be the mission manager," he said. "But I'd like you to be part of all of the training. It will help me if we prepared side-by-side. Can you do that?"

I was taken aback by the invitation.

"Will, you there?"

"Yeah, Mike," I said. "I'd like that. In fact, I'm just organizing my research material for you to look at, you know, whenever you have the time. Also, we have to come up with a physical training regimen. And, we'll need to go out to Kansas. And, I was also thinking, . . ."

"Whoa," Mike said. "You're overwhelming me. Everything you're saying's okay with me. Just let me know what you want me to do, I'm ready. You're the boss."

Maybe this was going to work out.

The moment I signed off with Hanly, I dialed Bill Reed's number.

"Bill, Will here," I said.

"Yeah?" he said, some hesitancy in his voice, before he added, "I'm really sorry about how the selection went."

"Not a problem," I assured him. "I trust Jerry and his committee—I'm sure they did the right thing. Our job is to prove them right."

"And?" Bill asked.

"I need you to help me prepare Mike. We need to plan a

work schedule for him."

"Is that what Mike wants?" he asked.

"I just got off the phone with him," I said. "Give him a call and get back to me."

He called me back in thirty seconds. "Let's do it," was all he said.

Chapter 10

Now that Mike was the next "animal" to jump, I gave my full attention to reviewing the test data for the test the earlier animals. Was our testing adequate to prove that time travel was safe? I was looking for any conclusions the doctors might reach about one particular side effect from the trips.

I reviewed the medical reports for each animal we'd sent, looking for any evidence that the time jump had compromised it in any way. The animals' EEGs seemed normal, and their blood tests showed no changes I could see. Even the animals' immune systems seemed unimpaired.

None of the data seemed to address my concern—how old was the animal when it returned. No one seemed to be looking for unusual aging. Without looking at that issue, they, or we, had certified the device as man-rated. Since I was now responsible for that man, I took a personal interest in the issue. When I questioned one of the doctors, he told me the data showed no reason for concern, that unusual aging would have caused changes that the testing would have revealed. I hoped, from Mike's sake, he was right.

The "device," as we generally called it, was unimpressive. Worn on the ankle, it weighed less than a pound and looked like an oversized pocket watch. Despite my engineering experience and my immersion in the project, I didn't know how it worked. I knew it relied on quantum mechanics and the uncertainty principle, and that it bypassed the argument that time travel would require the energy of a black hole to work. Most importantly, the method we were using didn't disassemble the traveler's body and put it back together somewhere else in time. That was a great comfort.

The project had been a two-step process. First, the theoretical scientists had set the stage by doing the calculations and writing the script for the trip. Once they had the principles in place, STRP was created to implement it. It was a process similar to the development of the first practical computers—the theoreticians had all the ideas in place, but it took some kids in a garage to take the second step by putting it all together and making mini-computers practical. None of us engineers were theoreticians. We were the Jobs and Wozniaks, and STRP was the equivalent of Apple. Like those first computer marketers, we didn't really need an in-depth understanding of the theory.

We expected the mission to stress Mike both physically and psychologically. With only weeks to go, our plan required him to prepare his body by working out and running at least three hours each day.

The psychological preparation was more guesswork than science. We had to harden Mike to both the unknown stresses of the time travel itself and to the cultural disorientation from dropping suddenly into another century. However, we were certain that he was going to experience things we couldn't predict. The only solution was to generally strengthen his psyche by imposing stressful situations on him in the hope he'd be able to handle whatever came his way.

Beyond that, however, he'd be the test animal for all future missions. We needed to learn everything we could, including, in detail, the side effects he consciously and unconsciously realized. The only way to know, aside from Mike's reports, would be to have as thorough a baseline of Mike's mental state before he left. I scheduled extensive testing by our team psychologist to establish that baseline. The psychologist told me that if Mike was mentally sound when we started, the tests would certainly destabilize him. For Mike's sake, I hoped she was joking.

As Mike's condition peaked, we would bring in experts of all sorts, including sports physiologists, to measure his physical condition. By the end of testing, Mike would feel like a white mouse. Despite all the assurances, testing, and preparations, I could never quite rid myself of the nagging question of how old Mike would be when he returned.

Mike would have to find time for road and weight work, and the psychological testing. We planned extensive counseling to follow each testing session. I was uneasy imposing on Mike that he bare his soul to the psychologist, but she assured me and, I, in turn, assured Mike, that none of the details would be available to others. She would only release evidence of any change, if any, that later testing and counseling revealed.

Not wanting to rely exclusively on my research, we scheduled hundreds of hours of private tutoring from the best experts we could find. I scheduled meetings for Mike to meet separately with a half a dozen of the best experts on the late nineteenth century West and Midwest. I'd bluffed Dolan about my in-depth knowledge of the West, but I found that, from Mike's program, what I believed was a deep knowledge of the West was rather surface.

"Is Mike going to be able to handle all this?" Bill asked me while we watched Mike's reflexes being tested. "I'm afraid he's going to rebel."

"As long as I don't ask him to do anything I'm not doing, he won't complain," I said. "It wouldn't hurt for you to train with us."

Bill studied my face to see if I was serious.

"God willing, you and I will go on a future mission and we'll need to prepare. Nothing else we can do can put us in the best position to get the next missions than training for this one."

I can't say Bill showed much enthusiasm for the idea, but I took his rolling of his eyes skyward as agreement.

We met with professors specializing in Kansas fauna, flora, and geology. Mike studied hard, but I still feared that, like me, he'd be unable to tell buffalo grass from big bluestem. We flew to Kansas and did most of our nature studies in and around modern-day Dodge City. After spending hours in class at Dodge City Community College, the professors took us on daily field trips to experience different aspects of southwestern Kansas.

Before going to Kansas, I worried we weren't doing enough to prepare Mike. But once there, I felt we were on the right track, that Mike was the right man for the mission, and Bill and I were the right men to support him. When he succeeded, we all succeeded. However, in the privacy of my thoughts, this was still my mission—even if I wasn't jumping.

During our second trip to Dodge City in the middle of June, my cell phone rang as we were flying in a helicopter west of Dodge. I flicked it off when I saw the call was from Jerry Knorr. An hour later, I called him back.

"We have a problem," he said.

My whole body froze, but I was sure we could solve any problem. I walked into the field away from the others as my heart started pounding, and put on a brave front.

"Can't be too bad," I said.

"Dolan's talking about canceling the mission."

"Why?" I asked, my body back to freezing.

"His stated reason is that we're not ready, and that it would be foolish to risk Mike and the whole project if we had a disaster."

"We're not going to have a disaster," I said.

"No," Jerry agreed, "we're not."

"Jerry, listen to me," I said. "He doesn't make this decision. Your committee does."

"Yeah," Jerry agreed unconvincingly.

"Okay, Jerry, come clean. What's going on?"

"Well," Jerry spoke carefully, "there seems to be a hint that we can go on the mission if . . ."

When he paused, I finished his sentence, ". . . if I'm out of it."

Jerry sighed audibly into the phone.

"I get the picture," I said. "He's playing me against everyone else."

"Something like that," Jerry agreed.

"Why does he care?" I said. "He's gotten his way. I'm not going to Dodge. What more does he want?"

"I think he doesn't want you around to thwart his schemes."

"God damn it," I spit out. "He's already taken the mission from me, now he wants to rub salt in."

"He had nothing to do with you not being chosen," Jerry said without conviction.

"How's the wind blowing?" I asked.

Jerry took a few seconds to answer. When he did, he was back to his measured tone.

"We're getting tired of his machinations," he said. "I'm with you all the way. My sense is everyone else is, too. In principle."

"But," I said, "they're willing to sacrifice principle for the practicalities. They think he could affect future crew selections."

"They're afraid of him."

We were both silent for a few moments. I spoke first.

"Your committee put me in charge of the mission," I said. "It's up to you guys—your call."

Again, silence. Good silence this time.

"That's what I wanted to hear," he said, his voice lilting a little for the first time. "If you'll defer to the best interests of the project—"

"Of course, I'll do whatever—" I said before he interrupted.

"—Mike's going to Dodge City next month . . . and you'll be there to tell him when to push the button."

I laughed. I sensed Jerry's confusion over my laughing.

"Jerry, Mike's already in Dodge City. I'm looking at him right now."

"Are you willing to make a permanent enemy of Dolan?" he asked.

"Only if you are."

"I'll get a unanimous vote," he said firmly. "Dolan will have to close down the project if he fights us."

"Thank you, Jerry," I said seriously.

"Not yet," he said but I could hear in his voice that the mission was on.

When I ended the call, I sat down in the grass for a few minutes, finding myself drained and shaking a little. I had confidence in Jerry, but I was still uncertain how this was going to play out.

"You okay?" one of the professors said, walking up to me.

"I think so," I said.

"Your face is gray, and you look like you've lost your best friend."

I gave him a grim smile. "No, I lost my worst enemy, and my best friend is the one who's losing him for me. Everything's going to be fine."

I wanted to believe that.

I briefed Mike and Bill. They both voiced full support for me, but I sensed, from Mike's eyes, he might sacrifice me to save his mission. Nevertheless, I took him at his word after repeating my deference to what Jerry and his committee decided.

We returned to our studies, but our minds were in Washington instead of in the lounge where we were meeting. After about forty-five minutes, the professors called an early recess, sensing we weren't getting much from their efforts.

Before we left, the professor who questioned me after Knorr's call walked up as I gathered my notes.

"Okay, tell me what's going on," he demanded politely.

I glanced into his face and saw determination, but I also saw someone I could trust.

"A little bit of Washington politics," I said.

"And?"

"Confidentially," I said. He nodded. "There's some conflict between me and the director, and he threatened to cancel the mission if I'm still managing it."

"Hmm," he said.

"I think everything's going to be okay, but it's still unnerving," I said. "If I don't step aside, I'll look like I'm in it for myself. If I give in, the project will be compromised."

"It's not your decision," he said. I stopped short.

"Now, I know why you're a professor," I said. "That's how it's being handled."

"Good," he said. "As you said, everything's going to be alright."

He walked away. I felt better.

Chapter 11

We made one more field trip before returning to Washington—to visit the exact site where Mike would arrive. We trekked a quarter mile into the middle of a sorghum field to reach the spot. Since sorghum wasn't native to Kansas, we hadn't studied it, and didn't know what to expect. We found ourselves up to our hips in a medium-height thick grass that looked like wheat on steroids. Our guide from the college informed us that grain sorghum is mostly used for feeding livestock, and most of the crop was shipped overseas. No wonder we'd never heard of it.

When our GPS confirmed we were at the spot, we stopped and I turned 180 degrees to get the lay of the land. Except for the Arkansas River to the north, all we saw was more sorghum. It would be grassland in 1876, just as it was grassland in 2010. The only difference was the grass in 1876 was likely to be sparse prairie grass eight or ten inches high, rather than the dense cultivated plants we were seeing.

"What's over there next to the river?" Mike asked, pointing a couple of hundred yards to the north.

"That's a gravel pit," the guide said. "But there's no river anymore. Ever since Colorado dammed it, we don't get any water. There's not much rain out here—maybe twenty-one inches a year. With Colorado damming the mountain runoff, we're left with nothing."

"Will there be water in the river when Mike's there?" I asked as we walked through the gravel farm to the riverbank. The riverbed was still there, but it was dry and full of weeds and stunted trees.

"Oh, yeah, there'll be a river. It won't be deep, but it'll be three or four times as wide. They narrowed the channel with these embankments after the flood of '65."

"You're sure it'll have water in 1876?" I asked.

He shrugged. "You can check it with the weather people at the airport," he said with a laugh. "I don't remember that year too well."

Before we boarded our flight at Dodge City Airport, we visited the weather bureau office next to the small airport's parking lot. The chief meteorologist pulled out the original reports and found that June 1876 was a little drier than usual, but a wet July made up for it. As our twin-engine plane lifted off the runway, I hoped that, when he jumped, Mike wouldn't arrive in 1876 in the middle of a rainstorm.

When we returned to the STRP campus in Washington, it was in a maelstrom. The turmoil was over control of both the first mission and, ultimately, of the entire program. Of course, it centered on me. The light was blinking on my answering machine when I entered my room.

"You are to meet with Director Dolan at 8:45 tomorrow morning."

It was his secretary's neutral voice conveying his stern mandate. I didn't look forward to the meeting.

I entered Dolan's office intending to take the neutral

position I'd taken with Jerry Knorr.

"Sit down," Dolan said. I saw no indication what tack he would take. I sat down.

"This program is in great jeopardy," he began. "If we don't resolve the problems immediately, the project will be scrapped and all of us will be out of work.

"You're aware, I'm sure, that I've recommended delaying the first mission until we can work out some technical problems and firm up the protocols."

"I don't know the details," I said.

When I didn't add anything further, he played his cards.

"I have to consider the long-range interests of this project. As director, I answer to Congress and to the President. We cannot risk a failure."

"There won't be a failure."

"I appreciate your confidence, but your involvement has isolated you from the overview I have. I get reports every day, and they concern me."

"In what way?"

He brushed my question away with his hand.

"I'm entrusted with this program, and I have to make the tough decisions."

"That's not exactly true."

He seemed startled and, momentarily at a loss for words.

"You're called the director," I said. "But you're no more than an administrator. You make sure we're funded. Everything else is decided by the people with the expertise to make the right calls."

Again, he brushed his hand, not quite as confidently this time.

"I don't intend to debate this with you," he said, but he did anyway. "Since my ability to secure funding depends on us succeeding, I must be sure we don't have any debacles. I have to be sure the decisions are right."

"I assume you didn't call me in to argue about the decision tree," I said.

"Will, let me be blunt. *You* are jeopardizing everything we've worked for."

"It's not my decision anymore than it's yours," I said. "I don't have a vote." I let that fact hang in the air before I dropped it on Dolan's desk with a thud. The thud was, "You remember, John, we didn't want any appearance that self-interest could affect decisions. This project is too important to have decisions made by someone who stands to gain by them."

I stared at him. He tried to return the stare, but he got my point, and he had no answer. He gathered some papers off his desk, straightened them, and, still not looking at me, said, "I don't know where we're going to find the funds to complete Mike's training. Thanks for coming in."

He dismissed me with that threat, his curt manner failing to hide his desperation.

I called Knorr when I returned to my cell.
"Let's take a walk," I said. "Gym door in five minutes?"

When Jerry and I left the gym, I asked about developments.
"Dolan's not getting much support," Jerry said, "but everyone's looking over their shoulders. Paranoia's everywhere. The rumor is that someone's in Dolan's pocket, and the mission is going to be sabotaged."

"Any chance of that?"

"I don't think so," he said. "But I'm as paranoid as anyone."

That wasn't reassuring. I recounted my meeting with Dolan.

"That's good to hear," Jerry said. "He wouldn't be pressuring you if he had things under control."

"Keep me advised," I said as we separated.

Chapter 12

With less than a month before launch, I felt confident the mission would go off as planned. Dolan had quieted down, Jerry was no longer worried, and Mike was doing great. Things couldn't be working out better.

After taking Sunday off, Mike, Bill, and I were to meet at 8 A.M. on Monday morning to go over the schedule for the week. Mike arrived on time, but as 8:15 approached, Bill was nowhere to be seen. Since Bill was the most punctual of anyone in STRP, I became worried.

"Bill," I said into the phone, "where are you?"

I didn't like the pause that followed.

"Oh, look, Will," he said. "I'm going to have to drop out. I've neglected everything else I'm supposed to be doing for the last month or so. I just can't continue."

Neglected everything? There was nothing else to neglect. His only job until Mike returned from Dodge was to support him and his mission. The excuse was clearly a fabrication. Was this Dolan's man? Was he trying to undermine the mission somehow? I didn't see how.

What was going on? Working on the mission was a big benefit to both Bill and me. It gave us a leg up for the next mission.

"Is there something you're not telling me?" I asked, rather than accept the lame excuse.

"No, Will," he said, feigning enthusiasm, "I'm all for Mike's mission, but I know that you and he can get him ready. You don't really need me."

I'd known Bill for half a decade, and I knew him to be a standup guy. I couldn't seriously entertain the suspicion that he'd sold out to Dolan, but I also couldn't buy his reason for dropping out.

Mike shrugged when I passed on Bill's excuse. He didn't seem as bothered as I was, and he seemed okay with going forward without him.

"Did something happen between you and Bill?" I asked.

"Not a thing," Mike said. "He's been great."

I believed him. Without any other option, Mike and I finalized the plans for the week without Bill, and I sent Mike on to the gym, promising to catch up to him within the hour.

"Jerry, Will here," I said into the phone. "Bill's dropped out and he's not giving me a story I can buy."

"What'd he tell you?"

I filled Jerry in, but he was of no help. He seemed in the dark but, like Mike, he didn't see it as a problem that would affect Mike's preparation.

"Just keep at it," he said. "You and Mike will do just fine without him. But I'll talk to Bill and see if I can find out more."

When I hung up, I sat for a few minutes trying to riddle out what was going on. I was inclined to see Dolan in every shadow but, like Mike and Jerry, I didn't see that Bill pulling out jeopardized the planned July launch. Nevertheless, I had that uneasy feeling in my gut that another shoe was about to drop, and I had no idea whose shoe it would be or when it would fall. Time to turn to Joey.

"This isn't like Bill Reed," I told Joey. "He's solid. It's not like him to jump ship like this."

"W-e-l-l-l-l," Joey said, temporizing while he thought. "Let's turn to the old question asked in every crime novel—*cui bono?*"

"That's the mystery here," I said. "I don't see anyone gaining. Not Bill, not Dolan, not anyone."

"Maybe the question is inappropriate then," Joey said. "Maybe there's no crime to solve. Maybe Bill's having problems at home. Maybe one of his kids is in trouble. Maybe he's got a mistress demanding more time."

"No, no, and no," I said. I didn't really know anything that justified my certainty, but I did know Bill. None of those possibilities was likely. Now, I started thinking like Sherlock Holmes when he said something to the effect that when you eliminate all other possibilities, what remains *has* to be the answer, however improbable it may be. My problem was that I'd eliminated all the possibilities and had nothing left—nothing probable and nothing improbable.

"Screw it," Joey said. "Do your job and let it go. Just don't depend on Bill again."

I reluctantly accepted Joey's advice and returned to my work with Mike.

Despite brushing off my concerns, Mike didn't seem to have his heart in the work anymore. The whole week, he seemed to be going through the motions rather than tackling the work as he had so up to Bill quitting. All the while he was slacking off, he voiced his understanding that we had to continue to work as if the whole project depended on us doing it right.

By Friday, I, too, was losing heart. We'd solved all the technical problems and we'd apparently prevented Dolan from taking over, but we were dying from within. Bill had disappeared completely, and only part of Mike was still with me. Why was I the only one who had any commitment to this mission?

The next morning, Mike called me as I was shaving.

"Will," he said and took a breath, "I'm not feeling up to it today."

"What's wrong?" I said, letting panic slip into my tone.

"Hell, I don't know. Just a little bit of a cold or something. I'm just feeling punk."

"You have to get to the clinic right away," I said. "Launch is twenty-nine days away. We've got to keep you healthy."

"Don't worry about it," he said. "I've already talked to the med people. He says I need rest."

"You sure?" I asked.

"Look, Will," he said. "Do me a favor. Go through the workout and meetings today for me. Later, you can fill me in, and it'll be as if I didn't even miss the day."

I didn't see the benefit that Mike would get from me training, but I didn't want to argue with him. Besides that, this was my job and I had nothing else to do anyway.

"Okay," I said uneasily. "Sure you don't need anything?"

"No, just do the job for me."

When I finished shaving, I called Jerry Knorr. "Jerry, the whole program's falling apart around me. First, Bill. Now Mike's sick. Are we going to be able to do this mission?"

"Sure we are," he said. He sounded confident. "Just a couple of setbacks. Do what Mike said and keep it on track."

I hung up feeling a little better, but I still felt Dolan was behind developments, and that he had a master plan to derail the mission. I considered confronting him but, instead, called Fity.

"What're you hearing?" I asked.

"Nothing," he said. "Bill's out. No big deal. Mike's under the weather. So what? If the launch was tomorrow, I'd be worried. Not four weeks before he's supposed to jump."

"You think I'm overreacting?"

"Something like that."

I'd now spoken with four of the team. The only ones I hadn't sounded out were Jim McDonnell and Kevin Keane. I was going to call them, but I replaced the receiver without dialing. As paranoid as I was becoming, I no longer believed that "a conspiracy of books and people hid the truth from me."

I still felt lonely, but I went about the training just as Mike asked.

Chapter 13

After I put in a full day of working out and planning, I dropped into Mike's room before going to dinner. He was in bed and didn't look good.

"Still not feeling well?" I asked.

"I'm hanging in there," he said without conviction. "I'll be back to work tomorrow."

"What'd the doctor tell you?"

"Just to rest like I told you this morning," he said.

"He didn't tell you what's wrong?"

"Maybe he implied I'm overworked," he said.

"I don't buy it," I said. "I've done everything you've done, and I'm feeling fine. Have you had any contacts with anyone who's sick?"

Mike shook his head. "Nah, I'm just a little tired. No big deal."

Mike's indifference to the situation baffled me. Maybe I was overreacting.

"No dinner tonight?" I asked.

Mike considered it briefly before saying, "I don't think so.

Maybe I'll join you later if I feel better."

I didn't believe him, but slapped him on the leg as encouragement.

I ate with the rest of the team, and none of them seemed concerned. They were more interested in talking about baseball or the hockey playoffs than Mike Hanly. I let it go.

During the next two weeks, Mike missed three more sessions and I grew increasingly alarmed. With just seventeen days to go, I confronted him. "I need to talk to the doc about this, but he won't talk to me. Will you give him the okay?"

"No," Mike said firmly.

"Am I missing something here?" I asked, my anxiety now up a notch. "I'm the mission manager. I'm entitled to any and all information that affects the mission."

I didn't mean that as sharply as it came out, but Mike's refusal was puzzling. Nothing he could have said or done would have raised my suspicions more than his abrupt refusal.

"Give me until Friday," he said. "If I'm still not feeling well, we'll talk to him together."

I reluctantly acquiesced. Despite appearances, he had to be feeling the pressure of the impending launch. He needed me to bolster his spirits, not add to his stress.

Friday morning meant Mike was just fourteen days from launching. It also meant, as it turned out, another call from Mike as I was getting ready. I expected another cancellation.

"Will, it's time we talked to the doctor," he said as soon as I lifted the receiver.

"Not feeling well again?" I asked.

"It's more than that?" he said. "See you at the dispensary." He hung up.

Sure that my suspicions had been justified, and with my blood pressure rising, I dressed quickly and made my way down the hallway. This wasn't going to be a happy meeting.

I arrived before Mike and greeted the doctor. "What's going on with Mike?" I asked.

"Let's wait for Mike," he said. "I think he'd prefer to tell you."

We waited uncomfortably for Mike to arrive. It seemed forever as I waited, sweating and agitated, angry with the doctor, and worried about Mike.

When he arrived, he seemed more relaxed and happier than I'd seen him in weeks.

"Sorry about the mystery, Will," he said, shaking my hand. "I'm glad to get this over with."

The doctor brought us into his office and, as soon as we sat down, we both looked at Mike.

"Will, I can't go to Dodge," he said with no further ceremony.

"What do you mean you *can't* go?" I asked, my voice high with tension. My world was collapsing around me.

"I have a condition that makes it impossible."

As much as I wanted to yank it out of him, I let him go on.

"Have you ever heard of Meniere's?" he asked.

"Yeah, Alan Shepard," I said. "Grounded him for fifteen years."

"Right," Mike said. "I'm grounded just like him. When I get a bout, it makes me sicker than any food poisoning, any flu. I can't even stand up."

"It's that inner ear thing," I said.

"Yeah, it's bad."

I turned to the doctor for help. "Can't you give him some medicine?"

The doctor shook his head. "No one knows what causes it. And none of the medicines does much good. There's no way Mike can do the mission."

I was without words to deal with this setback.

"When did you get it?" I asked.

"About a month ago," Mike said. "Surprisingly, you were never around when I had an attack. I've had about eight attacks so far, and they'll continue until they do surgery."

"No offense, doctor," I said nodding my head toward him, "but, Mike, you have to see a specialist."

Mike pursed his lips, "I have, two in fact. I have Meniere's."

I looked from Mike to the doctor and back. "Well . . . where does that leave us?"

Mike was lounging back in his chair. He looked healthy to me. He crossed his ankle onto his knee. I wanted to scream with frustration. How could he be so accepting of this?

He seemed to be enjoying my distress. He let my question hang in the air for a few seconds before answering me.

"Well, as I see it, the mission goes on schedule, without me."

"But you're the man. You've trained and studied for it," I argued. "It can't go without you."

"Well, it can," he said calmly. "Bill and you did exactly the same training as I did. Unfortunately, Bill's out of the picture now. That leaves you."

I was confused and disoriented, and didn't grasp the significance of Mike's words.

"What?" I asked irritably.

"You're fully trained. It's your mission now."

"Me?" I said. "Jerry's committee rejected me."

"No, they didn't," Mike said. "They just chose me ahead of you. No ever suggested you weren't qualified."

"And Bill? Does he know?"

"He knows."

"How long?" I asked.

"From the beginning," Mike said. "He was with me when I had my first attack."

"Why didn't you tell me? Why didn't he? And why did he

bail on us?"

Mike turned to the doctor to include him in his disclosure. "This doesn't leave this room," Mike said. "If this came out a month ago, Dolan could have pressured Jerry's committee to substitute someone else. Maybe they wouldn't have folded, but keeping it secret until now means there's only one candidate."

"And Bill?"

"He didn't bail. He stepped aside to narrow the options. Since he's missed a few weeks of training, he's out of the picture."

It all fitted together now. Mike hadn't said it, but I was sure that Jerry, Fity, Jim, and Kevin were in on it also.

"And Dolan?"

"He's a shit," said Mike, "but he has no argument for ousting you."

Tears started coming to my eyes as I appreciated what these guys had done for me.

"You really have Meniere's?" I asked.

Mike gestured toward the doctor.

"He really has Meniere's," the doctor confirmed.

"And you don't think Dolan can delay the mission?" I asked Mike.

"He'll get no support," Mike said. "The guys are united. They're behind you a hundred percent."

"You've talked to them?"

"Every one," Mike said. "And they've all heard a recording you haven't heard."

Mike pulled out his miniscule digital recorder and laid it on the table. He pressed the button. In a slightly scratchy and reverberating recording, I heard Dolan's familiar voice.

"Mike, you're on this mission because of me. I tried to work with Barrett, but he could never quite see the light of day. You don't have any choice or you'll end up like Barrett, without a mission and without a future."

Mike's voice, from closer to the microphone, answered.

"I'm here because the jump committee chose me. Not you."

"That's what you may think. Barrett wouldn't play ball and he suffered the consequences. Now, here's what you're going to do. You are going to gather anything in Dodge City that could be of value, Masterson's pistol, anything related to Earp, whatever—steal it if you have to—and bring them back. I'll sell them and you'll get a cut."

"I'm not going to do that," Mike said on the recording.

"You damn well are," Dolan said. "Or shall I make sure Reed replaces you?"

"Just try."

"Let me sweeten this for you," Dolan said. "Work with me on this and the next three missions. We'll make a killing and, then, I'll retire with a recommendation to the President that you replace me. You'll step into a very lucrative position, and I'll continue to sell the increasingly valuable treasures for you. For a cut, of course."

"And you think Bill would go along if I don't?" Mike asked.

"I know for a fact he will," Dolan said.

Mike turned the recorder off. "I spoke with Bill within hours of that conversation. He had me share it with the rest. It solidified the guys against Dolan."

"Why didn't I hear it then?" I asked.

"We already knew you wouldn't side with Dolan and, frankly, we worried you'd be upset by his assertion that he influenced my selection over you."

I didn't react to his explanation.

"Will, Dolan's a liar," Mike said. "Jerry would never be part of that. You have to know that."

"Yeah," I said. "I do know it, but Dolan has his ways."

"You should have been there when Jerry, Jim, Kevin, and Fity heard him say he got you dumped. You'd have no more doubts."

"You're right," I said. "I trust them."

"One final thing," Mike said. "Dolan's threats have nothing to do with me pulling out. The Meniere's is real, too real.

"You're it, and Dolan can't do a thing about it."

Chapter 14

"No, no, no," Dolan screamed. "I won't put up with it."

"You have no choice," Jerry replied.

"I do have a choice," Dolan replied, leaning across his desk to get as close to Jerry's face as he could. "We're not sending a second stringer on the first mission."

Jerry stood up, eyed Dolan for a moment, before saying quietly, "He's going." He paused again before adding, "And Barrett's not a second stringer. He's as good as we've got."

"Over my dead body," Dolan shouted to Jerry's back as Jerry walked out of his office.

That's how Dolan took the news, at least according to Jerry. I'll have to take his word for it. I leaned back and joined my hands behind my neck, smiling as Jerry recounted the story.

"I didn't think you'd be hurt by Dolan's reaction," Jerry said.

"We'll ultimately be judged more by our enemies than by our friends," I said. "Dolan's a good enemy to have. Where do we go from here?"

"You keep on training and avoid Dolan," Jerry said.

"We're all solidly behind you, There's nothing Dolan can do about it."

"He'll try something," I said, still bemused by Jerry's handling of Dolan's rage. "He doesn't know his limitations and he won't give up so easily."

I didn't know how to handle Bill Reed. I was ticked that he'd withheld Mike's condition from me, but I knew it must have been hard for him.

"Whose idea was it?" I asked when I first saw him after meeting with Mike and the doctor. We were in the weight room just after lunch on that same Friday.

"For what?" he asked.

"To set up Dolan so he couldn't scotch the mission."

"I guess Mike and I came up with it," he said.

I didn't believe him.

"You're lying," I said. "It was you."

I said that quietly so that no one else could hear the accusation. In fact, the banging weights covered most of our conversation.

"Why would I lie?" he asked, affecting hurt.

"Mike wouldn't think to ask you to step aside," I argued. "You could've had this mission."

"I don't think so," Bill deflected. "You had to be the next choice. Dodge was your show."

"Until Dolan strong-armed the committee into nixing me," I said. "Dolan would have pressured them again, and you would have gone."

"You're wrong," he said, keeping a straight face.

"Then, why did we need a charade to delay the disclosure until the last moment? And why did you have to disappear from training?"

"I was busy. It had nothing to do with it," he said.

He knew I wasn't buying it.

"Are you too busy to help me finish training?" I asked.

Bill smiled in defeat, even flushing a bit. "I'll make the time," he said. We shook hands and sealed the deal.

With the committee backing me, it was my job to get ready. That night, I sat down with a pad of paper and outlined what I needed to do. Two weeks didn't give me a lot of time. The first thing I had to do was adjust my thinking to being *the* man. Still only hours from being thrust into the spotlight, I was only gradually getting comfortable with it. I needed Joey to ground me.

"Joey," I said into the telephone, "I've been canned as manager of the first mission."

"Oh, God, no," Joey said. "Dolan again?"

"No," I said, affecting my saddest tone. "In fact, Dolan's livid about it."

"What? He hates you. He's got to be doing back flips."

It wasn't fair to continue misleading Joey, so I told him the whole story. He interrupted me with exclamations. "No kidding!" "Great." "Wow."

When I finished, he'd calmed down and asked the obvious, "How's Mike taking it?"

"He's great," I said. "Keep in mind he's known for a month. I'm the only one who's been hit with the surprise. Well, me and Dolan."

"So Jerry told him to stuff it?"

"That's what Jerry tells me."

"We have to celebrate," Joey said.

"Can't. I'm in training and can't spare the time."

"Time? Did I hear the word 'time'? In a couple of weeks, you'll discard a hundred and forty years, just throw them away like they never happened."

"Yeah, but I'd be an idiot to skip back to 1876 without being ready. I have to start tonight."

"Is Mike going to help Bill get you ready?"

"It didn't come up, but I'd be disappointed if he didn't. He'll help all he can."

"Congratulations," Joey said, before adding a somber note. "But beware of the feeble-minded program director. He won't go quietly."

Chapter 15

The next day, although still somewhat in shock, I reapplied myself to my studies and workouts. Despite my best efforts, I'd lost my edge from my conditioning while I prepared Mike. Now, it was different. The mission depended on me, and I couldn't slack off and give Dolan any encouragement. He had to see I believed the mission would go on schedule.

The jump doctors turned their attention from Mike to me and had to monitor me constantly. The first step was to give me a complete examination. I'd had a good relationship with them throughout out preparation, but I sensed a change in their greetings when I arrived. I tried to ignore it. I would have felt better if Mike's doctor was part of the examination team, but he wasn't.

"How're you feeling?" the flight physician asked.

"Great. Just fourteen days to go," I said.

When they didn't confirm that, I knew something was up. It started immediately.

"Your blood pressure seems a little high," the primary said, averting his eyes.

He examined my retinas next.

"How'd you sleep last night?" he asked.

"Fine," I said. "A little excited about taking Mike's place, but I was out in fifteen minutes."

He listened to my heart and, again looking away, asked another of the doctors, an internist, to listen. After he did so, they looked at each other with concern.

"Do we have a problem?" I asked.

"Oh, probably not," said the team doctor. "Just a few anomalies that will probably resolve themselves."

"Tell me," I demanded.

The internist sighed and took a seat in the corner of the small examination room.

"Will," he said in his best condescending manner, "your fitness is a combination of your physical condition and your mental state."

"Forget the prologue," I said. "What anomalies are you seeing?"

"You're now under a lot of stress," he said with a condescending look. "People handle it differently. Some can't handle it at all. We're concerned that the stress is affecting you physically. Your blood pressure has risen. Your heart rate is elevated, and I don't like what I'm seeing in your retina."

I seethed quietly, making my blood pressure and heart rate jump even higher. Moreover, since I was seeing red, my retinas probably didn't look good either.

"I'm feeling fine and, until just now, I was handling the stress just fine."

Rather than argue with me, the internist exchanged glances with the flight physician and patronized me, "As I said before, it'll probably pass by next week, and everything will be back to normal."

I dressed and left without another word. This was Dolan's doing.

"Joey," I said into my cell phone, "get me a doctor's appointment as soon as possible."

My brother hesitated at this unusual greeting. However, he knew me well enough to know there was a good reason.

"What kind of doctor? And how soon?"

"Immediately. I need a complete physical, including stress tests."

He called back in ten minutes. "Tomorrow at 10. Doctor Strand at Karen Clinic in Georgetown. Everything okay?"

"I think so. Just want to confirm it."

"And with Dolan?"

"Still up in the air," I said, "but what I hear is encouraging."

I made a point of collaring Jerry Knorr after dinner and I filled him in. "It's Dolan bullshit," I told him. "He's trying to go around your committee. If I'm physically, or mentally, unfit to go, it doesn't matter what you guys decided."

Jerry looked at me appraisingly. "Hang in there," he said. "The guys are behind you. Dolan's not going to get his way. Just relax."

I agreed, but I was feeling the stress the doctors created by their bogus findings. They might turn out to be right after all.

For the first time, I didn't sleep well that night. I worried my newly agitated state would lead Dr. Strand to confirm the project physicians' findings. I was in a Catch-22—if I worried about their findings, they'd say I was anxious; if I didn't worry, they would say I was dissociating under the pressure. Damn that Dolan.

I made it almost twenty minutes on the treadmill before my heart rate peaked and I started falling behind the curve.

"Mr. Barrett," Dr. Strand said after examining me, "you're in excellent health as far as I can tell. We pushed you hard on the stress test and the results look like a cross-country runner's. I'll get the blood test results back in a couple of days and then I can be sure."

"What about my blood pressure?"

"Very slightly elevated, well within normal limits."

"Any unusual sounds from my heart or lungs?"

Strand studied me before answering. "No," he said, drawing it out slightly. "Should there be?"

I shook my head.

"When the blood tests are in, I'll need a detailed report of your examination and your opinion about my fitness."

"I can do that, Mr. Barrett, but what's this about?"

"I can't say. All I can tell you is that someone wants to prevent me from doing a job and I suspect he's pressuring a doctor to say I have a physical problem."

This made Strand visibly nervous. I could almost see the sweat starting on his forehead.

"I'm not getting into a spitting match with another doctor . . ."

"No, you're not. I'll give your report to the other doctor before he can give a bad report, and it'll give him a way out. He'll have to pass me once he knows I've been certified as fit."

He searched my face, seemingly looking for assurance.

"You'll be saving his license," I said.

I had Bill pick up the full report from Strand and made several copies. When I went for my next examination, I brought the original with me. I exuded confidence as I walked in.

"Ten days to go," I said. Again, the two doctors were distant.

Before they began their examination, I hit them with the report.

"Your comments last time gave me concern," I said, forcing them to look me in the eyes. "To get assurance, I just had a complete physical, stress test and all. I'm in perfect health."

I stared them down. To their credit, they didn't flinch, but they also didn't show the relief the results called for. Finally, the internist spoke.

"Well, that's not a surprise. You're young, strong, and well-conditioned."

The other doctor asked if I had the report. I gave it to him, including the EKG, blood tests, and lung capacity results. He took them to his desk and studied them. An awkward silence ensued while he scrutinized the blood tests. I kept my eyes on the internist next to me, just to make him feel more awkward.

When the primary finished with the report, he held it up, almost as if he were offering it to the internist.

"The Karen Clinic. They do fine work. I see no reason to question Doctor Strand's opinion. It's all documented."

The two doctors looked at each other for just a fraction longer than was needed. In that short time, they had a meeting of the minds.

The internist turned to me and said, "Let's get some updated readings and confirm what Doctor Strand found."

They took the basics and agreed all was well.

"I think we all feel better about that," I said.

I thought I saw a look of relief on their faces when they nodded their agreement.

I called Jerry when I got back to my cell.

"Just in case you were wondering," I said, "the doctors say that I'm completely fit."

"Never doubted it."

Now that the days were getting short and I'd foiled the medical trap—and Dolan failed to intimidate my colleagues—he had to be feeling the squeeze. I spent my spare moments trying to think as he would. What would he try next?

I came up with only two possibilities: a psych disqualification or outright sabotage. I was confident we could deal with both. I wasn't confident, however, that I could think like Dolan. What other ideas could his Machiavellian mind conjure? If I was confident in anything, it was that Dolan would come up with the unexpected.

Chapter 16

The next hurdle was the psychological clearance, with a meeting with the psychological team scheduled two days after stuffing the Strand report down the medical doctors' throats. If all were well, now just eight days from launch, I'd be in the clear.

I found the team psychologist, a female, and two psychiatrists seated behind the conference room desk when I walked in. They welcomed me with smiles, but no warmth. I suspected they were already feeling the strain. Dolan was pushing them from one side, and, undoubtedly, they knew about the failed medical ambush.

"Let's be clear on this," I said. "This is just a formality. I'm ready to go and, not that I doubt your qualifications, I've just received a complete evaluation by my own team."

The three looked at me, all without expression.

"Why'd you think that was necessary?" the team psychologist asked.

"To take the pressure off you, Doctor, and you, gentlemen. It would ruin you professionally if you sent an unstable man on a mission. However, if you *and an independent team* cleared me, no one could second-guess you."

I opened my palms to them.

"We still have to give our opinions," the team leader said.

"And what is that opinion going to be?"

She glanced in turn at each of the others and fingered the file in front of her before she spoke.

"We need to ask you some questions."

"Go ahead."

She went through a charade of interrogating me, after which she glanced at her associates.

"Anything else?" she asked the others.

When they shrugged, she said, "You seem fine. Now, may I have a copy of your independent evaluation so we can attach it our report."

"No."

My refusal startled each of them.

"May I ask why not?" the leader asked.

"If you make your report after seeing mine, you could be accused of rubberstamping those findings. No, doctors, you don't want anyone to be able to say you were influenced in any way."

"Uh, that's . . . a good point."

"We're finished?" I said, standing up.

They remained seated and nodded without enthusiasm. I chuckled to myself, wondering how they would explain all this to Dolan. I didn't feel sorry for them.

Now, in my naivety, I saw only one last potential hurdle—sabotage. Combating that wouldn't be as easy. The most obvious way would be to tinker with the device or its software. However, I was more afraid of him tinkering with me—an accident or, more likely, poisoning. The more I thought about poisoning, the more I sweated, since I had to eat a couple of dozen more meals served by Dolan's kitchen.

However, I had a plan.

ဿ ဿ ဿ

The problem was I needed too many people to make my plan work. I could count on Knorr, but I needed more. We would need at least two others, and we didn't know who, if anyone, was in Dolan's pocket.

"Jerry, I have to rely on you," I said as we worked out on the rowing machines. "I have to stay healthy if I'm to make the first jump. I'm concerned."

"Seems like your only illness is the same paranoia infecting the rest of us."

"What's new?"

"Dolan's still raving about stopping the mission. Says he'll take down the whole program if he has to, if that's what it takes to stop you."

"I'm hurt," I said and theatrically dropped my chin onto my chest.

Jerry laughed, but his heart wasn't in it.

"He means it," he said after a polite pause. "In public, he puts on his bland, bureaucratic face, but, behind closed doors, he's out of control. I've seen him turn purple while he screeches."

I turned serious. "He wouldn't be acting out if he had things under control. His venom may be alarming, quiet confidence would worry me more."

"Now, how do you think he'll attack you?"

"A test to my digestive system," I said.

"Eating in the cafeteria could be an occupational hazard?"

"Yes, and we'd never know when or how," I said.

"You need a court taster," he said.

"In a way," I said. "If we rotated meals after we got them, . . . Or if I never got my own meal, . . ."

"Possibilities, but if we rotated, someone would get sick if they tried."

"They wouldn't try if we did it openly. They would know there was no way to identify my meal."

"How would we explain why we were trading meals?"

"Maybe we don't bother giving an explanation."

"The worst would be that everyone would think we're idiots. Dolan would see poisoning wouldn't work."

"Well, save a place at the table," Jerry said.

"And a couple of others? Who?"

"Bill and Fity?"

"They're as good as any," I said. "But I would be just as comfortable with Jim or Mike."

"Your choice," Jerry said. "Whoever you like."

"Bill and Fity."

Aside from poisoning, the only other sabotage I could imagine would be a contrived accident, but I doubted Dolan would go to that length. Nevertheless, I was extra careful in the weight room, and I crossed streets with my head on a swivel.

Dolan and I avoided each other most of the remaining days. The jump team, as we called the Flight Committee, had given him a final decision confirming I'd make the first trip. Now, it was just a matter of time.

"Will," Dolan said, coming up behind me. "Got a minute?"

I was relieved he wanted to meet. It might mean he was getting desperate. We walked to his office in silence.

"Will, believe it or not, I'm excited about your trip," he said. "I can't wait for it to happen."

He tried without success to put on a face to match his words.

"I agree with your concerns about misusing the project for personal gain, but I wonder if you would bring back one thing for me."

I still didn't say anything.

"It's nothing of value. Would you just get me Wyatt Earp's signature on something, say like a newspaper or a menu from the Long Branch?"

I shook my head. "I can't imagine what Wyatt Earp would say if I asked him to sign a menu."

Dolan opened his mouth to say something but stopped, his eyes glazing over. I guess he couldn't imagine what Earp would say either.

"Let's stick to the mission plan," I said, and left before he could get into a rant.

Chapter 17

Training took over my life. I studied, ran, lifted weights, went to class, and made lists. As my date with destiny approached, my energy waned. I was overtraining. Still, I pushed on.

Classes and books gave me the fundamental knowledge I needed about nineteenth century culture and idioms. I read every article and book on the West I could find and reread them as soon as I finished. I ran slide shows of all of my digital pictures from my Dodge trip and tested myself on animals, plants, and geological features found in southwest Kansas. I meditated on the trip for hours at a time. I pictured myself in Dodge City, envisioned the buildings I'd seen in old photographs, and injected myself into the scenes. I mentally walked down the board sidewalk, and imagined the sound of my boots on the wood planks and the talk of the people I passed. I visualized opening doors, walking into shops, and touching the clothes and other goods I'd find in those shops. Then, I'd mentally leave the shop and, when I stepped back out into the street, I'd listen to the horses shuffling at the hitching posts and to the wagons slowly rumbling down the street through the white dust. I inhaled the smells of the horses, of their ubiquitous droppings, and of the sweaty, unwashed people. I felt the heat of the Kansas summer, and found myself sweating despite the air conditioning in my room.

In my meditations, I met women and men of the nineteenth century, all wearing the simple clothes of the time, and I talked with them about the weather, the cattle herds just outside town, and the cowboys crowding the streets south of the tracks. I found everyone friendly and tolerant of the influx. I also imagined how appalled they'd be about the terrible massacre of Custer's men in Montana just over a week earlier.

My exercises were designed to acclimate me to the strange environment I'd visit so precipitously. I knew it was working when I found myself dreaming in the 1870s.

For weeks, I wore only the clothes that I'd wear for my transport—a white linen shirt, dark woolen pants held up by suspenders, and, underneath, cutoff long johns that buttoned up the front. On my feet, I wore thin white sox and a pair of ugly brown work boots. We knew enough not to have me wear cowboy boots.

Every night, I washed my clothes in primitive soap to fade the fabric. Over time, the whites took on a dull urine-yellow, and the dark pants faded into a non-descript gray. The suspenders looked more rose than red as the launch date approached.

I kept notes on the garb I'd encounter, more for my familiarity, since I'd travel with just the clothes on my back. However, I'd need the information if I had to replace any of my clothes while there.

Finally, I briefed myself on what the people of Dodge would, and wouldn't, know. I'd call attention to myself if I referred to events or people that happened after 1876. The Civil War and Lincoln were okay; the Spanish-American War and the assassination of President Garfield were not.

I made detailed lists of books, songs, events, and people to separate the "okays" from the "no-nos." Then, I studied the hundreds of items on each list to create a schizophrenic Will

Barrett—part pre-1876, part modern man. The destination committee detailed protocols of how I should present myself, and fashioned an unverifiable personal history for me.

Whenever I wasn't studying or meditating, I worked out. Besides controlling my weight, I also needed outdoor conditioning. I didn't expect to have to ride a horse in Dodge but, to be safe, I rode at least an hour every day through the trails surrounding campus, always using a western saddle. A side benefit of the riding was that it put wear marks on my clothes in the right places. It also darkened my pale Washington skin and gave me a tougher Western appearance. At least, I thought so.

I also walked a lot. Modern belief to the contrary, walking was the most common means of travel in the West. Unless one could afford a train or stagecoach ticket, walking was the only way to get anywhere, since few people owned a riding horse.

We targeted July 3rd for my launch.

I didn't see Dolan for days after he'd asked for Earp's autograph. The less I saw of him, the better I felt.

However, just a week before I was to leave, his secretary left me a message that the Board would meet the next morning at eight. She gave no reason.

I asked several of my colleagues, but they were equally in the dark. I didn't sleep well that night.

We gathered in the conference room at 8:00 but Dolan wasn't there. At 8:10, he walked in. In contrast to our casual dress, he was wearing a gray suit, white shirt, and tie. He also wore a grim look on his face. We quieted down.

With overwrought gravity, Dolan spoke. "We have a problem."

He paused theatrically and pursed his lips. He must have practiced this routine in front of a mirror.

Finally, he said, "As you may know, I have a source in Senator Talbot's office. And, as you certainly know, Senator

Talbot has considerable power in her position on the Senate Appropriations Committee. In any event, as ranking Republican on the committee, she has a great deal of influence on the committee's decisions."

Dolan paused again, letting tension rise in the room. Despite resenting his manipulations, I was becoming increasingly concerned.

"Our budget's in grave danger," Dolan said, drawing out 'grave.' "Talbot feels she needs a very spectacular journey to support renewing our funding."

No one reacted. Dolan nodded, his self-satisfaction barely disguised behind his sham look of sadness.

When no one rose to salute his report, Dolan added further muscle to his 'information,' "I'm told the Senator is appalled we're going to Dodge City." He said the last words with reluctance and disdain. "And feels she can no longer protect us if we treat this important project so cavalierly."

He repeated his grim theatrics as he looked at all of us. Although everyone maintained a manner of respect, I didn't sense any impact from his charade. It was time for me to speak. As I opened my mouth to do so, Bill Reed interrupted me.

"She's not suggesting that the Senate would completely abandon this project?" he asked.

"Oh," said Dolan dramatically, "that's exactly what I'm told. She's been our biggest supporter. Without her support, Appropriations would pull our funding out of the budget. Then, there'd be no chance it would be replaced. With our black status, there's no independent support on the Senate floor."

Here, Dolan put his head down, almost as if he were fighting back tears. He shook his head before bringing it back up.

"Remember, gentlemen," he said. "We're a big secret. Only half a dozen Senators even know we exist."

It was Bill's turn to speak again.

"John," he said in a sober tone, "this information is very

troubling. We're grateful that you've come to us with your concern. I'm sure that there's not a man in this room who doesn't share your distress over this information."

We all turned toward Bill. We didn't expect this attitude from him.

"If we lose the funding," he continued, "we and America will lose the benefit of this great enterprise."

Now, it was his turn to pause. Dolan was the only one nodding in agreement with him. The rest of us were sitting like statues, stunned by Bill's words. Had the mole just appeared?

"I don't see we have any choice but to do what's right for America," he said with increasing enthusiasm. Dolan grew more animated along with him

"That means that we maintain the integrity of this program and," another pause, "we tell the politicians to continue doing what they do best, screwing up the country, and leave us alone. I move that we go to Dodge, and that we do it on the schedule we set."

You could almost feel the whole room breathe out. Dolan, too, breathed out, deflated by the punch line, the rest of us with relief.

There was no reason for a vote, but Mike Hanly jumped in quickly. "I second."

There was no further discussion. The vote was unanimous. Dolan stared blank-faced as the tide whipped around and knocked him to his knees. He spoke not a word as we rose from our chairs and streamed from the room.

We were going to Dodge City.

Chapter 18

Now that I was in Kansas, *nineteenth-century* Kansas that is, the air scorched my whole body. I'd forgotten how hot Kansas could be in summer. Blowing across the plains like a hair dryer on high, unbuffered by any moisture, the blasts roasted my skin. The nonsense that dry heat was more tolerable than humid heat could only come from someone who'd never been out in a 100+-degree day in Kansas—or stuck his head into a hot oven.

Summer in Kansas, and there by my own choice. I'd say Never again! but that wouldn't be true. I was thrilled. I'd dreamed my whole life of doing something important and adventurous, and this mission was my fulfillment.

Kansas in July isn't my idea of paradise. Kansas at any time is anything but paradise. Winter or summer, Kansas has a hellacious climate. With no ocean breeze to temper the extremes, the heat and cold abuse the land and its people. For all its faults, I loved Kansas and the Old West, and my heart welled with gratitude that my colleagues had let me go. Kansas was the real Old West and it afforded the best climate, bad as it was, of any of the mythical frontier states.

Only a hardy people could have pushed the frontier through the western states, and only the hardiest of them would have stayed in such a climate. Outcasts, losers, if you will, but tough people, tough as the barbed wire that tamed the vast land.

All of those thoughts crossed my mind as I scanned the over-exposed, and overheated, land that greeted my arrival on the 3rd day of July 1876. I stood in the temporal middle of the so many famous events—the Gunfight at the O.K. Corral was still five years in the future, Sitting Bull just finished massacring Custer's 7th Cavalry a week earlier, and the declining Wild Bill Hickok still roamed rustic towns on the way to his brutal murder. I was born in 1983 but I now stood in blistering heat 107 years before my birth.

The *Space Time Research Project* needs some explaining. Theorists knew the *how* of time travel for almost a hundred years before I left on my mission in 2010. The way to do it hung in the air, low and close to the ground, waiting for someone to pick it. The secret lay hidden in the concept called the Uncertainty Principle formulated in 1927 by a German physicist, Werner Heisenberg. His thinking led the theory of quantum mechanics.

It took Dr. Loren Wright to harness the implications of the Uncertainty Principle and make time travel happen. In 2005, he peeked into the wonders of particle physics and saw time travel. If the world were fair, Wright would have been the first traveler. Wright's premature death gave me the privilege.

My engineering education prepared me for my brief careers on the Mars voyages and STRP, but quantum mechanics was beyond my reach. Although it had carried me back to nineteenth century Dodge, I'm still foggy on the details.

The specific of the Uncertainty Principle that permits time travel is that time is an illusion. All time—the past, the present, and the future—exists simultaneously. My understanding of time travel peters out at that point. At least I have an excuse. I'm in 1876—Heisenberg won't be born until 1901 and he won't propose the Uncertainty Principle until 1927. Not only does 1876 not have

93

the Uncertainty Principle, this romantic time doesn't have light bulbs, movies, or practical typewriters.

Wright's solution of the age-old mystery meant time travel was just a transition from one 'now' to another. As with most of nature's mysteries, time travel became easy once scientists solved the riddle. With the help of Heisenberg's theories, Wright proved that time had no past or future, and that even *now* was an illusion.

When Loren Wright cracked Heisenberg's code, he created the equivalent of the self-starting engine. And he called his invention a Time Machine. And because of Mike Hanly's illness and to Dolan's dismay, I became the first traveler sent back in time by the *Space Time Research Project*. The acronym, STRP, officially pronounced "Sterp," was corrupted into "Strip" and, as the first traveler, I became the first "Stripper."

Although my body was in Kansas, my thoughts returned to Washington. I reflected on my good fortune that the destinations committee chose my proposal of Dodge City in 1876. My arguments convinced them that this brief historical moment was important.

Wyatt Earp helped me sell Dodge. Earp, along with other later-famous lawmen, was a policeman in Dodge City in 1876. I was eager to meet him. However, I couldn't arrive in the middle of town, popping out of nowhere on Front Street. That might scare the horses and require impossible explanations. We chose coordinates that dropped me several miles west of town, specifically, 37° 44'34.75"N 100°04'43.55"W. The landing site was distant enough from Dodge to be sparsely populated, but close enough that I could walk to town.

As heir to eons of dreams, as a figurative son of H. G. Wells, Einstein, and Heisenberg, I stood, in the middle of tall pale, dry grass in a prairie dog village. I searched for some dramatic utterance, my own "That's one small step. . ." but my mind focused instead on how thirsty I was. "I thirst" was already taken, said under far more dramatic and important circumstances.

STRP sent my pampered twenty-first century body to Kansas. It was now up to me to find a way to survive. This soft, modern man was hot, thirsty, and sweaty. I wouldn't live long if I didn't get away from the chirping prairie dogs, away from the scrutiny of vultures, and find food, water, and shelter.

I saw scattered copses of trees in the distance along the river. Trees meant water and protection from the sun—and I needed both. Water might also mean farmers and settlers. A ranch or farmhouse couldn't be far.

Chapter 19

I stood in the middle of a prairie dog village but the animals had disappeared into their holes when I appeared. Now, they re-emerged, one at a time, watching me warily. They chirped loudly, whether at me or to each other, I couldn't tell. Over their noise, I could hear unseen meadowlarks twittering as I scanned the untouched land. Aside from the vultures spiraling overhead, the abundant life encouraged me. The vultures made my stomach tighten as they patiently gazed down, soaring and waiting.

"For God's sake," I said bravely. "I just arrived. I'm not about to die yet." The vultures took no heed and continued their aerial dance in the unclouded pale blue sky.

Despite all my conditioning, I was wearing down quickly, and I suspected those ugly creatures above were experts on my chances for survival. I despaired of fooling anyone else if birds hundreds of feet in the sky recognized me as a greenhorn.

Now, my eyes betrayed me, and I wasn't thinking right. Whether I was weak from the stress of the first jump or whether it was an unusually brutal hot sun above, I didn't know, but I could focus neither my eyes nor my attention.

"Discipline! Discipline!" I said, pressing my dried lips together hard. "Get yourself together."

My efforts to steel myself gave me some degree of control. I reminded myself what I needed to do—get shelter, water, and food. Now, I fell back my training to channel my thoughts on those essentials.

Although my eyes still weren't working, my mind reluctantly and lethargically listened. Everything was distorted, as if I were looking through heat waves rising from a distant highway. I squinted, blinked repeatedly, and rubbed my eyes, but nothing helped. When my mind started drifting again, I knew I was in danger of heat stroke. If I didn't get to water and shelter quickly, I'd die, and STRP would never know what became of me.

We'd never thought to have me carry water, since I'd arrive only a couple of hundred yards from the river. It never crossed our minds that the combination of the jump and a very hot day could impair me so quickly.

I needed to get out of the heat to the trees, which I guessed was a little more than a half mile away. I willed my legs to move, and I struck out northeast, toward the shade and the water I desperately needed.

I was no longer sweating—and my pulse rate was elevated. Sick to my stomach and dizzy, I was tired beyond words, but I forced myself to keep walking. My legs were heavy and pained, but I couldn't stop. If I did, I'd die. The vertigo was overwhelming as I plodded forward.

Keep walking I said to myself. Just keep walking.

I stumbled over prairie dog hills and staggered into unseen hollows in the grass, but I walked on. Painful step after painful step. I couldn't stop or let myself fall.

I wasn't thinking right, but I knew I was in mortal danger. I kept my eyes on the ground, wary of anything that could cause me to stumble. Still, my eyes let me down. Grass, dirt, hills, all waved in hallucinations of heat. I glanced up, but the trees seemed even farther away now—vague, dark shapes out there, so far away that I'd never reach them.

One step at a time, I told myself. Meanwhile, my body was telling me to sit down and rest. "No! No!" I shouted through a parched mouth. "You'll die. Keep walking."

One step . . . one more . . . one more. I touched my forehead—it was cold and dry. I couldn't feel my fingers, maybe because my fingers were tingling. I vomited violently, my stomach heaving in painful spasms.

I had to stop while my insides poured out onto the prairie. I took a couple of deep breaths, wiped my mouth with my sleeve. Feeling slightly better, I straightened, relocated the trees in the distance, and willed my feet to lead me on.

I vomited twice more as I progressed—each more painful and less renewing than the first. Now, my feet tingled like my hands making it hard to feel the ground. However, each step, each vomit, brought me closer to the trees.

I never gave up, thank God, and now I could see individual trees, and see the darkness under them. A hundred yards to go, a hundred or so more steps. All the while, the sun beat down on me and stole my strength, sapping my energy, so that each of those hundred steps became progressively more taxing.

Now, you can sit and take a rest, my evil side whispered. You need to rest or you won't make it.

"No," I screamed. "No, Goddammit."

I started counting my steps but lost count before I got beyond ten. However, when I sluggishly raised my head, I saw I was almost there. Twenty more steps, that's all. I was able to count twenty steps this time, but I still wasn't to the trees. Twenty more, that's all.

As I finally approached the copse, it grew larger than it first appeared. The humidity wafting from the trees lifted my spirit, but I was still a dead man walking, and my focus was worse than earlier. Desperate to get out of the sun and into the cool, shaded respite, I tried to quicken my strides. Despite my efforts, I seemed to be walking in place, and I feared I'd never make it.

I lost count, but my steps brought me to the edge of the trees. I bumbled into the branches and collapsed in the magnificent darkness. Even in my agitation and confusion, I gratefully felt the coolness. I lay on my back and spread my arms and legs to get rid of as much heat as I could. I clawed at my shirt buttons and laboriously pulled it free of my body. I was so pained that I wanted to die, but I fought back again. It took even more effort but I unbuttoned my pants and pulled them down below my knees. I needed air. I needed to get rid of the deadly heat.

I lay on the ground panting and disoriented, but I never lost consciousness. I couldn't let myself go, since I was having trouble breathing and was sure I'd die if I passed out. I'd lost all sense of time and didn't know if I lay there for twenty minutes or two hours. In time, the crisis passed. I knew I was going to make it when I felt a cooling breeze blow over my face and realized I was sweating again—a wonderful, joyous sign that the heat stroke had retreated. Although I was no longer nauseous, I remained dangerously weak. I had to get water, or I'd go into shock and never recover.

I raised my head and looked through the trees toward where I thought the river would be. It was still thirty yards away. I had to get up.

I had to get up—but I couldn't. My arms and legs were too weak. I couldn't even roll onto my side. Again, I panicked. Now, death was not just a reality—it was imminent. I passed out in surrender.

Chapter 20

I didn't die. That was the good news. The bad news was that, when I woke up, I wished I had. I'd been without water for hours and my whole body hurt, a deep to-the-core hurt I'd never felt before. My arms and legs felt paralyzed. However, with water just yards away, I couldn't give up.

I took some deep breaths to prepare for one big effort. Three breaths and I was going to get up. The oxygen gave me some strength, but it also renewed my dizziness. Nevertheless, after the third breath, I rolled onto my side and pushed myself into a sitting position. The blood ran from my head, and I almost passed out again. I fought it, and determined to get to my knees after three more breaths.

On hands and knees now, I would at least be able to crawl to the river if further efforts to stand failed. But I did the three-breath routine again and tried to get a foot under me—I couldn't. I noticed a small tree trunk a few feet away and crawled to it. Leaning my shoulder against it, I wrapped my hands around it and started pulling myself up. After scraping and sliding on the tree, I managed one foot, briefly. When I struggled to get my other foot in place, I weakened and fell back down onto my knees. I despaired, but clenched my teeth—I wasn't going to give up.

I clawed at the tree trunk again, my hands barely able to get any grip. Slowly, I struggled up the tree, and my shaking legs were under me. I had to hug the tree to keep from falling again. Slowly, falteringly, and painfully, I put my weight onto my legs. I was standing—barely and tenuously. I leaned lightly on the tree, hunched over, too pained to straighten. I teetered for a few moments, afraid to move away from the support. Accepting this as the best I was going to get, I pushed away from the tree, tilted toward the river, and stumbled and staggered, with halting steps, deeper into the trees.

I faltered several times and had to use passing trees as supports. But I never stopped, and when I reached the riverbank, I crumbled to the ground and tumbled down the embankment into the water. I sucked in as much water as I could. My lips were cracked, and I swallowed with difficulty. But, slowly, gradually, I gulped enough water to fill my stomach.

Fortunately, the river was shallow, only a foot or so deep, or else I might have drowned. As it was, I lay on my back with my face just above the surface. When I'd recovered sufficiently, I turned onto my hands and knees, took one last draught and pushed myself up—a far better imitation of erect posture than I'd managed moments earlier. I was stronger now and able to climb the bank. I was only on the bank a couple of seconds when my stomach cramped and I folded forward in pain. I started retching again.

Fortunately, the vomiting itself wasn't as painful or dangerous this time. I'd simply drunk too much, and my stomach couldn't handle it. I recovered quickly and clambered back into the river to replenish the water I'd lost. I drank more abstemiously this time, and I actually felt alive when I reclimbed the bank, alive for the first time since I'd arrived.

I looked around and saw no evidence of people—no houses, no animals, and nary a sound. Whatever birds lived in my small forest watched me silently.

The trees stretched about seventy yards along the river and appeared about thirty yards deep. After the skittering and cacawing I'd heard on the prairie, the silence was deafening—nothing, absolutely nothing. I was grateful, however, that the cocky vultures, if they were still around, were out from my sight, blocked by the canopy of trees. Even in this seemingly lifeless domain, I felt exhilarated, because those glorious, green, and protective trees shielded me like a cool tent.

I walked east along the riverbank, hoping for any sign of inhabitants, but I saw none. My eyes were back to normal now, but they detected no evidence that any human being was nearby. I walked with care, silencing my steps to match the empty stillness of this natural church. My stiff, cramped legs stiffened as I tried to keep my steps quiet. My stayed alert, hoping a human being, any human being, was nearby. I breathed deeply of the moist air to calm my nerves.

Even in the quiet, I sensed life hiding in the shadows. I marveled at the contrast—all the sounds in the hot sun and now, in the damp tree cover, no sounds at all. I inhaled again, this time to enjoy the damp smell of life and decay. I knew aggressive jays likely dominated the cottonwood patch, and that, any minute, a roost of them could threaten me with their harsh call. But I heard not a sound. I knew that hawks must also be watching my every move—unless they were all out controlling the prairie dog population.

With each step, my hopes ebbed as my search revealed nothing. I stopped to consider my plight. I was alone. I'd expected to find settlers nearby, but this grove of trees was my only hope for miles. My scanning of the area, the flatness as far as I could see, convinced me I was some distance from any other possible habitation. After what I'd suffered in the sun, I didn't intend to expose myself again. I'd wait until late afternoon when I was more likely to survive a long trek.

After I'd made my plan, I took no more than a few steps in the darkness when I sensed something. And it wasn't a bird. Did I hear something? Did some movement catch my eye? I froze in mid-step and listened. At first, nothing. Then, I heard hushed singing, perhaps a female voice. I swung my head around to find the direction of the sound. I advanced a few more steps and listened again. The sound was clearer, ahead of me and to the left—a woman singing. I walked on, gingerly lifting my feet and replacing them onto the dead leaves. I hoped she wouldn't hear my approach. That she continued singing, although sporadically, heartened me. I crept closer, a few feet at a time. The singing echoed euphonically through the trees now. After a score of mincing steps, I neared a clearing, but still couldn't see her.

Then I caught a glimpse of movement near a corner of the clearing, just sixty feet or so away. I stopped and slid behind a tree. I peeked out and saw something unexpected. The "voice" was nude. I could see her only with some difficulty because she stood knee-deep in the river under an awning of branches. The sun flickered onto her pale skin as the leaves flailed in the westerly wind. Her image flashed like a strobe light from impenetrable green shade to bright yellow sunlight. When the branches blocked the sun, she disappeared completely, only to reappear, sometimes in comely bits and pieces, occasionally, completely revealed.

My chest pained me as I paused and watched her, and listened to her song. She crooned a song that blended hope and melancholy, a brave tune reminiscent of an Irish ballad. She sung of tears watering the flowers of tomorrow and the futility of letting today's troubles stifle faith in another day's promise.

She interrupted her song to crouch and drown her head in the stream. When she did so, she revealed her figure, her long, strong legs, her tight, rounded bottom, and her healthy, full breasts. She looked too twenty-first century, too much a product of the gym and a careful diet, to live in the 1870s. Even her complexion disoriented me. The period photos of the nineteenth century West were shades of grays or, at best, sepia tones. This nightingale projected vibrant life, a very young woman, perhaps in her early 20s, with soft, pink skin and long dark-wheat hair, a *Playboy* centerfold ready to be photographed on her rural farm.

I watched her in awe and relief.

Chapter 21

The woman went on singing. I was safe. Only snatches of the words reached me, but the timbre of her voice came through clearly. She sang with a light, pure effect, much like the sound a fine crystal wineglass makes when tined. I still couldn't recognize the song, but I could tell that she sang of life's ongoing battle between hope and despair.

I watched her like a voyeur, which I certainly was, and felt a cold sweat of shame. My responses, both physical and emotional, peaked as she ran her hands over her tight flesh. I blinked and shook my head, embarrassed by what I was doing. I was intruding like a twelve-year-old upon this woman's privacy, and I knew better. I also feared that her husband, or father, might find my presence a bit threatening if he found me skulking behind in the trees.

I crept back the way I came, moving as silently as the dry leaves allowed. I still hadn't seen her house, but I knew it must be nearby. I'd find it when I returned later.

Watching my centerfold basking in the cool stream made me thirsty again. I retreated through the far side of the small forest and headed west along the riverbank, careful to keep the trees between the woman and me. I dropped down to the river when I was far enough away not to be seen.

The stream was far wider now than the dried bed I'd seen in the twenty-first century. Perhaps three hundred yards wide, but shallow, the water drifted past me heading east toward my bathing beauty.

I carried a small packet of powder to purify drinking water. The animal bacteria in this, or any, "pristine" stream made the water undrinkable by someone with a twenty-first century stomach. I'd drunk it earlier unpurified out of desperation, but I knew I'd pay for that later. Now, it was time to start being careful. As I stood above the river, however, I realized I had no container to hold the water during the purification.

I considered damming a small amount of water into a cupped-out hole but discarded that idea—the water would sink into the dirt before I could treat and drink it. I lifted my hat and scratched my head as I looked around for a solution. As I waved the hat to cool myself, I realized it was the solution. Movie cowboys used their hats to water their horses all the time—I could use mine as a bucket.

I slid down the few feet to the water, scooped the hat full of water, and hurriedly dropped in a few pinches of PUR powder. I swirled it to speed the process. Although PUR powder usually took thirty minutes to work, I had a high-speed version that purified in just five minutes, but even that was impractical because my hat wouldn't hold water that long. A ten-gallon hat works better in the movies than in real life. I waited about two minutes and gulped what remained. I suspected I might suffer later for my haste but, until I had a proper container, I had to put my caution to the side and keep my body hydrated. I filled the hat twice, gave it the scant PUR treatment each time, and drank all I could hold.

I had to give my Jayhawk beauty the chance to finish her bath and to dress before I ambled up for the 'first time.' I wanted my appearance to be as non-threatening as possible and was confident I'd be well received unless I gave cause for alarm. I was looking forward to seeing the woman again, but I needed to kill some time. I decided to keep away from the trees for fear of detection and found a scrawny bush that would give me sparse shade. I tilted my still-wet hat over my eyes and closed my eyes. I didn't sleep; my nerves wouldn't allow me to relax enough for that. When a respectable amount of time passed, I returned to the river and repeated my purification process. Grateful that I wasn't having any stomach distress, I set out toward the woman's oasis.

As I re-approached through the trees, I was able to see a structure now that I knew it had to be there. As I approached the far edge of the woods, I saw a small compound—a tiny sod house with one door and small windows, and a one-story barn nearby. The barn was only about fifteen feet on a side, with a rough corral next to it.

The compound roosted at the edge of the river like a chicken laying an egg. The two undistinguished shacks sat low on the bank as if they were hiding in the shadow of the trees. The house's sod bricks were decrepit, so worn from wind and weather that they seemed on their way toward returning to the ground. The weathered boards of the barn had darkened from age and they caused the barn to blend into the dark green trees, lost to all but the sharpest vision. A stranger passing a hundred yards away might fail to see either building unless the trees attracted him and he came closer.

Even then, he might assume they were abandoned. The buildings had a barren look about them, uncared for and uncaring. Given a few more years, they might succumb to nature, crumbling until no sign remained they ever existed.

The house was larger than the barn, but it stood only about seven feet high, barely half the height of the barn. Neither the barn nor the house was larger than a modern family room. The barn had no windows, just a hinged door hanging askew on the east side, its

107

door barely high enough for a horse to pass through.

The house door faced south, looking past the barn just to its west and the edge of the trees. I imagined that a house's back door opened to the riverbank on the far side. The front door hung on rusty hinges, opening outward. It stood slightly ajar, revealing a few inches of the dark interior. The lintel was low, so low that a full-sized man would have to remove his hat to enter and, even then, he'd bump his head unless he ducked.

The house had a small window on the west side, with a shutter hanging from the top. Small sticks propped the shutter open to let air and a little light inside.

The small corral almost joined the two buildings. Attached to north side of the barn, the corral fence reached tentatively toward the house, failing by the width of a narrow alley running along the west side of the house. The barn and house both fronted on a dusty area that served as a front yard.

There was neither activity, nor evidence of recent activity, anywhere, but small clues hinted that someone lived there: a dozen or so chickens pecked at invisible seeds in the thick dust covering the yard; the barn smelled of recent animal use; and a water pump near the barn wall was dripping water into a short trough.

My heart rate increased as I stepped from the protection of the trees. Once out of the trees, I could see down to the river through the drooping wire of the corral—the bathing spot was now empty. I listened for the woman or other occupants, but heard only the clucking of the chickens. I had an uneasy feeling in my stomach. I wasn't ready for this.

"Hello," I shouted.

I waited, but heard nothing, not even the chickens any longer.

"Hello. Anyone here?"

Silence again. I advanced slowly and glanced left toward the barn. The barn door was open, but it was quiet inside. I couldn't see anything in the dark interior. I looked to the right past the house for movement. Nothing.

I was about to shout again when I saw the front door of the house open a few more inches. I couldn't see who'd moved it, but someone watched me from just inside the door. I waited.

I took in the dilapidated condition of the whole place before I brought my eyes back to the black void between the cabin door and its jamb. With sweat pouring out of every inch of my skin, I waited for the man, or woman, to become visible. A few seconds passed without further movement. I worried that the hidden figure might be pointing a gun at me. I decided I should break the stalemate.

"Hey, I need some help," I said, not sure what help I needed.

Still nothing.

"I just need a little water." That sounded thin, considering that I was standing less than fifty feet from a river.

The door moved a few more inches, and I could now see something in the shadows. I waited.

The door inched open, and a woman stepped into the narrow opening. It appeared to be the same woman I saw bathing, but she now wore a rough white apron over a plain cotton dress that covered her from neck to ankle. She also wore a hard, merciless look on her face. She faced me at an angle, one hand on the door and the other behind her.

"What do you want?" she asked without wanting an answer.

The hardness of her voice stunned me. Even her face, the soft, ingenuous face I saw earlier, had taken on a brittle quality that discouraged any conversation.

"Sorry to bother you, Ma'am," I said. "I lost my horse this morning."

"What do you want?" she repeated.

I considered her position and imagined what she saw—a stranger dressed in rough-hewn work shoes, dark wool pants held up by cloth suspenders, and a collarless linen shirt. My hat, fresh from bucket duty, didn't make me look any more respectable. She might see me as a dangerous drifter or, perhaps worse, as a poor imitation of a late nineteenth-century drifter. An imposter with bad intentions.

"I need water," I said, "and a little food if you can spare any. I can pay for it."

She remained unmoved. I noticed she was barefooted. Her stern young face was still remarkable, but it reminded me of the Dorothea Lange black-and-whites from the Dust Bowl—hollow and hopeless. She blinked once, seeming to think over my request. She looked beyond me, searching for accomplices.

I wondered where her husband, or father, was. I concluded neither was nearby and that she was alone. She gave me a penetrating look, and seemed to read my thoughts.

"My husband will be along anytime now," she said. "He's on his way back from town."

I didn't believe her. She was alone and had to be very frightened.

"Water?" I asked. My spit was thickening, and I was having trouble speaking clearly.

She tilted her head toward the pump. I nodded my thanks.

Well water was safe to drink since the ground filtered out harmful bacteria as the water percolated toward the table. Although I drank my fill only fifteen minutes earlier, I was painfully thirsty again. I bounded to the pump to show her that water was my prime concern. I doffed my hat and threw it to the ground. I needed only a few strokes of the handle to draw the water, and I used both hands to push the icy water into my face and mouth.

I drank my fill and, picking up my hat, turned back toward my first Kansas contact. She hadn't moved. We were only about twenty-five feet apart, and she continued to glare at me as if I were a registered sex offender.

"I thank you for the water." I stepped from the pump to increase my distance from the woman. "I'm really sorry to have bothered you."

We stared at each other. My attempts to soften her attitude with politeness and friendliness weren't succeeding. Now that I was certain she was alone, I understood her fear, and I knew that she might overreact if she felt more threatened. The thought crossed my mind that, if I was going to die in the nineteenth century, it may as well be at the hands of this attractive woman.

In planning this visit, we'd worried about my Washington accent, but I no longer worried after hearing her challenge. She, too, had an Eastern accent, one not that different from mine.

She didn't acknowledge my thanks, but continued standing at the door, calculating the danger I presented. She could see I didn't have a gun since she'd seen me front and back already. I waited, shrugging my hands.

Without any change in her expression, she exposed her right hand for the first time. In her fist, she held a large pistol; it appeared to be a Colt Single Action Army. She held it awkwardly, with her pinky clenched against her palm. I tensed to run, but knew she could knock me down with one shot at the short distance that separated us. Instead, as my heart turned to liquid and my face went hot with fear, I stood still. I searched her face for some sign of her intentions.

Chapter 22

The standoff didn't last long, but any time when one's life hangs in the balance seems like forever—especially if one's prospects lay in someone else's hands. I tried to put myself in this woman's shoes (if she had shoes on, that is) and concluded that, from her point of view, shooting me offered a considerable upside—safety. On the other hand, not shooting me didn't seem to offer much.

I could see in her eyes we were both thinking the same thing. Both of us knew she was alone and vulnerable, and only one of us knew I was harmless. The only downside to shooting me was she'd have to bury me. That gave me small consolation because, for all I knew, she had strangers buried all over her land. I hoped she was philosophically opposed to killing strangers for no reason but, from what I'd heard, killing was easy after the first one.

She was still watching me with that hard look. The look didn't scare me as much as the fear that lay just under the surface. She wouldn't be dangerous if she weren't so terribly afraid.

As the seconds passed, I found my breathing slow, and my heart beats return to normal. To my surprise, I felt a certain elation, possibly because I was still alive. No, that wasn't it. I was enjoying the moment—the feeling of my life being at risk raised my spirits, maybe in the same way a rock climber feels during a particularly dangerous transition. A smile approached my lips, but I squelched it. I didn't want this woman to feel I was mocking her.

In my euphoria, I studied this woman's face again. God, she was beautiful. Nothing enhances beauty like vulnerability. Since I'd seen through the cold exterior, I could now look at the transcendent beauty of her eyes, skin, and features. She was incredibly beautiful. Adrenaline does strange things to us—one of them being to make us stupid.

"Ma'am," I said after we'd studied each other for too long, "excuse me for saying this, but you are the most beautiful woman I've ever seen."

I said it with the utmost sincerity, but I knew, as I finished those words, that they might be the last words I'd ever speak. An awful pause ensued—and my life moved closer to the edge. I took a deep breath and reflected on what I'd just done. Involuntarily, I was nodding my head. I still felt the euphoria, and I was glad I'd spoken the truth. I let the smile reach my lips this time. I smiled because I'd survived, at least so far, the most frightening moment of my life, and acknowledged to myself that I'd been just as afraid of the woman and her beauty as I'd been of her gun. I'd spoken the truth, and I wasn't afraid anymore. That, of course, didn't mean that I wasn't about to die.

But I didn't die. The woman's face cracked. Her eyes became confused just before her harsh look dissolved before my eyes. She was still staring at me, but tears welled in her eyes and, suddenly, tears ran down her cheeks.

I slowly spread my hands out from my waist. "I mean you no harm," I said quietly.

She nodded her head and blinked tears from her eyes. The nod was so tiny that the blinking was the larger of the two movements.

113

"I'd have already shot you if I thought you did," she said. She tried to keep her voice hard and flat, but it came out sounding brittle.

I didn't move as she eyed me. She held the pistol pointed down at her side, and I was reassured to see the hammer wasn't cocked.

"What happened to your horse?" she asked. It wasn't a friendly question. She was trying to regain the upper hand.

"Some hard cases took it from me just west of here," I lied. "Took everything I had."

"How were you going to pay for the food?" she asked.

"I have a little money in my boot and some inside my pants."

She questioned me again. "Why're you coming through here?"

She was asking questions to buy time. Her tears were drying, but she wasn't fully composed yet.

"I came out from the East a few months ago looking for work as a reporter," I said. "I couldn't find anything in Colorado, and thought I'd try around here."

"Doubt it," she said.

She put the gun into a pocket in her dress and told me, "Sit against the barn, and I'll bring you something."

As I waited, I thought about what I'd just seen. Although I'd hit a nerve, there was still a tough man inside that soft feminine body. I didn't have to wait long before she came out carrying a bundled rag. I noticed that she held the food between her thumb and the first three fingers of her hand, just as she'd held the gun. She must have injured her pinky and couldn't straighten it. I recalled, without any comfort, that a permanently curled finger is sometimes called a trigger finger. I didn't want to be thinking about trigger fingers just then.

I admired the way she walked across the yard. Her grace made me forget how hard and abrupt she'd been just minutes before.

She slowed as she got near me, but came close enough to reach the bundle out to me. Inside was a chunk of bread and a hard, dry piece of meat. I devoured the offering as she watched. I didn't realize how hungry I was until I had the food.

"This is good," I said. She nodded. She stood ten feet from me and never stopped watching me. She'd dried her eyes, but they were still red. They made her look helpless, but I knew better.

"Would you really have shot me?" I asked.

I saw a glimmer of humanity return to her face. My question apparently confused her, but she answered anyway by pursing her lips and nodding her head. I believed her.

"My name's Will," I said. I didn't get up or offer my hand—best not to do anything she might see as threatening.

"Tess," she said, some distance in her voice.

"That you in the trees earlier?" she asked.

I looked at her with new respect. She had radar before it was invented.

"Yes," I said. "Sorry I came up on you like that."

She accepted my apology. I gathered that my earlier retreat had inclined Tess to trust me. If I'd wanted to take advantage of her, that would have been the time. Of course, when I watched her, I didn't know she was alone, didn't know how defenseless she was.

I finished the brief meal and thanked her again. I stood slowly to hand her the rag. I reached out, making a point of keeping my distance.

"Can I get more water before I leave?"

Without taking her eyes off me, she stepped back, giving me a path to the pump. She tracked me as she would a dangerous animal—not with fear, but with a wary eye, studying every movement. I hadn't been studied like that since I lied to my mother when I was ten years old.

I cranked and drank, and wiped my hands on my pants.

As I turned around, I apologized again.

"I'll be on my way, if you just point me toward Dodge."

Her look told me she didn't think that was such a good idea. She stared me down some more.

"You need a place to sleep tonight," she finally said.

Her offer flustered me. "What about your husband?"

"He'll understand," she said flatly.

She surely knew I'd already figured out there was no husband.

"You can sleep in the barn," she said. "I'll bring you some food just before dark." She paused a beat. "If you come near the house, I'll kill you."

Not exactly Best Western hospitality but it was a start. Now more familiar with what were good manners in Kansas, I nodded my head. As she walked off, I said, "I'm sorry I upset you earlier."

She didn't turn, but I got a hesitation and a slight nod in return. Then, she went into the house. I was still standing in the yard when she re-emerged. She had her stern look on again. "You leave tomorrow," she said and turned before I could acknowledge her order.

Chapter 23

I stood for another moment after Tess closed the door behind her. Her order that I leave in the morning was both so abrupt and unexpected that I thought she might come out again and tell me to leave immediately. When she didn't reappear, I shrugged my shoulders and sat down against the front of the barn. She was beautiful but baffling.

With nothing better to do, I took a more careful inventory of the place. The house was larger than I first thought but had, I suspected, only the one room. The door opened outward and had no doorknob. It was probably hung to swing in to the jamb and could only be locked, if at all, by a bar inside. Since the one window was small and largely blocked by the shutter, the interior had to be very dark.

The roof was flat, pitched toward the back, making the house taller in front than the back. Even then, the front couldn't have been more than seven feet high. The exterior walls were very rough, looking more like old adobe than sod bricks. Stacked erratically around its exterior were the debris of rural life—nothing specific, but either items of character or items of junk, depending on one's view. The homestead reminded me of an aging animal hiding under the trees from the punishments of life. I could almost hear the walls crying they'd had enough and would welcome death.

The barn was no less forlorn. It stood at a right angle to the house, just southwest of it, with the near corner only fifteen or twenty feet from the near corner of the house. Its door was tall and narrow, barely large enough for a horse to duck through. The smell told me Tess had a horse around somewhere. At least, the smell gave the barn some semblance of life. When I peeked inside, I saw an open area just inside the door with the floor covered several inches thick with soiled hay. Aside from a couple of bales of hay, that open area was the homestead's attic, the place where the unusable artifacts not left around the perimeter walls of the house were deposited and forgotten. The back half, dark and shadowy, had two, side-by-side stalls, each taking up half the width, with a crude wall about my height separating the two. In the left stall, the hay was trampled and stained, leaving me to believe that Tess's unseen horse spent its nights there. A trio of rough trusses supported plank board roof. Whatever wasn't lying about on the dirty floor had been lifted onto the crosspieces, probably to preserve a pathway for the horse to pass.

The corral was rustic and covered most of the area between the two buildings. If the barn was the capital of a reversed letter "L," the corral was the down stroke and the house was the horizontal leg. The reversed "L" sat on the riverbank facing east. About twice the size of the barn, the pen was fenced on three sides by widely spaced posts connected by four strands of wire. The north side of the barn formed the fourth side of the corral. A battered, flimsy gate attached to the corner of the barn closed the opening into the corral.

A dozen or so chickens moved around the edges of the yard, still a wary of me. The compound tucked into the edge of the woods against the river. Even with the comfort of the trees and the stream, the whole place cried out its loneliness. As far as I could see, there were no other houses nearby.

The homestead was bleak. Tess was not farming the land nor was there anything else that might produce income. The shabby house needed plaster, and the barn was little more than an enlarged outhouse. Weeds sprouted in irregular patches throughout the corral. I speculated how this woman supported herself, but couldn't find evidence to justify any guesses.

I turned my thoughts to Tess. Although her slim figure said that she was just out of her teens, her face already showed signs of aging. Her long hair, tied in a bun in back, looked dark when wet, but it had dried to a variegated blonde like dry hay. The color matched the washed-out tan on her face.

She carried herself with a gracefulness out of place in this rough setting. Although she seemed to know she was attractive, she was as worn out and neglected as the buildings. I felt sorry for her, wishing her better. She shouldn't have to treat every stranger as if he had the plague.

I was speculating about the woman and projecting thoughts into her head, but I knew nothing about her. I saw her as if through a grimy window. Behind her fear and despair, however, her green eyes shimmered when she momentarily forgot her despair. She had a fine complexion that was worn raw from grit and sun. She had moments where a radiant smile almost surfaced. Underneath the plain dress and the frontier dirt, the woman faintly glowed with life. Despite all that, there was drop-dead gorgeous woman underneath.

Tess's desperate plight was weighing on my shoulders, and I shook myself to dislodge it. I brushed the dust off my shirt and stood up. I hoped I wouldn't frighten Tess if I wandered around. I felt her eyes watching me from the dark of the house and made myself as benign as possible. I strolled away from the barn across the small yard, taking an angle that I hoped would look like neither an escape nor an approach to the house.

I'd surveyed everything in short order. My only find, just over a rise, was the cow pasture. A dozen cows lifted their heads like a chorus line when I came into view, but they soon lost interest in me and resumed wrenching up grass. I also saw an auburn horse in the distance, but he showed no interest in me.

Between the house and the stream, I noticed a small garden full of greens, reds, and yellows—healthy plants to look at them. In contrast to the rest of the place, the garden was neat, orderly, and well-tended.

My tour took less than ten minutes, and I was already so wearied by rural life that I wanted to knock on the door and ask if Tess could come out to play. My tour was disheartening, and I began to entertain doubts about this mission. Perhaps, Dolan was right that this dreary place and dull time didn't justify any mission, much less the first. That thought shook me to the core and renewed my faith in Dodge City—if Dolan disapproved, it had to be good.

Tess must have seen me returning because she came out of the house and waited for me. She watched me as before, silently, non-committally.

I returned her gaze when I got close enough to see her eyes. I looked for some relaxation in her mien, but I wasn't sure I saw it. The staring contest grew uncomfortable, so I risked a conversation. I thought it best to start with something unthreatening.

"Can I ask you some questions about the town?"

She nodded.

"How far is it?" I asked.

She scrunched her face up, thinking how to answer me.

"Across the river and over the rise," she said tilting her head toward where I knew the town to be.

That didn't help me much, but I realized she didn't think in terms of time or miles. Of course, I knew the answers to my questions, but I had to play the out-of-town rube.

"How long would it take for me to get there?"

"A bit," she said but added, "You'd be pretty tired if you tried it there and back in one day."

Well, it sounded as if she wasn't going to let me borrow her horse to go to town. No surprise there. However, it also sounded as if she expected me to come back. Had she forgotten her command that I "leave tomorrow"?

"How big is Dodge City?"

She didn't seem to think much of my questions because I got another confused look from her.

"Not big, not small."

Overwhelmed by her details, I almost asked her if I could quote her on that. However, I hadn't noticed she had any sense of humor, and my sarcasm wouldn't foster further conversation.

"Big enough to get lost in?" I asked.

"Not likely," she said.

"I've heard people talk about a lawman named Wyatt Earp," I said. She didn't respond. "Heard of him?" I asked.

"Don't have much dealing with the law," she said. I took that to be a "no."

Since my cover was as an unemployed reporter, I asked about the local newspaper. That seemed to strike a chord with her.

"It's called the *Dodge City Times*," she said. "Comes out once a week. I get to read it during the winter."

"Only during the winter?" I asked.

"I don't get to town much during the summer," she said.

She was talking pretty well now, even if the information was sparse.

"I don't understand," I said. "Why is summer different?"

"I teach in town," she said, "but school lets out as soon as the crops come in, and it won't reopen until the Texans leave."

The cattle drovers wouldn't fully abandon the town until late October.

We'd been standing facing each other for some time now and, although the day had cooled, I was tired from my walks.

Aside from the bench against the barn, the yard was without chairs. I felt awkward about suggesting it, but I needed to get off my feet.

"Is there someplace we could sit?" I asked. "I'd like to hear about your life here."

A quick darting of her eyes told me my suggestion made her uneasy. She asked me to wait while she went into the house. She returned seconds later and had her pistol back in her hand. This time, she cocked the hammer and pointed it at me. I raised my hands in alarm. The look on her face convinced me to keep my mouth shut.

Chapter 24

"You said the men took your horse and gear," she said, her voice brittle and angry.

"Yeah," I cocked my head to the side, trying to understand why she was revisiting my story.

"Well, that looks like a gun there in your boot," she said and gestured at my right calf with the barrel of her pistol.

"That's no gun," I said hurriedly. This was going to take some explaining.

She stared at me, her gun still cocked and pointed below my waist. I stood frozen with fear, my heart thumping against my chest. My inclination was to show her it was nothing to be concerned about—but I checked myself, knowing any sudden movement could be my last.

"Can I show you?" I asked, my voice shaking. I'd never had a gun pointed at me before today, and I didn't much like it.

She nodded with a flat expression. I moved slowly and raised the right pants leg. I revealed what looked like an oversized pocket watch Velcroed to my calf. Fortunately, it didn't look anything like a gun.

I looked at Tess for assurance. She seemed satisfied, lowered her gun, uncocked it, and dropped it in her apron pocket. She seemed embarrassed.

"Sorry," she said. "I can't be too careful out here alone."

She probably didn't mean to admit she was alone, and I didn't think it politic to point out her slip.

"What is that?" she asked almost civilly.

Of course, the project knew that someone in Kansas would eventually see my device, and we had a cover story ready.

"It's a newfangled thing, just developed to help me get around," I lied. "I was born with a weak right leg, and this makes it stronger."

"How's it work?" she asked.

"I don't know," I said. "I'm not sure it does much, but I leave it on just in case it helps."

She didn't ask about the Velcro. She just nodded.

I couldn't tell her the device was my link to 2010, and that I'd be stuck in 1876 if I broke or lost it. It was true that it helped me get around, if time travel is "getting around," and that I didn't know how it worked. I just lied about my weak right leg.

The CrossChron, as we called the device, was simple in appearance. There were no dials and no flashing lights. Four pressure pads were inconspicuously located in the face. I punched in a sequence to activate the transporter. The battery would last about two weeks, and we planned for me to return every week to assure it didn't run down so far that I couldn't make it back.

"I have no gun," I said to reassure Tess.

Probably to show she believed me, she went back into the house and returned quickly. I didn't see the pistol again. She returned to her chores without further comment.

I sat uselessly against the barn and watched Tess as she worked. I was so focused on her scrubbing the wash that I didn't notice two riders come into view a few hundred yards away. They stopped at the crest of a low rise, their horses stomping the ground. Angled toward each other, the men talked. I got a bad feeling when one of them gestured toward me. Still leaning against the barn, I watched them with an empty feeling in my chest.

After a few minutes, the men spurred their horses forward. They kept their eyes on me as they approached. My pulse quickened when they both drew rifles from their scabbards and, almost in unison, worked the levers to chamber rounds.

They came forward ominously. I rose to my feet, my whole body tensing, butterflies in my stomach. I could see them better now. Rough looking, with crusty pants and shabby cowboy hats, the men hadn't shaved in weeks. Their horses glistened in the sun.

The men never took their eyes off me as they approached. I, in turn, never dared look away. When they were thirty yards or so away, the lead rider spoke.

"Raise your hands," he ordered as he pointed his Winchester at me. This was the second time I'd had a gun pointed at me in one day, and I still didn't like it. I didn't think I'd get used to it.

The man wore a dark hat and had a bushy dark mustache that partially covered the angry look on his face. I raised my hands with a jerk. Suddenly dripping with sweat that ran off my forehead, I clenched my eyes to clear the burning salt. My heart pounded against my ribs, and I felt myself getting faint. I realized I wasn't breathing and took a deep breath to stay upright.

The cowboys came in closer, their horses now moving abreast. Now the second rider pointed his rifle at me. He examined me quickly and announced, "That's one of them. Can I shoot him now?"

This one had an excitable manner, and he seemed eager to use his rifle on me, if only for the fun of it. Of the two, he scared me the most. He was tall and powerful but didn't seem to have much self-control, the type to incite a fight under any circumstance. He was probably typical of the cattle-drive cowboys—raised in rural Texas with little or no education and willing to join a brutal cattle drive just to find some excitement. My appraisal of the kid gave me increased concern—an immature, uneducated bully, looking for excitement and pointing a Winchester at me was not promising.

Despite their coarse looks, neither of the men looked much out of his teens, although the mustachioed one looked a year or two older than the other. Underneath the dirt and rough beards lay a callowness, which increased my fear. They both had a world-weariness beyond their years and an empty look to their eyes that made me suspect their horses were smarter than they were. A nod from the first man, and I would be dead. I felt myself losing control of my body.

Before the first man could respond to the question, Tess hurried across the yard. I hadn't noticed her, but she must have been watching.

"What's the meaning of this?" she demanded. She rushed toward me, her eyes wide with excitement, and her face flush.

When the men didn't answer her, she forced herself into the small gap between the horses and me. I could have reached out and touched her, except that I dared not lower my hands. I felt foolish having a woman protect me, but, under the circumstances, I was grateful for any help I could get.

She pushed at the neck of the nearest horse and demanded, "What are you doing on my property, and why are you pointing those guns at this man?"

Both men reluctantly acknowledged Tess by touching their free hands to their hat brims. They didn't lower their rifles.

"Speak up or move on," she said.

"Well, Ma'am," the older of the two said. "Some rustlers shot one of our boys this morning, a few miles from here. They didn't get none of our cattle, but they made a run for it." He gestured toward me with his rifle, "And this here is one of them."

Tess half turned and looked at me over her shoulder before speaking.

"No, he's not," she said to the men before ordering me, "Put your hands down."

Seeing the men shrinking before her, I lowered my hands very slowly. I slid a few feet along the barn wall so I was no longer behind Tess. The younger cowboy followed me with his eyes and his rifle, letting the other man deal with Tess.

The horses snorted and backed up a couple of steps as Tess pushed at the closer one again.

Tess raised her voice and pointed her finger toward the men.

"Now, it's time for you to leave," she said, sounding like a teacher speaking to wayward students. "Turn those horses around and get off my property. This man is my guest and he is certainly not a rustler."

Tess's orders cowed the men, and they left them unsure of what to do. With his rifle still pointed at me, the younger man glanced at the other, his horse jumping slightly as he did so. I stared at the muzzle of his gun, petrified that a twitch of the cretin's finger would send a bullet into my chest.

"Cam," said the younger man, his voice rising an octave, "let's just kill him and get back. Ignore the bitch—"

He barely had that word out of his mouth before Tess jumped all over him.

"How dare you!" she said. "If you speak like that one more time, I will get my gun and put a bullet through your filthy mouth." Considering how she greeted me the day before, I was surprised that she didn't have her pistol with her.

Looking at me but talking to Tess, the other man said, "We're not so sure. Blaine here apologizes for his manners."

In fact, Blaine showed no such contrition, but he wasn't inclined to confront Tess or to lobby further for my immediate execution.

After challenging the wise-mouthed youth, Tess returned her disdainful look to the first man.

"Well I am sure," she said. "You have no right to come onto my land and pull your guns on this man. Put those rifles away."

The men looked at each other, their certainty about me visibly wilting under Tess's orders. Cam looked sharply at Tess, resentment on his face. Although I couldn't see Tess's face, I could tell from the man's manner that she was giving him no reason to believe he could win this battle. After deliberating for a few moments, he relented, lowered the rifle's hammer with his thumb, and slipped his rifle into its scabbard. Blaine hesitated a second before reluctantly following suit. I could see his respect for, or his fear of, the first man draining from his face.

"Now, look at this man," Tess said, gesturing over her shoulder. "This is a rustler?" She sniggered when she asked the question.

"Look at his clothes." She grabbed my shirt. "Look at his boots. And, my God, look at his face." Her voice rose. "Does this look like a man who steals cattle?"

The men looked at me, but said nothing. Their horses took a few steps in place, anticipating they were about to leave.

"Get off my property," Tess said again.

The men exchanged glances and delayed briefly to save face. When Cam reached his hand up to his hat brim, I knew the confrontation was over. He turned his horse. Blaine glared at me with anger, but he, too, touched his hat at Tess, and turned his horse. They moved off without another word.

Tess stood in place as she watched the men retreat. The men began arguing when they got beyond our hearing, but, since they continued on their way, I didn't care.

Tess turned toward me. She looked flustered and tired from her exertion. I could see both fear and relief in her eyes.

"Thank you," I said.

"Well," she said with a huff, "whatever you are, you're not a cattle rustler. I guess we'll settle what you are later."

She looked at me intently, shook her head, and stalked off.

I found myself shaking after she left. The blood drained from my head, and my arms and hands felt like they were asleep. My stomach, weak under any circumstance, was about to heave. I slid down against the barn wall and put my head between my knees. I didn't want to embarrass myself by throwing up.

Chapter 25

Tess's rescue confused me, and her ridicule of my clothes embarrassed me. Our careful attention to details hadn't fooled her. Nor, I gathered, did my city tan make a convincing case of someone who'd ridden around the West for several weeks.

She didn't believe the smallest part of my story. Nevertheless, she didn't shoot me or run me off. She even came to my defense. I must have looked like a lost dog to her. A harmless lost dog.

I considered following her to explain myself. I decided not to since I didn't know what I'd say. Tess would question me when and how she wanted. Besides, I needed time to improve my story.

When my hands stopped tingling and blood returned to my head, I returned to the bench next to the barn. I pondered that, but for Tess's intervention, I'd be dead or on my way to a lynching. I owed her my life. How would I repay her?

When Tess brought me food a few hours later, I watched her eyes for how I should act. They betrayed nothing. She conducted herself as before the men arrived.

"That was kind of you," I said. I immediately regretted referring to the incident—I should have let her decide when she wanted to talk.

"What was I supposed to do?" she asked contentiously. "Let them shoot you or drag you off?"

I shrugged.

"Weren't you frightened?" I asked.

Tess turned toward me, a look of wonder on her face. "Of course, I was," she said. "They would have killed you."

"I meant weren't you frightened for yourself?"

She thought a moment about that. "I don't know," she said, clearly finding my question unexpected. "Anyone with a gun scares me, but," she paused as if trying to recall what she was feeling during the confrontation, "I wasn't thinking about me. I couldn't stand by and let them take you."

"Why not?" I asked. "It really wasn't any of your business."

I saw I was intruding. Her defenses came up.

"They didn't belong here, and I didn't want them around," she said with finality. Her justification sounded as lame as my cover story.

"I don't know that I belong here either," I said.

"Are you a cattle rustler?" she asked, making a point more than asking a question. She spoke with a forced assertiveness to avoid explaining her courage. Or was she avoiding talking about me?

"Well, no," I said and averted my eyes to the ground.

"You're here because I let you stay here," she said.

"I'm a guest?" I asked, repeating what she told the men.

"You're a guest," she agreed. "And when you want, you'll tell me who you are and why you're here," Tess said, looking me in the eye.

She spoke with the same no-nonsense tone she used earlier, but her eyes betrayed her eagerness that I explain myself. She still barked, but the threat of a bite was gone. In that moment, we connected, and my chest welled with an overwhelming gratitude.

I nodded my head. She walked off.

For some reason, she trusted me, and she'd wait for the truth until I was ready. I wasn't sure what my story would be. My first story didn't convince her. I knew my next one needed to be a heck of a lot better . . . or the truth.

I offered to help with some of the chores.

"What are you good at?" she asked, not kindly but without malice.

I felt myself blush. Neither my twenty-first century life nor my engineering background gave me skills useful to Tess.

"Can you feed the chickens?" she asked.

"Of course," I said, perhaps too insistently. "Just tell me what you want me to do, and I'll do it."

Tess cast a condescending glance at me. I must have appeared defenseless because a motherly look came over her face.

"Let me show you where the seed is," she said, moving toward the barn. "Just spread it around the yard. Don't drop the seeds all in one place or the chickens will fight more than eat."

I could do that job. She filled a wooden bowl with the seed and handed it to me. I accepted the bowl and looked into her eyes. She looked back for a moment before she blinked.

"Well," she said. "Feed the chickens."

We had evolved to where we were avoiding things. In such a short time, we already had so much to avoid.

I fed the chickens. At least, they were grateful. I couldn't say the same for Tess. My help made more work for her.

I scattered the seed around the small yard, but I finished in about five minutes, and again had nothing to do. After returning the bowl to the seed bag, I approached Tess as she knelt next to the river, washing clothes.

"Finished?" she asked. When I nodded, she searched

around for a simple task I might be able to do. "Can you drive some nails into the fence?" she asked.

"Sure," I said. I asked where the nails and hammer were, and I made the most of the task. I felt like a boy doing busy work to stay out of the way.

Later, when we were standing under the trees taking a break, Tess addressed the five-hundred-pound gorilla.

"You don't have to tell me," she said. "But, if you want, you can tell me who you are."

When I went to speak, she interrupted me. "Just tell me the truth. If it isn't going to be the truth, don't bother."

We looked at each other. She meant what she said, and I knew I needn't explain myself. If I refused, she would accept my decision, but she wouldn't put up with another fiction.

"I can tell you," I said. "But you're not going to believe me."

She turned toward me but looked more through me than at me.

"If you tell the truth and I don't believe you, that's my problem," she said. "If you story tell again, that's your problem, whether I believe you or not."

She sensed I wanted to tell her, and she questioned me.

"You're not a newspaper man, are you?"

"No."

"And you didn't lose your horse to hard men, did you?"

"No."

"So, now I know what you aren't and how you didn't get here," she said.

I shrugged in acknowledgment.

"Your clothes and boots are new, and you're not used to wearing your hat."

"At least they fit," I said. She didn't laugh.

"And you obviously haven't spent a lot of time in the sun,"

she said.

"I don't look like a cattle rustler, huh?"

She shook her head, a poignant sadness in her manner.

"It all looks put on to me. But you don't seem shady." She spoke quietly. She paused and added, "Snake oil salesmen never do."

"I wouldn't know what snake oil is," I said.

"What I can't figure out," she continued, "is whether you're here for a reason or whether you just happened on SouthFord."

"Just happened on it," I said.

"Is there someplace you're heading?"

"Just Dodge City," I said.

"Then, why are you hanging around here?" she asked.

"Maybe, it's the company," I said.

I said it sincerely, but she ignored the comment and the sincerity in my manner.

"What could you want out here? A ranch with a mortgage and few animals. The chickens, the horse, and the cows can't be worth more than a hundred dollars. And, believe me, I don't have any money stashed around here."

"No," I said. "I don't suspect you do."

We fell silent before she spoke again.

"Are you the tall, silent stranger who arrives in town, and no one ever knows your past?"

"Maybe, I don't have a past," I said. "Maybe, all I have is a future."

Tess's eyes focused in the dust as she digested my riddle, knowing my words had meaning.

"Can we sit somewhere?" I asked.

Chapter 26

"We can sit here," she said and moved toward a couple of stumps near the far corner of the house.

We sat about eight feet apart. When I turned to her, she had a stern look, which I took to mean she wouldn't tolerate any fairy tales. I wasn't inclined to try her patience, but I needed to soften her a little before I revealed anything.

"How'd you end up here?" I asked.

Tess studied me for a moment, perhaps weighing whether she should bare her life to me. I guess she decided she should.

"We came here from back East in October," she said. "I was to teach, and Wiley would make a fortune somehow or other." She paused and her eyes lost focus. "He got killed in a wagon accident in May." She said it so quietly that I barely heard it.

I waited for her to continue, but she had nothing more to say. She returned to the present and looked at me. For the first time, she looked soft and vulnerable, almost fragile. I averted my eyes and coughed to cover my unease.

"How'd you end up with this?" I asked, waving at the ranch.

"We had some money and the place was available," she said wistfully. "Someone abandoned it, from what I heard. They called it SouthFord."

"You making it?" I asked, apropos to nothing.

She only shrugged. I thought she was going to cry, but no tears came. Still, the hopeless look on her face made me wish I were back in Washington.

"And you?" she asked.

I shouldn't have told her, but her vulnerability and lack of pretense touched something in me and I just couldn't lie to her—not then. The Heisenbergs would never understand why I confessed.

"I'm from Washington."

She still looked weary when she asked, "How'd you really get here?"

I inhaled and looked at her. Her sad eyes compelled me to admit what I'd pledged never to do.

"I came back in time," I said. "From the year 2010."

She stared at me with those sad eyes, smiling wanly. "Yeah, and I'm Marie Antoinette, and I escaped from Paris just before they chopped my head off."

"She wasn't blonde," I said. I was dispirited from Tess's circumstances, but I forced a smile.

"How do you know?" she asked. She didn't smile. "Did you visit 1793 before dropping into Kansas?"

I shook my head with a resignation. I desperately wanted to win her confidence, but everything I said separated us more.

"I'm tired," she said. "It was nice talking with you."

She didn't mean that. She was a weary young woman, who didn't have the energy to entertain my nonsense. I had to gain her trust.

"Will you hear me out?" I begged. "Just give me five minutes."

She hadn't gotten up. She looked at me blandly, giving me

another chance.

I bared my leg again and pointed to the Velcroed device. "You've never seen anything like that, because Velcro wasn't invented until the 1940s. And that isn't a contraption to help me walk. It's a CrossChron and it allows me to move through time," I said too earnestly. "I'm the first to try it. I'm twenty-seven, and I got to make the trip because I promoted Dodge City as the first target." I didn't bother explaining about Hanly getting sick; it didn't matter.

She looked at me without commitment. I was sure she was thinking, if she believed anything I said, Why would anyone choose Dodge City?, but she was discreet enough not to say it.

"Let me tell you what's going to happen in the next several years," I said, my last shot, at least at this sitting, to convince her to believe me.

"A few months ago, a man named Bell invented the telephone in Boston," I said. "It's kind of like the telegraph except that you can talk to someone far away. And next month, Wild Bill Hickok—you've heard of him—will be shot in the back of the head in Deadwood, Dakota Territory."

She remained sitting on the stump. That encouraged me.

"And I asked you about Wyatt Earp," I said. "Well, he's going to move on, ultimately to Arizona, and become the most famous lawman in the West."

"And what happens to Dodge City?" she asked, not believing anything I'd said.

"Well, it's a mixed bag," I said. "The big cattle drives from Texas are just starting, but they'll stop in four or five years when the railroad reaches Texas, and the cowboys don't have to drive the cattle up here anymore."

I looked at her, eager for her to believe me. She only shook her head slowly, not refusing to believe but refusing to look foolish.

"Are you a drummer or something?" she asked.

"No," I said. "I'm not selling anything."

"Why would you come to Dodge City of all places?" she asked. I guess she was not as tactful as I thought.

I pursed my lips. It would be harder to explain the mission to Tess than it had been to convince the committee.

"You might find this hard to believe, but, in our time, we see the West as the most romantic and interesting period in American history. We make movies about it, read novels about the West, and make heroes of people like Earp, Hickok, Billy the Kid, and even Jesse James.

"The train robber?" she asked about James with a backward jerk of her head.

"Yeah," I said, "one and the same. And, by the way, a man named Bob Ford will kill him in Missouri in 1882."

"That's a good story," she said. "But, as you can see, there's nothing romantic about living in Kansas in 1876."

I'd lost Tess and couldn't blame her. Hollywood could make a small, rough ranch in the middle of nowhere look fascinating in a movie, but the reality was nothing like a movie set.

"What's a movie?" she asked. "You said you make movies about these people?"

I didn't know how to explain movies but I tried, "They're like the pictures you see in town, you know, the paper photographs, except that they move. And you can tell a story with them, kind of like going to a play in the theatre."

"Why not just go to the theatre?" she asked.

"Because they can make copies of the movie, and show it many places at the same time without the actors being there."

"Is life better in the future?" she asked, just playing along.

"Well, in some ways, it is," I said. "In some ways, it's not. Like, for instance, there will be two terrible world wars in the 1900s."

"No worse than the Civil War," she asserted.

"Not for the United States, but a hundred times more

people died in Europe in each of those wars than died in the Civil War.

"But, it's not all bad," I hurried to explain. "In the future, you won't ride around in wagons, at least not wagons pulled by horses. Everyone has what we call a car, and it has a motor to make it move."

"And people aren't killed in wagon accidents anymore?" she asked.

That set me back. But I told her the truth. "Well, they are. In fact, more than 30,000 people die in car accidents each year in the United States. But it's not as bad as it sounds, because everyone drives about 10,000 miles a year and more than ten times as many people live in the U.S. in my time."

"Is Will your real name?"

"Yes," I said. "Well, my real name is Williamson but I don't go by that."

"Why not?" she asked. "I like it."

"It's pretty stiff," I said. "And, besides, my mother always called me 'Sonny' when I was growing up. So, I don't use the full name much."

She looked at me for a moment before she spoke.

"I like you," she said softly. "I just don't believe you. And I still don't know why you're here. There's nothing to steal from me, except my horse and the cows."

"I don't want your horse or your cows," I said.

"I believe that," she said quietly. "I have some chores to do." She got up and went into the house. I sat for a while and thought about how stupid I must have sounded. I could never convince anyone I came from the future, but I never thought I'd have to.

Most of all, I didn't think I'd meet someone like Tess, someone I'd want to convince.

I didn't see Tess again until dusk. I did more exploring. I

looked inside the barn and found that my sleeping quarters were about what I expected—dark and airless. From the smell, the hay hadn't been changed in weeks. I decided to let the horse decide where we'd sleep. If he'd go in there, I would, too.

I wandered about the small garden. All of the plants were doing well. Tess had small patches of lettuce, cabbage, carrots, potatoes, corn, and some plants I didn't recognize. I assumed she fertilized them with the byproduct of her cows, but I didn't see an irrigation system. In the Kansas heat, the garden could only be productive with a lot of water. Although the river was just feet away, but it wouldn't water the crops on its own.

The corral wasn't in good shape despite my earlier efforts to repair the fence. Some of the poles were broken or fallen and, here and there, the wire still needed my attention. In fact, the whole place needed work. The barn had never seen paint and the sod brick walls of the house were decrepit. Both structures seemed resigned to sinking into the ground.

I still hadn't seen the inside of the house, but it had to be as dark and airless as the barn. I hoped it smelled better. I couldn't imagine how Tess slept inside without any breeze. The barn wouldn't be much better, and I'd find out soon if the horse convinced me to sleep in the barn. I didn't know if it was safe to consider the alternative of sleeping outside.

Chapter 27

Dusk settled in as Tess emerged from behind the house carrying a large bowl and a block of cornbread. A filigree of the steam rose from the bowl and drifted over her shoulder as she walked toward me. I searched her face, without reward, for a clue to her thoughts.

"Thank you," I said when she handed the bowl to me. I lifted the wooden spoon and leaned over the bowl to savor the smell of the meal, surmising it was a vegetable stew made up mostly of cabbage. My stomach was empty, and the stew smelled, and looked like, a feast to me.

Tess said nothing as she watched me attack the food. I couldn't guess her thoughts, but I wanted to get into her head, to understand her, and, ultimately, to win her confidence. The time-travel story had fallen like a rock in the river. I thought it best not to aggravate her further by insisting it was all true.

I broke the silence. "Would it be safe for me to sleep outside?" I asked.

"Probably," she said, not taking her eyes from me. That was all I was getting on that.

"I'd like to go into Dodge City tomorrow," I said.

Tess continued to scrutinize me, but said nothing. I realized my statement didn't require an answer.

I continued, "How's best I do that?"

She didn't understand my question, or chose not to, since she answered, "You'd cross the river and go east on the Trail."

"The Trail?" I asked.

"Santa Fe Trail's just across the river. Bring you to town."

As if it related to what she'd said, she asked, "Are you married?"

"No," I said. She looked at me blankly. I added, "I was, but it didn't work out."

"Why?"

I didn't want to talk about it, but I also didn't want to make an issue of refusing.

"Why?" I said, repeating her question. "All sorts of reasons, I guess. She said my work became my mistress, that it was more important to me than her."

"Was it?"

"I don't know," I said. "My brother agreed with her. So, I guess she was right."

"You believed your brother, but not her?" Tess said. She didn't wait for my response. I had none and felt her disapproval.

"Did you love her?" she asked.

I was already weary of this topic. "Yes, I loved her," I said and stopped. "But I guess I loved my ambition more."

"Any children?"

"No. How long would it take me to get to Dodge?"

"Where does your past wife live?" she asked.

"Washington," I said. "Could I make it in an hour?"

"Maybe," she said.

She was annoying me now, and so I asked, "Could I borrow your horse?"

"Don't know what good it would do you," she said. "I

don't have a saddle."

"What's the horse for?"

"For the wagon," she said.

I looked around and didn't see a wagon.

"It's broken," she explained quietly.

I realized her husband was killed in the missing wagon.

"I'm sorry," I said. "I shouldn't be asking."

"Does your wife know you traveled here?" she asked.

"Ex-wife," I said between slurps. "And, no, she doesn't. This whole thing is very hush-hush. Just about nobody knows I'm doing this." I added pointedly, "I never see my ex-wife. We don't have anything to say to each other. And, if we did, my work would be the last thing we'd talk about."

We sat in silence for a time. When I finished the stew and bread, I decided to clear the air. "I apologize for being short about my marriage, but it brings back bad memories. My father abandoned my mother for who knows what reason. When my marriage fell apart, I realized I'd done the same thing to my wife. I've never felt good about it."

"Maybe you're not your father," she said.

I looked at her, but she gave no indication of what she meant. "My father was abusive to my mother. What I did was almost as bad."

"Would you marry again?"

"What, and abuse another woman?" I said. "I doubt it."

Against my better judgment, I changed the subject back to why I was in Kansas. "My work consumed me completely. I ate, drank, and slept Mars and, then, time travel. I was a very boring person."

Tess didn't say anything, but the Mars comment caused her to flinch in confusion.

"My work seems important to me, but maybe it isn't," I added. "Are you impressed talking to the first time traveler?"

She rolled her eyes and shoulders in a very modern-looking

way, eloquently signaling her lack acceptance of my time-travel story.

"I didn't think so," I said. "Look," I added a little too sharply, "I know you don't believe me, and I don't blame you." I took a breath and tried to take the edge off my voice. "When I go back, I'll return with something that'll convince you."

As soon as I said that, I thought, Why am I trying to so hard to convince her? I'm much better off if she thinks I'm lying, but I so wanted her to believe me. I decided to change the subject.

"Are you going to stay here after what's happened?"

She inhaled deeply and let it out in a quiet sigh. "I don't have anywhere else to go."

"No relatives back east?" I asked.

"None to speak of, and, besides, I don't have the money to go back," she said desperately. "They don't pay teachers much."

I asked about her teaching.

"Sixteen children in the school, from five or six up to twelve years old," she explained.

"A one-room school?" I asked.

My question confused her. "Yes," she said, "of course. None of them has any interest in learning. Their parents aren't educated, and few of them believe learning will help their children. Most of them are satisfied if their children can read and write," she said glumly. "And I mean just barely."

"Do you like teaching?"

She brightened at my question. Her face colored, and that spark of beauty re-appeared.

"I do," she said with conviction. "It's just that no one seems to care out here."

I nodded, sure she was right.

"You're an educated man," she said, more as a question than a statement.

I nodded again.

"Did you graduate from high school?" she asked.

"And college," I confirmed. "And I have a Masters and a Doctorate."

Her eyes opened wide at first, but then they narrowed with skepticism.

"No," I said. "It's true. I'm an engineer. They needed someone with a technical background for this thing."

"What's an engineer?" she asked. Undoubtedly, she pictured the guy driving the train.

"An engineer," I explained, "is a scientist who applies scientific theory to the real world."

I could see she didn't understand what I meant.

"How about this," I suggested. "The scientist knows that heat turns water into steam and it expands. The engineer designs an engine that uses that expanded water, steam, to make a train run."

"Do you make engines?" she asked, trying to figure me out.

"I work on time travel," I said lamely. "I know you don't believe me, and, frankly, it's all pretty amazing to me, too. But here I am."

"Yeah," she said, "I'm here, too, and that doesn't make me an engineer."

I smiled, impressed with her quick wit. "Or a time traveler from the future either," I added.

"You don't look any different," she said.

"No, people aren't much different in the future," I agreed. "We're a little taller and heavier, but otherwise the same."

"But you ride in carts instead of wagons," she jibed.

"Cars," I said. "Yeah, we ride in cars. And work in offices, and that's probably why we're heavier."

"You're not heavy," she said, her first real comment on me.

I explained that the average height and weight had increased, but not everyone was tall or fat.

"The average man today is about 5'7½" or 5'8". In my time, the average man is almost 5'11". However, Wyatt Earp is as tall as I am. The difference is that I'm just a bit taller than average for my time; but he's very tall for this time."

"How could you know how tall Mr. Earp is when you've never met him?"

"He's a folk hero in our time, and we know a lot more about him than anyone except his family does today," I explained. "And Hickok is also tall, but Billy the Kid and Jesse James are not."

Her dilemma was evident on her face. Part of her wanted to believe me, but she didn't want to look like a fool.

"It's a good story," she said. "I just can't wait to see this Wyatt Earp and have him be five feet tall."

Tess had watched me intently as I ate and talked, but now she was rocking side to side. I knew our conversation was over. She looked one last time into my eyes, said, "Good night," turned and walked back toward the house.

I called after her, "You never told me if it was safe to sleep outside."

"Should be," she said without turning. "I'll bring you a blanket."

Chapter 28

When I awoke to the call of the rooster, I felt like a pioneer. First light was just coloring the yard, and I'd slept like a mountain man. I felt good—about myself, about Kansas, and about Tess. She and I were developing a rapport—even if she didn't know it yet. I looked toward the house and saw she was up. A faint orange light slipped through a small crack around the shutters, probably a candle burning. I heard some movement and a low clanking behind the house. I was in no hurry to get up, and I waited for her to appear.

She swung around the side of the house a few moments later, her dress rustling as she walked. She carried a plate and a metal cup in her hands. She saw me studying her as she approached, but it didn't seem to bother her.

She would have been self-conscious if she knew I was remembering her as I first saw her—a voluptuous bather. She didn't look as sexy in her plain dress and bare feet, and I was struggling to put the two images together.

"I thought you'd want some breakfast," she said.

She handed me the plate as I sat up. It was weighed down

with three fried eggs, fried potatoes, and a couple of sausage patties. I wasn't hungry until I saw that feast.

I thanked her and cut one of the eggs with the heavy fork she gave me. While I did so, she filled the cup with water from the pump.

"Oh, this is good," I said when I tasted the egg. It tasted like an egg fresh from the farm should taste, not at all like the eggs I ate in the twenty-first century.

"The eggs are fresh, only laid yesterday," Tess said, reading my thoughts.

She'd already eaten and stayed with me while I ate.

"This is good," I said again as I attacked the food. My enthusiasm pleased her. "I notice you walk around barefooted a lot?"

Tess looked at me, visibly surprised at the question.

"It just seems strange," I said, regretting the words as I said them.

"Don't need boots around here," she said.

I shrugged. "I guess I'm just used to people always wearing shoes outside the house."

"Just wears out the shoes," she said.

I turned my mind to more practical matters—I had two problems to solve and little time to do them. First, I had to get into Dodge City and record my experiences. If my only report back to Washington were that I ended up at a dreary sod house and met a pretty girl, this would be my last trip.

Second, I had to find a way to contribute to my stay if, indeed, I did remain at the homestead. I wanted to stay, and I suspected Tess wanted me to.

The problem was that I lacked any skills helpful to her—I knew nothing about farming or ranching. I had money, but I wouldn't be comfortable paying rent while Tess did all the work.

"It was very kind of you to let me sleep here last night," I said. "I need to get on to Dodge City today."

She looked distressed.

"I'd like to come back, if that's possible."

"Why do you have to go to Dodge? And why today?"

"I know you don't believe me, but I'm a scientist, and I'm here to get information and report it back."

"I thought you were an engineer," she argued. Our first argument, a good sign.

I laughed. "Yeah, I'm an engineer," I acknowledged, "but we have delusions about being scientists and, sometimes refer to ourselves that way. And I'm here as a scientist."

"Harrumph," she said.

"I'd like to come back," I repeated.

She apparently didn't believe me. She turned away and started toward the house.

"I need your help," I said. She stopped, and turned toward me.

"I don't know what help I can be," she said and walked on.

After giving Tess time to accept my need to go to Dodge, I approached her as she worked in the garden. She heard me come around the house and looked up.

"Could I do some work around here to pay you for your kindnesses, and then, maybe, go into Dodge tomorrow?" I asked.

We reached a compromise—she found some work for me and left me to it. As the day developed, I was glad I hadn't wandered far from the ranch.

The wind was blowing all day, stinging my eyes with dust and grit. It wore me down under its onslaught. I'd read about what the constant wind on the plains did to the early settlers. However, reading about the wind and experiencing it were different things. After several hours of Mother Nature leaning all her weight on me, my strength waned. The constant keening of the wind reached inside my head until I thought it'd never leave. I tried covering my ears with my hands, but it still reached me, albeit at a lower pitch but still piercing, reverberating between my ears as if my head were an empty canyon. I wanted to scream for it to stop, but knew my voice would barely reach my lips before being lost in the shrieking.

The gusts tortured the trees, thrashing their branches about, which added to the cacophony. The barn whistled and groaned. For the first time, I knew why people described wind as like the sound of banshees. I began to believe that banshees were real, and that they'd taken up residence in my head.

When Tess and I were working near each other, I drew energy from her. The wind didn't seem to bother her. She only struggled when we tried to talk. The howl made conversation all but impossible, and I saw frustration on her face after several efforts to say short sentences to me.

The wind blew constantly at about twenty-five miles per hour with gusts that knocked me about. Once, after almost falling to the ground when a gust knocked me off balance, I looked at Tess with a questioning look. She smiled slightly and shrugged her shoulders. I took that to mean this wasn't unusual, and that I'd better get used to it. With no alternative, I emulated Tess and went about my work as best I could. The wind was just another part of this difficult frontier life that Tess endured daily, and it deepened my admiration for her toughness—and it reminded me how soft I was.

Early in the afternoon, everything changed. The sky darkened in minutes and lightning discharged like flashbulbs across the southwestern sky. When the wind died down suddenly and the clouds took on a strange greenish color, I got a bad feeling.

I heard what sounded like pebbles pelting the barn and house, and then felt them hitting me with painful strikes. It was hail. I never dreamed that I'd see ice pellets covering the ground in the middle of summer. As I took shelter inside the barn, the hail changed to rain.

My eyes darted around the sky as I tried to figure things out. Tess was out of sight behind the house, and I couldn't look to her for reassurance. The wind resumed wailing as dramatically as it had stopped, and I saw swirling leaves in the sky. The wind's howling now doubled in force and the pressure in my ears changed. Even with the wind banging against the barn, I felt as if I was in a vacuum. I stumbled out of the barn and started across the yard to find Tess. Just then, she hurried around the side of the house, a crazed look on her face.

She gestured impatiently for me to follow her. Her look told me I'd better hurry. I pulled my hat against my head and ran after her. When I got to the east side of the house, I found her struggling against the wind to lift a square wooden door that angled slightly up from the ground. She was losing the battle. I came up next to her, grabbed an edge, and braced my body to force the door against the increasing tempest. I was just able to hold it open a couple of feet off the ground. With her dress billowing around her, Tess threw herself onto the ground and rolled under the door. My shirt and pants were flapping around my limbs as the wind screamed its defiance at me. I fought to keep my feet under me so that I had some leverage with the door.

My effort was sapping my strength, and I was about to release my hold when I felt the door rising slightly. As it came up, now maybe six inches higher than when Tess crawled through, I could see that Tess was underneath it, pushing it up with her back. She caught my eye and signaled me to duck in. I fell in and found myself on my hands and knees on hard packed dirt in a room no more than eight feet square. Calling it a "room" was generous since it was only three or four feet high. The door slammed shut and bucked until Tess worked a heavy beam into a slot on its back and angled the ends into openings in the doorframe.

I fell back, breathing too hard to talk. The room smelled loamy, and I concluded we were in a root cellar. It was much quieter inside, but I could still hear the wind pounding on the door, bouncing it with all its might. Enough light worked its way around the door for me to see Tess collapsed on the dirt floor next to me.

We were both lying on our backs.

"What's going on?" I shouted between coughing and gasping. Fear, as much as exertion, caused me to breathe so hard. Despite the protection from the full fury of the wind, I still had to shout to be heard.

"Nothing much," said Tess, who was gasping as much as I was. "It's a tornado."

That accelerated my heart rate again.

"My God!" I shouted. I'd already guessed what it was, but hearing the word confirmed my worst fear. I never dreamed I'd be in the middle of one.

Tess touched my arm, and that quieted me down instantly.

"Nothing to do but ride it out," she said. "It'll pass."

She'd caught her breath now, and she spoke in a calm manner.

"Suppose it takes the house and barn?" I asked.

I could feel her shrug. "Not much we can do about it," she said.

"Are we safe here?"

"Not if it came right over us," she said. "Otherwise, we'll be all right."

I marveled at her calm, and convinced myself I should act brave. As Tess pointed out, there wasn't much I could do anyway. Her words may have convinced me, but my heart wasn't listening, and it continued to pump torrents of overheated blood through me until I thought my head would burst.

As we lay there, the wind buffeted the door mercilessly, peaking and ebbing in its ferocity. In the distance, I heard what sounded like a rapidly approaching freight train. When it reached its peak, the roar was so loud that I could almost believe that a train was right outside the cellar rushing toward Dodge. I covered my ears, but the earth vibrated violently beneath my back. I was sure we were going to die and I reached out for Tess's hand and gave it a squeeze. I was still holding it when I felt and heard the freight train retreating. Then, suddenly, the roar was gone completely and all was quiet. The silence was so startling that I felt like I was floating in space. My ears were still ringing from the residual effect of the freight train, but the wind was gone.

"Is that it?" I asked, probably speaking too loudly.

"I think so," Tess said but she remained still.

"Can we go out?"

"Let's give it some time," she said calmly. "Could be just a lull. Let things quiet down."

When the wind didn't renew itself, Tess sat up and removed the bar holding the door. I was kneeling next to her as she put the bar aside and I pushed the door open.

When I stood up, I inhaled deeply, clearing my lungs of the moldy air from the cellar. The earth seemed renewed. The air felt clean and fresh, and there was only a slight breeze. With the door pushed fully open, we stood in the cellar, our legs still below the ground. Tess maintained her calm as she surveyed the house.

"Well, Toto," I said. "I guess we're still in Kansas."

Of course, Tess had no idea what I was talking about.

"How often does that happen?" I asked.

"Not too often," she said, then adding, "but too often."

"Have you ever taken a direct hit?"

"Wouldn't be a house here if we did."

"How close do you think it was?"

Tess looked around and clearly had no more idea than I did.

When I surveyed what I could see from behind the house, I realized that there was one big difference between a nineteenth-century Kansas tornado and a twenty-first century Washington hurricane—debris. Aside from some tree limbs, there was almost nothing to clean up. Although I couldn't see the horse or cows, I assumed that they'd found refuge and were okay.

I helped Tess out of the cellar, and I leaned down to look inside before I closed the door.

"Root cellar?" I asked.

Tess nodded her head.

"I hadn't noticed it before."

Tess gave me one of those looks that said if my comment required an answer, she didn't know what that answer was.

"How can you live in place where tornadoes threaten your life and property?"

I shouldn't have said that.

"This is my home," she said and walked off.

Chapter 29

It had dawned on me during the night that Tess'd said she had no saddle and, currently, no wagon.

"How do you get to town for supplies?" I asked when I saw her in the morning.

"A neighbor carries me," she said. She seemed serious. I wanted to tease her about her face cracking if she kept it like that. I wanted to see her smile, something I hadn't yet seen.

"A beau?" I asked, cocking my head.

"A neighbor, I said."

Considering that she lost her husband so recently, my comment was inappropriate. I'd wear out my limited welcome with further gaffes like that.

"When might you be going again?" I asked, returning to business.

"Should be soon," she said. Big help that was.

"Is that today, tomorrow, next week, or in September?" I asked.

"Today," she finally said reluctantly.

It was time for some humility. "Would it be possible for

me to ride along?"

"Could be," she said. "You'll have to ask him."

"When might he be by?" I asked.

As I was asking, I heard a wagon creaking and jostling in the distance.

I looked around, but couldn't tell exactly where the sound came from. There was no discernible road, no trail or path that led to the yard. I didn't have to wait long, however, since a horse's head soon arose like the sun behind a rise no more than a hundred yards away. Soon the horse's dark, muscular torso followed and, in time, I saw the head of a man. I couldn't tell much about him at that distance.

He apparently saw me, because he stopped the horse. They, the horse and the man, and presumably the still unseen wagon, just sat there. The horse shook its head, and expressed impatience with a loud neighing.

Tess nodded toward him in an easy manner, and that seemed to allay his doubts as the horse started up again. The wagon came into view, slowly appearing as if it was on a stage riser.

The driver jostled in his seat as the wagon lurched forward. I looked for evidence of a trail or even of ruts that he might be following, but I saw nothing. He rode the prairie like a small boat rising and falling on the waves of a grass sea.

The man was small but stocky and, although he looked to be in his 40s, I couldn't be sure since people aged quicker out here than in my time. He wore a straw hat and dirty overalls.

Tess waited until the horse was almost upon us before acknowledging him. She gave him a small semaphore with her hand, her pinky tucked under.

"Howdy, Tess," he said evenly, speaking to her but watching me. "Everything okay?"

I could tell immediately that, like Tess, he wasn't talkative. Tess nodded amiably, also looking at me, in a manner that made my chest clutch.   Suddenly, she seemed so self-assured and feminine, and it made me jealous.

Despite my discomfort, I thought I should interrupt the staring contest. I walked around the horse toward the man.

"I'm Will," I said reaching up with my hand.

"Lester," he replied, taking my hand reluctantly. His grip was anything but firm.

Lester wore glasses, the type we called Granny glasses, and a suspicious look on his face. I was still jealous, but no longer intimidated about meeting my first frontiersman.

He looked from me to Tess and back. Tess said nothing. I had nothing to say, until I remembered that Lester was my ride into town.   If he decided three was a crowd, I'd be in for a long, difficult walk.

"I need a ride into town," I said as non-threatening as I could. "Would it be possible for me to ride with you and Tess?"

Lester scratched his neck, twisted his face, and looked at Tess. He seemed to be looking for Tess to tell him what to do. I guess she signaled him in some way.

"Could do that," he said without any enthusiasm.

The wagon was right out of a Western movie, big wheels, a boxed body, and raised platform for sitting, but it was smaller than I expected. The seat was just a platform without sides or any backrest, not even the sloped three- or four-inch frame I would have expected. The whole wagon was only about three feet wide and no more than ten feet long. The back wheels were four or more feet high and noticeably larger than the front wheels. They took up most of the wagon's length.

The box was painted green, and showed little sign of weathering. The horse looked strong and healthy, and had no reluctance to snort and swagger its displeasure at the waiting. The harness seemed older than the wagon and horse but, while well used, showed no signs of fraying.

"Can you give me a minute, Lester?" Tess asked as she

picked up my plate and cup and turned toward the house.

Lester didn't answer, but Tess took that to be a 'yes.'

Tess's departure left Lester and me alone. He kept his thoughts to himself, but his expression told me he had questions on his mind. He had a short, somewhat unkempt graying beard that failed to hide his displeasure. Maybe, he just didn't like surprises.

When Tess returned minutes later with a small cloth bag in her hand, Lester got down from the wagon to help her up. Despite the compact dimensions of the wagon, the seat was still a good five feet off the ground and Tess had to climb up using a small step that projected forward of the front wheel. Even the step was more than two feet from the ground and it was not an easy climb. But Lester held her arm in a gentlemanly manner as she struggled on board. She took a seat on the left side of the platform as Lester followed her up. In spite of his bulk and short stature, he clambered up with agility.

When they were settled, they looked at me expectantly. I asked what I was to do by gesturing toward the wagon bed. Both Lester and Tess just looked back at me, which I took to mean I could climb on if I wanted. I was afraid the horse might start moving but I used the back wheel as a ladder and pulled myself into the box.

The confined area offered no comfort for me, and neither Tess nor Lester made any suggestions. I tried sitting sideways but that put my knees in my face and the sidewall was too high for me to support myself with my elbows. There was no back to the bed and I couldn't rest against the bench since that would have me leaning on Tess or Lester. This was going to be a long trip into town.

Lester headed east for a short way and then down to the river. We splashed into the water but, despite the great width of the river, the water never rose higher than halfway up the axles, leaving me dry by half a foot. When we climbed out of the riverbed, the horse shook himself off before pulling the wagon onto land. Lester clicked at the horse, and we slowly rose up a gentle slope. Not until we reached the top did I realize that the rise was the track bed for the Atchison, Topeka, and Santa Fe railroad. We clattered across the tracks very slowly, so slow that I found myself warily looking in both directions for fear that a train would come while we were on the track.

Only a few hundred feet north of the track, we came to a wide, worn area—the Santa Fe Trail. It showed signs of disuse and was starting to grow over, but it was flatter and smoother than the land leading up from the river. Even on the worn trail, the ride was bumpy and every thump was transmitted to me. Within minutes, even at a walking pace we travelled, I had scrapes and bruises on my arms and back from trying to hold myself in place. I tried bending my knees and lying flat, but my head took an intolerable beating. Tess and Lester had it much better, but I didn't envy them as I watched them bouncing and jarring in unison on their platform. Tess held on tightly to the outside of the seat to keep from falling off. They didn't talk to each other.

As we bucked eastward toward Dodge City, I had time to think. Beside my discomfort, my first thought was a minor panic. I hadn't thought to ask Tess not to say anything about the time travel. Even if she only joked about it, I didn't want Lester or anyone else to become too inquisitive. My cover wasn't good enough to survive serious questioning. I especially didn't want Wyatt Earp demanding answers as his hand twitched toward his gun.

Chapter 30

Lying in the wagon bed, I couldn't do anything to stop Tess from talking to Lester. Fortunately, small conversation didn't seem to be part of their relationship.

Despite my discomfort, I tried to take in the sights. I'd moved to the back of the box to face forward so that I could look to either side and had to hang onto the sides to avoid being pitched out the open back. After we forded the river, there wasn't much to see, just rolling prairie land with occasional sparse brush.

I didn't see another homestead for a good fifteen minutes. When the next one appeared it was like Tess's place, an undistinguished sod house, though larger and better kept. From a distance the sod layers looked like bricks and, seen that way, it wouldn't have been out of place in twenty-first century Kansas. The Santa Fe Trail showed increasing use as we moved toward Dodge. Although the railroad had replaced the trail for long-distance freighting, the trail had enough local use to keep it from disappearing into the grasslands.

In time, other houses appeared, set back from the trail. I gathered that we were approaching Dodge City and looked ahead for town, but I saw nothing.

Worn out and beaten up from sitting, I dropped onto my back and looked up at the sky. As the back of my head bounced around, I saw a sky that was no different from the ones I saw in Washington. The same blue, the same clouds, the same sun. Here, however, the dryness caused the clouds to be thin and wispy, and thousands of feet higher than clouds in the damp, humid East. Of course, there weren't any jet contrails at 35,000 feet cutting through these clouds.

Just about the time when my tired and jostled body was urging me to ask, "Are we there yet?," houses started popping up with greater frequency. I sat up and could see the town ahead as well as the slightly elevated railroad tracks still running parallel to us on the right. Since I knew the town's history, I didn't have high expectations for Dodge City.

Founded in 1872 as an offshoot of Fort Dodge, Dodge City sat on the Arkansas River northwest of, and five miles from, the fort, just outside the no-saloon line. Fort Dodge replaced the abandoned military outposts that protected the Santa Fe Trail. The earlier forts, Fort Mann and Fort Atkinson, had been located three miles west of the then future Dodge City. Although we'd crossed the river near where they would have been, I didn't see any signs of them. The U.S. Army abandoned the earlier forts and, in 1864, built Fort Dodge farther east where the "wet" and "dry" Santa Fe Trails split. We were approaching Dodge on the wet trail, the one that followed the river. The dry trail was a shorter and quicker route but had no access to water for considerable stretches. The Atchison, Topeka, & Santa Fe rails reached the area in 1872, the same year that Dodge City was established. Aside from taking traffic from the trail, the railroad had little impact until 1876, the very year of my visit, when the rails, and the ban on Texas cattle in eastern Kansas, diverted the cattle drives to the western part of the state. The cattle were starting to arrive as we made our way into town. Before the cattle drives ended in the early '80s, five million head would ultimately pass through town.

As we rattled into the outskirts of town, the smell reached me first. The town smelled like a dirty wet dog. Dodge City was about to become famous as a cattle drive destination but, in 1876, it was still making money from buffalo hides. Hunters had wiped out the buffalo herds in Kansas, but the Texas hunters still dragged their hides into Dodge for shipment east. At the peak of buffalo hunting a couple of years earlier, stacks of hides would stand ten feet high on the streets waiting to be brokered and shipped. As we lumbered into town, there were still a few hides piled along North Front Street. I gawked at the buildings as I recalled the town's history. My visit in 2010 had prepared me to expect the town to climb, however modestly, up the north bluff rising from the river. All the buildings were the standard false-front wooden structures common to the West, but the owners painted them in a variety of bright colors. Some of the accounts of the trail cowboys said they could see the bright colors of the storefronts from miles out as they approached. The streets were dirty and dusty, but there was a greater sense of order than I expected.

Dodge was little more than a one street town, extending east and west for three blocks. Streets extended north from Front Street, but there were only scattered houses along them. Unlike Hollywood's western towns, however, Dodge's main street only had buildings on the north side, set back and across the street from the railroad tracks. Front Street ended abruptly at the east edge of town where the depot stood between the parallel tracks. A second Front Street ran parallel to North Front Street, just south of the tracks, and was marked by an assortment of smaller, less well-kept buildings. Like a sentinel, the tiny city office/jail stood in isolation alongside the track in the middle of the expanse between the two Front Streets.

The "other side of the tracks" was exactly that. Except for the Great Western Hotel and a livery stable, all of its businesses were saloons and houses of ill repute mixed in with decrepit shanties. Some of the south side buildings were relatively new but most had never seen a coat of paint and were already badly weathered.

Dodge hired Wyatt Earp as a deputy marshal in May 1876, but he was really the marshal in everything except the title. He'd hired four deputies—Bat Masterson, already famous for the Adobe Walls siege, Bill Tilgman, later a famous lawman, James Masterson, brother of the more famous Bat, and a man named Neal Brown. That was a lot of law for a town of no more than a thousand permanent residents, but Earp knew he'd need help when the young cowboys roved the streets. In an attempt to separate the riff-raff from the respectable citizen, Wyatt instituted a deadline at the railroad tracks. Men could carry guns on the south side of the tracks, but no guns would be tolerated on the north side.

In fact, visible guns were not common anywhere in the West. Although almost every man had a gun of some sort, he kept it at home and rarely wore it on the street. More often than not, that gun was a shotgun, because that was best for hunting. The idea that Western towns like the fabled Tombstone had a dead body for breakfast every morning was a creation of some Easterner's imagination. Like Dodge's north side, Tombstone later banned guns from its streets, and for the same reason as Dodge— Wyatt Earp forbade it. In fact, the most famous gunfight in history, the Gunfight at the O.K. Corral resulted directly from the Clantons and the McLaurys wearing guns in town. Virgil Earp, his brothers, and Doc Holliday confronted them behind the O.K. Corral in an attempt to disarm them. And, yes indeed, they did disarm them.

Earp had arrived in Dodge after being fired as deputy marshal in Wichita. When Larry Deger, the Dodge marshal, showed no interest in doing his job, Dodge City Mayor Hoover hired Earp to be Deger's chief deputy. According to Earp, Hoover wanted him so badly that he agreed to pay Earp $250 per month, more than twice Marshall Deger's salary. However, Dodge records show Earp never made more than $85.

Dodge City was surprisingly big for a town of its small population. Not city big, but Western prairie big. I expected one street lined by shabby wooden buildings with only outhouses behind them. (The outhouses were indeed there. I couldn't see them, but I could smell them from any place in town.) Instead, I saw the railroad tracks running through the heart of an orderly town. Hitching posts lined the street on North Front Street, and small corrals were spaced between the scattered buildings on the south side of the tracks.

After spending the last several days at SouthFord, the activity on Front Street overwhelmed me. Some children were playing tag around some hitched horses, and I found myself anxious that one of the skittish horses would accidently step on one of the children as they ran through their legs. The snorting and whinnying horses didn't scare the boys in the slightest and somehow they escaped the dancing hoofs. With the loud wagons rumbling through town, the squealing children, barking dogs, and clouds of dust, Dodge was as busy as downtown Washington. I tried to take it all in, the sounds, the jostling and hurrying, the smells, and the foreign feel of this exciting Western town. The *piece de resistance* came when one of the hitched horses, now free of the tag-playing kids, dropped his load onto the street just as we passed by. I looked at Tess and Lester to see their reaction, but they ignored it. When I looked around, I saw pungent evidence that such things happened all the time. To these people, the horse's action was apparently the same as exhaust from a car or bus in my time.

I tried not to gawk, since my cover didn't include being a reverse hick who'd never seen a Western town before. After Lester pulled the wagon into the wagon corral, I clambered out of my chamber and hurried to help Tess climb down. She seemed to like the gesture.

"I see Rath's store over there," I said. "Can I pick up some things for you?"

I thought Tess would appreciate the offer but I was wrong. After being isolated at the ranch, she was eager to get onto the street, to see people, and to spend some time in the shops. When she declined, I asked her permission to wander around a little. She didn't care.

I stepped onto the dusty, hot street and looked across the tracks. I wanted to visit the part of town that gave Dodge its nicknames of "Sodom," "Queen of the Cowtowns," and "Bibulous Babylon." Not just yet, however.

I knew that Bob Wright was a political force in town, and Wright and his partner, Judge H.M. Beverly, would soon own Rath's store. Wright would buy the store and build the Wright House Hotel a block north on Chestnut Street from profits he'd made on the Santa Fe Trail and from business dealings in Texas. Even though Rath still owned the store, it was already Wright's place and most citizens already called it that.

Behind the sign "General Outfitting Store" was a two-story wooden structure less than twenty feet wide with a small wooden awning projected from the front.

The famous Long Branch Saloon stood two doors east. I half expected to see Marshal Matt Dillon and Miss Kitty walk out. The large sign said only "Long Branch" and ran the width of the white building. It didn't say "Saloon," but the smell of liquor and beer advertised its business adequately.

Mayor George Hoover's store book-ended the Long Branch on the east side. Hoover and Wright were polar opposites, disagreeing on every issue. His store, monikered "G.M. Hoover, Cigars," filled the street with the smell of tobacco, mixing with the stale liquor/beer smell from the Long Branch. With the alcohol and tobacco on Front Street, the stinking buffalo hides wafting in from the side streets, and the horse urine and manure perfuming the streets, Dodge City made an immediate olfactory impression. The people added to the smell, too. It seemed Tess was the only one who bothered to bathe.

Avoiding two women coming out of Wright's store, I stepped up the small step onto the wooden sidewalk and opened the door. A bell jingled above me as I stepped in.

It was small inside, far smaller than the average 7-11 of our time, and so dark that it took my eyes a moment to adjust. Shelves lined the side walls, carrying a limited amount, but wide variety, of goods. Wooden barrels and tables cluttered the middle of the room and a low counter ran up the right side.

A short, portly man with muttonchop sideburns behind the counter watched me as I took the place in. I greeted him, and he acknowledged me with a nod and a small, uncertain smile.

"Help you?" he asked.

"Yes, sir," I said. "I need a tote bag and a few other things."

He quickly provided me with the bag, as well as sox, skivvies, and a second set of clothes.

"New in town, I take it," he said.

"Yes," I said. "I'm looking for a job as a reporter. I'm hoping that the *Times* needs someone."

The clerk's whiskers seemed to take over his expression as he fought to suppress his disapproval. His look lingered on me a moment before he leaned down and, using a short, fat, well-bitten pencil, added up the tab.

"That's a dollar for the shirt, two for the pants, six for the jacket, 25 cents for each pair of sox, and 50 cents each for the underwear. That's $11.75," he said dotting his calculations with a flourish.

I displayed the tote bag to remind him to add it. That made my bill $13.50, which seemed like a lot of money for 1876. I pulled a $20 gold certificate out of my back pocket and put it on the counter. The clerk looked at it warily and sniffed a bit before he picked it up, acting as if it were confederate currency. His hesitation intimidated me, but I knew that our staff had researched the money carefully. The U.S. Mint printed $10,000 in the vintage currency for my trip and then aged it to make it usable. There was no possibility this disapproving clerk in backwater Dodge could know that it was, in a way, fake money.

He held it up, leaning toward the dim light from the window to look it over. Then, glancing toward the back of the store, he said, "Officer," getting the attention of a man in a black felt sombrero standing nearby, "could you take a look at this."

I watched the man approach us. Not much older than I, he looked like he'd lived several lives more than I would ever see. He made my blood thicken and my lungs freeze up. He was blond, stood over six feet tall, and he was hard. Even his striped trousers looked like they were made of iron. His eyes were like granite, light blue but utterly without emotion. I outweighed him by twenty pounds or so, but I backed involuntarily as he neared us. He watched me as he approached.

The clerk handed him the bill, and he went through the motions of inspecting it. But he wasn't looking at the money; he was scrutinizing me. I tried not to act nervous, but he had me pegged. I didn't like being near this man.

With his piercing eyes still riveted on me, he handed the money back to the clerk and nodded. His eyes never left me.

The clerk, as intimidated as I was, hurriedly pulled a drawer out from under the counter and made change. The officer and I were in a kind of staring contest, and I was losing.

"You should take some of that money over to the Alhambra," the man said to me, his tone neither friendly nor hostile. "They have a good faro game over there."

That seemed like a good suggestion to me. I nodded. I would have agreed with anything he said. I turned to the clerk as the man started toward the door.

"Thank you, Mr. Earp," the clerk said to the retreating figure.

Holy shit, I thought, turning to watch the man leave, that's

Wyatt Earp. He certainly had a presence.

I pocketed my money and took my time rolling up my clothes and cramming them into my bag. I was in no hurry, since I wanted nothing more to do with Officer Earp for now.

I shouldn't have been surprised he promoted the faro game at the Alhambra Saloon, since he and Bat Masterson ran the game. I would have been easy pickings for them, even at such a simple game. I agreed with Earp when he suggested I visit it, but I didn't intend to spend the taxpayers' money at his game. In fact, I decided I'd already had enough of the famous Wyatt Earp. I temporarily decided against trying to sit down with him for an interview. I knew now why he lived into his 80s.

Chapter 31

I was still shaky when I exited Wright's store. As I stepped out into the blinding, baking sun, I searched the street for Tess and Lester, but didn't see them.

I was standing in front of the store when a man approached from my right, walking in the middle of the dusty street. He was well dressed, walked with a slight limp, and carried a cane. The limp didn't slow him any. He looked vaguely familiar.

"Wyatt," he yelled past me. "Hey, Wyatt."

I looked to my left and saw Earp only twenty feet beyond me, leaning against a hitching post outside the Long Branch. He didn't seem pleased to see this man.

"What do you want, Bart?" he asked. The man was Bat Masterson. The cane was a new accessory, the result of a gunshot wound he'd suffered in January. Although the legend held he was nicknamed "Bat" because he used the cane to slug people, the story was the creation of a dime-novel writer. "Bat" was his family's corruption of "Bart." Although Masterson used William Barclay Masterson as his full name, Wyatt apparently knew Bat's real name was Bertholomiew Masterson.

I turned with greater interest toward the gimp and now recognized the face, even though I'd never seen a photo of him this young. Earp had just hired him as an assistant marshal. He and Earp had forged a relationship when they were buffalo hunters in the early '70s.

Masterson was shorter than Earp, probably no more than 5'9", stockier, and with darker skin and hair than the fair Wyatt. He seemed more genial than Earp, and wasn't put off by his friend's manner. I gathered this was Earp's usual way of treating people, even his friends

As Bat hurried toward Wyatt, I noticed the limp was more severe than I'd first thought. When Masterson noticed I was watching him, I decided to move on. I didn't wait to be introduced.

As much as I wanted to see Dodge City, I wanted to see Tess more. I found her in York, Hadder, & Draper's, a general store a couple of blocks east of the Long Branch. When she saw me enter, she involuntarily smiled. I smiled back, glad to be welcome. I waited nearby as she bought small sacks of flour and cornmeal, and I carried them to the wagon for her. Lester was nowhere in sight.

I asked her, "Do you think I have time to drop into the newspaper office?"

She looked around to make sure she wouldn't be overheard. "Why on earth would you do that?" She asked with a shrug. "You're not really a reporter, and you're not really looking for a job."

I felt like a schoolboy being chastised by the teacher. I found myself rocking side to side in arguing with her. "Let me just drop in and talk to them. It wouldn't look good if I didn't."

Tess waved her hand as if she thought me silly. Before allowing me to go, she thought to ask, "Have you found your famous Wyatt Epps?"

"Earp," I corrected, opening my eyes as wide as I could.

"I've seen enough of him."

She tilted her head in a question.

"He's a hard man," I said emphatically.

Tess nodded without being completely sure what I meant. I gestured down the street, indicating I was heading to the newspaper office.

As I walked off, I wondered when Tess and I got on the footing that I had to ask permission from her. I wasn't worried about being left behind—if they left without me, I could handle the walk and find my way back.

I felt safe leaving Tess alone at the wagon. Women moved freely along the street, and this part of Dodge didn't seem particularly threatening. Apparently, she felt the same way. I came to learn that Dodge had an unwritten code that a woman, any woman, was to be treated with the utmost respect on the streets of town.

The *Dodge City Times* was located in a small building that stood on Chestnut Street near Bridge Street, a block off Front Street. I knocked on the door before entering. Inside, I found a frail man wearing a black vest over a white shirt. He sported a small hat on his scraggly hair. He looked warily at me through gold wire-rimmed glasses as I opened the door.

"Yes, sir?" he asked.

I introduced myself and told him I was a writer. He didn't tell me his name, but I later learned he was Walter Shinn, one of the owners of the paper.

When I told him I'd like to report for his paper, he said, for no apparent reason, "I don't know." I waited for him to explain.

"Where have you worked before?" he asked.

I told him that I'd worked for both the *Washington Post* and the *Baltimore Sun*. It wasn't altogether true, but I did *read* both of them. I knew how to write and, if given a chance, I was certain I could convince him I had experience.

He looked around the small office as if he would find an

answer there. He needed my help.

"How about this?" I suggested. "You give me a short assignment, lend me a typewriter, and I'll rap out a 200-word article. If you like it, hire me."

"Typewriter?" he asked.

Damn, I forgot that typewriters weren't in common use yet. I didn't know when they were invented, but I did know that Mark Twain wrote the first book on a typewriter, *The Adventures of Tom Sawyer*, only the year before.

"Lend me a pencil," I corrected myself.

"Well," he said uncertainly, "I don't have any stories that need writing right now."

I suggested we make one up. "It's just a writing test," I said impatiently. "You don't have to publish it."

He still didn't get it. How, I thought, could someone so utterly lacking in imagination run a paper?

"I have an idea," I said. "I just ran into Wyatt Earp and Bat Masterson. I'll write a small piece on them."

I cocked my head and raised my eyebrows, asking him to confirm my brilliant idea.

"Well, okay," he said reluctantly. He looked around the room again. "There's really no room for you to sit in here."

"Just give me some paper and a pencil. I'll write outside."

It took Perry White a few minutes to scout up the necessary equipment, but I was on my way out the door soon enough. I had to write fast since Lester and Tess might be waiting for me. After comparing him in my mind to Clark Kent's editor, I was tempted to write a short piece about Superman, but thought better of it.

Dodge City is facing an invasion. Because eastern Kansas is off limits to Texas cattle, dozens of large herds of Texas cattle are driving toward our peaceful city. The cattle themselves may never run down our streets, but the so-called "cowboys" driving them will. They will be looking for some action when they come into town.

Dodge has never faced such a threat. The buffalo hunters were few in number and relatively well behaved. Texans do not have the same reputation. Dodge City life, as we know it, could be compromised when this foreign horde tries to impose its will on our fair city.

Fortunately, they will not get their way. No city in the United States has a more capable police force than Dodge City. Our estimable marshal, Larry Deger, and his street soldiers, Wyatt Earp, Bat and James Masterson, Bill Tilghman, and Neal Brown, will be more than up to the task. Earp, the assistant marshal and acting lieutenant on the streets, has a quiet way of controlling even the most rambunctious character. His associates will surely learn from his example.

It is no exaggeration to suggest that the police force guarding our safety and our way of life has the potential to go down in history as the finest staff ever to wear badges. With their firm hands, these men will assure that the Texans do not abuse their welcome.

It wasn't a great piece, and I felt guilty about having the benefit of hindsight, but it would do. I re-entered the office and handed it to Shinn. He didn't seem to know what to do with it.

"Aren't you going to read it?" I asked.

"Oh, yes," he said, adjusting his glasses.

It took him but a minute.

"Okay," he said. "That's very good." He tried a smile. "I'm sure the marshal would be pleased."

"Well?" I asked.

He looked confused again.

"Are you going to hire me?" This man was an idiot.

"Well, as I told you," he stuttered, "I don't have any stories needing writing. My brother and I do all the work ourselves."

Having done what I was to do, I shook my head and turned to leave. As I opened the door, I told him that he could publish the article if he wanted. "If you give me a byline, the name is Will Barrett."

I knew I should return to the wagon, but the Alhambra Saloon drew me like a magnet. I wasn't sure I'd ever make it back to town and wanted to see the haunt of Earp and Masterson. Fortunately, the distances were short in Dodge and my hurried steps carried me to the Alhambra in less than two minutes.

The House of Earp was a big disappointment. The Alhambra was a weather-beaten shack even less impressive than the Long Branch. Hedged in by Collar's Dry Goods on one side and a barbershop on the other, it was just another storefront masquerading as a bar. A standard twenty feet wide, the saloon had a single glassed door under a tin awning overhanging the planked walkway.

I saw no light or activity through the windows or door, but I approached anyway. The door was open. I stepped into a gloomy and quiet room. A dark wooden bar ran up the left side with a crude painting of a semi-nude woman centered over it. She looked only vaguely Mediterranean enough to justify her scanty oriental garments. I presumed the painting was in color, but I couldn't tell for sure in the darkness.

Four round tables were scattered in the front section and running in a row toward the back wall. I looked for the faro table, figuring that Earp would get the prime location near the front. Sure enough, I found a round table with thirteen spades, two through ace, pasted to the wooden top of the first table. Six chairs surrounded the table.

Looking at the cards reminded me of the colorful words associated with this primitive game: punter (the bettor), banker (dealer), and bucking the tiger or twisting the tiger's tail (playing faro). Masterson later wrote a tale about Earp that might have happened right at this table. As Bat told it, a tough man complained of being cheated at Earp's table. Called into the fray, which was escalating into a mob protest, Wyatt took the dealer aside and was assured that the deal with straight. He then returned to the hard case, pulled him outside, and falsely confirmed the dealer had cheated him. However, Earp said, he couldn't return his money because it would look like the unhappy punter had intimidated Wyatt. Satisfied that Wyatt had acknowledged his claim, the man backed down and even had a drink with Wyatt later.

I touched the table for a few seconds as I pictured the scene of Earp's diplomacy. After absorbing history through my imagination and my fingertips, I left to catch up with Tess.

As I left the Alhambra, I tried to eavesdrop on conversations on the street. It wasn't as easy as I expected, but I did hear passing references to the military disaster a week earlier. "Custer was always a fool . . . It probably isn't as bad as the newspaper's reporting. You know how the paper always . . . It puts us all in more danger . . ."

I hustled back across the tracks to the wagon and found Lester standing quietly with Tess. The horse was drinking from a trough as I approached. I apologized for holding them up but they didn't seem concerned. Tess acknowledged my apology with a smile, but Lester just turned and mounted the wagon. I helped Tess onto the bench seat, threw my bag into the bed, and climbed aboard. Lester started up without waiting for me to settle.

I spent most of the uneventful ride back thinking about Wyatt Earp, wondering what made him so hard and, as Masterson described him, "utterly fearless." Aside from Masterson and Doc Holliday, Earp enjoyed two long relationships during his life, one with a prostitute named Mattie and a second with a traveling actress named Josephine "Sadie" Marcus. After he met Sadie in

Tombstone, he spent the rest of his long life with her. He never married either woman.

For the most part, Earp stayed on the right side of the law. Aside from his faro tables, which he ran wherever he lived and which were probably as crooked as the average game, he was always a lawman with side businesses. He owned a silver mine in Tombstone with his brothers and rode shotgun for Wells Fargo. Ultimately, after the Gunfight at the O.K. Corral, he went on his "Vendetta," a yearlong retaliation against the men who killed his brother Morgan and maimed Virgil, the eldest Earp brother. In the eponymous movie starring Kevin Costner, one of his sisters-in-law said to him: "You're a hard man, Wyatt Earp." He *was* a hard man and none of Henry Fonda, Kevin Costner, Kurt Russell, or the mild Hugh O'Brian came within a hundred years of catching the essence of his stone heart.

When Lester dropped Tess and me off at SouthFord, I thanked him profusely for the ride and put out my hand to shake his. He didn't seem to want my thanks, or my hand, but he took both unenthusiastically without looking at me. He hadn't said a word to me all day.

Chapter 32

As Lester rumbled away, I ran to the water pump, pumped as fast as I could, and inhaled the strong stream of cool water that flooded into my hands. I'd drank no water since breakfast, and my mouth was sticking together.

Sloppage dripped from my face when Tess joined me at the pump. She had a smile on her face. "Have a good time today?" she asked, obviously as invigorated as I was exhausted.

I smiled back and gave her a firm nod. I did enjoy it. I saw a lot and even met, or almost met, two famous Western heroes.

"You didn't seem very thrilled about your Mr. Epps," she said.

"Wyatt Earp, you mean," I said. "Well, yes and no. He's an intimidating guy, but I'm still happy I met him. I wouldn't want to be at odds with him."

"Was he bigger than life itself?" she asked gaily.

"Not the least disappointing," I answered. "But I'm not sure about interviewing him for the *Times*. He didn't talk much, and it might make for a short article."

"Are they going to hire you?" she asked.

"The *Times*? I doubt it," I said. "The idiot running it didn't seem to recognize my talent."

She laughed and, when she did, she jettisoned the hard, worn-out look. I liked her like this, but I checked myself as I watched her. I couldn't get involved with this woman—it would be disastrous for her and the mission. However, for the moment, I relaxed and enjoyed the pleasure of seeing her so happy.

The day in Dodge had taken its toll on me. I wasn't sure if it was the jostling in the wagon, the hot sun beating down on me, the adrenaline letdown after all the new experiences, or a combination of all three. Whatever, I was beat. I carried Tess's purchases to the front door, took my leave, and retired to the shade of the barn where, after rearranging the junk to create a space, I promptly fell asleep.

I awoke as the sun was setting and the shadows were lengthening. I again drank my fill at the pump, the cool water satisfying me more than any iced drink in Washington had ever done. Tess heard me and came out.

"Need anything to eat?" she asked.

"Sure do," I said, "but I don't want to put you to any trouble."

She ignored my comment and brought me some bread, a ball of hard cheese, and a knife. I made myself comfortable on the bench in the shadow of the barn and ate the entire half loaf she'd given me. The cheese disappeared along with it. I felt bad as I was finishing it, realizing how much bother and expense I was to Tess. She didn't know money wouldn't be a problem, but she bore my imposition without complaint.

We ate dinner a couple of hours later as dusk turned into night. Tess served simple, satisfying food. I didn't miss the twenty-first century supermarket fare in the least.

After dinner, Tess let me clean the few pots and plates in the river. It was fully dark by then, and I spent half my time watching the stars and the moon reflecting off the water as I sent ripples out from shore.

When I finished, Tess came out and we stood together in awkward silence before she spoke. "Are you afraid being out here all alone?" she asked.

I cocked my head, at a loss to put her question in perspective. She studied me, making me feel awkward.

"Well," I said trying to buy time, "I'm no different than you. You're all alone, too."

"It's not the same," she said. "Even though I'm only here a short time, I belong in Dodge. People know me, I'm part of the community."

"And I'm 1500 miles and 134 years from home and don't really belong?" I asked.

"Yeah," she said, adding, "If what you tell me is true."

I thought about her question before answering. "Part of me is comfortable," I said. "You've made me feel welcome, and I almost feel like this is home."

In the dark, I couldn't see her face clearly, but her body language told me she blushed at my words.

"I know I'm imposing," I said defensively. "I'm just a temporary guest."

"No," she said. "It's not that. It's . . ." She trailed off, apparently unable to explain what I was.

"However, there's a part of me that's very uneasy. My project has invested a lot in this mission, and I'm afraid I'm screwing it up." Now, it was my turn to blush. "Sorry about my language," I said. "That's a term that's pretty common in my time."

She ignored my vulgarism and its related apology. "Why do you think you're not doing what you're supposed to?"

"It's hard to explain," I said. "Coming to Dodge was my idea, and I have to prove to Dolan—that's our director—and, maybe, some others, it was a good first target. I have to bring back something to justify myself."

"Bring back?" she asked. "Like what?"

I waved my hand vaguely. "That's just it. I don't know. It's not going to go over well if I return and write up a two-page report that says that I met a pretty girl, stayed at her homestead, and visited Dodge City to find it just like in the movies."

"What are you supposed to do?"

"That's what has me scared," I said. "As much as we've prepared for this mission, I don't know what I'm going to do that's going to silence my critics."

"Dodge is pretty dull, isn't it?" she agreed.

"No, it isn't," I asserted, perhaps too forcefully. "Dodge City is everything I'd hoped it would be. I can't put in words what I experienced when I first saw the town, what it was like to walk down Front Street, to see the people, to run into Wyatt Earp, . . . It made my heart beat faster. It was so exciting that I felt like a little kid. I just wanted to run my hands through the dust in the streets, to rub my fingers on the store fronts, to talk to everyone I saw." I felt silly talking like that. I took a deep breath and looked away.

"Find the words," she said.

"Words?"

"You can put that feeling into words," she said. "I got goose flesh just hearing you talk like that."

"You mean goose bumps?"

"Goose whatever," she said impatiently. "I've never heard anyone talk like that—making dirt and wood sound exciting. All you have to do is convey that feeling to them."

"They're engineers," I said dejectedly.

"And I'm just a school teacher," she said. "And I've walked in that awful dust and passed those plain store fronts a hundred times. Yet, you made me excited about it. If they've any heart at all, they'll understand and share your enthusiasm."

"You think so?" I asked, unsure if she was mocking me.

"They'll understand," she said.

I hoped she was right, but I couldn't think of any way I'd

convince anyone that dirt and wood siding were exciting. I appreciated her words, but I was falling back into my insecurities when she interrupted my thoughts.

"Tell me about the future," she said.

Tess set out a blanket on the sparse grass next to the house and we both lay down. I kept my distance.

"Why?" I asked. "You don't believe me."

I speculated that she thought I was just a clever writer imagining wonderful things. At least, I assumed that she found me a little clever.

As we looked at the stars blossoming in the sky, I asked what she wanted to know.

"Oh," she said. "Tell me what the people are like."

"People don't change," I said. "People will be the same as long as we're on earth. There are good people and bad people, smart people and dumb people. I already told you people are bigger in my time, however," I continued.

"Are they good-looking?" she asked.

"The same as now," I said. "Except there's no one in my time as pretty as you."

She dismissed that with a snicker. "Are the people nice?"

I almost laughed at that question, but realized that, maybe, they weren't.

"There are problems just like now. Half the people hate our country, and more than half the children grow up without both parents. It's a very self-indulgent time, a lot of selfishness."

"Worse than now?" she asked cautiously. Her face took on a concerned look.

"In some ways," I allowed.

At a loss for what to say, she changed the subject.

"Tell me about books," she asked.

"Nothing's changed," I said, "except you can listen to books as well as read them, and you can read them off a computer screen. But most people still pick up a bound book."

"I don't know what a computer screen is, but don't bother explaining," she said. "What kind of books do they read?"

"Like now, all kinds. We still read the great writers of today—Twain, Dickens, Tolstoy, Dostoevsky. But new books are written all the time. A lot of great books will be written in the next hundred years. Some of them will be famous forever."

"What about houses?" she asked.

"For the most part, not much different, except we don't have sod houses anymore," I said, looking toward her house. "Every house has indoor plumbing—no more outhouses. But the biggest change is in the cities, where some buildings stand almost 2000 feet high."

"I don't believe that," she said with no confrontation in her voice. "I don't know anything about buildings, but a building that tall would fall down or be blown over by the first wind. And how would anyone be able to get to the top?" she asked, thinking that she'd clinched her argument.

"They use elevators," I said. "An elevator is like a room that's connected to the top of the building by a cable. People get in on the bottom floor and a motor pulls them up to wherever they want to go. Elevators were invented about twenty years ago but I guess you've never seen one."

She still didn't believe me, but she didn't argue the point further. "Tell me about the carts," she said.

"Cars," I said. "Well, everyone has a car. There are no horses in towns anymore. They're only found on ranches."

"And farms?" she interposed.

"No, not even on farms," I said. "Farmers use tractors, kind of like strong cars, to do the work horses and oxen do now."

"How big are the cars?"

"Oh, that varies a lot," I said. "Most cars are less than twenty feet long but some busses can carry three or four dozen people and they're about sixty feet long. And there are trucks over a hundred feet long that carry goods around the country."

Since I was spinning tall tales for her, I decided to really get her attention. "Besides riding in cars, when people have to go long distances, they fly."

"Fly?" she asked with a puzzled look on her face. "How do they fly?"

I regretted bringing the subject up. How was I going to explain this? "Well, there are these things called planes, airplanes really," I answered. "They have wings and go very fast. You can't imagine how big they are. One plane is so big that it could carry most of the population of Dodge at one time, more than 600 people."

I knew she didn't believe that. As I said, a plane that big can't be imagined.

"How big is that plane?" she persevered.

"You're never going to believe me again," I said, "but that plane is over 200 feet long and weighs about a million pounds."

"Yeah," she said, clearly dismissing that nonsense. "And what makes these cars and airplanes move?"

"Engines," I said. "A car engine is about half the size of a horse's body, no, smaller, but it produces a lot of power."

"Like a train," she asked.

"No, not that much," I said. "But cars are smaller and lighter than trains and don't need as much power."

"Do they go as fast as a train?"

"Faster than today's trains, but some trains in my time can go over 200 miles an hour, about four times as fast as the fastest trains today."

"And the airplanes, they have engines, too?" she asked.

"Yes," I said slowly. "But they're completely different. They have what're called jet engines. A jet engine pushes the plane like the air rushing out of a released balloon."

"And you're going to tell me these elephant-size planes can go 200 miles an hour?" she said, scoffing at me.

"Well, actually, they go closer to 600 miles an hour and

they aren't elephant-size. They could carry a couple of hundred elephants."

"I understand," she said. "You have airplanes that can make elephants fly and go 600 miles an hour."

I didn't expect her to believe me.

"What do people eat?" she asked. "And don't tell me that they eat airplanes."

"No," I said, laughing. "They don't eat airplanes, or elephants either."

"People can eat almost anything they want. We have markets almost half the size of Dodge that have any kind of food you can imagine."

"But not airplanes or elephants?"

"No."

"Tell me what you'd eat on an average day," she directed.

"For breakfast, maybe fried eggs, bacon, and toast. For lunch, a sandwich with meat, lettuce, and tomato in it. And for dinner, maybe some meat, potatoes, and a vegetable."

"Do people grow their own food?" she asked.

"Good question," I said. "No, they don't. In fact, this very area we're in—Kansas, Nebraska, Iowa—becomes the most productive food producer in the world. It's called 'The Breadbasket of the World.'"

"Of the world?" she asked.

"Believe it or not," I said. "A good portion of the world is fed on wheat and corn grown within 400 miles of here. This is the best farming soil anyplace on earth."

"I can barely grow enough to feed myself," she said. "And I was blaming the soil."

"Well, they dump a lot of fertilizer on it," I said.

"My cows give me enough of that. That can't be the problem."

"But how do people in Washington or other places in the world get the food?" she asked, and then answered herself.

"Trains, right?"

"Not exactly," I said. "Cattle are still probably moved by train, as is grain, but most of the processed food probably travels by truck and on huge ships to go overseas."

"Do people still get sick?"

"That's a losing battle," I said. "Science has developed some marvelous medicines that should cure anything. But nature stays one step ahead of the cures.

"Some diseases have been stopped, like smallpox, polio, and malaria for the most part. But people still get the common cold, and influenza hits every winter. Then, there're some terrible new diseases. One is called AIDS. It attacks the body's defense system and the victims suffer a terrible death."

"Do they still sell snake oil?"

I laughed at the question. "Yeah, they do. But they call it vitamins in my time."

"And people buy these vitamins?" she asked.

"Yeah, just like they buy snake oil now."

"How are babies born?"

"Same as now," I said. "Still a difficult and painful experience for women."

"Do husbands and wives still . . .?

"Exactly the same, thank God," I said. "However, it's not just husbands and wives anymore. More people live together without being married than are married."

That quieted Tess down. But not for long.

"What are the biggest differences from now?" she asked.

I thought a moment before answering.

"Better and more food, easier transportation, instant communication, and air conditioning."

"Air conditioning?"

"Almost everyone's house is cooled in summer and heated in winter."

She didn't ask how that was done. She'd had enough for

one night.

"The one thing that has remained the same is that a beautiful woman is still the most enjoyable and interesting thing on earth," I said. "That'll never change."

Tess looked at me sharply in the dark, stared for a few seconds, and then looked away without saying anything. I shouldn't be playing with her like that. We had no future, and it would be cruel to lead her on.

Chapter 33

Although Tess didn't believe a word I told her, she and I settled into an increasingly comfortable routine. She went about her usual activities and I contributed as I could. My twenty-first century skills translated poorly to 1876. Instead of skills, I knew what technology to use to get jobs done in my time. Since none of that technology was available in nineteenth-century Dodge, I was useless—especially since I wasn't hardened to physical labors.

I'd lifted weights and jogged, and carried little fat, and thought I was in good condition, but none of that helped with the ranch work. My arms tired quickly from hammering nails and my back ached from cleaning out the barn. My whole body strained from carrying water for the small garden. The realities of nineteenth-century work disabused me of my twenty-first-century conceits. I was, in truth, a soft product of a different time.

There was one thing I could do for Tess—clean up. Both the yard and the barn badly needed straightening up. I'd noticed Tess taking little steps to brighten things, and I offered to help.

"What are we going to do with the stuff?" she asked.

"What do people usually do with things they need to throw

out?"

"I guess they throw them in a wagon, take them someplace out of the way, and dump them," she said.

I must have made a face that showed I didn't approve because she added, "Well, what do you suggest?"

"Dodge must have someplace where they accumulate stuff," I said. "We'd need Lester to let us load it in his wagon."

Acquiescing to my twenty-first-century sensibilities, she said she'd ask him. I took that to mean it was okay for me to go to work. I started in the barn and, in a few hours, I had cleared it of three-quarters of its useless thing. I piled it in the yard to the left of the barn door. When Tess came to inspect, she shook her head.

"Do you need any of this stuff?" I asked.

She shook her head, then added, "Looks like two hauls with Lester."

She seemed pleased, especially after inspecting the inside of the barn.

"Does it look better?" I asked.

"It looks better than my house," she said.

"We can work on that after I gather the stuff from the yard," I said.

My comment caused both of us to react. I hadn't been inside the house, and it represented her sanctuary to both of us.

"Maybe, you can just bring the stuff you don't need outside, and I'll put them with these things," I said.

"We'll see," she said.

She did give me credit for the clean-up, increasingly so as the place started looking more kempt. However, she still took pleasure in seeing me strain doing things she did with ease. She seemed to approve my physique while enjoy its limitations. I, on the other hand, greatly admired *her* physique, but I also marveled at her strength and endurance. She looked fragile, but had a physical and mental strength hidden under her smooth skin. I found myself working harder to try to match her. I kidded myself that I studied her because she was part of the historical West I was to observe. I knew, however, that despite my professional responsibilities, I was being drawn to her, and—just as important to me, I thought she was attracted to me.

Now that it was cleaned out, the decrepit condition of the barn itself glared at me. It felt like a burr in my shoe, so I proposed painting it. That, at least, I could do. Reluctantly, Tess agreed and let me get paint from Dodge, along with the necessary equipment. All I needed was a short ladder, a few brushes, and turpentine. It didn't seem like much but, since I had no other way to get to Dodge, I had to walk in and to carry back myself. I managed by making a kind of travois of the ladder, tying the paint and turpentine to it, and dragging the contraption behind me.

Even applying three coats, I finished the job in less than a day. I felt that, for the first time, I'd contributed something by cleaning and sprucing up the barn. The dark red paint made the barn, and the whole compound sparkle. More importantly, Tess sparkled along with it. The house needed even more attention but I had no idea how to repair a sod wall.

"I don't know how to fix a sod house," I said as we were eating lunch.

"Neither do I," she said.

"It needs some work," I said, trying to be as diplomatic as I could.

Tess didn't respond.

"I can afford to pay for someone to come out and do it," I said.

Tess looked at me with a mixture of emotions on her face. "What are you going to use—money from your boot?"

"Getting money is no problem."

"What do you plan to do—telegraph back to your time for a loan?"

"You find someone to do the work, I'll pay for it."

Tess continued to feed and house me, if you count the barn

as housing. She never asked me to contribute beyond my embarrassingly meager work around the place. I had money, but her equivocal reaction to my offer to pay to fix up her house made me reluctant to offer her money directly. I didn't want to make our relationship a financial one, and I didn't want to call attention to her sparse finances. She let the offer on the house pass, and neither of us discussed money again.

After four days, we'd fallen into a routine both of us accepted. I was happy, very happy, to be at SouthFord, and Tess suffered my presence without explanation or complaint. Reflecting on my good fortune and grateful for the place to stay, I was reluctant to ask how long I was welcome. I feared she was waiting for a polite way to suggest I move on. I didn't want to make it easy for her.

Adding to my fears was that I needed to return to Washington. The batteries on the device were deteriorating every day, and the one-week deadline was looming.

I thought this was a good time to tell her. "I need to go away for a day."

Tess's face went blank. I couldn't read her reaction. Despite myself, I wanted to believe she was distressed about my announcement. That possibility thrilled me. Another possibility, however, was that she was relieved that now she didn't have to tell me to leave. I couldn't tell because, in that feminine way, she simply accepted my announcement.

"My first trip was supposed to be short," I explained to fill the awkward silence. "I need to go back to be checked out, and get the device recharged. If everything's okay, I'll come right back."

"When's 'right back'?" she asked. Her question might have been polite conversation or true interest. I couldn't tell.

I told her that, in theory, I could return at any time without any lapse of time. In practice, however, the device was programmed to move forward in both eras at the same rate. As a result, I'd arrive back in Washington later by exactly the same number of days as I spent in Kansas.

"I should be back soon, maybe tomorrow evening," I said. "It shouldn't take long to clear me." Maybe, I was saying the wrong thing, forcing her to tell me I wouldn't be welcome when I returned.

"You intend to return then?" she asked.

"Am I welcome?" I choked on the words, fearful of what she would say.

She nodded, but without commitment. I didn't know how to interpret her *Mona Lisa* look. Was it concern about never seeing me again or distress that she'd ultimately have to deal with sending me on my way when, and if, I returned? Overall, I should have been relieved by her lack of enthusiasm—one less complication to deal with. If she weren't interested in me, I could dowse any incipient torch I was carrying for her.

However, I wasn't thinking like an engineer. I wanted her to care, one way or the other, that I was leaving. And Tess? Like women of every age, she evidenced only a passive acceptance of what was beyond her control. For now, I tried to accept that I wouldn't know her intentions until I returned.

"I'll tell you what," I said to bolster my prospects. "When I come back, I'll bring you some things from the future, things you'll like."

Tess got up and returned to her work without another word.

Chapter 34

I didn't wait until I'd left to begin worrying. I started even before Tess disappeared behind the house. As I watched her walk away, I felt my future receding with her, leaving me alone in the yard, alone in the world. Her indifference to my departure was a blow. I'd expected to have to justify my departure, and to have to assure her I'd return. Instead, my justification, and my attempts at assurance, fell on apathetic ears. Tess's casual turning to her tasks struck me as a turning away from me. And, damn, I didn't want her to have a life without me.

What was I saying? I'm Will Barrett, and I live in the twenty-first century. I'm just passing through Kansas and the Old West. At best, I had hoped to make a few acquaintances here to help me understand how these people thought. Instead, I was aching over Tess, a woman I yearned to fathom and to understand, but someone, I realized, I didn't know at all. I glanced at a chicken strutting by and knew I understood the chicken better than I understood Tess.

The day seemed to darken as I struggled with my disappointment. Still standing near the barn where Tess had left me, I felt tired and heavy. I couldn't focus. I tried to convince myself that Tess was only a momentary infatuation. I depended on her so much that I'd fallen in love with her in the same way female patients so often fall for their doctors. What was I saying? The "L" word? Had I really given my heart like a fifteen-year-old to the first attractive woman who showed kindness to me? In a word, yes.

I had nothing to do until I left, so I sat in my customary spot against the barn wall. I rested my chin on my fist and gave in to my juvenile thoughts and emotions. In my funk, I speculated about what Tess would do after I left. Soon, I'd convinced myself that she blew me off so easily because I wasn't the only man in her life. Whoever else had intentions toward her, and she would undoubtedly know who that was, had to observe widow deference—he had to wait a respectable time before actively pursuing her. I, on the other hand, having neither decorum nor respect, had stumbled into the middle of her mourning period. Now that I'd ended Tess's bereavement by being seen in public with her, I'd opened the door to the other man—or men—who were waiting in the wings.

Surely, as soon as I left, a prospect would be calling at her door. In all likelihood, Tess would be relieved to be free of the lame time traveler, and open to any townie who appeared. Knowing that men would be flocking to her door, Tess would forget me within ten minutes of my jump. But twenty-five or thirty years in the future, she'd be telling her grandchildren tall tales about the strange man who appeared off the plains and claimed to be from the twenty-first century. Her grandchildren would listen in awe but, like Tess, wouldn't believe a word of the story.

"Aw, Grandma," they'd say. "There wasn't no such man. You're making that up."

"No, I'm not," she'd say earnestly, "that's the truth, cross my heart."

Her grandchildren would search her still-beautiful face for a twinkle or the start of a smile, but none would come. Within a few minutes, the children would lose interest in the whole idea and ask if they could go to town to see the horseless carriage. Grandma Tess would sigh, stand up, and fluff out her matronly dress. "It's the truth," she'd say.

As the grandchildren ran off to play, one of them would yell back, "If he was real, then why didn't he come back?"

In my imagination, the question would startle Tess, tears would come to her eyes, and she wouldn't be able to answer.

Or so I hoped. Twisted thoughts from a despairing mind. Twisted but vivid—I couldn't rid myself of the image of the little blond boy turning around as he ran off, one suspender hanging off a shoulder, asking, "Then why didn't he come back?"

Chapter 35

As the sun was setting, Tess came over to sit by me. At first, she didn't say anything, but sat quietly, deep in thought. Not knowing what she was thinking, or feeling, I waited for her to break the silence.

"Could I ask you some questions before you leave?" she asked quietly. There was a tone of finality in the way she asked, as if she had prefaced it with, "Since I'm never going to see you again . . ."

"Sure, anything," I said.

"Is it ever going to get better?"

"Is what going to get better?"

"The world, life, my life," she said, despair seeping into her words.

"Yes," I said, trying to sound upbeat, "it's going to get better. Despite the wars, the world in my time is a brighter place with a lot to make people happy."

"Would you rather live here or there?"

I understood what she meant, but I hesitated to give the honest answer, which was "I'd rather live wherever you are." The conversation didn't invite me to talk about my passion for her.

"There's a lot to be said for the here and now," I said instead. "But the world I come from is a lot more comfortable."

She thought for a moment before speaking.

"I look at the children in my classroom," she said, "and I feel so bad for them—they'll have such hard lives—so much struggle, so much pain, and so little joy."

"Don't feel like that," I said. "They're going to see wonders—inspiring things that will make them feel good about being human."

"You're sure?"

"I'm sure," I said. "The children you teach could live to—let's see—about 1940 or 1950. In that time, they'll see diseases cured, they'll see cars and planes, and they'll see men—and women—start to understand the universe."

She didn't seem encouraged.

"Your own children will see even more," I added. "They could live until 1960 or so. In that time, they'll see rockets launching satellites into orbit around the earth, maybe even men going into space. They'll see jet planes flying across oceans."

"And those things are good?"

"Things aren't good or bad. It's what men do with them that matters. I think anything that expands men's horizons is good," I said. "You're a teacher. Your job is to encourage these small minds to blossom so they can solve difficult problems and invent wondrous things. For all we know, your children may be the people doing these things."

"Will there be enough food for everyone?"

"Food will never be a problem in this country. There'll be enough so no one has to go to bed hungry, although, in fact, some people do."

"How will these children learn to do these things?" she asked. "How could I teach them if I don't know how?"

"You don't have to teach them everything. Teach them to love knowledge and show them how to get it."

196

"How to get it?"

"Teach them to love reading and to love learning," I said. "In my time, anything you want to know is at your fingertips. If I were sitting in front of my computer, I could get almost any information I needed by pressing a few buttons. I'd have access to millions of articles that would provide the information."

"All in your computer?"

"Well, no," I said, dragging out the 'no' as I thought about how to explain the Internet. "My computer would be connected through wires, like telegraph wires, to a place where all the information is stored." Then, to add to the confusion, I added, ". . . or connected without wires."

"Will stupid politicians learn to work together?"

"You're talking about the way Wright and Hoover fight about everything here in Dodge?"

When she nodded, I told her the truth. "No, stupidity and fighting go with politics. That's not going to get better."

"Are the Indians still a problem in your time?"

"Not in the way you think. They don't fight against the white man anymore."

"Babies die all the time around here," she said. "I assume they still die in your time?"

"Some do," I said. "But infant deaths are few in my time. Most babies die now because of disease. In my time, they get medicine injected into their systems that protect them from most diseases."

"That's good," she said. "I love babies. What about the Civil War?"

I didn't understand the question.

"The southern states still hate the northerners," she explained. "Will that ever end?"

"Yeah, for the most part," I said. "Lincoln saved the country. The South and the North will always have somewhat different cultures, but they learned to get along. Gradually, southerners came to think of themselves as Americans again."

"What about slaves? What happens to them?"

"Well, there are still difficulties," I admitted. "They aren't slaves anymore, of course. We're still working on fully integrating them into society but, even in my time, there are problems."

"It doesn't sound like it's much better," Tess said.

"It is better," I said, perhaps too vehemently. "Despite what I've said, most black and white people are doing their best to work together. Still, there's racial conflict, and blacks tend to be poorer than whites. But even the poor have things unimaginable to you— they're all wealthy by today's standards."

"You think my life will be better?" she asked, bringing me back to reality. Ultimately, all of her questions were pleas for hope—hope for her and hope for her children.

"Tess," I said, "you have a lot to look forward to. You're going to live long enough to ride in a car, maybe fly in a plane. You'll eat better food and it'll be a lot cheaper. And you'll have a refrigerator to keep the food safe. You'll see movies and will live to see television invented. You'll listen to the radio and be able to hear someone singing or talking thousands of miles away."

Tess didn't understand everything I was saying, but she listened.

"And your children will have it even better," I added.

"Will it make them happier?"

"No one can guarantee they'll be happy. That's up to them. What I can assure you is that they won't have to struggle like you do now."

"But, planes, cars, rockets," she said with a small shrug. "What do they have to do with happiness?"

As an engineer, I always think that technology is progress, that people will be happier if they have a better TV. I saw her point, but I wasn't going to concede.

"All we can do is improve the human condition," I said. "We can make their homes more comfortable, and make it easier for them to move about. If you reduce the struggle, they have a better chance to find their happiness. You make the best of what you have. Teach that to the kids in your classroom, and teach your own children to do the same."

"You keep bringing up my children," she said. "I don't have children, and who says I'll ever have them?"

"You'll have children," I said in a manner that would brook no argument. "And they're going to be the most beautiful and smartest children who ever lived."

Even she had to smile at that. I reached over and squeezed her hand.

"We'll talk some more when I get back."

Chapter 36

I didn't sleep well and awoke early with an empty feeling. After indulging my self-pity for a couple of hours, I had to plan my jump to Washington, and to consider what I'd bring with me when I returned to Dodge. My thoughts centered on what I could bring back to wow Tess, but I also wanted to carry back the tools to document Dodge for STRP.

Our experiments confirmed I could travel through time with relatively small items attached to my body. For instance, my clothes had traveled with me. Thank God. However, we didn't know the carry-on limit, or the consequences of exceeding that limit.

I planned to tape a number of items to my legs and arms for my return jump. I didn't think the Heisenbergs, or Dolan, would approve the contraband, but early astronauts often carried unauthorized items into space while management looked the other way. Aside from Dolan, I expected a lot of blind eyes to my innocent cargo. I'd encourage them to focus on my *iPad* and digital camera, since those items would further our mission objectives.

I got up from my pity-perch and stretched to get some blood flowing. I couldn't continue to dwell. As I did so, the cause of my distress emerged from the house. She looked at me for a moment, her face devoid of expression. Was she angry with me? Disappointed? Sad that I was leaving? Glad to be rid of me?

Tess kept her feelings to herself but now, as I looked into her face from across the small yard, I saw a look of despair had returned to her face, the same heartbreaking look I saw when I first met her. Despite myself, I experienced schadenfreude, that guilty joy one feels at someone else's pain. In this case, her pain meant she cared about my leaving. I hoped.

She'd changed since my arrival, dramatically and for the better, but I'd failed to see it until now. Although I'd spent every minute of my time with her searching her face for evidence of her thoughts, I'd missed the obvious.

I reflected on what I should have been noticing. The despair had all but disappeared and, in its place, she had a depth I'd never seen in another human being. She seemed to have a higher knowledge that transcended schooling. It made my education and even my twenty-first-century experiences seem trivial. Instinctively, I found myself deferring to her in so many ways unrelated to my guest status in her home.

As I thought, Tess had crossed the yard and stood, like a sphinx, in the dust. She stopped about six feet away and continued to look at me.

"I'm looking forward to telling my people everything I've seen," I told her. It was probably the wrong thing to say.

"I'm glad," she said. She didn't mean it.

I wanted to tell her how hard it was for me to leave and that I'd miss her terribly but . . . I just couldn't. I wanted to get her talking about her feelings, but . . . I just couldn't. A wall prevented both of us from saying anything meaningful. We stood in the shadow of the barn, awkwardly looking at each other. It was time to leave.

For lack of anything better to say, I told her I'd have to hike out into the plains, away from the trees and house because my jumping-off place would be the target when I returned from Washington. She didn't see the logic until I asked her to picture how enjoyable my return to Kansas would be if I arrived in the middle of a tree trunk, my arms and legs flailing outside while my head and body were trapped inside.

Tess laughed uncertainly at that. I couldn't be sure what she believed at this point. Time travel wasn't an easy sell, especially in a time when a steam engine is high tech.

I pointed at Tess and said, "I *will* be back." It drew an enigmatic smile.

"I hope so," she said. "Maybe I'll be taking my bath in the stream when you return." She said it without emotion, as if it were a script, something she was supposed to say.

"Now, that'll guarantee I'll come back." I tried to be jocular, but my tone was somber.

That exchange was encouraging and, although I was reluctant to leave, I didn't want to make too much of this. Traveling 134 years in an instant isn't the same as flying to Mars, is it?

Tess's smile was stale by this time. There was pain in her eyes, and I still didn't know what to say. I didn't want to presume she was going to miss me—she was probably just going to miss the company. I had no words to make her feel better. I would be back—if I could.

I didn't know where our relationship stood—if we had a relationship—but I didn't think it'd reached the point where a hug was appropriate. I gave a weak, waist-high wave and walked off.

My return to Dodge wasn't as assured as I'd made it seem. Washington can be capricious, and I feared the project might decide we'd learned all we could. I hoped not.

When I was a good 400 meters from the house and trees, I

stopped and looked back toward the house, but Tess was nowhere in sight. Disappointed, I scanned my surroundings, perhaps my last look at suburban Dodge City. I said my goodbyes to the hundreds of pairs of prairie dog eyes watching me, leaned down, lifted my right pants leg, and pressed the seemingly blank front panel. I took a deep breath as I hit the fourth quadrant. When I finished inhaling, twenty-first century air filled my lungs.

Chapter 37

I was spaced out when I arrived in the twenty-first century. Or, perhaps, timed out might be more accurate. Going almost instantaneously from the endless plains to congested Washington would disorient anyone. I arrived where I'd left, in the campus gymnasium. Fortunately, the gymnasium was empty when I appeared. I needed to settle down before I faced the intense celebration, and questioning, that would result from my successful voyage.

I stretched a little as I adjusted to the different 2010 light streaming through the high windows. I listened to the usually unnoticed background growl of city noises—cars, people, doors, and planes. When my fret lag fell to an acceptable level, I walked toward the lab.

As word spread about my return, the halls filled excitedly. Everyone, from the janitor on up, ran out to grab my hand or hug me. Everyone had to slap or bounce me along the hallway in the exuberance—I was living proof of an historic accomplishment.

The joy was genuine and caught me up. I put on a happy face for my fellow scientists and the support staff. We'd succeeded, and I was happy about that. However, I experienced the celebration as through a glass darkly. The fact was that I wasn't happy to be back. I already missed Kansas—and I missed Tess.

The other celebrants cleared a path when Dolan arrived. As he approached, I was unnerved to see what appeared to be genuine happiness on his face. When the badger is happy, the prey better be wary. I accepted his handshake and pats as if they were genuine, but I wasn't about to turn my back to him.

Dolan hastily assembled a debriefing team to interrogate me. Of course, the questioning would center on my arrival in Kansas and the sensations of traveling back more than a hundred years. The good news was there wasn't much to report. Despite my initial reaction to the heat, I felt good physically, and I decided not to relate how despondent I was about coming back. I didn't yet know if my melancholy might be partly a product of the experiment.

My encounter with Dolan prepared me for the confrontation that had to be lurking in the shadows. I wasn't so naïve as to believe that all was well and good since I'd made it back and everyone, or nearly everyone, was thrilled at our success. I braced myself to face the problems Dolan was sure to create. I feared his vindictiveness, and I, and the mission, were certain targets.

The debriefing panel was the first evidence of his plan. Not only did he appoint the three Board members most susceptible to his will, but he also made himself the chairman.

Ed Fitzgerald was a capable and honest team manager, but he also had ambitions for an early mission. Even without the natural jealousy about me getting the first mission, he would be sensitive to the political winds swirling around the selection of the next Stripper. Ed was shrewd enough to know that the Board would be reluctant to challenge Dolan a second time. Without any duplicity, Fitzgerald was in Dolan's pocket.

Jim McDonnell was the second appointee. He was a programmer and had written most of the code that I rode to the nineteenth century and back. Without his genius, I would never have left the twenty-first century. His vulnerability was technical. Since his code had already successfully completed the Dodge mission, he'd want to apply his skills to the next target. He had no investment in redoing the West.

Finally, Bill Reed was our ethical consultant. His focus had been, from the beginning, on minimizing the impact of our missions. His mantra, like the dictate in the Hippocratic Oath, was "First of all, do no harm." He was my ally in so many ways against Dolan, but he was vulnerable to the argument that short missions would do the least harm.

As soon as I learned the composition of the debriefing committee, I began referring to them as the FMR Committee (for Fitzgerald-McDonnell-Reed). It didn't take me long to start thinking the initials stood for the "Frustrating My Return" Committee.

Fundamentally, I trusted all these men. Even leading up to my launch, when we feared that someone had sold out to Dolan, I couldn't imagine any of them betraying me or the program. I'd literally lived with these people for months. We'd all committed ourselves to STRP and had an almost obsessive commitment to its success. However, despite our common aims, we all had niche agendas, resulting in a diverse Board with differing ideas and talents. As a result, it was also a Board susceptible to the Machiavellian machinations of John Dolan. I kept that in mind but, like it or not, the FMR Committee would decide my future.

I was given a couple of hours rest before the interviews. While lying in bed, I prepared myself for the battle instead of resting. I would avoid referring to the trip as "my" mission. I repeated ten times: "our mission, our mission, our mission . . ." Dolan would jump all over an inadvertent "my" to convince the others my arguments for returning to Kansas were self-serving and didn't reflect an objective appraisal of the value of the mission.

Just as I could be realistic about my fellow STRPers, I knew they had their opinions about me. I was the youngest member of the team, save one, but I was the lead engineer because of my experience with the Mars program. While I was secretly proud of my *wunderkind* reputation, I knew it drew resentment.

My older brother, Joey, had ragged me since I was four or five that I only lived to be rich and famous. My work on the Mars missions, work that put me on the cover of *Time Magazine*, brought both respect and ill feelings. I couldn't deny my ambitions—I wanted to succeed every bit as much as I wanted STRP to succeed. In promoting my ideas and, perhaps, in promoting myself, I'd alienated some on the Board and, perhaps, had given the impression I didn't consider their contributions to be of equal value.

To offset those challenges, I intended to separate myself from any emotional plea. I would stress only that the mission was incomplete. STRP's objective was to penetrate the past and gather data to enhance the historical record. Through no fault of mine, my brief journey to Dodge hadn't yet resulted in usable data. I'd spent only a few hours in Dodge and would need days or weeks to gather the data we sought. Any fair and objective evaluation had to conclude the Dodge City mission needed more time—more time to perfect our methods and more time to gather data itself. I could only hope I'd get an objective evaluation from FMR.

I knew Dolan would be there as I presented my case, and he'd be sitting there, ready to destroy it. That is, if he hadn't already. I feared more than anything that he wouldn't challenge my return to Dodge. If he remained silent, I'd know that I, and *my* mission, would be doomed.

Chapter 38

I entered the debriefing unrested and uneasy. I faced Dolan and the committee with tired eyes and muddled thinking. We shook hands, and I was encouraged that all three FMR members were smiling and still excited to see me.

Three doctors sat along the wall of the small conference room. They didn't stand when I entered, but they never took their gazes off me. I assumed Dolan invited them. They were to examine me after the debriefing, but I didn't expect them at this meeting.

With two video cameras running, Dolan turned the initial questioning over to Ed Fitzgerald. He made it simple: "Summarize the mission."

I told them everything I could recall about my time in Kansas. Well, perhaps not everything.

I spoke as an engineer reporting his observations. I described my condition upon arrival in Kansas, my near-fatal reaction to the heat, and my struggles to reach the trees. I reported the several reasons I headed toward the trees—relief from the sun, access to water, and hope of making contact nearby.

I told them everything—except what I thought and felt about Tess. Unless I revealed myself through body language, Tess would appear in the report as just one of a few dozen Dodge City contacts. Like the innkeeper in the Christmas gospel, she'd be a footnote to history.

I spoke for about thirty minutes, taking questions along the way, and was surprised at the details I recalled. I hadn't taken notes and had been concerned that I'd forgotten a lot. A careful draftsman—and I intended to be one—could frame a report from my monologue that would fully justify the mission. The FMR members seemed satisfied and pleased.

Dolan seemed pleased, too. However, I suspected, he wasn't pleased for the same reasons as the committee members. He confirmed my skepticism as soon as he spoke.

"Well, Mr. Barrett," he said officiously, "it seems that we've had a very successful mission, and the data you've provided will help us plan future missions. Let me give you the opportunity, however, to explain why we should expend further efforts on Dodge City."

His words would appear, on the recording, to be a generous offer to give me the final say. His manner, however, was anything but generous. He laced his words with condescension, implying that Dodge was a dead issue, and we were just writing the final page of the report.

Trying to sound objective, I explained that the most vital information wouldn't be found in simple observations such as the appearance of the town or the amount of dust on the streets. We needed to establish protocols for future missions, to devise non-intrusive methods for insightful interviews, in-depth observations, and even recordings and photographs. I argued that my cover as a reporter allowed me to garner information without raising suspicions or interfering with history. I proposed that, while they planned future missions using my preliminary experiences, I return to Dodge for a two-month fact-gathering period with periodic transitions to update our methods and results.

"The techniques we develop in Dodge, and the lessons we learn there, will be the foundation for all later missions. If we don't mine this target for all there is to learn, both historically and scientifically, we risk setting back the entire project for years to come."

Before adjourning the debriefing, Dolan made his own statement.

"Mr. Barrett, you have the thanks and congratulations of everyone on the Board and, ultimately, you will have the adulation of the world," he said in what sounded like a planned speech. "We all respect your arguments that we haven't met one hundred percent of the objectives of this mission. We could, perhaps, at considerable expense, gain additional, but very marginal data. The entire Board must decide whether we resume your mission, but I think many of us believe we're at the point of diminishing returns. Each additional journey to Dodge will result in less and less return, while the vast history of the human race would have to wait because we tied up resources on this mission. We've succeeded in this limited mission, and it *is* time to move on. We'll give you our recommendation in the morning before proposing it to the entire Board."

With that, and with a glance at the doctors, he called the meeting to a close. I saw the looks the doctors returned to Dolan, and I didn't like my prospects. I'd noticed the doctors getting subtly agitated as I answered questions. They took notes as I spoke and exchanged looks among themselves at certain points.

When I left the room and walked to the infirmary for my post-jump physical, they remained with the committee. I saw that as strike two, and found myself perspiring lightly as I walked down the hallway for what I now believed was a rigged examination.

The lead doctor gave me a brief physical examination and asked, in various ways, how I felt. He queried me about visual loss or hearing loss during the mission, whether I had felt unusually hot or cold, and whether I had any trouble breathing. He asked how I slept, and whether I ate or drank any more or less than usual. Did my heart rate seem unusual? What about my elimination of wastes? I answered all of his questions honestly. I'd experienced nothing unusual—except Tess. And I wasn't going to tell him about her.

When he finished, he left, and the psychiatrist and psychologist continued the evaluation. Their questions were more intensive. After I answered their questions, all of which was again recorded on video, I took several written tests.

I left for dinner even more depleted. The debriefing and examinations were more taxing than the mission itself had been, and I feared the doctors would attribute the stress of the evaluations to the mission itself.

I called my brother on my cell phone when I returned to my room after dinner. Of course, he was relieved I was back. I gave him an abridged version of what I'd told the debriefers. I didn't begrudge him the time, nor did it tax me, since I felt the love and warmth of his enthusiasm.

Although the project was Top Secret, I could tell Joey anything. He'd been the project's computer/electronics expert until he'd left six months before to work for a private defense contractor. He remained a consultant for STRP and had full access to the campus and to project information. Using the vernacular of secrecy, he had the "need to know."

My selection as the first STRPer and his immediate departure were only coincidental. Joey was my biggest supporter, and he harbored no jealousy of my success.

"Will," he said grimly when he resigned, "I've gotten you this far. I've done all I could for you. Now, you're on your own."

We both laughed, knowing that there was a lot of truth to what he said. He had pulled me along since we were little. He protected me from bullies, helped me with my school projects, convinced me to go to engineering school, and used his influence to get me into STRP. I'd built a strong résumé on the Mars mission, but I never could have gotten into STRP without Joey.

"You've always wanted money and fame," he said when I called him after my appointment to the project. "You can thank me later for getting you into a secret program that pays a government salary."

Then, speaking more seriously, he added, "Dad would have been proud of you."

I nodded. Our dad was a vague memory to me. Our mother had raised us alone after he disappeared. Perhaps, that explained my reliance on Joey—he was both a brother and a father to me. I remembered telling Joey, "I'm going to be somebody so that Dad will be sorry he left us."

I was only about four when I said that, but, even then, my soul burned with ambition. Our mother didn't earn enough to give us luxuries, and the other kids pitied us as the boys whose father had abandoned them.

As much as it pained me not to have a father, I felt even worse for our mother. He'd treated her so badly that his leaving was, in some ways, a blessing for her. It gave me a profound respect for the difficult role women play in society. I saw how male selfishness burdened women. I vowed never to abuse a woman as Dad had.

"Will," Joey said, when I finished telling him about my mission, "I'm so proud of you."

That meant more to me than if my real father said it. I always had Joey's support, but I still craved hearing it.

Chapter 39

Much as I wanted to tell Joey about my mission, I had another reason for calling him.

"I need some things," I said. "Can you help me?"

In addition to my *iPad* and the digital camera, I read him the items I wanted from a list I'd made just before my call.

"I need them quickly," I said. "I could be returning anytime." I'd implied to Tess that I'd be gone only one day. I wanted to be back that quickly, and I wanted her to want me to come back.

"I'll see you in the morning," Joey said.

My brother visited the next morning. He pulled a plastic bag full of my "incidental" cargo out of his small duffle bag and poured it out on my bed. Nothing he brought was more important than the roll of duct tape, that magic cloth that would hold the precious cargo to my body and, if I calculated right, allow it to travel with me.

Joey knew better than to ask about the items. He'd seen so many of my adventures that all the stories ran together. As much as he influenced my life, he was glad to be a character actor in the movie of my escapades.

"So tell me about Wyatt Earp," he said enthusiastically.

"You never want to meet your heroes," I said, looking up from the contraband spread on my bed. Since he wanted me to go on, I'd have to shoot down his blimp.

"He was everything we've ever read about him," I started. "He was tall, charismatic, and tough. That's the good part."

"And the bad?" asked Joey.

"The bad part was he was tough," I said resignedly. "He was as hard as a nanotube. His blood had to be icy blue."

"Did he beat anyone up while you were there?"

"No, he didn't have to," I said. "Everyone was too afraid to cross him."

I said that, realizing Joey couldn't possibly understand. None of the books I'd read prepared me for the reality. My account would sound the same as the historical record, but Earp couldn't be explained. He had to be experienced.

I tried anyway. "Imagine a tall, lean young male. Imagine he dresses impeccably and moves like a professional athlete. Imagine further he has a handsome, unmarked face with clear blue eyes and blond hair. Give him a presence that makes everything in a room stop as soon as he walks in. Then, give him intelligence and an insight into human nature few psychologists have. And let him have a rigid value system, with the courage to back up any affront to those values."

I took a breath and looked Joey right in the eye, "And now imagine that he has no soul whatever," I added, "that he doesn't care if you live or die."

I stopped and let it sink in. "That's Earp. You know how we feel about cancer?" I asked. "How it's arbitrary and merciless? That's how Earp makes you feel. You're utterly subject to his will and you have no idea what drives that will."

Joey didn't say anything at first, and then he asked, "Did

you ask for his autograph?" He was kidding.

"I got away from him as soon as I could. But let me tell you a story I heard. The way it's told, someone hired Clay Allison to kill Earp. You know who Allison was, one of the murderous sociopaths who roamed the West."

"Yeah, big guy, over 250 pounds and always got drunk before he killed anyone. Didn't he shoot something like four or five lawmen?"

"That's the guy. Well, as I heard it, Allison came to Dodge and, while he was drinking, bragged he was there to kill Earp. When Earp heard of the threats, he planted himself outside the Long Branch and waited for Allison. When Allison came out of the bar, he saw Earp and confronted him. Earp, leaning against the wall, stood his ground even when Allison came so close that he was actually leaning on Earp's right arm to prevent Earp from drawing his gun. When Allison reached for his own gun, he felt the muzzle of Earp's pistol, which Wyatt held in his left hand, pressed into his ribs. After a few seconds pause, during which Earp stared Allison down without a word, Allison backed away."

"And that was the end of Allison?" Joey asked.

"No," I said. "He didn't give up so quickly. He got on his horse and started out of town, riding south on Bridge Street. Suddenly, he twisted his horse around, got it into a full gallop, and headed back toward Earp. He found Earp standing in the middle of the street with his Colt pointed straight at him. That was enough for the bully—Allison wheeled his horse back around and raced out of town over the bridge. Earp reportedly holstered his gun and returned to business as if nothing happened."

"You didn't see this?" Joey asked.

"Naw, but, from what I saw of Earp, I believe it."

"Now," Joey said letting out a deep breath. He'd already had enough of Earp. "What's this stuff for? Lady friend?"

That wasn't a hard guess, considering what I had him bring. "Her name's Tess."

"Do you really think they'll let you bring the *iPad* back?" he said. "Fat chance."

"I don't plan to ask," I said.

Chapter 40

Joey checked my cargo calculations. Before leaving the project, he'd prepared a chart for estimating how much a STRPer could carry with him safely.

"It's just a guess," he said. "And we don't know what will happen if you try to carry too much."

"I know, I know," I said. "Just tell me if all of this is going to make it."

He looked over the items on the bed, hefting a few.

"Yeah, I think so," he said without enthusiasm.

"Great," I said. "Your brother's life depends on not overpacking and you *think* so?"

He shrugged. That was all I was going to get from him. Actually, I got a lot more. Joey protected me like a parent, and he wouldn't let me take an unreasonable risk. His shrug gave me a lot of confidence that I would make it safely back to Dodge.

I called Dolan's office to ask when I'd meet with the FMR committee.

"Oh," his secretary, Janice, said, "didn't they tell you? They rescheduled it to tomorrow. I heard Mr. Dolan telling the

President they wanted more time to evaluate the information before deciding."

She paused, waiting for my comment.

"How does it look?" I asked her in a near whisper. I could trust Janice to give me the truth.

Her voice took on a theatrical tone. "Yes, Mr. Barrett, I'll keep you advised."

I knew that, one, Dolan was near her desk as she spoke and, two, the news wouldn't be good. She'd call me when she could to fill me in.

"They're not going to let me go back," I told Joey when I replaced the phone.

"What'd she say?"

"Nothing," I said. "That's just it—Janice would've been encouraging if it looked good. Judging from her tone, I've seen the last of the Old West."

Joey and I went to lunch with our heads down. I saw a couple of Board members across the small cafeteria, but neither of them came over to say anything. They nodded and smiled, but there was no reassurance in their smiles. I felt like a man going to the guillotine, and any smiles I received were only to reassure me that it wouldn't hurt. This was going to hurt.

Just after Joey and I returned to my room, someone knocked on my door. The committee wanted to see me. What happened to the delay until tomorrow? Joey good-naturedly punched my arm as I went leave.

"Give 'em hell," he said.

I was the last of the team to arrive. I looked around the table at the faces of the six men I'd teamed with. They still seemed elated, but I got a watery feeling in my bowels. I wasn't going to like this meeting.

Dolan took over as soon as I sat down. "Will," he said with a pasted-on smile, "we're very pleased with our success in Dodge

City and realize we're sitting with a very important historical figure, no pun intended."

Everyone hurrahed and clapped. "You're no different than Columbus, Magellan, Lindbergh, Gagarin, and Armstrong." Heads nodded around the table.

I tried to enjoy the recognition, but I knew the next sentence was going to be, "But, Orville, we regret to have to tell you—we're taking your plane away."

Dolan ran on about the data we'd gathered, the theories we'd verified, and the opportunities we'd opened.

Looking around the room, he continued, "One of you is going to witness Christ being executed. Someone at this table is going to be in Dealey Plaza in '63. And soon."

I wanted to scream Give me the bad news, NOW, but I didn't say a word, even as Dolan continued for another five minutes. Finally, my patience exhausted, I inquired.

"Where do we stand on the second phase of Dodge?"

Dolan looked down at his hands before answering.

"We want to evaluate what we have so far," he said. "The doctors need to monitor your condition for a couple of weeks to determine if there are any as yet undiscovered effects from your mission. We also want to review and discuss the results of the voyage to see what more we can get from this target."

"Weeks?" I said. "The doctors want to monitor me for a couple of weeks?"

I asked the question pointedly, but I carefully avoided becoming adversarial. Dolan would use any hostility as evidence the mission had impaired my stability. He was baiting me, and I couldn't take the bait if I was to have any chance of going back to Dodge.

The delay would likely mean nothing to Tess. If I returned, they could, perhaps, reprogram my arrival to any date. I could arrive the day after I left. However, I knew my chances for returning diminished with every passing minute. Right now, my chances were less than five percent. In a couple of weeks, they would be zero.

"Look, John," I said, "the doctors say I'm fine—no evidence of any emotional or physical problems. The data from Dodge so far is just preliminary. When I go back, I'll gather pictures and information that'll knock Congress's eyes out."

I could see in Dolan's face that I was talking to myself.

"Will," he said evenly, "you're overreacting. We haven't decided you're not going back. We just want to make a considered decision when all the information is in."

He put his palms out in that universal gesture of How can you question that?

I looked across the table for support from my fellow engineers. I got none.

Chapter 41

Joey knew before I said anything.

"You're not going back, are you?" he asked.

"How about if we kill Dolan and send his remains back to ancient Egypt," I said. "Let 'em embalm him, and we won't have any language problem then."

Joey didn't say anything as I paced. I wanted to throw things and trash the room. The rational part of me said I still couldn't act out. Dolan probably had bugged the room, or even installed a video camera hidden in the air-conditioning grate. Whether my fears were paranoia or reality, I needed to act on the assumption that Dolan knew my every action.

I sat down and acted like an adult. "Acted" was the operative word.

"Joey," I said quietly, "I believed Dodge was the best first mission for STRP. And I believe completing that mission is essential to future missions. The methods I develop there will make Rome, Greece, and Egypt so much more productive."

Joey squinted at me. He knew I was talking to someone else. He also knew I still wanted to trash the room.

"I need a walk," I said.

We left my room, exited the building, and headed toward the exercise trails. Joey was quiet, knowing I'd talk when I was ready. We were well clear before I was able to talk sense again.

"I wouldn't be surprised if Dolan's got my room bugged," I said. "I can't take a chance."

Joey nodded, waiting for me to continue.

"Dolan gave me some bullshit about needing a couple of weeks to evaluate my condition and the data before deciding on my return. He has no intention of letting me go back."

"Dolan's a jerk," Joey said. "But he doesn't have a vote. Everyone knows he's got his own agenda."

"Dolan does, however, have a lot of influence over who goes on the next mission," I said. "Everyone's trying to position themselves to be tapped, and stepping on Dolan's toes isn't the way to move up the list. He's using me as an example of what happens when his toes feel bruised."

"Dolan's making the decision on Dodge, you think?" Joey said. "When will you know?"

"I know now," I said. "I'm already on the spit, and I'll roast gradually. A week or so from now, Dolan will stick a fork in and announce I'm done."

Chapter 42

Dolan held all the cards, but he apparently couldn't convince the rest of the committee to leave me hanging as long as he wanted. After a couple of days, Janice called me.

"This is the death sentence?" I said when she told me the committee wanted to meet with me.

"Yes," she said.

When I walked into the room, I found only Dolan willing to look me in the eye.

"Dodge is dead," I said before I sat down.

"We don't think there's any need for you to return," he said, his throat sounding like it was clogged with phlegm.

My chest tightened. I scanned the faces around the table. Everyone looked back without expression. They knew Dodge was my pet destination, and that this decision was devastating to me.

Dolan also knew what my reaction would be, and paused to allow me to reply.

"I do *not* think we should do that," I said, fighting to mask my anger. "First, we've had only one successful trip. Cutting the mission short would be like sending Alan Shepard up for fifteen minutes and shooting for the moon on the next flight."

Dolan shrugged to indicate the decision had already been made. He didn't seem to want to get into an argument.

"Second," I continued, "I have arrangements in place for my return and, more importantly, I have ideas for getting data we'll never be able to get otherwise."

They listened in silence. Not a good sign.

"I was only there for a week," I pled. "Give me a week more, and we'll prove the feasibility of controlling the missions in time and place. And, while I'm there, I'll gather hard data that will convince any critic."

That last point was my strongest argument, and I could see a reaction to it. So far, the only evidence that I'd travelled back in time was my report. I'd carried no recording equipment, and we had no proof I'd gone anywhere, much less to a different time. Even if I was believed, my reports were little better than contemporary newspaper reports.

"Your last point is a good one," Dolan conceded. "We'd like to have better documentation. That's why we're going to provide the next traveler with non-incriminating tools that will bring back proof."

"Did I mess up in some way?" I asked.

Dolan had won and now played the gracious winner. He assured me I had performed perfectly, and that I would be considered for future voyages. That was damning with faint praise. I felt like Gus Grissom after his *Liberty Bell 7* Mercury capsule sank in the Atlantic. On the one hand, Grissom was given every groundbreaking flight thereafter (except Glenn's orbital flight) until he died in the launch pad fire. Nevertheless, he was widely known as the only astronaut to screw up and lose his spacecraft.

"If I return to Dodge for four days with still and video cameras, we'll guarantee our funding for the next ten years," I argued. "A lot of Senators relate to 1876 Kansas who don't identify with ancient Egypt or even 1960s Dallas. You need to reconsider, especially since there's almost no cost to send me back to Dodge."

That said, I got up and walked out of the room. I returned to my room and told Joey the decision.

"You aren't going to let them get away with this?" he asked.

I had little choice. I was only one of seven members of the committee, and I gathered the other six sided with Dolan. Their reasoning wasn't completely wrong. Dodge City—been there, done that.

"I made the strongest arguments I could—low cost and documentation," I said. "Maybe I swayed three of them."

I didn't want to sit around in my room. "Let's go to the lab," I said. "I want to visit my CrossChron."

Technicians were disconnecting my device from test equipment when we arrived in the lab. Despite my arguments to Dolan and the committee, the device had recorded information that proved I'd traveled through time. However, the proof was technical and would do little to keep the attention of the shallow minds in Congress.

I glanced at the half dozen or so devices in cases along the wall, each device an exact duplicate of mine. The only difference was that mine had the number "7" painted on its face, my tribute to the seven Mercury astronauts, all of whom had "7" in their capsules' names. It also reflected that our team—Hanly, Keane, Barrett, McDonnell, Fitzgerald, Knorr, and Reed—also had seven men.

The technicians deferred to me as if I were an alien. More than Dolan's comparisons with Columbus and Armstrong, the techs' behavior conveyed to me the historical significance of what I'd done.

"Can I touch it?" I asked. They nodded uncertainly,

reluctant to tell me what I could and couldn't do. I already viewed the device as Glenn must have felt about his *Friendship 7* capsule—a relic of the past he'd never again use, but which would be associated with him as long as recorded history.

As I touched the smooth cover, I thought of Tess and hoped she wanted me back. If so, I was going to disappoint her.

Joey gave me some distance, leaving me to contemplate the CrossChron alone. My reunion wasn't doing anything for me except make me angrier. I turned to Joey. "Let's get out of here," I said.

I left the lab feeling worse than when I left the latest meeting.

As I left, I mumbled over my shoulder, "I'll visit it again later. Don't lose it."

I meant the last comment as a joke, but the techs didn't think it was funny. Either that or they sensed my mood and were afraid to laugh.

"Feeling better?" he asked as we walked the few steps to my room.

"No," I said. I needed to talk. "I promised my 'lady friend,' as you call her, I'd be back. Am I Dad all over again?"

We both sat in silence for some time before Joey turned on the radio and increased the volume.

Finally, with a casual air, Joey said, "Why don't you just put the device back on, hit the buttons, and go back."

"They'd never let me," I said

"Who said 'let you'?" he asked.

"Did you see the techs' faces when I joked about losing it?" I asked. "To them, it's like Lindbergh's plane."

"Yeah," he acknowledged, "but they're obviously afraid of you."

We went to the cafeteria for lunch. I saw several of my teammates eating together but, aside from brief nods, they avoided eye contact. I didn't get the impression any of them were rallying to my side.

Joey and I ate in silence. I pushed my food around on my plate as if it were a jigsaw puzzle. None of the pieces fitted together, no matter how I arranged them. When I looked up from my puzzle, I peered past Joey into the distance. My body may have been in 2010, but my mind, and heart, was in 1876.

Joey finished his lunch and sat silently, letting me drift in time. I apologized for my behavior and suggested we go for another walk.

Once outside, Joey spoke for the first time since we entered the cafeteria. "What are they going to do if you go back on your own? Are they going to telegraph Wyatt Earp to arrest you?"

Even I smiled at that. A good line, even if Earp's name still unnerved me.

"No," I acknowledged, "but they might send the FBI back to get me."

"Yeah," Joey argued. "I can just see Earp letting them step on his jurisdictional toes. He'd buffalo them in a half a second, take away their guns, and throw them in jail."

That would be a scene to watch: arrogant, officious FBI agents confronting the toughest lawman in history. Joey was right. If they tried to take me into custody on some ridiculous tale of time travel, Earp would jail them before they could explain what FBI stood for.

We walked along the exercise trails for a while, losing ourselves in the trees surrounding the campus. I felt more at home in the forest than I had at any time since my return.

I wasn't thinking clearly. Thoughts were running through my mind faster than I could process them. The cancellation of my mission was only part of my problem. No matter what I told Dolan or the doctors, the trip had muddled my thinking. I was in no condition to make a decision that would affect the rest of my life.

But Joey was. However facile he seemed on the surface, underneath he had a sharp mind and uncanny wisdom. His instincts were good and his judgments about people were rarely wrong.

"Now, Joey," I began slowly, "I'm just thinking out loud. No one else is around, just you and me."

I had his attention.

"Let's look at my options," I continued. "First, I can accept their decision and be a team player."

"You could," he said skeptically. "You've always been a team player."

I ignored Joey's comment. "Number two, I could marshal my arguments and seek another hearing."

"These guys may be good engineers," he said, "but they're more likely to be certain than they are to be right. They're already certain." He paused for a couple of seconds. "And they also very well may be right."

"Are they?" I asked.

"Are they right? Probably. Dodge was your gig anyway. There's nothing magical about it from a scientific point of view."

"Okay, okay," I said. "We'll keep that option on the table even if we both know it's dead."

"Three, we could barge into the lab with a Single Action Army and steal my device."

"How about *you* sneak in and smuggle it out in your jockstrap?"

"Okay," I allowed. "I make a substitution. Any others?"

"Maybe, you could threaten to go public with the whole project."

"Yeah" I was the skeptic now. "I can see the headline on the *National Inquirer*: 'Deranged Engineer Claims Visit with Wyatt Earp!!!!!'

"Remember," I pointed out. "I have no proof whatever. Why would anyone believe me?"

Going public wasn't a strong option.

"Okay, skipping the *Inquirer* headline, what do we have?

Four options? Submission, re-argument, theft, and whistleblower."

"I'm not impressed," Joey said. He was always honest with me.

"Let's narrow it," I said. "The weakest is going public. Let's drop it. What's next weakest?"

"It isn't weak," Joey replied. "But is accepting their decision even an option?"

"Not one I like," I said. I tried to clear my mind of my promise to Tess that I'd return. "That leaves re-arguing my case or stealing my device. We've already killed the re-argument."

When Joey didn't say anything, I didn't know what he was thinking. We walked on, side by side, both of us looking at the trail ahead.

I tried to think of other options. "How about negotiating a deal in which I submit now on the assurance that they'll let me go back in the near future?"

"Sure," Joey responded. "They'll pat you on the head, say 'Sure, Will,' and the closest you'll ever come to Dodge City again will be *Gunsmoke* reruns."

"How about re-arguing first, and then, if they refuse, we steal the device and I take off?" I asked.

"As Tonto once said, 'What's this 'we,' white man?' If 'we' steal it, you leave for 1876 and only one of us goes to federal prison," Joey said.

When the trail was leading us back out of the forest onto the campus, Joey suggested, "How about this? You accept the rejection for now, but ask for a meeting tomorrow morning. That'll give you a night to sleep on it."

I nodded. I didn't want to wait another twenty-four hours, but it was sage advice. I needed to be thinking clearer. And I also needed time to plan the heist, if it came to that.

I called Dolan when we returned to my room. Without elaboration, I asked to meet with the committee in the morning. Dolan didn't ask why. He suggested 9:30.

I ate dinner as if I'd need energy. Now that we had a plan, I felt better, despite how grainy the plan was. When we left the cafeteria, Joey and I paused in the hallway and looked at each other. Neither of us spoke.

As Joey extended his hand, he looked me in the eye, commitment all over his face. He rocked his head so resolutely that his shoulders joined in the affirmation. His confidence reassured me. He turned and left.

The last thing he said to me was "If you hijack the device, there goes any chance for fame and fortune. Keep that in mind."

Leave it to Joey to reassure me on one hand, and then remind me I was about to forfeit my lifelong dreams.

Even though "we" weren't going to steal anything, I might need help in getting the device out of the lab. I didn't ask Joey if he'd be back in the morning, and he didn't say.

I retired early, knowing (or was it hoping?) I might have a very long, one-hundred-and-thirty-four-year day tomorrow. Before falling asleep, I thought of Tess. She was like a time magnet, drawing me back. Or was it a Will magnet? Either way, she was a force that reached me in 2010.

Chapter 43

I awoke early and enjoyed a solitary breakfast in the cafeteria. No one bothered me. I didn't see any of the men who would decide my fate. They'd decide if I was a scientist on a mission or a common thief on a joy ride. I didn't care which it was.

I arrived in the conference room ten minutes early to convey the message they were coming to *my* meeting, not me coming to theirs.

In minutes, the group had formed. I didn't wait for Dolan to start.

"Gentlemen," I said formally, "I've asked for this meeting to revisit our discussion yesterday." They looked at me without expression. I saw no evidence of what they'd discussed after I left the day before. I put that on the table.

"I don't know what went on after I left yesterday," I said in a challenging manner. "Because I wasn't here." I stopped and looked each of them in the eye. "I also wasn't here when you met—while I was on a mission—and apparently made a decision that affected, no not affected, *cancelled* is a better word, my mission. That wasn't right.

"It wasn't right for several reasons," I continued. "I'm a member of this team and have been since the beginning. As far as I know, we're all equals." I looked at Dolan to see if he wanted to argue about that. "As equals, we're all entitled to be heard and to vote. Apparently, someone here thought otherwise while I was away, away on a mission you approved.

"Keep in mind, I am the only one who's ever voyaged through time. No one sitting at this table, except me, has risked his life by strapping on the device and saying goodbye to this world for perhaps the last time. None of you has done anything except plod forward in time one second at a time. That makes me an expert. I should've been heard before any decision was made."

I was getting going now. No one made a sound, not so much as the clearing of a throat.

"Third, this team committed to going to 1876 as the maiden voyage. And we did so after long deliberation and discussion. Yes, it was my destination, but *you* picked it as the first mission. It was this team, not me, that made the commitment to Dodge City, and that commitment was to a series of trips to perfect our procedures, to establish guidelines for future voyages, and to determine what equipment we could, and should, use on future missions. None of that has been done.

"Historically, the precipitous decision to cancel Dodge is all wrong. Orville and Wilbur didn't pack up their plane after the first flight. They flew it several times before a gust of wind destroyed it. NASA didn't move on to Apollo after Shepard or even Glenn flew. No, they had a plan and they adhered to that plan and, on each succeeding flight, they learned more, sometimes things that were unexpected, but proved invaluable later when they moved on to the Gemini and Apollo programs.

"And, let me remind you, both the Wright Brothers and NASA were in races, the Wrights against Langley, and NASA against both the Russians and Kennedy's deadline. Yet they made a plan, and they stuck with it. Why? Because it was good science, and because it was good planning.

"If we, and I use 'we' advisedly, adhere to our plan, if we make two more trips to Dodge City, as we planned, we'll reap the rewards. Every future mission will be better for it. This project will be richer and more successful. Gentlemen, we are running in the sands of Kitty Hawk with Orville, and stepping into the footprints of Armstrong on the moon, and we don't have the option of deviating from the sound example they've given us. It's time to return to Dodge City and complete this the first voyage through time that man has ever made."

I sat back and looked at each of them with a challenge clearly written on my face. I looked at Jim McDonnell, the blond Scot; Jerry Knorr, the dark Norwegian; Ed Fitzgerald, the Yogi Berra of our group; Bill Reed, the thoughtful, deferential one; Mike Hanly, the bright Thoreau type; Kevin Keane, the erudite genius; and John Dolan, the titular, brooding headmaster. They all returned my gaze without commitment.

"Where do we go from here?" I asked quietly.

Dolan cleared his throat and everyone turned toward him. "Very well said," he started. His manner already told me he wasn't going to rally to my side. "You made some very good points." Here we were, drifting into lingering death again.

I interrupted, addressing Reed instead of Dolan, "Bill, are you going to let this program degenerate into a Jimmy Carter presidency?"

Everyone knew what I meant. I wasn't questioning anyone's motives or their intentions. I was making them face the insanity of making decisions out of context with the design of the project.

"We all want what's best for the project—" Bill answered. I interrupted him.

"No one is questioning anyone's motives," I said

forcefully.

Reed didn't want to continue. That told me that he wasn't on my side either.

Kevin generally kept his position hidden until he had to reveal himself. Not because he was still formulating it, but because he knew that nothing anyone else said was likely to persuade him to change.

"Kevin," I said. "Have you thought this decision out?"

Keane looked off into space, seemingly searching his thoughts. Of course, he'd thought it out. He just didn't come to the same conclusion I did. I didn't bother waiting for him to speak.

"Jim, Fity, Mike, Jerry," I said to each in turn, "I gather that you still want to abort this mission."

They didn't bother answering. Their silence spoke for them. The meeting was over.

"Gentlemen," I said, as I rose from my chair to leave. "Thank you for meeting with me and for hearing me out."

Although I'd intended to force them to discuss the decision in front of me, I knew I hadn't changed any minds, and I respected them too much to embarrass them further. Besides, I had an option.

As I returned to my room, I passed the glass-walled lab. I saw Joey inside studying my device. He glanced up at me and smiled. I smiled back, feeling better already. My option was apparently already underway.

Since Joey seemed to have everything under control, I continued to my room. He arrived less than five minutes later and didn't bother to knock.

"Come on in," I said gratuitously.

"How'd it go?" he asked, equally gratuitously.

"Well," I drew out the word. "I made an eloquent, iron-clad argument for my returning to Dodge."

"And they shredded it," he said.

"They didn't even bother," I said. "Their minds are made up. Churchill couldn't have convinced them to send me back."

Joey turned my radio on and increased the volume. He sat down next to me and whispered in my ear, "Are you going back?"

I studied his face. He raised his palm toward me before putting his index finger to his lips. I nodded. "Only if I can do it without them," I replied whispered back.

"You're the only one who can," he said. He stood up and pulled up his pants leg. There was No. 7 strapped to his leg.

"My God," I cried, probably too loudly. "Be careful. You could end up in the nineteenth century."

Joey touched his finger to his lips again, but a smile came to those lips.

"Only someone who knows the sequence can travel without a travel agent," he said.

I couldn't resist asking. "How'd you do it?"

"There was only one tech in there, and he treated me like I was part of the royal family. I distracted him and substituted one of the spares for this."

"But they've probably already noticed the spare doesn't have the '7' on it," I said.

"It does now," he bragged. "I made a decal last night."

We agreed that they wouldn't wise up until someone resumed working on the device. That could be hours, or it could be minutes. I couldn't wait for the knock on the door.

Now that the choice was real, I became frightened. I was making the biggest commitment of my life, and it wasn't to science. It wasn't to fame or fortune. My commitment was to Tess.

I stripped off my shirt and pants and instructed Joey to duct tape all my baggage to my legs and torso. We hoped the items would travel with me. He finished in less than ten minutes, and I redressed, albeit in twenty-first century clothes. I strapped the device to my right calf.

"What's going to happen to you?" I asked Joey. "No one else could have taken it."

He insisted he had a cover story. "It probably has at least a two percent chance of fooling them," he added.

I couldn't risk hiking to the gym to jump. It was dangerous, but I decided to launch from my room. I hugged Joey, tears running down my face. I knew he'd sacrificed himself for me, sacrificed his future to give me a past. I would worry about him as long as I lived, and I'd never know what became of him.

He'd never know what became of me either. Unless . . .

I thought for a moment before sequencing. "Joey, they probably have old newspapers from Dodge on line. Look for them. If all goes well, I'll get a job at, or freelance for, the *Times*. I'll write to you and tell you how I'm doing. Maybe, you'll be able to find them. It just a thought, but I just hope you're not reading the papers in Leavenworth," I added.

We separated. I took a deep breath, and leaned down to my device. Just before hitting the fourth quadrant, I said, "Love you, bro." And the twenty-first century disappeared.

I missed Joey even before I reached Kansas, but my heart was buzzing with the thought of seeing Tess. I hoped that she hadn't forgotten me in the last 134 years. Upon my re-arrival in Kansas, I was greeted by the scurrying and chirping of now-familiar prairie dogs—I was as happy to see them as they were to see me.

Chapter 44

I arrived in Kansas in the same field I'd arrived in before, and, as with my first arrival, the heat baked my flesh. To the southwest, however, dark clouds were gathering. Ah, the joys of summer in Kansas—heat, drenching rain, lightning, and, sometimes as a bonus, a tornado. I had to get to shelter fast to avoid getting drenched, and, fortunately, I knew the nearest shelter hid in the gallery forest a half mile away. Unfortunately, with bad weather approaching, the nearby homesteader wouldn't be bathing when I arrived. Damn!

As I hurried toward the trees, I grew increasingly insecure and voiced my fears to the deaf grasses: Will she want me back? Has she thought it over and decided I should leave?

I sweated more from fear of her rejection than from the heat, and I prayed she wouldn't greet me with the grim face I saw the first time. I so wanted her acceptance, and I hoped my small cargo of twenty-first century toys would win her over. I needed her to believe I wasn't a charlatan.

A symphony of thunder pursued me as I raced the storm to Tess's house. The smell of rain reached me just as I hit the edge of the woods. When the wind switched direction, now blowing toward the storm, I knew I had less than a minute to cut through to the house. The small forest was much darker than my last visit, and I couldn't see the house until I was almost out. When I emerged, the yard was almost as dark as the forest. Nothing moved as I came out a few dozen yards from the barn. I didn't see Tess anywhere.

I took a deep breath, inhaled the wonderful animal smells, and reveled when the chickens, recognizing me, resumed clucking. I ran my hand over the rough wood of the newly-painted barn to make sure it was real. I paused to take in the homey, still somewhat dilapidated condition of the house.

I crossed the yard to the house and knocked on the front door. I'd never been this close to the house before. I heard some movement inside the house. My heart raced as I recalled the six-shooter she brandished to greet me the first time. Would she challenge me again? I didn't want to face an armed blonde again, and I couldn't be sure, with the vagaries of time travel, she'd still remember me.

"Tess, it's me," I said.

The door opened immediately and Tess's face brightened the day. She was smiling, and she was happy. So was I. She lunged into my arms and held me in a fierce grip. We'd never hugged before. She felt womanly and wonderful.

Without letting go, she leaned back, still smiling, to study me with sparkling eyes.

"I told you I'd be back," I said.

"I know you did," she said, still smiling. "I just didn't believe you."

She hugged me again and, as the storm hit and rain pelted down, she dragged me into the house. First hug, first welcome into her home. I was glad to be back.

I could see little inside the dark single room. Although the shutters were partially open, and there was a candle burning inside a chimney lamp, the details of the room were no more visible than they would be in a cave. I was surprised to find the interior walls whitewashed, but it helped little with the dark storm outside. Tess looked me over as I adjusted to the room.

The furnishings were even sparer than I'd expected—a rough table and two mismatched chairs to my left, and a narrow bunk along the right wall were the only furniture. A few primitive shelves filled the back right corner. A small door led out back to the "stove" and the river. Next to the door was a pendulum clock that seemed too large for the room. The floor was of unfinished planks. Despite its simplicity, it smelled of Tess and of cooking, and it felt warm to me.

"Interesting clothes," she said over the clatter of large raindrops on the metal roof. I could hardly hear her.

I looked down, and remembered I was still dressed for the twenty-first century. My golf shirt and tan cotton pants were out of place here in Kansas but my shoes . . .

"I had to leave in a hurry," I said.

"What are those?" Tess asked, laughing as she inspected my shoes.

"They're called running shoes in my time," I answered, explaining nothing. "I know they look ridiculous to you but, in my time, everyone wears them."

She looked quizzically at me.

"Yeah, they're ridiculous," I said. "But, I swear, everyone wears them."

Tess shook her head, all the while wearing that endearing, and rewarding, smile.

"I still have the clothes you bought last week," Tess said, "but you didn't buy any shoes." She shook her head before adding, "You can't wear those into Dodge."

We decided she'd have to go on a shoe run for me. But Tess wasn't finished commenting on my garb.

With a slight blush, she said, "I don't know how to say this, but you seemed pretty lumpy when I hugged you."

"Oh, yeah," I said. "I carried a few things with me." With the storm threatening, I hadn't thought to check on my cargo. I pulled the golf shirt over my head. Tess didn't stop me.

She stifled a giggle behind her hand when I took off my undershirt. I had the wonders of the twenty-first century taped to my chest and back.

I winced as I tore off the first tape. "This is shampoo. Ever heard of it?"

Tess was familiar with the word, but didn't know exactly what it was.

"Ah," I said, as a magician might, "this will turn you into Rapunzel. It will turn your beautiful hair into gold."

Her eyes asked a question.

I grew pedantic, explaining, "Soap turns your hair into straw. You'll look so glamorous after one shampoo."

I ripped another strip of duct tape off, leaving a pair of red welts on my stomach.

"And this," I said, holding up a plastic bottle of white liquid, "will moisturize your overworked hands." I poured a little into my palm and gestured toward her hands. When she tentatively extended them, I rubbed the cream into each hand in turn. I've had sex that was less intimate than rubbing her hands.

As Tess continued rubbing her hands together when I stopped, she showed a look that revealed she was feeling more than the moisturizing of her palms. I didn't hurry her, letting her savor the moment.

"Smell your hands," I told her. She sniffed at them and, then, took a second deeper breath and savored the perfumes in the moisturizer.

"And next," I said with a flourish, yanking more hair off my chest with the duct tape, "is an invisible shield from the sun." I detached the tape from a dark green bottle.

I explained to her that the sun damaged her skin and that

the sunscreen, one of the scientific wonders of the twentieth century, would protect her from the dangerous rays. She was back to not believing me. Or not caring. Sunscreen wasn't as romantic as shampoo or hand cream.

"What's that?" she asked and pointed at a small black case under my arm.

We were standing close and shouting over the clatter of the rain on the metal roof.

"This is going to be complicated," I said as I retrieved my *iPad* from the tape. "Can we sit down?"

I didn't show her all the wonders of *iPad* right away. I started her with the simplest.

"Put these in your ears," I said, handing her ear buds. "And don't be frightened by what you hear."

I played two songs for her: *More Than a Woman* and *Nom Dimenticar*. I watched her eyes start with distress at first, then confusion and, finally, with a sparkle of childhood discovery. She looked at me with feeling when she started listening to the words.

"There's more in this box," I said, holding the *iPad* up, and retrieving the ear buds, "but that's enough for now."

I hated to deprive her of other *iPad*'s wonders, but I knew I had to preserve the battery. I called her attention to a silver case a tenth the size of the *iPad*. "And this, too, is wonderful."

I turned my tiny camera on and, pointing it at her, I warned her not to be afraid when it made a bright light twice. I took a picture and checked it on the back display before showing it to her.

"You're going to like this," I said, moving over to her side. "I know I like it."

She inhaled sharply when she saw the bright color picture.

"Isn't she beautiful?" I asked.

Tess looked at me for my meaning, but she already knew how I felt about her.

"How did you . . .?" she started.

"Now, do you believe I'm from the twenty-first century?"

Chapter 45

Tess nodded distractedly and returned her delighted gaze to the display, making no effort to hide her glee.

While she focused on the picture, I removed a package of condoms and put it in my pocket. I answered Tess's questioning look by explaining it was for later. I turned around and asked her to rip other objects from my back. When she hesitated, I said, "Go ahead. Just yank the tape fast."

She removed the manila file first and put it on the table.

When she saw what I had taped to my waist, she turned me to face her. "What's that?"

"A little loose change," I said.

"How much?" she asked breathlessly.

In fact, I had $10,000 in 1870's currency strapped to my back. All of it was legitimate U.S. currency expertly aged at the Mint.

I saw her calculating in her head.

"I make $85 a month," she said. "And that's only for ten months. It would take me a whole year to make that much."

"A little more," I corrected, "but, yes, it's a lot of money."

"Did you rob a bank?" she asked, turning serious.

I assured her it was clean money. "I would, of course, have a little trouble explaining it to Mr. Earp. We're comfortable," I said.

"We?" she asked.

I didn't answer her. I wanted her to have a sense of security, but I didn't want to buy her affections. I'd said enough, and she'd heard me.

"Now, I'm hungry," I said, ending the discussion, "I haven't eaten in 134 years."

After lunch, Tess said, "If I'd known you were coming, I'd have taken a bath."

I took her words to be purposely ambiguous. I hoped she was suggesting she'd have liked me to watch her again. I didn't ask. She didn't say.

Not getting any reaction from me, Tess continued, "So how was the twenty-first century?"

"Not good," I said. "They wanted to cancel this mission and move on."

The statement struck Tess as if an ice pick had been stabbed into her heart.

"Well, why, how?" she stammered. "Then, how are you here?"

"I hijacked the device and came on my own," I said. "I probably can't go back."

"Hijacked?"

"It means to steal or take something illegally."

I spoke as calmly as I could, but I couldn't hide the tension in my voice. She measured me, and my words, for a few moments, then nodded her head, accepting that as the case.

"I'm worried about what you'll do when you run out of shampoo," I said in a most serious tone.

Tess burst out in an engaging laugh. I liked seeing her laugh.

"Won't you miss your friends and family?" she asked.

I shrugged. "A little, I guess, especially my brother Joey."

"And your lady friend?" she asked.

I didn't know what to say. I wasn't going to say that my "lady friend" lived in the nineteenth century—that would've been too bold. I shook my head with a slight smile.

Tess turned serious again, "Are you in any trouble?"

"Probably," I said. "I haven't thought it out, but I must've violated a number of laws."

I hesitated, seriously reflecting on the consequences for the first time. Things happened so fast in Washington that I was too distracted to give any thought to the consequences of what I did.

"I'm worried about my brother, and I know I'm through with the project. They'd never forgive this."

Tess became somber—she appreciated my situation. For one brief moment, I entertained remorse, selfish remorse. I felt empty about forfeiting everything I'd worked for since my dad left us.

The moment passed when I looked up at Tess's face. That face, that woman, caring about me was all I needed. I'd done the right thing. She touched my hand as we looked at each other.

"I'm glad I'm here," I said, and I meant it.

Tess went to retrieve my store-bought clothes from the barn. I tried to stop her from going out in the rain, but she ignored my orders and was out the door before I could restrain her. While she was gone, I looked down at my Reeboks, wondering if I could just cover them with dirt and mud and go unnoticed. I didn't think so.

I considered plans for replacing them. I could ride partway to Dodge with Lester and Tess, have them drop me off outside town, and come back for me after Lester bought me some shoes. A possibility. Of course, that would mean Lester would have to know I was a little strange. He probably knew already. Just not how strange.

Tess returned before I moved on to plan B.

Chapter 46

Tess returned as wet as if she'd swum across the river. She'd held my clothes under her arm to keep them dry.

"I'll change outside," I said to avoid an awkward situation ,but Tess didn't cooperate.

"No need," she said definitively, tilting her head at the sound of the rain. "And, besides, you've already seen me wearing less. I won't be shocked."

I quickened at her words, both in memory of watching her bathing in the river and at the prospect of disrobing in front of her. I hoped it wouldn't show when I took off my pants. Tess sat down, and I turned away before dropping my pants.

I glanced over my shoulder at her and found her smiling, obviously enjoying my embarrassment. She didn't put on a Victorian show of averting her eyes. She sat there, elbow on her knee, and brazenly watched me change. She made me feel *she* was from the liberated age and *I* from the staid nineteenth century.

I wasn't accustomed to an audience while I changed and found myself nervously sneaking peeks at what she was doing— which was watching me. She made no conversation but gave an interested look at my underwear. She'd never seen Jockey undershorts before.

When I'd redressed in appropriate garb, the rough clothes felt good, but those frivolous Reeboks looked even worse when I put them back on.

"When're you going to town next?" I asked.

"Not until Sunday, for church. Can you wear them that long?"

"As long as I don't have to explain them to any guests," I said.

"We don't get many guests," she said. "Now, um," Tess said, "you're not the only one who needs to change."

Indeed, Tess was so wet from retrieving my clothes that a puddle had developed under her chair.

"I'll wait outside," I said.

"Yeah, that's a good idea," Tess said. "Then, you'll come in wetter than I am and have to change again. A really good idea."

"How about if I promise not to peek?"

"That wouldn't be fair. I peeked at you."

She started unbuttoning her dress, looking me in the eye. She turned away from me before she reached the last button. She peeled off her soaked cotton dress, letting it drop to the floor. Except for her boots, she was completely and utterly nude. I found myself breathing harder as I looked her up and down. Her pure white skin was majestic, and, even in her incongruous boots, she was everything I thought I saw when she was bathing. Fortunately, she was still facing away and didn't see me looking her over.

"You okay?" she asked over her shoulder.

"I'm not peeking," I lied.

"I need your help," she said. "I forgot to get a dry dress out. Could you get one for me?" She gestured toward a shelf over the bed. There was only one dress there.

"And could you bring a towel?" she asked as I started back.

I walked stiffly and awkwardly as I approached her with the dress and cloth. She stood there, one heel off the floor and her knee turned in. They must have invented that pose before the time of Christ. She turned her head and looked at me over her shoulder.

"Dry my back," she said, leaving me holding the cloth out toward her. I reluctantly did as she asked. I stopped at her waist. "All the way," she ordered. I carefully dried her all the way to her boots. She took the towel from me and finished drying herself.

"I thought of you while you were gone," she said, making no effort to put on the dress.

I didn't respond. I was only a foot or so from her and could feel the heat of her body.

She continued, "I thought about how your hands would feel on my bare back."

She looked over her shoulder, catching my eye. "I'm still thinking about that," she said. She looked into my eyes as she waited for me to act.

I touched her skin lightly with my fingers and gently traced her ribs to her waist. I felt her shudder ever so slightly. Her back expanded as she took a deep breath. I thought I heard a murmur. I stopped. She froze.

Time seemed to stand still. I stood there at a loss, while Tess seemed in control, completely at peace with my uneasiness. She continued to stand there, at once both vulnerable to my advances and powerfully in control. Fortunately, while back in Washington, I'd made up my mind that I would refrain from entering into any improper relationship with Tess. I regretted that her letting me stay at her ranch had put her in a very questionable position and, undoubtedly, was the gist of gossip in Dodge. I'd compromised her enough. I wanted her to be able to hold her head high when she went to Dodge. In addition, I didn't want to do anything that would undermine her teaching position. It was different for me. I had no reputation to protect—except hers.

When I didn't continue, Tess let out a sigh. But she didn't

turn around or do anything to call further attention to my inaction. She merely put on her dry dress, buttoned it up, and turned to face me. That joyous face was now very serious, and I knew that my best intentions had made matters worse.

I couldn't tell Tess why I was so resistant to get into an intimate relationship with her. Some things are too private to share. The fact was, however, that Joey only recently had revealed a family secret to me: he told me how Mom and Dad had come to get married. As Mom's sister, our aunt, told the story, Dad had taken advantage of Mom when she was only seventeen. It was only a fling for Dad, but Mom had a huge crush on Dad, who was six years older, and she trusted him. If Mom hadn't become pregnant and Dad weren't forced to marry her, it would have been a one-night stand for him. Maybe that's why he was never committed to the family; maybe that's why he abandoned us. Maybe . . . A lot of maybe's in the story, but there was one certainty that came out of it—I wasn't going to do to anyone, and Tess above all, what Dad had done to Mom.

Chapter 47

The rain stopped and a bright sun replaced the dark clouds.

"Let's sit outside," Tess suggested.

Although I remained committed to acting respectfully toward Tess, I was completely at a loss about what Tess was thinking. I didn't know what was going on inside her, and my head was fighting a battle with my instincts. My instincts told me my chivalry wasn't as selfless as I pretended, but, rather, was a selfish imposition of my standards on her. I worried that Tess didn't see me as the hero I was trying to be. Maybe I was like the Boy Scout who insisted on helping an old woman across the street, only to find she never wanted to get across.

Despite my good intentions, I felt inadequate and didn't look forward to what Tess might be about to tell me. We exited through the back door, the one on the river. Facing north and shadowed by the trees clustered on the river, the back of the house didn't receive the warming sun. The smell of wet trees, muddy soil, and stagnant water filled my lungs as Tess led me to a narrow bench at the back of the house. I looked through the darkness of the trees to the sunlit prairie across the river. Just then, the wind rustled the trees, peppering us with droplets from the still-wet leaves. The scents of the river and the hay-like smell of the plains grass briefly replaced the pungent moist smell of our immediate surroundings.

To my surprise, Tess was past what had happened, *or not* happened, inside. She asked me about events in Washington.

"You believe me now?" I said, immediately regretting my tone.

"How could I not, after hearing the music and seeing the likeness you took," Tess said. She sounded resigned to the truth, rather than excited about it.

"Are you going to tell me what happened when you went back?" she asked.

"I don't exactly know," I said. "The director resents that I chose the destination and got the first mission. My guess is that, while I was away, he convinced the others to cut me short."

"Are you hurt?" she asked.

When I didn't answer her, Tess reached onto my lap and took my hand.

"Did you try to convince them?"

"Yeah," I said. "I think they decided it should be an Alan Shepard flight, and that we needed to move on to other things."

"Alan Shepard?" Tess asked.

"Yeah, the first American in space. He only flew for fifteen minutes."

"Space? What are you talking about?"

I explained to her that we had evolved Fourth-of-July rockets to be big enough to carry men out of the atmosphere and around the earth. I decided to hold the moon and Mars for later.

"He flew in the rocket for fifteen minutes?" she asked.

I could tell from the way she asked that she thought fifteen minutes was a long time.

"Shepard only flew for fifteen minutes but, since then, other men have flown away from earth for months on end."

"Then, why did he fly for only fifteen minutes?" she asked. She couldn't grasp what I was saying and, so, I tried to keep things simple.

"It was just a first step, and he flew on a very small rocket that couldn't fly fast enough to stay up longer," I explained. "But, that's not the point. It was his brief, very brief, moment of glory. Fifteen minutes of fame, as they say."

"And you stole the device?" she asked.

"Joey actually stole it for me. He taped the cargo to my body, and off I went," I said. "Or came, depending on which way you're looking at it."

"And now, you're my problem," she said wearily.

I didn't like hearing our situation phrased that way. I'd mishandled my return so badly, and now I could foresee the day when I might have nowhere to go, no place where I was welcome—not in Washington, not in SouthFord.

"I'm worried for you," she said.

I didn't know how to take that, whether it meant what I feared or that it meant she cared about me.

"Stop worrying," I said, rubbing her hands. "Joey and I even joked about them sending someone back to get me. We decided that Earp could handle anyone they sent."

I laughed, but there was no joy behind it. Earp could handle anyone Dolan sent, but he couldn't help me with Tess. I was on my own here.

I felt the magnitude of what I'd left behind. Not that I believed the progress of the next century made mankind, or me, happier. I was missing the security and comfort of my time. I was never going to sleep in my own bed again.

Tess sat quietly and, after some time, I took my leave. My heart was heavy as I returned to the barn.

Chapter 48

I didn't accompany Tess to church that Sunday. The stores wouldn't be open and I couldn't appear in my Reeboks. So I stayed out of sight when Lester picked Tess up.

Come Wednesday, however, Lester drove his wagon up again, and I climbed into the wagon's trunk. My feet were bare. Tess was to tell Lester I'd lost my shoes when I parked them too low on the riverbank and the river swept them downstream. I assumed she told him but, riding in the back, I didn't hear it.

I needed new boots, but I also had another mission. I remained uneasy around Tess and wanted to smooth over any hard feelings I created after my return.

Upon arriving in Dodge, I went directly to Mueller's boot shop and told the same story about my lost boots. I looked over the limited choices and finally found a couple of pairs of work boots that fitted me reasonably well. "Reasonably well" meant that they weren't too tight where they were tight and not too loose where they were loose. I bought both pairs, taking the extra pair in case I "lost another pair to the river." Or in the twenty-first century.

I was walking down Front Street, breaking in one pair of my new shoes, when Earp headed toward me. I changed course to avoid him.

"Hey," he yelled. I turned reluctantly.

Earp glanced at my new shoes as he walked up.

"You're Barrett?"

I didn't like this. "Yes?" I said.

"You wrote the article?" he said. It wasn't a question.

Until then, I didn't know that the *Times* had printed the piece. I nodded. He glared at me, seeming to be at a loss for what to say.

"How come you know so much about me?"

I wasn't going to let him see how much he intimidated me. "Don't know that I do," I said. "You didn't like the article?"

Earp glared again. I feared he was going to buffalo me for challenging him.

"No," he said reluctantly. "You want the facts, next time you come to me."

This was a challenge—and an opportunity.

"If you want to talk," I retorted, "we can schedule it right now."

He didn't answer. We glared at each other before he leaned toward me—enough to scare me. I'm sure I turned white, but I'd misinterpreted his movement. He was through with the conversation.

He turned and walked past me without further comment. I stood in the street for a few moments, my heart still pounding. I looked over my shoulder, but Earp was gone. I felt sweat dripping off my brow and wiped it off. I looked around to see if anyone had watched our encounter, but I didn't see anyone looking at me. I headed away from Earp, still breaking in my new boots. I didn't feel the boots pinching my feet as much now that I'd stared down Wyatt Earp. I doubted he saw our conversation the same way.

I continued down to Hoover's Cigar store, and bought

small sacks of penny candy for Tess. She rarely enjoyed such luxuries. I tucked them into my bag along with my spare pair of boots. As I left the store, I tried to think of something else I could get her, and realized she might like a nice pair of shoes of her own. Her beautiful legs shouldn't always be in work boots or, just as often, barefooted.

I returned to Mueller's and looked at the even more limited stock of women's shoes. Mueller kept his eye on me.

"Need something?" he asked, as if he hadn't just sold me boots thirty minutes earlier.

With his help, I found an acceptable pair of black buttonhook shoes that were a compromise between work and church shoes. They cost me $2.25, a bargain if they'd make Tess happy. I hoped they'd fit her. They went into my cotton bag along with my shoes and the candy. As I was leaving, Mueller spoke. "You're living out at SouthFord," he said.

I hesitated with my hand on the doorknob, not turning toward him. Mueller didn't wait for me to answer before continuing, "Mrs. Christie's a nice woman. Children love her and we think highly of her."

I waited again, barely turning my head to acknowledge he was addressing me.

"People wouldn't take kindly to anyone mistreating her," he said. After a pause, he added, "Or taking advantage of her."

"No," I said, still not looking at Mueller, "I don't expect they would."

I left the store, uncertain if I should take offense at the comments. I was gratified to hear him speak well of Tess and glad that people were concerned about her—even if I caused their concerns.

I crossed in front of the Long Branch to visit Wright's store, still named Rath's General Outfitters, which was the Nieman Marcus of Dodge. If anyone in Dodge had what I needed, it would be Wright's, as everyone else called it.

"I need a galvanized tub," I told the clerk.

"How big?"

"Big enough for me to take a bath in."

When he showed me what he had, I was taken aback. I'd expected a plain elongated galvanized tub but found myself looking at a bona fide <u>bath</u>tub. It was an enameled affair only about a foot high and two feet across with a high back on one side. It was only about four feet long, and I imagined myself sitting in it, barely covered with water to my waist, with my knees up to my shoulders. Or would I let my legs hang out? Either way, I didn't see any dignified way to use the contraption.

"That's a bathtub?" I asked.

"Yes, sir, that's a bathtub," the clerk replied, confused by my question. "The best made."

I paid him the $3.50 price and put it over my head to get it out the door. I staggered down the dusty street, weaving to avoid people more respectable than I.

By the time I reached the wagon, I dripped with sweat, my feet were raw, and my arms and shoulders were stiff and cramping. I grunted the ungainly metal up into the bed and leaned against the back wheel to catch my breath. I wanted to explore Dodge further, but that would be another day. I climbed into the wagon box and stretched out as best I could. That included hanging my legs into the oversized bucket.

I removed my dusty shoes and tried, with little success, to loosen them up by flexing and bending them. My socks, to my surprise, weren't bloody. I couldn't wait to get back to SouthFord and put on my Reeboks.

As I lay there, I thought about the mission. I was eager to get pictures of Dodge, but I couldn't walk around town with a sleek twenty-first century digital camera. I needed to build a blind for it first. My plan was to make a cast or splint for my arm and hide the camera in the material. I'd given Tess a shopping list of the items I could use to build the blind. I imagined how, on my next trip, I would walk around, secretly recording Dodge City and its 800 or 900 residents. I hoped that these infernal boots would soften before then.

I'd hidden my camera and *iPad* back at SouthFord where no intruder would happen upon them, and I'd pulled the battery out of the camera to keep it from draining.

Lester returned to the wagon before Tess. Although he acknowledged me and glanced at the tub, he said nothing. I tried to strike up a conversation. He looked at me as if he were deaf. After a few tries, I confronted him about it.

"Lester," I said as politely as I could. "Is it that you don't like me?"

He shook his head, dismissing my question.

"I only asked you where you were from," I said.

"Don't know why you'd want to know," he said after an annoying hesitation.

"Just trying to get to know you a bit," I explained.

"Why?"

I had no answer for that. I threw my hands up and went back to lying in the box. Lester took the feedbag off the horse and led him, along with the wagon and me, to the water trough. The horse drank noisily.

Tess returned about a half hour later. Her arms were laden with foodstuffs, and she had two store clerks carrying more heavy bags for her. At my insistence, she'd indulged in what was, to her, a spending spree. Before we left SouthFord, I reminded her we were rich and could afford anything she wanted, but warned her to be discreet so as not to raise suspicions about where the money came from. It would be hard for her to buy luxuries, but this was a start.

She gave me a quick look when she saw the tub, but didn't comment. I tried to get her eye as we loaded her purchases into the tub but, without being obvious, she avoided looking at me.

Tess hadn't bought all we needed, much less all she could

have. As modest as the increase in her buying seemed to me, Lester looked askance at the bags, but he didn't comment. He climbed up onto the bench after helping Tess up, and we headed out of town.

I knew that, with the candy, shoes, and the spending spree, I was trying to buy myself into Tess's good graces, but it was all I had. My charming personality hadn't yet worked its magic.

When we arrived back at SouthFord, I helped Tess climb down from the wagon and dragged the tub, loaded with parcels, onto the ground. As soon as the tub hit the ground, Lester flicked the reins and drove off.

"Thanks for the ride," I yelled after him. I think he nodded his head. Maybe not.

He hadn't gone fifty feet when Tess exclaimed, "What on earth is this?"

"I worry about you bathing in the river," I said. "What with spiders, snakes, piranhas, Indians."

"Have you gone out of your mind!" she said.

"Feel like a nice hot bath?" I asked.

Tess shook her head and started toting the food in. Deep down, I was sure, she liked the idea. If she did, however, I couldn't tell from her manner. I decided to hold the candy and shoes until her mood improved—if it ever did. I stood in the yard, wondering what I'd do with the tub if she told me to leave—and take my junk with me.

After I carried the rest of Tess's purchases into the house, I lugged the tub around to the back, and set it down about ten feet from the bank. With the water handy and the cow chip fire nearby, I would be able to make this a memorable event for Tess.

Chapter 49

After we ate, I filled the kettle and hung it over the fire. While it heated, I dumped a few buckets of water from the river into the tub. After I added five kettles-full of boiling water, the bath was finally ready. Inside the house, Tess pointedly ignored me.

"Tess," I yelled. "Oh, Tess. It's bath time."

She came to the back door and stood there, a bemused look on her face. That was better than I expected.

"And you think that I'm going to take off my clothes in front of you and get in there?" Tess said with a wry smile, leaving me wondering if she'd gotten modest all of a sudden, or if she was playing with me

"I have another treat for you," I said and pulled a bar of soap from one pocket and the shampoo from another. "This is going to be the best bath you've ever had."

I explained to her how to use the shampoo, not that it took much explaining, handed her the bottle and soap, and walked away. "I'll be in the barn. Yell when you're finished," I said. "I'll want to smell you and see your dazzling blonde hair."

She shook her head, but her smile gave her away.

"You won't peek?" she said. More games?

"Not unless you want me to," I said. I waited a beat before adding, "No, I won't peek." I walked to the barn.

It hurt to leave. More than almost anything in the whole West, I wanted to watch Tess take a bath. But that would be selfish. It was more important that Tess luxuriate in this first bath in her new tub.

I killed time clearing more junk from the barn and organizing what little was left. As I worked, I paused occasionally to listen to Tess making waves in the water. I knew the bath had been a success when I heard her singing, singing for the first time since I'd come upon her bathing in the river. The proof was that her song was no longer the melancholic tune I'd remembered—this time, there was a joyous lilt that lifted my heart.

After she'd been in the tub about fifteen minutes, I heard her call for me. When I ambled around the corner of the house, she was standing gracefully in the tub with a poor excuse for a towel barely veiling her modesty. She looked at me as if I was supposed to do something. She looked wonderful and, although she was covered, just barely, I couldn't hide my admiration. Her radiant smile, in turn, confirmed she'd enjoyed her bath, and it crossed my mind that she was repaying me with this display, semi-modest though it might be.

She feigned being embarrassed about the situation.

"I just don't know how to get out of this tub," she said, not even trying to convince me she was distressed. "Could you help me?"

I played along. "I've never seen a woman wearing only a towel before," I said. "I don't think I better come any closer."

"If you don't," she said, almost batting her eyelashes, "my feet are going to shrivel all up like prunes and, when it gets chilly tonight, my skin is going to be full of goose pimples."

Laughing, I gave in and went over to her. She extended her

hand and had to let go of part of the towel to take it. I couldn't help myself. I peeked as Tess made a futile effort to cover herself as she stepped out.

"Lovely," I said, "like a cover girl."

"What?" she asked with wide eyes, suddenly seeming to be distressed by the situation.

"I'll explain later," I said. "You're positively lovely." I turned away so she could dress.

I kicked myself for making that comment. I was probably being too tough on myself, but I'd resolved to treat her with the utmost respect. It was simply not respectful to comment on a woman when she is undressed—even if she purposely displayed herself. Tess's reaction was, as always, inscrutable, and I found myself feeling unsure of whether she'd staged the display.

Tess cleared her throat, a signal she was presentable. I turned and looked at this wonder. Even with her blonde hair wet and dark, she was glowing and beautiful.

"This may sound rude," I said, "but do you mind if I use your bath water before I return it to the river?"

"It's getting cold," she said.

I gestured for her to go inside as I started to undress. "If you didn't heat it up, nothing could."

I didn't linger in the tub. The water was cool, but I felt like a prince in our new tub, even with my knees sticking into the air. When I finished, I dried off and put on the same clothes I'd worn all day.

I suspect that Tess was spying on my bath, but I didn't say anything when she appeared at the door just as I finished dressing. Daylight was thinning, and the filtered light that reached us was a soft orange.

Tess had brushed her hair dry, and it looked like very fine gold thread. In the soft warm light of impending dusk, she looked enchanting. When she smiled, I thought, When God looks in a mirror, this is what she sees.

I checked my enthusiasm long enough to ask her, "Tell me the truth—did you like your bath?"

Enlarging her smile into a quiet, winsome laugh, she ran into my arms. "I loved it," she exclaimed. "I loved it. I feel so feminine."

I hugged her tightly to me, feeling her warmth and her body against my chest.

"You're always feminine," I said into her ear. "You're always beautiful."

Tess ran her fingers under the hairline at my neck and kissed me just below my jaw. She pressed her hips against me.

"I like that," she whispered to me. Was she talking about the bath or the hug?

"I love you," I said as I disengaged us. I held her at arm's length to look her over. Here was my own princess dressed in Kansas plain that only made her more sensual. I felt unworthy.

As if she could read my mind, she cocked her head and said, "You told me you'd explain the 'cover girl' comment to me."

"I did, I did," I said. "Let's pull out the *iPad*."

We entered her house through the back door and I recovered the *iPad* from its hiding place behind a burlap bag of rice. Tess reached for the ear buds but, as I waited for the *IPad* to boot up, I told her she wouldn't need them.

When the display came up, I clicked on the Photos app to open one of a series of pictures Joey had loaded for me.

The first picture showed a *Cosmo* cover featuring a petite redhead looking directly into the camera lens with her body at forty-five degrees. The look in her eyes said Aren't I beautiful?

I showed it to Tess. Her mouth and eyes opened wide. She looked at me and then back at the picture.

"My God," she said, trying to catch her breath. "I can't imagine."

"Isn't she beautiful?" I asked.

She looked at me again, her eyes full of confusion. She

looked back at the *iPad* screen, her eyes seeming to be having trouble focusing.

"You're more beautiful than she is," I said. "God gave you gifts. You should appreciate them."

She put her hand over the *iPad*. "I shouldn't be looking at that," she said.

I kissed the back of her hand as I lifted it away. "I shouldn't be looking at you," I said. "You're so heavenly. It's a picture from a magazine called *Cosmopolitan*. It puts the prettiest girls in the world on its covers. None of them are as pretty as you."

I advanced the *iPad* to the next photo, another *Cosmo* cover, this one of an exquisite blonde displaying a remarkable amount of cleavage. She, too, looked brazenly at the camera.

"How can you look at those things?" Tess asked. Her voice was skittish.

"Do you mean, how do I react to looking at them?"

Tess nodded, even though it may not have been her question.

"No easier than it is for me to look at you," I said. "You interest me far more than these pictures."

Tess examined the picture, but I could tell she was thinking about what I'd said. I switched to another picture, one more revealing than the previous two. I didn't let on, but I could see that Tess was agitated. I never even considered that the girls would be exciting to her. She had to know I enjoyed looking at the photos with her.

I showed the balance of the photos to her and she watched them in silence. When she'd seen all of them, I turned the *iPad* off and put it away.

When I turned back to Tess, I took her face in my hands, kissed her forehead, and told her, "You're my cover girl."

Tess uneasily put her arms around me. I'd never before found her so unsure of how to act. Fortunately, she showed no fear of me. She knew I would neither take advantage of her nor hurt her in any way.

Later, we sat in the dark outside the house. After sitting quietly for some time, she broached a subject that, from her constricted voice, must have been on her mind for hours.

"How did those girls feel having their likenesses taken like that?"

I didn't answer her right away. It was a very good question, one that I could answer in many ways. After considerable thought, I turned the question on her.

"You're a woman," I said. "How do you think they felt?"

I couldn't see Tess's expression in the dark, but knew I'd hit a nerve. Without seeing her, I felt her tense. She didn't answer right away, but her small nervous twitches told me she was preparing to respond.

"They seemed happy, pleased to judge by their faces," she said. "But that could be only for the camera." She thought a moment. "Were they forced to do that?" she asked.

"No," I said. "I don't think so. As hard as it might be for you to understand, there's considerable prestige in appearing on a magazine cover."

"Then," she said slowly, "if they weren't forced to do it, they must have done it so people could see how beautiful their bodies are."

She thought more before going on.

"Are the girls shady?" she asked.

"No, though modeling has a tinge of not being respectable, kind of like being an actress," I said. "They don't work as escorts, if that's what you mean."

"Escorts?" she asked quietly.

"Ladies of the night," I said. "Their personal behavior mightn't be completely respectable, but they're celebrities of a sort."

"Do they get married?" she asked.

Ah, now we were getting to what Tess was really thinking.

"Most of them do," I said. "Generally, they marry inside their culture. Not the best of men."

"Would you like to have your picture published like that throughout the world?" I asked.

I shouldn't have asked that. I was being intrusive again. However, Tess didn't hesitate.

"Maybe," she said. "But I would want to have more clothes on." She turned toward me. "Would you want to take pictures of girls like that?" she asked.

I shrugged as if it were a stupid question. But I didn't want to embarrass her, so I added, "I think every man would."

Neither of us spoke for some minutes. We were on shaky ground, and I didn't want to cause a landslide.

"Did looking at them make you want those girls?" Tess asked.

Now, this was getting personal. I wasn't exactly a wowser. (Oops, that's a word that wouldn't be invented for twenty-five years and Tess couldn't guess it meant a puritanical person.) I hesitated a long time before answering, fearful of Tess's reaction. But she asked, and I assumed she wanted an honest answer.

"Them and you," I answered.

I still couldn't see Tess in the dark, but I realized my answer had to confuse her. I owed her a more direct reply.

"Yes," I said. "Looking at them reminded me of how beautiful a human being can be. But that was only a small part of it."

She remained silent. I went on.

"Looking at them with you made it all the more interesting." There, it was out.

Again, Tess was quiet. Yet I could feel she was more relaxed than when the conversation started.

"Why?"

My heart froze. I didn't want to answer that. She was

being downright rude to ask that.

"Tess," I finally said. "Do I really have to answer that?"

She didn't make me answer it. However, she asked another question, "Why did it matter if I was looking at them, too?"

I had to answer that one.

"Because you're so beautiful," I said.

"So?" Tess asked, not even deflecting my statement.

"Your reaction just made it more enjoyable," I said.

I knew she didn't understand, and I wasn't about to try to explain it to her. There are reasons for many things and, being an engineer, I always think in terms of reasons. Almost always. This was a matter of feelings and respect. I owed it to Tess not to go into too many details.

"Did you look at *Cosmopolitan* where you lived?" she asked.

"No, it's a woman's magazine," I said. "I'd just look at the covers at the newsstand."

She dropped the subject. I'd suffered through a draining twenty minutes, and I knew I wouldn't sleep well. Nevertheless, I announced my retirement and stood up. I reached down, took Tess's hand, and lifted her to her feet. I pulled her to me and, when we hugged, she couldn't have missed the degree to which I enjoyed our conversation. We parted uneasily. I again felt I'd set up a situation to arouse Tess's interest and attention, and then left her hanging. I felt I was continually making things more awkward between us. I couldn't blame her for being confused about my thoughts and intentions.

Lying in the hay, I was restless. I wasn't getting any rest under my blanket, so I decided to take a walk. I knew I had to be quiet to avoid alarming Tess, so I opened the barn door only a few inches to slip out.

I stepped as lightly as I could toward the river. The moon was almost full, and I could see my way easily. Aside from a few cicadas chirping and the fwopping of an occasional bat passing overhead, there was silence. My steps crunching in the dust sounded like a stampede passing through the yard. As I passed near the house, I heard Tess through the open window. I froze in mid-step, not ten feet from the house and afraid to move further.

I heard Tess again. She was crying, a quiet whimpering sound which I found heart breaking. There was nothing I could do about it without scaring her.

I stood there, feeling utterly dejected. My arrival had only caused her pain. I didn't exactly know why she was crying but I had to be the cause.

As I eavesdropped on her distress, I became more attuned to Tess's crying. It seemed to come in a rhythm. After a minute or two of listening to her, I realized that I shouldn't be listening outside her window.

I felt flattered that I might be on Tess's mind as she was trying to get to sleep. At the same time, I felt like a stalker. I had no right to be standing outside her window spying on her.

I resolved to absent myself, as stealthily as I could. Importunely, I trampled on a stone on my first step, and it snapped loudly out from under my boot. I made like a statue again and, in the silence, I could tell that Tess had stopped what she was doing. She listened for the noise I tried not to make. I held my breath and didn't move. My guilty foot was in place, but my other leg was extended behind me.

If Tess came to the window, she'd find me posing like a complete idiot a few feet away. I could never explain myself and, certainly, Tess would never again find anything attractive about someone who loitered outside the window of beautiful women.

But Tess didn't come to the window and, after almost a minute of imitating Lot's wife, I risked making my way to the barn. I covered the short distance on my toes, scrutinizing the dirt as best I could for any further stones. When I reached the door, I slipped in without moving the door and left it open the six or so inches rather than risking a squealing hinge.

After that misadventure, and after hearing what I heard, I returned to my blanket with my blood pulsing and my eyes wide open. I was certain now that I was making Tess's life more miserable. Perhaps it was time for me to move on.

Chapter 50

My emotions had swung to extremes since I'd returned. A lot had happened in a very short time—I'd abandoned the Project and couldn't return, I'd had good exchanges with Tess, I had bad exchanges with Tess, and, as a result, I was in limbo. I didn't belong in the twenty-first century, and I had no future in the nineteenth.

Under the best of developments, I'd remain in this century, and Tess and I would marry. The weakness in that scenario was that I had nothing to offer Tess. We'd never planned for something like this, since none of us expected me to remain for any length of time in the nineteenth century. Now, my deficiencies were a harsh reality—I had no job, no job skills, and couldn't even contribute to her ranch, farm, homestead, or whatever it should be called. I would be wronging this good woman by letting her take me on. I'd be a kept man on a teacher's salary.

My alternatives weren't any better. I could return to the twenty-first century and create another life, or stay in this century, leave Dodge, and seek my misfortune elsewhere. In all likelihood, the twenty-first century offered me prison time. Eventually, the authorities would find me, and I'd face charges. Of course, leaving Dodge for another nineteenth-century location had little promise, since I'd still suffer from the lack of frontier skills.

The biggest negative about leaving Dodge, however, was the guilt about abandoning Tess. I'd imposed myself into her life and would be a cad to leave her. Even the thought of doing so made my stomach turn. As a product of a broken home, and scarred for life by it, I couldn't break Tess's heart that way.

Now that I knew Tess had feelings for me, I would be no better than my father was when he left us. Neither Joey nor I ever understood why he left or where he went. If mom knew, she never let on to us. That uncertainty, one that Joey and I often spoke about, was the hardest part of all. If he left for another woman, if he had gambling debts, if he and mom couldn't get along, if, if, if . . . Any reason would have been better than not knowing.

I couldn't think of any explanation I could give to Tess that would satisfy her. As a result, I'd leave her with the same uncertainty, the same self-doubts that Joey and I had.

Yes, that was at the core of the pain our dad caused us—the guilty feeling that it was something I, or we, did that drove dad away. I felt guilty toward Mom and toward Joey for I don't know what. I even felt guilty toward Dad, for God knows what reason. It helped a little that Joey had the same feelings, the same regrets about whatever it might have been. Few things that a father could do would be more painful to his children.

If I left Tess, and it seemed inevitable that I had to at some point, I'd be doing the same thing to her. I had no confidence that a frank, heart-to-heart conversation would ever give Tess freedom from the pain I'd cause. Like my dad, I had created a situation both founded, and foundered on, selfishness.

Now I needed Joey more than ever. I imagined a conversation with him, perhaps attributing to Joey more benevolence than he would have had:

"Joey, I'm distraught about leaving Tess."

"Why do you have to leave her?"

"I have no way to support her here."

"Learn to do something. You're a bright guy."

"There's not much market for a twenty-first century engineer with computer skills."

"Maybe, she won't be as upset as you think. Are you, perhaps, flattering yourself?"

"I bumbled into her life and gave her hope. Now, all she'll have is a dreary future teaching kids that don't want to learn."

"That's your view of her life."

On second thought, maybe Joey wouldn't have been much help.

During a sleepless night, I decided to stop the charade before it got too much further. In so resolving, I knew what I had to do but I wanted to put it off. I felt like St. Augustine when he prayed to God: "Please, Lord, give me chastity . . . just not right now."

Chapter 51

I averted my eyes when I saw Tess in the morning. I felt her studying me. I knew I should look her in the eye, and act as if there were nothing to make either of us uncomfortable. But I was nervous and feeling guilty about invading her privacy, and I didn't want to embarrass her further. Of course, my shifty conduct was doing just that.

I saw no indication she sensed my uneasiness. She was calm and relaxed. Well, then, aside from my awkwardness, why shouldn't she feel relaxed?

I spent most of the next day building my camera blind. The blind needn't be an artistic gem or a technological marvel—as long as it worked.

My efforts resulted in a rigid frame that lay against my chest, hidden behind an arm sling, with a lens opening about the size of a dime. I could aim it with my body and snap the shutter by reaching into the sling with my free hand.

I planned my targets as carefully as my knowledge of Dodge would allow. I wanted, of course, to get some pictures of Earp and Masterson, but I knew they'd be the riskiest.

Tess wasn't altogether sure I should be trying to take pictures at all.

"Why take them?" she asked. "You can't do anything with them."

Considering my alienation from the Project, and the small chance I'd ever see the twenty-first century again, she was right. Nevertheless, the scientist/time traveler in me drove me to gather data, even if I could never report it back. I was committed, and I wasn't going be deterred, neither by logic nor by the woman I loved.

That evening, over dinner, I told Tess I had a special treat for her. Instead of watching the stars, we would watch the "stars." She became like a little child, all eagerness and impatience. She looked longingly at me, pleading with me to tell her more. I wouldn't give anything more away.

After we'd cleaned up and as dusk gave way to the vale of night, I retrieved the *iPad* from the barn.

"Remember when I told you about movies?" I asked.

She did.

"Well, I have one here on my *iPad*," I said. "Would you like to see it?"

She did.

"It's about something you might vaguely recognize," I said.

She couldn't sit still and fidgeted like a five-year-old on Christmas Eve. Finally, after prolonging her agony, I turned the *iPad* on. I selected "Movies" from the menu and pressed "WE."

Tess was already wearing the ear buds and wasn't surprised when lead-in music erupted in her ears. She glued her eyes to the small movie screen, and she laughed enthusiastically when the words "Wyatt Earp" filled the screen.

I sat back and watched Tess, my only concern being whether the battery would last the whole movie. Tess was understandably electrified when she saw "Wyatt" appear on the screen as a young man driving a cargo wagon. She constantly looked from the screen to me. She was either looking for my reaction, which wasn't on a par with hers, or to share her enthusiasm with me. I smiled back my enjoyment of her reactions.

More than anything else, this movie could bridge the gap between the two eras. Like all historical movies, it reflected both the past and the time when the movie was made. As much as the movie might seek to portray Wyatt Earp as he really was, it also depicted the Wyatt Earp that the 1990s wanted him to be.

I looked forward to seeing how Tess, an 1876 person living in Wyatt Earp's time, would react to a modern recreation of her era. I was also interested in seeing Tess's reaction to the movie experience itself. I knew that watching any dramatization, whether in a play, on TV, or in a movie, was a learned experience. Tess was unfamiliar with the shortcuts and implications movies use, devices so familiar to us we don't notice them.

Tess, and the *iPad*, made it through the entire movie. When the movie ended, she handed the *iPad* to me, took off the ear buds, and looked at me. She showed no emotion. I turned the *iPad* off, and waited for Tess to say something. She searched my face as if I were the one who'd just had my first, full-color 100-years-in-the-future media experience.

I cocked my head, asking her to say something.

Tess seemed stunned, unable to make any comment. I prompted her.

"How'd you like your first movie?"

"I don't know," she stammered. "It was so noisy and bright, and all of that movement. And I felt like I was spying on those people."

"Was it fun?" I asked.

"Yes, I guess so, except the hard parts," she said. "They were terrible."

"The hard parts?" I asked.

"Yes," she said thoughtfully, "when they hurt and shot each other."

"No one was actually hurt," I said. "That was make-believe."

My explanation confused her. She tried to frame a question but couldn't.

"There were no bullets in the guns, and the blood wasn't real," I said. Now, I reflected on the movie—how my generation brought assumptions into the theatre that Tess couldn't grasp. People in my time accepted violence more easily than anyone in the real West probably ever could.

I'd witnessed thousands of violent "deaths" in movies and on TV, all realistically portrayed in the most grisly detail. At worst, Tess might witness a couple at most. I'd seen hundreds of gunfights; Tess would never see one in her lifetime if she were lucky. Instead of me enlightening Tess, she was expanding my understanding of my times and of myself.

We talked about my time, how we'd become so isolated from real death, and how we substituted for it a steady diet of graphic brutality that should appall us. I acknowledged that our acceptance of this trivializing of human life made us less civilized than our ancestors.

The painful truth of what I was recognizing saddened me, and I moved away from it.

"What about Wyatt Earp?" I asked.

"I don't know him," Tess said. "Is that what he's like?"

The question was back on me—I'd met Earp and she hadn't.

"I know the facts in the movie are basically true," I said. "But the man . . . Gee, he's a lot harder than the movie shows him. If they captured the real Wyatt Earp on film, no one would want to see it."

"What about the movie's portrayal of the West?" I asked.

Tess looked at me and again bounced the question back. "You're here," she said. "Is this how the movie showed it?"

"No," I admitted. "It's not as action-packed as the movie

makes it seem. But books, stories, and movies always take the highpoints and ignore the rest. The movie covered about sixty years, and had to do it in two hours."

"Would my life be exciting if we put all the best parts in two hours?"

"You're exciting every minute of every day," I said. "But I don't think there's any way they could show that in a movie."

Tess flushed at my flattery.

"Well," I said. "I'm sorry your first movie experience wasn't all I hoped it would be. Maybe, I should've had Joey load in a love story."

"That would've been nice," she said, trying to salve my disappointment.

When I said nothing, she added, "You're my love story. I don't need a movie love story."

Her words left me speechless. I was about to retire on that upbeat note when I remembered I had one last thing to show her.

"Would you like to see cars and planes and trucks?" I asked.

She became reanimated. "You have pictures of them?"

I turned the *iPad* on, hoping that it wouldn't die on me. I went to "Photos" and found where the cars started. The first photo showed a huge traffic jam on a Los Angeles freeway.

"Oh, my goodness," Tess breathed out. "Look at all of them. Those are all cars?"

"You can see the drivers and passengers in them," I pointed out. "Some people sit in traffic like that every day going to work."

I showed her some photos of individual cars.

"As you can see, there are all kinds of cars."

"They're so pretty and colorful," she said. "So shiny."

I moved on to trucks. I showed her panel trucks, repair trucks, and eighteen-wheelers. She took them in without comment.

Finally, I showed her jet airliners, but I realized it was hard for her to see how large they were.

"See those windows, those little dark squares running down the side of the plane. Those are about twice the size of my head.

"The tail at the back is probably four times as tall as your barn."

I couldn't expect her to understand a jet liner.

Finally, out of courtesy I gathered, she asked, "How fast did you say they go?"

"Five or six hundred miles per hour," I said. "They can fly across the country from New York to San Francisco in about five hours. If Dodge is three miles from here, a jet could cover that distance in about ten seconds."

"I don't really understand," she said.

"No, I don't suppose you do," I said. "It's hard to believe."

I was out of tricks for the night. I hugged Tess good night and moved off in the moonlight toward the barn. When I hugged her, I could almost feel her tugging me to stay with her. I resisted again. Reluctantly.

Chapter 52

The following day, I reconsidered my camera blind. I relocated the frame for the camera inside my shirt, leaving the sling to cover the camera until I wanted to take a picture.

Tess was constantly on my mind, or in view, as I worked. I was mesmerized by her long legs, tight hips and waist, and those resplendent breasts loosely covered by her plain gingham dress. A breath-taking nude woman takes your breath away, and you never quite get it back again. And Tess didn't want me to ever breathe the same way again. As modestly and chastely as possible, she flaunted her barely hidden talents and piqued my interest, and my libido. She'd look at me until I had to look back and, after a pause, she'd look away. She'd make a gesture, or she'd walk in a way I couldn't ignore. Or she'd 'inadvertently' brush up against my arm or shoulder.

My thoughts vacillated among reliving her physical charms, recalling her smile and manner, and, as men are wont to, trying to fathom what she was thinking. The last was both the most intriguing and the most frustrating. I entertained the conceit that she was as charmed by me as I was with her, but I also considered the possibility that I was just a convenience for her. In my most paranoid moments, I even considered she might be no more than an assassin with breasts, that she had no motive except to torture and humiliate me for the fun of it.

A full day of such varied thoughts depleted me, but it brought me no closer to an answer. In truth, however, I loved every moment of the torment.

In late afternoon, I approached Tess with my left arm wrapped in the sling. Of course, she knew what I was working on. I showed her its various, and very limited, facets and soon had her heavenly face masked in boredom. However, in the few seconds it took, I had taken about ten pictures of her without her knowing it.

I renewed her interest marginally when I announced, "you ain't seen nothin' yet." I slipped off the sling, retrieved the camera from just above my belt, and, turning the display screen toward, played the photos for her. Not all of them were usable, but they proved my system was both practical and clandestine enough for prime time. I had to explain 'prime time' to Tess, but she got the idea quickly enough.

I had four large memory cards with me and could take thousands of high-resolution pictures. Tess was polite enough not to ask again what I intended to do with those pictures, and I studiously ignored the futility of my efforts.

It was time to put the show on the road. However, we not only had no road, we had no wagon to put on the road if we did. I suggested we get the long-missing wagon repaired or, if it couldn't be repaired, replaced. After all, we were rich, sort of. Besides, I didn't want to have to rely on good old electrifying Lester.

Without vetoing my suggestions, Tess didn't exactly acclaim them either. I suspected she still associated the wagon with her husband's death. I didn't ask her again, but neither did I change my plan.

I proposed that I walk into Dodge the next day and arrange for the wagon, and that, on our next joint visit, we lead the horse behind Lester's wagon and return to SouthFord in our own wagon. Tess acquiesced without enthusiasm. That was enough for me.

As usual, Tess and I spent the evening together and talked about all manner of things. Of course, the future came up several times. She asked about the World Wars again and what made them so terrible. I gave her the discouraging news that technology had made war worse, more widespread, and more destructive of human life.

"No war could be worse than the Civil War," she said.

I couldn't dispute that point. Of course, I was living just eleven years after the Civil War ended and frequent reminders of the war's devastation walked the streets of Dodge. We saw men wearing parts of both Union and Confederate uniforms and, worst of all, we saw men mutilated and dismembered. Because of the mixture of veterans from both sides, the War wasn't a fit subject for open discussion. I knew, as Tess couldn't, that even the future Gunfight at the O.K. Corral, fully sixteen years after the War ended, was largely a North versus South confrontation. The lawmen of the West, including the Earps, were mostly Yankees, and the cowboys were almost uniformly from the South, mostly Texas. When the Earps faced off against the Clantons, it was, except for the Georgia-born Doc Holliday, the Civil War all over again. And, as before, the North won.

Excited about trekking to Dodge in the morning, I slept fitfully that night. When I again wandered during the night, I remained close to the ranch for fear of wild animals, but I stayed away from Tess's house. What I'd heard was music to my ears, but it wasn't mine to hear. I owed Tess her privacy.

Chapter 53

I was up at dawn, aroused by the high-pitched hawking of nature's walking alarm clock, the rooster. I filled my tote bag with bread and salted beef, a canteen, along with my camera, the sling, and camera frame. I carried $50 with me as I kissed Tess goodbye and headed east.

After just over a half hour of walking, with the sun low and blinding, I was able to see Boot Hill, the highest point in town. I decided to eat my spare breakfast before entering town. With no trees to shade me, I sat on the riverbank, facing away from the sun.

I drank half my canteen before attacking the hard bread and even harder meat. After eating the salted meat, I needed a good part of the rest of my canteen. It was a good meal, and I felt rested and satisfied.

I rigged my camera, dressed my left arm in its wrappings and sling, looped my bag over my shoulder, and headed into town.

When I got to the plaza, the wide area surrounding the tracks, I made for the *Times* office first. The same non-entity, Walter Shinn, was there when I opened the door.

"You haven't paid me for my piece," I said.

Shinn acted as if he'd never seen me before.

"You remember the article I wrote about Earp?" I said.

He feigned great thought on my question. Finally, he remembered.

"Oh, yes," he said. "I threw a little of it in as a filler."

"I guess Earp reads your fillers," I said. "He seemed to have read it very carefully."

"That's nice to hear," he said.

"I believe you owe me for that piece," I reiterated.

Shinn wasn't exactly running to the cash drawer.

"Look, Jack," I said. "You're not the only paper in town. Do you want me to post signs about how the *Times* stole and published an out-of-work reporter's story without paying for it?"

The newspaper business wasn't yet fierce in Dodge. In a couple of years, at least four papers would compete for the very small audience. For now, however, the two-month old *Times* was already the biggest paper in town. But it didn't need any bad publicity as it sought readership, especially from someone who could write a compelling report about how Walter Shinn had cheated him.

Shinn saw the light. I called him "Jack" for emphasis. Just for spite, I took my first photos using my hidden camera. He never had a clue.

"I had no way of finding you," he said. "Of course, I intended to pay you. I think that two dollars should cover you for that article."

I had no idea what newspapers paid reporters in 1876, but I was sure I was entitled to at least double whatever Shinn offered.

"My calculation was that you owe me four," I said.

Shinn was taken aback. "That's way out of line," he said. When I didn't retreat, he continued, "But I'll pay you the four for good relations. That way, I'll be able to call on you in the future when I need something written. Your piece was quite good."

Fat chance, I thought. I took my four dollars and, as I

walked out the door, I said, "I understand someone named Klaine is thinking of starting a new paper. And Moore might restart *The Messenger*."

Nicholas Klaine would be in the newspaper business the next year, but Moore had disappeared after briefly publishing the first Dodge paper in 1875.

I didn't wait for a reaction. I couldn't afford to alienate Shinn completely, since I'd have to use his rag to communicate to Joey.

I crossed the street, took a couple of shots of the *Times* office, and snapped a few pictures of the people I passed on the street. I couldn't escape the influence of all the western movies I'd watched, and I found myself looking for shots that looked like the western towns they portrayed. Ah, I thought, the power of the media—I was trying to fit the real Dodge into the Hollywood mold.

I crossed the tracks to the marshal's office on the slim chance I could get pictures of Earp or any of the other later-famous officers working for him. As in all frontier towns, the productive people of Dodge owned the morning hours. The troublemakers and, therefore, the lawmen, kept late hours and didn't reappear until after noon.

The marshal's office was open, but there was only a kid there when I entered. He couldn't have been more than sixteen or seventeen. He dropped his feet off the desk when I opened the door, apparently surprised anyone would come in.

"Is Officer Earp around?" I asked.

"No, sir," the boy replied without conviction. "I haven't seen him yet today."

"Who are you?" I asked, as if I had a right to know.

"I'm Billy," he stammered. "I'm to get someone if anything happens."

"When will Officer Earp be checking in? I'm with the newspaper."

"Could be anytime now," he lied.

"I'll be back," I said and walked out before Billy could ask me any questions.

I took a few pictures while I was interrogating Billy but I wasn't sure if I had enough light to get anything useful. I shot some more of the tiny, isolated marshal's office from the middle of the street. A wagon almost hit me as I took the shots. Fortunately, the wagon was moving slowly and made a lot of noise as it approached. I had the added protection that a horse, unlike a car, wouldn't keep going with a person in its path.

I walked to the blacksmith/wagon shop at the west end of town where Tess told me I'd find her wagon. When I explained my errand, the man, who introduced himself as Mike Wagner, shook his head. He said Tess hadn't shown any interest in the wreck, and, after some hemming and hawing, he reported he'd salvaged a few parts from it before using the rest for firewood.

"I see," I said. "Well, Mrs. Christie needs a wagon. I assume you can provide her with one, and credit the parts you salvaged."

Wagner nodded, agreeing to the credit too quickly I thought. I also guessed his story about cannibalizing the wagon was less than true. More than likely, he'd fixed the wagon and sold it. Shrugging that off, I negotiated for him to build one, and we reached agreement at sixty-two dollars. For that, I got four wheels, a three-foot bench, an eight-foot bed, and the option of a one-horsepower engine, sold separately. I passed on the engine and gave Mr. Wagner $5 down. He'd have it ready in two days. I probably overpaid, but it wasn't as if there was any other wagon maker in town.

He asked how I hurt my arm. I hadn't given any thought to having to explain the injury, but I immediately contrived a tale. "I wrenched it trying to quiet a horse."

I left Wagner's and headed back to the *Times*. This time, I found it manned by a very young man. Although barely out of his teens, he greeted me professionally as I entered and introduced himself as Lloyd Shinn. His manner gave me another shot at establishing a relationship with the paper. I told him I had two matters to discuss with him. One was the possibility of working as a stringer, and the other was that I wanted to place an ad. He asked about my newspaper background. I implied more, but told him only about my brief, and bogus, experiences with the *Baltimore Sun* and the *Washington Post*. That seemed enough for Lloyd. He took my name and suggested I drop in whenever I was in town.

The second matter was the placing of an ad. He asked me to write out what I wanted it to say. I did.

> *Joey. All well. If can crank a torch, why not pad, kon, even PC? Surprise visit for Mom's birthday. Will contact. Will.*

Lloyd blinked when he read it. "These spelled right?" he asked.

I looked over his shoulder. "Yeah," I said. "P-a-d, k-o-n, p-c. That's right."

The Times charged subscribers $1 per year, but Joey would read it free on the Internet. Before I absconded from Washington, I'd spoken with Joey about me writing stories in the *Times*, but, just before I left, I realized ads would be more practical. We were sure he'd get access to them on the Internet, that is, depending on how many issues had survived long enough to be scanned in. If we were lucky, he could read my 1876 ad in the comfort of his 2010 home.

I re-read my ad before Lloyd took it. The cryptic content would be clear to Joey.

I continued taking pictures at every opportunity. By noon, I had as many as three hundred shots—three hundred shots I hadn't yet checked. I hoped some of them were usable.

Before leaving town, I bought some luxuries. A dozen

eggs cost me fifteen cents. I bought two pounds of buffalo meat that cost only five cents a pound. I also bought five yards of calico cloth for Tess. At seven cents a yard, I couldn't resist. The cloth had a small flower pattern on a peach background. In paying, I ran into a quirk of Dodge commerce—since money was so plentiful, the smallest unit of coin used was a quarter. The clerk rounded my purchases up to the next highest quarter. I shrugged and went along. I felt like a congressman spending taxpayers' hard-earned money.

As I passed the marshal's office, I again attempted to locate Wyatt Earp. He still made me nervous, but I now had an entrée. He knew I was a writer, and now I had a cover as a stringer for the *Times*.

My blood pressure jumped when we almost collided as I entered his office. He was leaving, and I barely missed hitting him with the door. I took the offensive.

"Officer," I said, "You may recall that I wrote that story about you for the *Times*. I'm—"

"I remember," he interrupted.

"Well, Lloyd just hired me to do some pieces. I'd like to do a fuller story on some things," I said.

"Why're you talking to me?" he asked.

"I'd like to make you the focus," I said. "And you told me to talk to you first before writing any else about you."

"Not likely," he said and walked past me out the door.

Billy, still sitting at the desk, watched me for a reaction. I shrugged and left. I'd been unable to take any pictures of Earp in the office because we were too close to each other. I shot a few useless pictures as he strode across the tracks to the north side of town.

I felt better after meeting with Earp. Instead of him intimidating me, I'd taken the initiative. He reacted to me this time. Of course, he wasn't receptive. Yet.

Chapter 54

I arrived at SouthFord just after one o'clock and Tess came to the door to smile me home. She stepped into the yard and gave me a brief hug. We walked in together, Tess clinging to me all the way. I didn't object.

I gave her the eggs, meat, and cloth. She didn't seem very interested in the cloth, but was appreciative that I thought of her. She gave me a short kiss on the cheek.

"How'd your picture-taking go?" she asked.

"We'll find out," I said.

As much as I wanted to see my results, I was reluctant to run down my nearly exhausted battery to view the photos. Nonetheless, I ran through them quickly as Tess watched over my shoulder.

"Hey," she said, chuckling. "They're so good."

Some of them were, but most weren't. I tried not to be disappointed. Ten good shots of 1876 Dodge was a coup, even if none of them showed Wyatt Earp—yet. I was sure I'd get him eventually.

Tess and I ate heartily—buffalo on the grill, buttered

potatoes, and corn. The buffalo meat was on the tough side, but I liked it. A little tenderizer and some aging would have done wonders.

After dinner, I told Tess I was going to sneak back to Washington. She lost all color in her face and didn't say anything.

"I'll be back," I said. "I have a plan now."

She waited for me to explain.

"I'm going to bring back some things to let me communicate with the twenty-first century."

I didn't go into details since they'd be lost on Tess. I also didn't tell her the jaunt was risky or that I feared being captured. If Dolan learned I was in Washington, I wouldn't have another chance to return.

My plan was to jump back when Joey could provide a cover for me. If it worked, I'd be off the campus in no time and Joey could help me put my plan into operation.

Before I left, I needed to hide the money. After giving Tess enough to support her for a month or so, I left the house to find a secure place. I didn't want her to know where it was in case my spending drew predators to the house. She stayed inside while I buried it.

Tess reluctantly accepted my decision to make another round trip, and I left the next day, my mother's birthday, taking my camera and batteries with me.

The chirping and vigilance of the prairie dog village was replaced by the silence of the gym in Washington. Joey must have come up with a plan to allow me to arrive unnoticed—he was up to one of his tricks. My job was to get out of the building and off campus as soon as possible. As I approached the gym door, I saw a bag next to it—Joey at work again—and found a fireman's uniform inside. I quickly changed, and headed out the main entrance. A real fireman stood just outside the door, and he seemed startled when I rushed out. He opened his mouth with a confused look on his face. I responded with a sweep of my hand indicating that everything was okay. He blinked and let me pass without a question.

Joey awaited me in an isolated stretch beyond the cordon in the parking lot.

"There must be some problem here," I said.

"Yeah," he said with feigned concern. "Someone called in a very credible bomb threat. They've been searching for a few hours now. It could be dangerous to stay this close."

I agreed, and we left in Joey's car. Once off campus, I told Joey of my plan.

"Got any cranks ready?" I asked.

"Just one," he said. "But it'll work with the *iPad*, the camera, and, with a lot of effort, a laptop. Do you really think you can carry a laptop back with you?" he asked.

"I hope so," I said. "Is it loaded with songs, movies, and PhotoShop?"

"Everything you could ever need," he confirmed. "I even included the recordings you made from your meetings with Dolan, and a few scanned documents. You never know when they'll come in handy. Oh, and by the way, did you know that Jerry Knorr had some recordings, too? They'll back yours up. They're on there too. Just look in the file called 'Scumbag.' I didn't know how to spell 'Dolan'."

I laughed. He was right. You never know when something like that might be useful.

"Burn a CD of the tapes and papers for, what shall we say, for posterity."

"Will do," I said.

"What are you going to do with the photos?"

I told him of my plan to have him reprogram the CrossChron so it would return to Washington at a location away from the campus. The beauty of my plan was that I wouldn't have to travel with the device. I could strap the device onto a dog or a sheep along with my Compact Flash Cards or CD's, or even the *iPad*. Joey would meet the animal, retrieve the information, and return the animal packed with whatever I requested or with anything he wanted to send to me.

The key need at my end was electrical power. While wandering in the yard one restless night, I had a spark of inspiration: I'd have Joey modify one of the miniature flashlight generators to recharge my devices. I could crank electrons into any of the devices whenever I needed.

We downloaded my photo collection into Joey's computer and ran them as a slide show. This was Joey's first look at the real Wild West. Seeing the photos through his eyes, I realized I'd done a creditable job during my one-day shoot.

I pointed out Wyatt Earp in the series on the street.

"That's his back, you mean?" he asked.

"Okay," I said. "I'll get better."

Some of the muddy interior shots pleased both of us. In contrast to the colorful exterior shots, the underexposed, colorless interiors looked like the few images that have come down to us from the era. They seemed realistic, whereas the colorful ones looked too Hollywood to be convincing.

When we had inspected all 373 pictures, we sat back. "Well?" I asked.

"Oh," Joey said with a shrug, "they're okay." Then, he lunged forward on his seat and put his arms out. "Will," he exclaimed. "They're great. This is an historical accomplishment."

I was gratified, and I agreed with him. Now that I was 134 years removed from Dodge, I appreciated how precious these pictures were.

"What if . . . ?" I began and looked directly into Joey's eyes.

He waited on me.

"What if," I repeated, "I brought back a miniature video camera?"

I opened my eyes wide, asking for a reaction. Joey shrugged.

"I don't know why not," he said after a moment's thought. "I could add another output from the generator to charge it. And you could transfer the recordings to the laptop, burn a DVD, and send them on your traveling pig."

"Tess doesn't have any pigs," I said.

We decided I shouldn't linger in the twenty-first century. STRP might be monitoring my CrossChron and know I'd returned. We had to move quickly.

Joey led me into his garage laboratory and showed me my generator. It looked like a slightly oversized computer mouse, black in color, with five wires coming out of it.

"No crank?" I asked.

"Cranks are passé," Joey said, releasing a flush handle and yanking it out three feet on a spring-loaded cord. "This pull cod will cut your work by eighty percent."

I counted my electronic devices and they didn't match the outputs. "Why are there five? I only have four devices."

"You've got five," he said smugly. "You forgot about the CrossChron."

I slapped my forehead at my stupidity at missing the device that was most important for me to ever return to Washington.

"I've marked the wires for each device," he explained unnecessarily. "Let me pry it open and solder in one more for the video camera." He did that quickly, using images and specs from the Internet to choose the right configuration.

As soon as he was finished, we headed across town to buy the smallest and most advanced high-definition video camera available. At less than twenty cubic inches and weighing less than a pound, the latest GoPro fitted my needs. We bought a few storage cards for it, as well as an external battery pack. All told, we spent less than $500 and had a technological marvel almost as impressive as the CrossChron.

I unpacked the camcorder in the car and started planning how I'd hide it. Since it was only slightly larger than the still camera, a small holster would do the trick.

I considered how to distribute the equipment on my body to make it back. I'd be carrying the video camera, the *iPad*, the still camera, several batteries, and, of course, the laptop. Joey had gotten the thinnest, lightest laptop he could find, but it was still bulky, weighing almost two pounds. We'd talked about skipping the laptop and relying on the *iPad*, but decided that the laptop still did more things than the *iPad* and did them better.

I was fiddling with the camcorder when we turned onto Joey's street. My heart seized up when Joey said, "Uh-oh." We had trouble.

Chapter 55

A nondescript car sat at the curb in front of Joey's house with silhouettes of two men in the front seat.

"Duck down," Joey ordered. I unhooked my seat belt and ducked forward.

I thought Joey would just continue down the street past his house but, to my surprise, he pulled quickly into his driveway. The garage door rumbled up as Joey sped up the driveway and pulled into the garage. Joey pressed the button to lower the door before he came to a stop.

"Go out the side door," Joey commanded. "Cut behind the house next door and knock on the back door of the second house down. Say I sent you and wait there until I call."

Before I even opened my door to get out of the car, Joey was on his way into the house.

"Hurry up," he said over his shoulder.

I ran to the side door, fearing I'd run into one of the silhouettes just outside, but I found the path clear. A middle-aged couple in the second house down welcomed me with only slightly quizzical looks. I sat down and enjoyed an iced tea while we waited for Joey's call. Aside from disclosing I was Joey's brother, I didn't explain further, and the couple didn't ask.

Joey didn't call for almost thirty minutes. I was sure the men were FBI agents and that the project had intimations I'd returned. Of course, they sent the Feds to talk to Joey, the person most likely to help me. I later learned the agents asked to search the house. Joey told them they could—if he could search their houses. They didn't push the point.

Now I was paranoid. They knew—and would do anything to thwart my escape.

"Suppose they've tapped your line," I said.

"They will," Joey answered, "but it'll take them time. We won't be able to use the phone in a few hours. Have the Boyds drive you to Home Depot. I'll meet you there in ten minutes." He hung up after assuring me he'd make sure he wasn't followed.

The Boyds carried out Joey's directions without question, even when I asked if I could ride in the trunk.

A young couple was passing the car when I unfolded myself from the trunk in the Home Depot parking lot. I smiled at them and brushed myself off. After scanning the parking lot, I shook hands with the Boyds, thanked them for their help, and hurried into the store. I headed for the electrical department, where I knew I'd find Joey.

He was already there, looking even more paranoid than I felt. He started walking as soon as he saw me.

"We'll put you in a hotel," he said without looking at me. "I've got eMail set up on the laptop and we'll use that until they catch on. You're not long for this world."

"Maybe not for this time and place, but . . ."

After slipping me a credit card, Joey dropped me off outside the Holiday Inn Express. He pushed my new laptop after me as I got out of the car.

The hotel had Internet service and, as soon as I reached my

room, I connected to the outside world. As it booted up, I inspected the credit card—Simon L. Morley. Leave it to Joey. Morley was the main character in *Time and Again*, probably the best time travel book ever written. I suspected he'd have used the protagonist in H. G. Wells's *Time Machine*, except Wells never gave him a name, always referring to him as the "Time Traveler." A credit card with "Time Traveler" on it would have raised a few eyebrows.

I checked the eMail immediately. Joey had already written to Simon.

Adjusting the device. Will disable the tracking so that the Project can't track you. Will also reset its 2010 return location. Any ideas?

I had none. We couldn't use Joey's house, nor mine. Even if I arrived safely behind closed blinds, they'd detect my presence through electrical or water use. One flush of the toilet, and I'd be in federal prison.

Besides, I probably wouldn't be the next return traveler. It might be a goat or a sheep, something about my size. It might even be a pig as Joey suggested. I didn't want any of them in my house. Even if they didn't use the toilet or the microwave.

As I watched the Nationals lose another game, this one to the Cardinals, I pondered possible target sites, but I drew a blank.

The site had to be out of public view, but easily accessible to Joey without causing suspicion. In addition, it had to be available at all hours of the day, since we couldn't control the arrival time precisely.

I felt like the invisible man in the several literary versions. The invisible man had the advantage of choosing his times and places and, in the modern version, he made the New York Athletic Club his roost. The NYAC had all the advantages—unoccupied every night, warmed and protected from the weather, stocked with food, water, and even toilet facilities. However, his hideout was eventually discovered, mainly, if I recalled right, because of the missing food he ate.

My traveler didn't need all of those advantages. We needed only privacy, accessibility, and availability at all hours. I fell asleep without finding a solution.

I awoke with a start in the middle of the night when I heard voices. Was I caught? My heart raced as I confusedly looked around the room. When I remembered I was Simon Morley and in a hotel, I got control of myself. The voices were from the TV, which I'd left on when I fell asleep. I turned it off, undressed, and got under the covers.

The scare prevented me from returning to sleep easily. I spent the time mentally reviewing areas near Joey's house that might serve as a staging area. There were few promising places. I approached the problem systematically. First, I listed what we needed. Besides being private and accessible at any time, it needed to have a predictable pattern of traffic and be free of any structure that could entangle me. The last was the most important. If I, or my courier, arrived a few dozen feet astray and in the middle of a wall, the result would be at best unpredictable and, at worst, fatal.

Although the project had used the gym, because of its large area free from any walls, I knew of no equivalent area that would be as free of unpredictable traffic. If there were an abandoned warehouse with large open floor space, we'd have our solution, but I could think of none.

I next considered the local parks but, as promising as they seemed, trees and bushes covered most of them. The trees that gave privacy also made them dangerous.

Before I fell back to sleep, I thought that I was close to a solution. The image of the parks wouldn't leave my mind, but I fell asleep before I put the pieces together.

Hours later, I awoke from a nightmare. In it, I was running from some faceless pursuers and, breaking from a forest, I came out into a large, open area. As I ran, I stumbled over flat stones spaced evenly on the ground. Just as my pursuers were about to seize me, I stopped, reached down to my ankle, and disappeared.

I awoke out of breath, whether from my panic or my sprint from the trees I couldn't be sure. I sat up and re-oriented myself to the now-familiar hotel room while I replayed the dream. I assumed I escaped using my device to travel to a different time. The woods were remnants of my earlier thoughts about area parks. The smooth stones were a mystery at first. Then, I realized they had writing on them.

The stones were grave markers and the open area was a graveyard which featured flush headstones. I had my staging site. Now, I only had to scout out which local cemetery had a large area with only such markers.

In the morning, I waited to hear from Joey. Even as Si Morley, I dared not leave the room. Just after 8:30, the phone rang.

"Candy store in thirty minutes," was all Joey said before hanging up.

I knew what he meant. I was only a mile or so from where we grew up, and we bought our candy and sodas at the local corner deli. We always referred to it, inaccurately, as the candy store.

I gathered my sparse belongings and headed for the door. I felt panic, as an agoraphobic must feel, as soon as I opened the door, fearing that someone would grab or follow me when I left this cocoon. I steeled myself, took a deep breath, and stepped out—no one grabbed me. I looked for anybody who might be watching. I saw no one, either in the hotel or in any unmarked cars in the parking lot.

I headed in a direction away from the candy store for a block, turned the corner, and immediately retraced my steps. If anyone were following me, either on foot or in a car, I should come face-to-face with him or her shortly.

Nothing. I relaxed and hastened to the store. When I approached it twenty minutes later, I didn't see Joey or his car. I slowed my pace, not wanting to arrive early and draw attention by standing around. As I approached the store, a gray compact car flashed its lights. I'd never seen the car before, and tried not to show any interest in it. The silhouette in the driver's seat might be Joey. I casually stopped opposite the car on the other side of the street, looked both ways, and crossed unhurriedly. As I checked traffic, I tried to see into the car. The figure raised his hand slightly—it looked like Joey. I surveyed the area for suspicious cars. None. I saw no one standing in place or reading a newspaper. Everything looked clear.

I tried not to quicken my pace as I approached the car from the front. It was Joey. I got in the passenger side.

"We okay?" I asked as I shut the door.

"I think so," Joey said before answering my unasked question, "I rented this. I'm worried there might be a tracking device on my car."

I nodded.

"I'm all set once we find a launching site," he said.

"How about a cemetery with a large area of ground-level headstones?" I asked. "Few people around, often surrounded by trees."

"Don't you think that a goat might stand out in a cemetery?" he asked.

"Not as much as he would on the Mall," I said. "People in cemeteries are usually in their own world."

"I know one that might work," Joey said. "Let's take a look. If it's good, we'll get the coordinates, and I can reprogram your device in a few seconds."

He took me to a cemetery only about five blocks from his house. We parked the car near the entrance. It was small, maybe ten acres, without a raised headstone in sight. There were a few scattered trees on the periphery, but none in the main area.

As we walked among the graves, I read the headstones. Most of them reflected few burials before the 1970s. That meant there'd be few visits to graves.

Joey and I looked at each other and nodded in agreement. He took a position near the middle, pulled out his hand-held GPS locater, and recorded the coordinates.

"Sure you have it?" I asked.

He was sure. We left quickly.

Joey dropped me off outside a restaurant, three blocks from the hotel. Still paranoid, I scanned my surroundings as Joey drove off. I saw nothing suspicious.

I entered the restaurant, took a table near the window, and divided my attention between the menu and the street. After I ordered my ham sandwich, I went to the men's room in the back of the restaurant. I carried my bag with me. I took my time in the restroom to spook anyone trying to watch me.

When I came out, I scanned the room for anyone keeping an eye on me, or studiously *not* watching me. Nothing. I returned to my table and ate my sandwich. The street still seemed reassuringly bland.

When I finished and paid, I left by the back door, emerging into a filthy alley. I looked for somewhere to sit while I waited for any pursuer to show himself. There was nothing in the alley that I would even touch, and I wasn't about to sit or lean against anything. The smell of decaying food convinced me to move on.

I headed away from my hotel and walked a circuitous route that should have flushed out anyone following me. I even stopped to look in store windows to use the window as a mirror for activity behind me. All I saw were me and some unconvincing wigs on Styrofoam heads.

When I got back to my room, I turned on the TV and lay down to think. Unless Joey had been followed, he'd be back at his house inputting the GPS location of the cemetery and disabling whatever signal the project used to track the device's location. I was no longer completely isolated: Joey had bought two burner cellphones we could use without any fear of being tapped. We knew, however, that the NSA had computers scanning billions of telephone calls looking for key words and could intercept our calls if we used flagged terms. Joey had recited a list of words we couldn't use: our names, travel, time, Dodge City, Kansas, project, launch, and a few dozen more that I'd already forgotten.

In my solitary confinement, I missed Tess and became increasingly anxious about being arrested before I could return to Kansas. I looked at the door, expecting a knock at any moment. I felt trapped since my room had only one exit. If the knock came, I'd never see Tess again.

Chapter 56

Joey called in mid-afternoon. "How was your lunch?" he asked.

I assured him it was okay and told him I was ready.

"I'll meet you at the restaurant," he said.

I was out of my room and in the hotel lobby in minutes. I checked out and headed directly for our rendezvous, taking no detours this time. My heart was beating too fast for my pace, my chest ached, and I found myself gulping short, shallow breaths. With my departure imminent, I imagined a disaster occurring every minute. I was certain I looked, and acted, as panicky as I felt.

Joey was parked at the curb when I arrived. I don't know if he saw my anxiety, but he reassured me that he'd been careful.

"I parked a block away from my house and climbed the back fence to get in," he said. "I didn't use any water or electricity except to work on the generator.

"Your laptop, the camera, the *iPad*, and the generator are all on the back seat. You'd better switch clothes and start taping them on. I don't want to be hanging around the cemetery."

I stripped off my shirt and pants and, after strapping on the device, I started taping things onto my limbs.

"*iPad* loaded?" I asked.

"Songs and movies," Joey said. "Everything you need—on the *iPad* and the computer, too."

I asked, "Are you sure that the device will transport everything?"

"No," he said evenly. "I'm worried about the laptop. But it's too late now."

I would be carrying more than twice as many tape-ons as before. The laptop alone would double the cargo mass the device had conveyed to date. I continued taping, attaching all manner of luxury items for Tess, but, as I worked, I worried that, by taking so many non-essential things, I was jeopardizing my chances. I kept taping anyway.

Joey and I refined our plan. I'd again use ads in the *Dodge City Times* to notify him of any transfer to the twenty-first century, encoding the date using a person's name. If I intended to send on the 14th day of the month, the person's name would start with the 14th letter of the alphabet—Nancy would be the 14th, Ophelia the 15th. Since we couldn't be certain of the time, I wouldn't try to signal that. However, we agreed I'd consistently transmit at around four P.M. Kansas time, in the hope that Joey would find a consistent correlation, and be able to meet the arrivals in the cemetery.

I planned to use small farm animals, such as a goat or sheep weighing less than my hundred and eighty pounds. I'd strap the device on its leg and tape the cargo tightly wrapped around its body inside a cotton bag. Then, I'd hobble the animal so that it couldn't go far if Joey missed its arrival.

I'd burn DVDs of my photos, videos, and any writing I did. In this way, the cargo would be minimal, no more than a couple of ounces of hard plastic. The return trips from Washington might be loaded up more. I'd ask Joey for various things I needed, but we didn't anticipate any problems with excess baggage. If I made it to

Kansas with what I had taped to me, it was unlikely that Dolly the Sheep would have much trouble carrying the modest parcels Joey and I intended to exchange.

When Joey received a DVD, he'd copy it and, after removing all possible fingerprints and DNA, forward it to the Project by anonymous mailing. The DVD's would provide the Project with all the benefit of my travels. Although I was a renegade from the team now, I felt a strong obligation to give back what I could.

The Project would naturally focus on Joey as the source of the DVDs and try to monitor his activities. For that reason, his visits to the cemetery had to be few and well planned. We considered hiring someone to make the pickups, but realized we couldn't. Clearly, we couldn't sandbag any such intermediary since he'd have to retransmit the animal using the device. Neither of us had the imagination to contrive a plausible story to explain that.

When I finished redressing in eighteenth-century clothes as we approached the cemetery, I was sweating. With my taping finished and my clothes back on, I was left to my thoughts. Joey had nothing to say, and we passed the last few blocks in silence.

We pulled up to the gates to the cemetery.

"Set?" Joey asked.

I nodded.

"Want me to come in with you?"

I wanted him to, but I couldn't think of any reason he should. I shook my head.

I opened the car door, and got out clumsily. Joey looked at me when I turned around before shutting the door.

"You're sure you re-programmed the device right?" I asked for lack of anything better to say.

Joey gave an almost indiscernible shrug. "I hope so," he said without conviction.

"I'll see you in the funny papers," I said. "Or you'll see me in the *Dodge City Times* anyway."

I tried to be light, but there was no jocularity in my voice or in Joey's face. This might be the last time we ever saw each other. Men don't say things like that to each other. I reached out my hand to him.

"Thanks for everything you've done," I said. I felt tears filling my eyes, but stifled them.

Joey gripped my hand firmly. "Take care of yourself," he said. "And say hello to Tess for me."

I was about to leave when a thought came into my mind. "Joey, did you ever consider the possibility that Tess and I might have children and that our descendents . . .?"

"Yeah," he said. "But, I don't know . . ." Yeah, I understood it was too much to think about. It was best just to drop the thought.

I winked at Joey and closed the door. As I walked through the gates, I felt like the tin man in *The Wizard of Oz*. All the items taped to my arms, legs, and body made me clunky and ungainly. I waddled more than walked the fifty or sixty yards to the middle of the graves.

When I arrived, I glanced around for any witnesses—only Joey. I pointed my index finger at him, leaned down to raise my pants cuff, and pressed the buttons.

Chapter 57

My four previous leaps had seemed instantaneous—I arrived before I could straighten from pressing the buttons.

Not this time. My body felt heavy and disjointed, and my mind empty. Things were going on that I had no control over. At some point during the transition, my stomach heaved, and I feared what would happen if I started vomiting in transition.

In time, perhaps in no time at all, I arrived in Kansas, the same flat grasslands. The same oppressive heat. The same interloper into nineteenth century Kansas.

At least, I assumed I was back in 1876. I wouldn't know until I arrived at Tess's door. I started hiking and, along the way, considered several possibilities, none of them good. One of them had me returning earlier than my first trip and having Tess confront me with her pistol again.

I abandoned my speculations on that note. I needed to get out of the sun quickly. But, first, I had to detach my cargo. I didn't bother to check whether everything made it.

A few pats here and there reassured me. I took off my shirt and ripped the tape to free the laptop. I pulled off the camera, pull-cord generator, *iPad*, and video camera next, and I stuffed them into my pockets. When I ran out of pocket space, I decided to carry the remaining items still taped to my legs.

By the time I reached the trees, the tape was irritating my skin. I was sweating into the tape and the sweat had no place to go. I was almost to the house and decided to leave everything in place until I got inside.

When I came out the other side of the thicket of trees, the house was only a few yards away.

"Tess," I yelled. No sound.

I didn't want to approach the house unannounced. "Tess," I yelled again.

Only silence came back—a deafening silence. Even the chickens and cicadas were quiet. I became worried. I paused in the yard and looked around. It reassured me that everything looked the same as when I left. I was probably in the right time. I was certainly in the right place.

With bile rising in my throat, I walked the last few steps to the front door. "Tess, it's me." I knocked. No answer.

I pushed it open. "Tess?" I asked. Nothing.

I entered and found everything in order—but no Tess. And no indication of where she might be. I put the laptop on the table and emptied my pockets of the rest of my electronic devices. I unbuckled my pants, dropped them, and started painfully ripping the tape from my legs. I was unstrapping the device itself when . . .

"Isn't that a sight?" Tess said.

I was facing away from the door, and I didn't hear her enter.

I straightened up, my pants still around my ankles.

"You almost scared me back to the twenty-first century," I said, a little breathless.

"Scared you?" Tess asked. "How do you think I felt opening my door to find a half naked man standing in the middle of my house?"

I went to pull up my pants as I turned. "I'm sorry . . ."

"Don't bother apologizing," she said. "Just give me a hug."

My pants fell back down to the floor as I hugged her, an awkward hug at best. I wasn't used to hugging beautiful women wearing only my underpants.

Tess was happy to see me—her face glowed and the smile wouldn't leave her face. After glowing at me for a long time, she looked on the table at all the items that I had off-loaded.

"Oh, my," she said. "This looks interesting."

"Have you removed everything?" she asked. There was a tone to her question. I cocked my head at her, questioning her meaning.

She became disingenuous. "Well," she said, "I thought that I felt another big item still attached."

I blushed when she said that. I tried to cover the blush by reaching down to pull my pants up. I clumsily tried to button my pants. The pants had no zippers, because they still weren't common in the 1870's.

Tess watched me with amusement as I fiddled with my pants and belt.

"You don't need any help with that?" she asked.

"Some other time, maybe," I said.

How tempting. How available—maybe. And how reluctantly I resisted, but I did.

"I've got a lot to show you," I said, looking down at the table.

"So I noticed," she said, looking from me to the table.

"Look at these things," I said firmly, but not rudely. "You're going to like them."

I was glad to be back, and flattered by her interest. However, my resistance to her had its limits.

Instead of inspecting my cargo, Tess sat me down while

she prepared a small meal. She even refused to let me go to the pump to get water. While she worked, I carefully peeled the duct tape from the items on the table.

When she brought my food to the table, she sat down at an angle. Her hands in her lap, she looked fully at me, her face still beaming.

"Shall I show you?" I asked, gesturing at the stack of twenty-first century items.

She really didn't care, but she let me show her what I'd brought.

"This is the big item," I said unnecessarily, hefting the computer.

"It's beautiful," she said, reaching to run her hand over the smooth red aluminum top.

"It's more than beautiful—it's a wonder."

I reminded her that I'd mentioned computers in my previous incarnation. She didn't really remember, but nodded anyway.

"This is a computer," I said. "It can do all kinds of magic."

Since she really wasn't interested, I cut my explanation short.

"This is a hand generator I'll use to recharge the batteries for the cameras, *iPad*, and laptop."

"Cameras?" she asked.

"Oh, yeah," I said. "This is a video camera. It takes moving pictures."

"Are you going to take more pictures of me?" she asked.

"Sure," I said. "Of course."

"I'll look forward to that."

She was a constant surprise. I wasn't sure I'd said the right thing. I thought it was what she wanted to hear, but I wasn't sure I wanted to commit myself.

"Joey put more pictures in my *iPad* and on the computer, too. Do you want to see them?"

"Yes," she said. "Are you going to show me the computer now?"

Of course, I would show her the computer. I turned it on.

While we waited for the computer to boot, I asked how she was.

"I missed you," she said. "It was lonely out here by myself."

"Good," I said. "I'm glad you missed me. When I was in Washington, all I thought about was you. And how not to get caught."

She leaned over the table to touch my hand.

The computer was up now. I searched the desktop for a downloaded website. I punched it, and watched it come up.

"This is just an example of what it can do," I said. "Joey went on the Internet and pulled down this information. The information is stored in the computer and can be accessed at any time."

Tess came around behind me. Joey had downloaded a huge number of pictures showing all the wonders of the twenty-first century in vivid detail. Tess didn't say anything, but her hand was on my shoulder and she stroked it lightly. Her other hand was on my back, then rose to my neck. She started tickling the nape of my hair.

"Are those pictures all real?" she asked.

I didn't know how to answer her. Why would she ask that question?

"Of course, they're real," I said.

"If I take a bath and get nice and clean," she said quietly, "will you take some pictures of me?"

I couldn't be sure if she intended the ambiguity I heard in her question—did she want me to take pictures while she bathed or after she was nice and clean? It was best to give a neutral answer, "Let me heat some water for you," I said.

"Maybe," she continued. "You should take your bath

first."

I didn't have to be a genius to see her point. I needed a bath.

I stirred the fire, added some cow chips, and went to the pump for clean water. I poured a few gallons from the pail to the kettle and returned to the pump for another pail full. When the second pail was in the kettle and heating, I made a few more trips and dumped the pails directly into the galvanized tub.

As I emptied the kettle into the tub, Tess came out of the house. She folded her arms, leaning against the wall. My look asked why she was there.

"Better get in before it gets cold," she said.

"Not with you there," I said firmly.

She shrugged and, apparently deciding against a standoff, walked back in the house. "I'll get you something to dry off."

I quickly disrobed and was in the tub before she returned. When she brought out some cotton cloths, I felt naked. There were no soapsuds in the bath water and I was completely exposed. I felt stupid with my knees sticking up out of the water. I did my best to cover myself as she handed me my "towels."

"I'll call you when I'm through," I said. She half smiled and returned to the house. I had my hands full with her.

I didn't get a chance to call Tess. I intended to call her only after I was fully clothed. Instead, as I was still standing in the tub drying myself, she appeared and looked me over from head to toe. I was turned away from her and unaware of her presence until she said, "Very nice."

When I turned, she did me the courtesy of at least blushing. With several mixed emotions, I barked, "Go away until I'm dressed."

Her concession was to turn away as I hurried into my shirt and pants. When presentable, I told her. She turned to reveal she had unbuttoned her dress all the way down to her waist. Although she was still completely covered, she dared me with her look. I smiled at her audacity.

"Getting the camera?" she asked. As I passed her, she pulled her arms out of the dress and she was bare to her waist. She was facing away from me, but we both stopped, not three feet apart. I couldn't help looking at her radiant skin and turned to look at her.

When I returned with the camera in hand, she was still standing where I'd left her. She heard me come out and half turned. Her arm blocked any indecency, but it was still beautiful.

"You're not going to take a picture of me like this?" she asked. Was that a suggestion or was it a prohibition? I couldn't tell.

"No, I won't take any pictures of you like that," I said, my voice slightly lower than I'd have liked. Was that the right answer? Tess didn't let on.

"Get in the tub," I directed, turning away to give her privacy. I heard the water splash against the sides of the tub as she stepped in.

"Are you covered?" I asked as I turned toward her. She was facing away from me sitting in the tub and didn't bother responding. I watched her for a few minutes.

Tess took great pleasure at shampooing her hair. Her whole manner took on a relaxed, sensuous quality. I could see that her eyes closed, giving her face a sexual look. I was glad I'd brought the soap and shampoo for her.

She opened her eyes and, looking over her shoulder, found me watching her. I guess I looked amused.

"Well," she said defensively, "it feels so good. Almost the best feeling ever." She paused for effect. "Almost."

I laughed and sat down against the house. I shook my head, appreciating how lucky I was. I enjoyed her bathing as much as she did.

I walked over to the tub, picked up the half-filled pail next to it, and warned her, "Close your eyes. I'll rinse your hair."

When I emptied the pail over her head, she sat up in shock. I looked away before I embarrassed her, or, more likely, stretched my sensibilities.

"Oh, that's cold," she exclaimed.

"I'm getting out now," she said, starting to stand.

I turned away.

"I need a cloth to dry off," she said.

I averted my eyes as I reached for the equivalent of a towel. I handed it to her without taking in the view.

"Are you shy?" she asked. "Is that why you're afraid to look?"

I didn't answer her.

"I can see you're interested," she teased.

After a few seconds, she came over to me and ran her hand on my arm.

"Will you give me a hug?" she asked.

She held the towel in her hand as she wrapped her arms around me. I found myself hugging a completely nude woman, and she happened to be the most beautiful woman in the world.

"What's holding you back?" she whispered in my ear. "Don't you find me attractive?"

I said nothing.

"Will you answer me?" she asked in a little girl manner.

"I don't want to do it until we're married," I said.

I felt her body stiffen.

"Marry?" she said. "Do you . . . Is that a proposal?"

She was at a loss for words, but she managed to get out something that sounded like that.

"No," I said. "It's really a proposition, just a means to get you to go to bed with me."

She ignored the irony in my words. She was clearly not in a humorous state of mind.

She pushed herself away slightly, still in my embrace, and looked me in the eye. Her face was grave as she searched me face to see if I was serious.

"I love you, Tess," I said. "Will you marry me?"

Her expression cracked, but she didn't answer right away. I clenched in fear that she was going to say no.

Finally she spoke, "Only if you sleep with me." Her face went from granite to that great smile.

"I promise," I said. "But only after we're married." I wasn't going to give in now after all the effort I'd made to restrain myself.

"Then, let's get married now," she said impatiently. "I can't stand it anymore."

"Imagine how good it'll be if we wait," I said.

I pulled away. "Stop that," I said. "That can only lead to disaster. Get dressed and let's have dinner.

"I found something while you were gone," Tess said. "It was a box of small metallic packages."

I blanched, knowing she'd discovered my secret cargo, the one item I refused to discuss with her. She cocked her head in a question. I couldn't tell if she was being coy, or if she didn't understand what they were.

"I'll show you what they are very soon," I said. "Be patient."

After she dressed, she came into the house. I was sitting at the table. She sat on my lap and put her hands loosely around my neck.

"Did you mean it?" she asked.

"Yes," I said. "Now, will you answer me?"

She laughed, "Of course, I'll marry you."

I kissed her. We were engaged. But I had no ring for her.

Chapter 58

After dinner, I told Tess of my plans. First, I'd dig up the buried money, and we'd take a train to Kansas City to put it in a bank. I didn't want to keep it in Dodge because, without any real banks, Mayor Hoover or Bob Wright provided the only safe place to keep cash. Either of them would keep locals' money in his safe. While my money would probably be safe either place, I didn't want anyone locally to know about our relative wealth.

Tess's immediate response was to plan a clothes-buying trip to Dodge for our visit to Kansas City. Typical woman—nineteenth century, twenty-first century, no difference. I didn't squelch her enthusiasm, but, as I left to dig up the money, she volunteered, "No need. I dug it up the day you left. It's behind the flour."

I looked at her in complete confusion. "How'd you know where to look? And why'd you dig it up?"

She looked at me in her superior manner. "It wasn't a very good hiding place," she said. "And any thug or savage looking around would have found it."

I sighed. I already knew she was going to be a handful. I

sat back down.

"I'm going to leave $3,000 with Wright and the rest in Kansas City," I explained. "I'll make arrangements to transfer money from Kansas City to Bob if I need it."

Tess had no interest in my plan for the money. She had shopping, and her future visit to the big city, on her mind.

I had two other plans, one for Tess, and one for me. I decided to keep my plan for her a secret. The other was for me to go to Dodge for the wagon and, while there, expand my photos of the Queen of the Cow Towns.

Before I could take more pictures, however, I needed to improve my camera blind and to devise one for the video camera. I couldn't keep wearing my sling without unduly drawing attention to myself. Besides, the sling was hot and uncomfortable in the oppressive heat.

I found the solution in my obsession with avoiding attention. I knew that, no matter how careful I was, I'd act oddly every time I took a picture. Whether I was standing still in front of a building or carefully watching people on the street, I stood out and, increasingly, I found people watching me. I concluded the solution was to flaunt what I was doing and accustom people to my picture taking.

I'd do it by becoming a photographer—I'd buy a vintage, wet-plate camera and modify it to conceal my tiny digital cameras. I could openly drag the heavy contraption through town and everyone would know I was taking pictures. With imagination, however, I could keep a secret of the type of pictures I was taking.

The unwieldy hardwood box camera could also camouflage the video camera. I'd designed a small leather case to hide the small camcorder, exposing only the lens and trigger. By attaching it to the side of the box camera, it would disappear from view. The video camera was only about fifteen cubic inches, about half the size of my fist, and I guessed the vintage camera would be about as big as a horse's head, maybe 1400 cubic inches. Attached to a box one hundred times its size, the videocam should be all but invisible.

First, I had to get the vintage camera. I kissed my fiancée goodbye just after dawn the next day and started for Dodge leading her horse. I draped the harness over the horse and hoped I wouldn't embarrass myself too much when I asked Wagner to hitch the wagon to it.

Dodge was busy when I arrived just before 9 o'clock. I was bemused that a mere 800 or 900 people could make so much traffic. Since geniality would be a professional asset to Will Barrett, Photographer, I made a point of smiling at and greeting everyone I saw. I'd been friendly before, but now I made a serious effort, and found it made my visit all the more pleasant.

I studied the faces I greeted. I came to know the people by their expressions and their responses to my greetings. Their lack of hygiene no longer bothered me. I'd earlier concluded that Tess was the only one in Dodge who bathed. That was enough for me—body odors in Dodge, soap and shampoo at SouthFord.

When I walked into Wagner's barn, he took only a moment to recall who I was.

"Will," he said. "It was Will, wasn't it? I've got your wagon ready."

He led me to a corner where he swept his hand across the length of the newly built wagon. He seemed very proud of his work, or was it just the normal showmanship of a car salesman?

"Isn't it great?" he asked, sounding like a TV pitchman.

"Yeah," I said as enthusiastic as I could. "It looks fine."

In fact, it looked like a wagon: four wheels, two axles, and a platform with a rudimentary seat. It was hard to get excited about buying a new vehicle that didn't even have the new-car smell.

"Could you hitch Tess's horse up for me?" I asked. "I've got some other errands to run."

I paid the balance of $57 and headed for a small storefront

on Chestnut Street near the *Times* office. I'd noticed a modest sign advertising "Quality Photography" when I was last in town.

I tapped on the door and admitted myself to a small room containing just a table and two chairs. The place smelled of several chemicals, all of which, I was sure, were toxic and would shorten my life by ten years. I heard some noises from the back and announced myself. In a few seconds, a small, thin-faced man in wire-rimmed glasses came in. He had a look of uncertainty about him.

"Welcome," he said. "Can I help you with a likeness today?"

I hadn't planned on that, but it sounded like a good idea.

"Yes," I said. "That's why I'm here. I'll also need you to take one of me and my fiancée when we're next in town."

He quickly moved his table against the wall, pulled down a painted backdrop from near the top of the rear wall, and moved a chair in front of it. He opened the front door to admit more light and set up his camera on a heavy wooden tripod next to it. I watched as he worked, gaining confidence that a behemoth like his camera would easily camouflage my tiny cameras.

He inserted a glass plate, and ducked behind the camera, reaching forward to focus the lens.

He ordered me to hold still, as he quickly replaced the focusing plate with a plate he'd prepared out back.

"Now, don't be startled by the flash," he said as he filled a hand-held trough with powder. "Look directly into the camera and don't move."

A second or two after the flash, he told me that I could move. He changed my position slightly, replaced the plate in the camera, replenished the flash powder, and, holding the flash pan above his head, had me hold still again.

"That will be one dollar," he said. "I'll have your picture ready tomorrow."

"If I paid you two dollars, could I have it today?"

317

My proposal took him by surprise, but he quickly recovered.

"Yes, I guess I could do that. Will noon be okay?"

That business out of the way, I broached my real objective—my quest for a camera, any old camera. My statement renewed his initial uncertainty.

"Well," he said hesitantly, "I don't mean to be rude but . . ." He stopped talking, seemingly out of words.

"Yes?" I prompted.

"Well," he began again. "If I were to sell you a camera, you would use it to take pictures, wouldn't you?"

"Yes," I said in enthusiastic contrast. "That was my intention."

Seemingly leery of offending me, he explained, "Dodge is a small town, and, as it is, I can't earn a living taking pictures without travelling to neighboring towns. Two photographers in southwest Kansas would be one too many."

I nodded agreement. He was right. Of course, he was right.

"That's a very good point," I admitted. "We could make a deal. I won't take any pictures for money, and won't sell pictures to anyone in Dodge or within a hundred miles of Dodge. In fact, I'll promise to send any potential customers to you."

"You would?" he asked, narrowing his eyes.

"I would," I exclaimed. "In fact, whenever I'm on the street taking pictures, I'll be a visible advertisement for you.

"Aha," I said. (I was the pitchman now.) "Why don't we paint your name and address on the side of my camera so that everyone would see it."

I put out my hand. "I'm Will Barrett."

He still wasn't sure about me, but was too polite to refuse my handshake.

"Micah Kincaid," he said meekly as I shook his limp hand.

I painted the camera ad in the air: "Micah Kincaid, Quality

Photography, 36 Chestnut Street, Dodge City. I'll even pay to put it there."

I knew that Micah wasn't such a rube that he didn't know the old saw that 'If something sounds too good to be true, it probably is'. I had to bargain hard now.

"Maybe," I said more seriously, "you might want to sell me one of your old cameras very, very cheap to make this an even deal."

I had him hooked. I tried to see his eyes, but his glasses reflected the bright windows behind me.

"I gather you have an old camera you don't need?" I asked. "Could I see it?"

Micah hesitated but, while his feet were still planted firmly on the floor, his spirit was already leaning toward the back room.

"Well," he said (he said that a lot), "I do have one I haven't used in over a year. It is pretty heavy, though."

"Does it have a tripod?" I asked.

"Yes," he said.

"And a decent lens and some plates?"

"Well," again, "yes, it does. But I don't have any spare developing equipment."

"Gee," I said. "That's disappointing." What did I care about developing chemicals?

"That's a problem," I continued. "But maybe . . ."

I put on my thinking face. I looked toward the floor, grimacing the whole time.

"I guess you wouldn't ask much for it?" I asked. "If I have to get that stuff myself."

He assured me I wouldn't have any trouble getting everything I needed from Kansas City.

"The train comes through here every day," he explained. "You could probably have what you need in a couple of weeks."

I was bargaining hard now. "Well, since you're not using the camera, and we're going to use it to advertise for you, and since it isn't a complete outfit,"

I picked my eyes off the floor and looked Micah in the eye, pleading for his sympathy.

"How about five dollars?" he asked.

I could tell from his manner that I could get it for three.

"Woo," I said. "That's a lot. Could you do any better?"

I asked the question in a way so he'd know I was a beaten man. He had a sale.

"No," he said. "No, that's the best I can do."

"Can I see it?" I asked. I just wanted to prolong his misery.

He hurried to the back and, after some clattering and banging, emerged with a huge fandangle over his shoulder. It was bigger than he was, without counting the dust and cobwebs.

It was heavy, ugly, oversized, and seemingly useless— exactly what I wanted.

"Five?" I said as he set up the tripod. It was so large that he had to fold up his current camera to give him enough room to set it up. It nearly filled the room. I guessed it weighed fifty pounds.

"Yes," he said firmly. "That's the best I can do."

"Do you have a plate box to go with it?" I asked. "And some plates?"

He nodded, eagerness leaking out of his mask.

I took my time checking the lens, tripping the shutter, and testing the tripod. I took the lens cap off and then the lens itself to show my experience. I tripped the shutter again. I looked in the back, inserted the sanded focusing screen, and adjusted the focus. I couldn't see anything—just fine for my use.

I turned away, reaching in my pocket for my purse. I discreetly pulled out five silver dollars and turned back to Micah.

"You drive a hard bargain," I said as I grudgingly placed the coins in Micah's hand.

He dragged the plate box out from the back. It was even

dustier than the camera. I didn't bother to look inside.

"You'll help me if I need it?" I asked. He assured me that he would.

I dragged my junk out the door, banging the plate box on the doorjamb. Several people gave me looks as I lugged my bargains down the dusty street to Wagner's shop. Little did they know that the elephant I was displaying would appear frequently on their streets, or that the elephant was a mask for a pair of mice—a mice, far more potent than the elephant could ever be.

Chapter 59

Wagner left his work, and ambled toward my new rig and me as I loaded my purchases. He seemed mystified.

"You gonna take pictures?" he asked, for lack of anything better to say.

"Sure am," I said. "I'm gonna take the best pictures you ever saw. Will you watch this stuff for a couple of hours or so?"

He vaguely nodded his okay as he inspected the camera and tripod. I headed back out to my next destination—Wright's General Outfitting Store. The clerk, who I now knew to be Gus, welcomed me as an old friend this time—he was getting used to me.

"I need a drill," I said, "some bits, screws, a screw driver, and some pieces of wood."

Gus quickly found the screws I needed and we settled on the bits. The drill and screwdriver were easy. The wood stumped him, but he eventually found some scraps I could use. We added a hacksaw, and my purchases came to just over three dollars. I paid and tucked the hardware into my canvas bag.

Before I left, I asked Gus where I could get a small holster made.

"Can't carry guns this side of the tracks," he pointed out.

"I'm glad you told me that," I said, already knowing about the ordinance. "But can you direct me to a good holster maker?"

He sent me across Bridge Street to the saddle shop. I'd passed it several times, but I'd paid it no attention.

A bell rang as I opened the door, and I was greeted by a stocky man with a square face and slicked dark hair parted in the middle. He wore a leather apron and carried a wooden mallet in his right hand. The smell of leather filled the small space.

"Help you?"

"If you make holsters, you can," I said.

"I do."

I pulled a small piece of wood out of my shirt pocket. I'd carved it the evening before to the precise size and shape of the video camera.

"I need a small holster to hold something like this," I showed him. "I need this handle to be open, and you'd need to put some holes for these notches here." The openings would accommodate the lens, the exposure sensor, and the on/off button so I could use the camera without taking it out.

"A holster for this piece of wood?" he asked.

"Yeah," I said. "And I'd like the leather to be light and thin."

He frowned while looking at the carving and I watched his black mustache dance on his upper lip as he inspected my woodwork.

"Gonna attach it to a belt?" he asked.

"No."

"Can do—a dollar-seventy-five," he said and looked for my reaction to the price.

"I was hoping for something under a dollar," I wheedled.

"You want a good holster?" he asked.

"Well, of course."

"A dollar seventy five."

"When could you have it ready?"

"Need it tomorrow, I could have it ready tomorrow."

I agreed to the price and promised to return.

"Pay in advance," he said.

Acting as if he were taking the last of my money, I handed it over to him. As he put the money into his pocket, I asked for a receipt.

He eyed me briefly before turning back to a shelf. He scribbled on a scrap of paper. When he handed it to me, I read it: "$1.75."

Good enough.

I was making progress, and would be in operation in less than a week. The wagon would make it easy for me to visit Dodge whenever I wanted, assuming Tess would let me take it.

When I emerged from the saddle shop, Earp and Masterson were walking together heading south across the tracks. They looked like the latter-day Laurel & Hardy, the lithe Wyatt and the shorter, stockier Masterson. Bat was talking up a dust storm and Earp just nodded. I needed to get to know them better—just not today.

I spent the next several hours scouting the town for good picture angles. I walked every street and stuck my head into every store and saloon. Just as important, I continued my study of the people. I cut short my observations as noon approached, so I could head home to modify the camera.

Before returning to Wagner's, I worked my way back to Kincaid's shop. My picture was ready, sitting in a dark frame on his desk waiting for me. Micah pointed toward it as soon as I walked in.

"It's good, isn't it?" he asked.

It *was* good. The focus was soft and the contrast muted,

and I found myself excited to have hard evidence that I, Will Barrett, had truly been in the nineteenth century.

"Yes, it is," I said. "You do fine work."

He wrapped it in some brown paper, and presented it to me. I paid him the two dollars I promised.

Realizing I wanted to take a copy back to the twenty-first century, I ordered another.

"Can you make me another copy?" I asked. "I'll pick it up the next time I'm in town."

For another dollar, he could. I paid him the extra dollar.

I picked up the rig at Wagner's, and headed back to the ranch. When I arrived, I called out to Tess. I wanted to show her my camera and tell her of my bargaining. She didn't appear or answer. I got worried.

"Tess," I yelled again. Nothing.

I jumped off the wagon and hurried to the house, leaving the horse and wagon in the yard. I opened the front door and called her name again.

"I'm over here," she said sleepily. When my eyes adjusted to the dark, I saw that she was lying on her bed face down.

"You okay?" I asked.

"I'm fine," she said. "I didn't think you'd be back so soon, so I decided to take a short rest."

I slipped out to unhitch the wagon, and gave the horse some water. After washing up at the pump, I returned to the house. Tess was still lying there.

I noticed that the back of her dress was unbuttoned all the way down to her waist. "What are you doing?" I asked.

"It's so hot in here," she said. "I just wanted to get some air on me."

"Hmm," I grunted for lack of better conversation.

"Could you rub my back a little," she asked her eyes still closed.

I tilted my head. Was this staged? I knew better than to let myself get hooked into her game—if that's what it was, but . . .

I sat on the edge of the bed. As I did so, Tess leaned up and pulled both of her arms from the sleeves of the dress, her near breast coming almost completely into view.

"Um-hmm," she murmured.

Here we go, I thought. I have the most beautiful woman in the West lying in the dark, half-disrobed asking me to rub her naked back.

"Are you trying to seduce me?" I asked.

She didn't answer me.

"Are you?"

"No. Could I, if that was my intention?" she asked rhetorically. When I didn't answer, she continued, "So what are you afraid of?"

By this time, I was running my fingertips along her spine.

"Mmmm." The sound came from her throat and carried the image of a smile on her face.

I put my palm on her back, held it there, and, unable to deny Tess, stroked her softly. She adjusted herself almost imperceptively.

I stroked her gently and with appreciation for the privilege, both physical and spiritual, of touching this precious woman.

Caught up in my caresses, I found myself running my hand over her entire back. When I reached her shoulder on one side, I ran across her neck and started down the other side. I didn't stop until I reached her waist. Then, spanning her narrow waist, I retraced my path up the first side. My hand soon wandered onto her sides, feeling the softness of her waist giving way to the countable ribs under her rich soft skin.

I caressed her for some time, covering as much of her skin as I could. I found, whether through my unconscious efforts or Tess's movements, that her dress, initially covering her below her waist, had slipped down. A fair portion of her bottom was exposed. Of course, my hand, having a mind of its own, fondled all of her bare skin.

Tess showed no reaction for some time. She'd invited me into the world of the mythic woman, into contact with that mystical quality of femininity that all women have. I was entranced—literally out-of-body and out-of-mind.

In my fervor, I found my hand brushing the sides of her breasts and stroking more and more of her ever-more revealed bottom. Although I tried to keep my focus on the emotional and spiritual experience, my body was along for the journey. I was breathing hard and longing to touch more. I had to stop, yet I lacked the will power. This was an experience beyond any I'd ever had. If nothing more ever transpired between Tess and me, I could have lived on the memories of this moment.

Fortunately for my resolve, Tess blinked. Her self-control weakened, and I gradually became aware that she was making noises—gentle, guttural sounds from deep in her throat. She started twitching and jerking involuntarily. Very small sounds, and very small movements, but they awakened me from my spell. I still smelled the perfume that clouds all men's minds, but I regained control of myself. When I stopped rubbing her back, Tess grunted her displeasure.

I took a deep breath, smiled to myself, and leaned down to her ear.

"If I don't stop now," I whispered, "your fiancé is going to be livid with you. You'll never be able to explain how you ended up completely nude being molested by a strange man from a hundred-and-thirty-four years in the future."

I kissed the side of her face.

"Please cover that beautiful body before I do something I'll regret," I said as I stood up. "I'll wait outside."

I stepped outside, still aroused, my heart beating rapidly. I leaned against the house and closed my eyes. That was as much as I could handle—it had summoned all of my resolve to walk out.

In a few moments, Tess came out, now fully dressed. Still

leaning against the house, I turned to look at her. She glared back, whether angry or frustrated—or both—I couldn't tell. I had no idea what she was thinking. Was she upset because I'd stopped—or because we'd gone too far? I had no idea how any man, especially someone as vulnerable to her as I was, could resist her.

I was fighting a battle, but uncertain who the enemy was. I desperately wanted to make love to her and, perhaps, she wanted me to, but it wasn't time yet. It had long ago gotten to the point where I was arguing with myself—and losing most of the arguments. Still, it was important to me—it would just have to wait until our relationship was resolved. I couldn't have lived with myself if I used her, and left her with only a memory when I returned to my normal life in Washington.

I was proud of myself, but also sympathetic with Tess. This beauteous human was offering herself—or was she?—to this ungrateful lout, and I had the temerity, not to say the stupidity, to refuse her. Shakespeare described me hundreds of years ago—I was, indeed, an arrant knave. I didn't know what arrant meant, nor, for that matter, what a knave was. But I knew I was one.

I thought it best to leave Tess alone for a while. I retreated to the barn, and began work on my camera.

Chapter 60

I'd already worked out the design for the still digital camera—I'd install a small frame inside the top right corner of the front panel to hold the camera, drill two small holes, one to give me access to the on/off switch, the other for the small lens to peek through. To finish it off, I needed to relocate the cable release to match the location of the shutter release on the smaller camera. The video camera was going to be even easier—I'd screw the holster, with the video cam inside it, to the right side panel.

My alteration of the camera work took me two hours. I lugged the tripod and camera outside, leaned my head inside the back drape, and using the LCD screen, framed the wagon I'd left in front of Tess's house. I slid in a plate for effect, and, standing erect, thumbed the plunger down. I could hear the nearly imperceptible, and completely bogus, click of the electronic shutter. I looked under the back drape and viewed the display of the picture. It looked good.

I inspected the front of the camera from several angles to get an idea what people on the street would see—the extra holes glared at me, because I knew where they were. A little stain would darken the freshly exposed wood inside the drill holes, and I felt satisfied that a casual witness would see nothing suspicious.

I looked around for Tess and found her hanging clothes on the line to dry. She didn't turn around as I approached.

"Tess," I said as if nothing had happened earlier, "I need you for a minute so I can take your picture."

She turned and renewed her glare. I kept a friendly look on my face.

"It'll just take a minute," I said.

"Should I take my dress off?" she asked sarcastically. "Oh, no, Mr. Mormon might take offense at that."

I acted hurt by her comment. I certainly wasn't going to point out that Mormons were anything but prudes. My approach worked—Tess softened.

"Okay," she said with a sigh, "but just a minute."

I posed her next to the wagon and went through my routine again. As soon as I went to take the picture, she unfroze her face and my coquettish fiancée appeared. It was a great picture.

"One more," I said.

As I was about to press the plunger, Tess raised her right leg, putting her foot on one of the spokes of the wheel. She hitched up her dress hem to expose her calf. Even in her bare feet, the pose made for a very sexy picture. I took the picture without comment, and thanked her.

Whew, I thought, nothing like a camera to break the ice.

As she walked off, I yelled after her, "You didn't say whether you liked the wagon."

"It's fine," she threw back over her shoulder.

As I packed the camera away, I wondered if Tess's efforts to seduce me would end. As hard as the trials had been for me, I hoped not.

I reflected on the fine line between being a rogue and a gentleman—I'd tried to be a gentleman, but I knew Tess could only see a selfish rogue. I was being selfish, but it was something I had to do. Sometimes, you can't win.

Dinner was tense that evening but, after we finished, I suggested we go to Dodge in the morning. She could shop for our wedding and for Kansas City, and I could take pictures. Tess assented without enthusiasm.

In the soft light of dawn, I clumsily hitched the horse to the wagon. Tess was getting ready as I loaded my camera, tripod, and plate case into the back.

I got up on the wagon seat and, after turning the wagon around, waited for Tess. She came out dressed for church, clearly intending to do serious shopping. I jumped off to help her up. She didn't speak.

When I climbed back on, I turned to her with a smile.

"We're going to have fun today, right?" I asked.

She studied my face and, apparently charmed by my enthusiasm, agreed. "Sure," she said. "Why not?"

I knew how to get her talking—ask her what she planned to buy. As we crossed the river and turned onto the Santa Fe Trail, I heard about dresses, shoes, hats, umbrellas, gloves, corsets, and other essentials for the big events. After hearing the list, I considered returning to SouthFord to stuff more money into my pockets. However, I feared Tess would take offense, and so I continued on, knowing we could get credit from the stores if we ran short.

When she was finished with her list, she pointed out that I needed a good suit and other clothes, and shoes, suitable for city wear.

"Could you get them without me?" I asked.

"You have to try them on," she said.

Recognizing she was right, I suggested we get my clothes last, just before we left town.

I pulled into the Ham Bell's livery stable, proud to arrive in the newest wagon in town. I didn't display my conceit to Tess, for fear that she'd see how truly shallow I am.

I helped Tess off the wagon, gave her most of my money, and we went our separate ways. Of course, burdened with my dinosaur camera, I would move more slowly than she did. As soon as Tess hit the ground, she trotted off across the tracks to north Front Street for what would certainly be the most expensive shopping spree of her life. I lagged behind, dragging my camera, tripod, and plate case from the wagon. I pulled the case strap onto one shoulder, leveraged the tripod and camera over the other, and headed toward the tracks behind her. I immediately doubted the wisdom of using fifty pounds of equipment to hide my two digital cameras, each weighing far less than a pound.

I set up next to the tracks and shot an oblique picture of the Long Branch with Wright's store and Hoover's Cigar store flanking it. Seeing me, a handful of cowboys, and even a few women, gathered in front of the saloon. Recognizing they would add to the picture, I signaled for them to be patient.

I switched on the digital camera, ducked under the black hood, and adjusted the zoom on my digital camera to frame it tightly. I went through the motions of inserting a plate in place of the focusing screen and stepped out in front of the camera, just off to the right side. I took the cable release between my fingers and, putting my thumb on the plunger, held up my hand for my subjects to stand still. I took three or four shots before I replayed my charade of switching plates. I took a couple more before waving my thanks to the gathering.

I swung my camera toward the northeast to photograph the corners where Bridge Street and First Street intersected with Front. The Alhambra appeared prominently on the left and was now stored in my camera's memory. I scanned the south, but there was nothing particularly photogenic across the tracks from this location.

I approached the Long Branch, dragging my equipment with me. I leaned it against the wall under the awning before going into the bar. I approached the bartender.

"Do you mind if I shoot a few pictures in here?" I asked. I'd initially thought of referring to his "beautiful establishment," but he would have laughed me out of the place if I had.

The bartender, a short rotund man with a bald head and mustache, looked at me with a look of disdain.

"This is a saloon," he said.

"I'll only take a few minutes, and I'll get out of the way," I said. It wasn't as if I was going to disrupt business. The Long Branch was open twenty-four hours every day, but there were only a handful of drunks in the place that early in the morning. I wouldn't have dared ask at night when dozens would be there.

The bartender wiped a glass on his white apron, shook his head, and turned away. The shake of his head looked more like disdain than a refusal. I retrieved my equipment, and set up just inside the door at an angle to the bar.

"Don't go shooting off any flash powder in here," the bartender added over his shoulder. "I'm not going to let you burn this place down."

"No flash," I said. "When I'm finished, drinks for everyone on me."

I wished I could've used the camera flash, but there'd be no way to explain it.

I set up the shot and read from the LCD screen that the shot would take a half second even at ISO 800.

"Could everyone hold very still," I suggested. As soon as they turned toward me, I pushed the plunger. I ducked under the hood for show, not bothering to change the plate. After swiveling the camera to get the tables to the left, I held up my hand again and shot another.

"Thank you," I said.

I moved the camera closer to the corner of the bar, and gestured toward the bartender, now standing at the far end.

"Could I get a couple of pictures of you and the bar?" I

asked.

Although he tried not to show it, he was flattered.

"Where do you want me?" he asked.

I positioned him, fiddled in the back of the camera briefly. I raised the plunger, said, "Hold it." I shot two.

"One more," I said.

I moved him in front of a customer and suggested he act as if he was talking to him. After replacing the plate with the focusing screen, I framed the two of them and shot them without the charade of inserting a plate.

I approached the bartender, and thanked him for his cooperation.

"Will three dollars cover drinks for everyone?" I asked, reaching into my pocket.

He looked around the room. "Might need four," he said.

He was gouging me, but it was worth it.

I packed up and called out to the patrons, "Thank you, gentlemen. Enjoy your drinks." As I left, there was a migration of the few to the bar.

After I left the Long Branch, I headed to the saddle shop to pick up my video holster. It looked good, and I thanked the man.

"Aren't you going to check to see how it fits?" he asked.

He had the woodcarving already wrapped in it and it fitted the carving perfectly. I didn't intend to try the video camera in his presence. I left the shop, leaving behind, I was sure, a sense that something wasn't quite right.

I found a secluded spot in an alley, and dragged my equipment in with me. I set up the bulky camera and leveled it. I pointed it out of the alley, and positioned the holster, now containing the camcorder, on the far side of the street. Holding the holster in place, I removed the camcorder, and, using two screws and a couple of large washers, attached the holster to the camera box. I reinserted the camcorder into the holster, checked its aim, and ran a short cord to the Nikon still camera. Joey had made changes to the Nikon to allow me to display the GoPro videos on the still camera's LCD. I worked the controls to shoot a few seconds of video. I checked the results and, to the extent that I could tell on the small screen, decided they looked sharp. I was glad I decided to go with a dedicated video camera. As good as the Nikon video feature was reported to be, GoPro seemed ahead of it on high-def imagery.

Now fully equipped, I loaded my equipment on my shoulders and headed south across the tracks. Time to document the wild south side.

Chapter 61

Soon after I crossed the tracks, I ran into trouble. As I was setting up, facing the Lady Gay dance hall, three young cowboys stumbled out. I could see trouble coming when one of them pointed at me.

The men unhitched their horses and two of them mounted. The ringleader, still on foot, led his horse toward me. The other men tagged behind on horseback.

"What do we have here?" the ringleader asked loudly to no one in particular.

One of the others answered anyway, "Looks like a tinhorn that doesn't belong."

"Hey, tinhorn," said the ringleader to me, "we didn't say you could take our likeness."

"No," I said. "You didn't. So I won't."

They were drunk, and looking to make me the butt of their meanness.

"Well," he said slowly, in what I took to be a Texas drawl, "that won't do. We don't think we can trust you."

He reached up to his saddle and released the rope. He

flipped the loop over my camera, and climbed onto his horse. With a cruel grin on his face, he said, "I think we better bring this camera back to camp to make sure you don't try to sneak a likeness. Right, boys?"

My heart was beating wildly. I pictured them dragging my camera down the street. There was nothing I could do to stop them.

Just when the ringleader was about to turn his horse, he was yanked from his saddle and thrown to the ground. Wyatt Earp stood over the stunned troublemaker. I hadn't seen Earp approaching, and I was as startled as the kid was.

Earp removed the rope from the camera, and wrapped the loop around the kid's ankle. The kid was lying on his back in the dust, dazed from the long fall from the horse. Earp tied the rope to the saddle horn on the now-empty horse.

"Now, I heard you talking about dragging something out of town," Earp said. "If I spook your horse, he's going to run for camp and take you with him."

The kid looked up with wide eyes. He knew that, if Earp carried out his threat, the dragging would probably kill him. He looked wildly to his accomplices for help. They were backing their horses away and offered no support.

"No, officer," he begged from the dust. "We didn't mean nothing. Just a little fun."

He was completely sober now. Earp gazed down at the kid. While Earp stared him down, the kid tried to get to his feet. Earp put his boot on the boy's neck and held him in place.

My pulse raced and my heart was thudding against my ribs. I stepped away from Earp, afraid he'd turn on me. This wasn't going to end well.

Finally, Earp spoke. "Or I could run you all into the jail and charge you with assault, public intoxication, and, probably, a number of other charges."

His voice was low and he spoke with calm, as if he were

seriously considering his options. All three of the cowboys were cowered now, and none of them moved or spoke. Even their horses looked frightened.

"You'd probably get away with a fine of $50 each," Earp added.

The ringleader spoke again, his voice quavering, "Sir, officer, we don't have $50. We were just joking around." His voice was forced, choked by Earp's boot on his neck.

"What's your name?" he asked the ringleader. Now, Earp's voice was firm. I thought it was firm before, but now I was thoroughly intimidated.

"Jake, sir."

"Jake, this man," Earp said, gesturing toward me, "is a citizen of Dodge City. The citizens of this town pay me a lot of money to protect them. I can't let pissants like you threaten and assault them."

"But, sir . . ." the ringleader interrupted.

"Shut up," Earp commanded, increasing the pressure of his boot.

"If I send this horse back to camp dragging you behind," he continued, "that's going to upset a lot of people minding their own business. And if I drag you to jail, you'd sit there until your cohorts raised enough money for your fines. In the meantime, Dodge would have to feed you."

The three men looked on with wide-eyed attention. Earp glanced toward the sky as he recited the problems with each of his options. He nodded his head slightly, as if he'd thought of another way out of the situation.

"Now, maybe," he said, looking sternly at the boy under his boot, "if you apologized to this gentleman, and each of you paid him, say, $10 for his trouble, he might not press charges."

The men nodded in unison before Earp finished his sentence. I nodded along with them. Wyatt turned and looked at me. The cowboys were already reaching into their pockets for money.

"Would that satisfy you?" he said, turning to me.

I wasn't expecting the question and didn't say anything. The cowboys turned anxiously toward me, waiting for my response. Jake strained to raise his head, his eyes filled with pleading.

"Yeah," I finally said, "that'd be okay." I continued nodding. The two quickly stood up in their stirrups and reached into their pockets before comparing what they each had. They didn't have enough.

"Jake, we need $15."

Earp was still pressing his boot on Jake's neck and he had difficulty finding his money. Fortunately, he had enough and handed it up. Earp lifted his boot, and collected the money from the three men. Earp turned and handed it to me.

Jake jumped to his feet, pulled the rope loop from his foot, and clambered onto his horse, gathering his rope as he did so. I watched Earp. This was theatre to him. As the men were about to ride off, he yelled at them.

"Hold up there," he shouted.

The cowboys reined their horses to a stop and looked back at Earp, fear on their faces.

"I don't think I heard your apologies," Earp said.

All three of the cowboys started apologizing at once, running on beyond what was necessary.

Earp cut them short. "Get out of here. I don't want to see any of you in town for the next seventy-two hours. Hear me?"

They yes-sirred together as they spurred their horses to a gallop and headed down the street without turning back. Even under the circumstances, their exit reminded me of the twentieth-century phrase of "getting out of Dodge." Here, I was watching it live.

As they rode off, I turned to thank Deputy Earp, but he was already thirty feet away, walking slowly down the street.

I yelled after him, "Thank you, officer." I don't know if he heard me.

I stood there, holding thirty dollars in crumpled up money. I didn't want it. After I took some breaths to calm down, I decided to donate the money to charity.

When my adrenaline returned to a normal level—that is, when my hands stopped shaking—I took pictures of the Lady Gay and of some of the other sites of the wild side of Dodge. I also ran a few minutes of video to capture some of the atmosphere—the sounds, and movements of the streets. I breathed easier when I was back across the tracks.

As I sat alone eating lunch, I reflected on how vulnerable I was, and how much my efforts to complete my mission depended on factors, and people, that I had no control of.

Chapter 62

Despite my encounter at the Lady Gay, I had a great day. By looking through the camera lens, I saw Dodge anew, as if for the first time. I was more attentive to the details, and I experienced a new and fresh Dodge City. Despite the difficulties and uncertainties, I was even more committed to documenting Dodge and its people, as well as to fulfilling my commitment to the Project.

The highlight of the day came in mid-afternoon. I spied Masterson sitting under an awning in front of the barbershop on north Front Street. Burdened with my equipment, I approached him, set my plate box on the board sidewalk, and leaned the tripod and camera against the wall.

"Officer," I said as I stepped up on to the sidewalk and extended my hand, "I'm Will Barrett."

"I know who you are," he answered amiably. He shook my hand without rising.

"Would you mind if I shot some pictures of you?" I asked.

"Now, why on earth would anyone want a picture of me?"

I couldn't tell him how famous he'd become. Instead, I

said, "I'm trying to document Dodge, and you and the other officers are a big part of the town's character."

"Why don't you take a picture of Deger? He's the marshal."

"In name only," I said.

Masterson flashed me a sharp look. It was no secret that he and Deger didn't like each other, but it seemed I wasn't supposed to talk about Deger's inattention to his duties.

"Then Earp's your man," he said. "He's the assistant marshal."

"I'll get him, too," I said.

Another look intimated what I already knew, that getting a picture of Earp wouldn't be so easy. His look vanished as fast as it appeared. His skepticism past, he acquiesced.

"What do you want me to do?"

"Just stay right there while I set up."

I did my usual fiddling and grabbed a couple of shots, asking only that he not look into the camera. I was pleased with the pictures and was about to move on when I realized I had a once-in-a-century opportunity. I reframed the digital camera to include the chairs next to Masterson and set the camera to timer. I pushed the plunger, turned on the videocam, and jumped into the chair next to Masterson.

"If you don't mind," I said, "I'm going to get a picture of you and me."

I turned toward him, as if I were listening to him. I hoped he wouldn't ask how I delayed the picture. I got a few more and quit, not wanting to press my luck. I returned to my seat, leaving the video camera running, and switched into my reporter role.

"I'm doing some writing for the paper," I said. "Would you tell me a little about yourself in case I have to write about the police force? And tell me about Dodge."

Although Bat was a fabled storyteller, he swept his hand across our view and said, "What's there to tell? Dodge is a no-account bunch of shacks stuck in the middle of nowhere. It's only here so soldiers have a place to drink, and so rowdy Texas cowboys can load their herds onto rail cars."

"Isn't that selling Dodge a little short?" I asked. "She isn't called the 'Queen of the Cow Towns' and 'Cowboy City' for nothing."

"Queen of the Cow Towns?" Bat snorted. "Now, that's something to be proud of."

"What about Officer Earp? Tell me about him."

He thought for a few moments, and I feared that he was through talking. But when he spoke, he opened up.

"Earp's a good man," he said. "I could tell you he's a good officer, but that wouldn't tell you much."

He became quiet again, as he organized his thoughts.

"Wyatt's the bravest man I've ever met," he said, staring into the distance as if reliving past events. "Everyone else has his fears, and can be intimidated. Not Wyatt. I've never seen any man cow him."

I took a chance by saying, "I don't mean to criticize him, but he is as cold as ice."

He turned his head toward me, and I felt my face flush. I thought I'd crossed a line. However, Bat was quick to react and even quicker to let the emotion go.

"He may seem that way," he said, turning toward the street again. He tugged on his mustache before continuing. "But he's got a good heart. He'd risk himself to save a stray dog."

"He's pretty brutal with the cowboys," I said.

He snapped his head, as if to ask how I could say that. His voice was firm when he continued, "Let me tell you, young man, he's the least violent officer I've ever met. It's easy to shoot a man. Wyatt won't pull his pistol unless he has to and, then, he'll buffalo a man before shooting him. That takes courage. He's saved many a cowboy's life by bloodying his head rather than putting a bullet in his chest. He ain't brutal. If anything, he's too gentle. It might get him killed one of these days."

"I noticed that he called you 'Bart'." I wanted to get Masterson to talk about their relationship.

"Aw, I don't like that," he said and shook his head. "He heard somewhere that 'Bat' came from someone mispronouncing 'Bart' and he digs me with it."

"Wyatt's got it right, doesn't he?" I asked.

He gave me another sharp look. "Bat comes from this here," he said. He lifted his cane, and shook it like a cudgel.

I knew he was lying, but I didn't know how to challenge him on it.

"But your family called you by your baptismal name, Bertholomiew, and didn't that get corrupted into 'Bat'?"

Masterson set his jaw. I'd invaded his privacy, and could lose him.

"Could be," he said, his tone closing the topic.

"If you don't mind me asking, how'd you get your limp?"

"It's nothing," he said. "I just got nicked in a shootout in January. I'll be walking right in a while."

I was thinking about what to ask next when someone walked up and took the seat on Bat's other side. It was Wyatt Earp. My throat constricted. Although our last contact was the brush with the cowboys earlier, I was still frightened of him.

Earp didn't say anything, not to me, not to Bat.

"Officer Earp," I said, my words tumbling out, "I want to thank you again for rescuing my camera this morning."

"My job," he muttered, still looking out at the street.

I was at a loss for how to talk to him. I wanted to question him, but he didn't invite conversation.

"I'd like to donate the thirty dollars to charity," I said. "Could you recommend one?"

"Give it to the firemen," he said without looking at me.

I leaned forward, and looked across Bat toward Earp. Earp's body kept its tension as he stretched his legs across the boardwalk. His face, except for his meticulous mustache, was freshly shaven. However, his eyes drew my attention. Not only were they a vivid blue-gray, but they moved constantly. He missed nothing that happened in the street. When I saw them focus sharply and follow movement on the other side of the street, I looked out, thinking that trouble might be approaching. Instead, I saw that Earp had seen a particularly attractive woman and was following her as she passed.

"Could I ask you some questions?" I asked with a catch in my throat.

"Yeah and have what I say end up in the newspaper?" he said.

Already, a difference between Masterson and Earp was apparent. Where Bat was articulate and spoke in complete sentences, Wyatt answered in snippets, and left the rest to implication.

"How about if I promise not to write anything you say?"

Earp didn't answer, but Bat turned to study him a moment. I don't know what he saw, but Bat turned back toward the street and nodded almost imperceptively. I took that to mean Earp would answer me.

"You and Bat met hunting buffalo?"

Earp nodded his head. Well, that was very quotable.

"What about Doc Holliday?" I asked.

Earp didn't answer. After a strained pause, he half turned toward me and said, "Don't know that name."

I flinched. The reports on when he met Holliday were spotty, and now Earp's response convinced me the reports were right that they'd met no earlier than 1877 or 1878.

"Sorry," I said. "Just a name I've heard."

I asked both of them, "Don't you worry one of these yahoos will take a shot at you just for fun?"

Neither wanted to answer that question. I suspected the possibility was too real to discuss.

Earp answered first.

"They're not here to shoot anyone," he said in a flat voice.

"But the cowboys are all southerners, sons of the Confederacy," I said, "and you're a Yankee to them."

Earp shook his head. "Civil War's over."

This interview wasn't going well. At least I had it on video, assuming that Earp was in the frame. Now I wanted some stills of the two of them.

"Officer Earp, would you mind if I took a couple of pictures of you and Mr. Masterson?"

Earp glanced at Bat, the look saying Where'd you find this fool?

I didn't wait for an answer. I hurried to my camera, fiddled briefly for show, reframed the digital camera, and took four shots. I didn't have to tell Earp not to look at the camera. He had no such intention. I felt sure I had some of the greatest historical pictures ever taken.

I thanked them for their cooperation and got my equipment—and myself—out of there as quickly as I could.

Chapter 63

Tess had a jaunt in her step as she walked down Front Street toward me. Judging from her manner, she'd spent most of the money I'd given her. However, I didn't see any packages in her hands.

"How'd it go?" I asked. I was conscious of Earp and Masterson behind me, probably watching us.

"Wonderful," she said gaily. "I even got a suit for you, but you have to try it on."

"You didn't buy anything for yourself?" I asked.

"Yes, I did," she said, as if this was the best day of her life. "I left them over at the corral."

"How much did you spend?" I asked.

"Well, you only gave me forty dollars," she pouted. "I had to buy the rest on credit."

'Forty dollars!' I thought. She probably never had that much in her hands at one time before today. And she didn't have it long this time.

"How much did you charge?"

She pouted slightly. "Only twelve dollars or so."

Fifty-two dollars was a lot of money to spend in one day, but I had enough in my pocket to cover the charged purchases, assuming that the 'or so' was just change.

After dropping off my camera at the wagon, we walked the short distance to Wright's, and I reluctantly tried on the suit. The jacket fitted just fine, but the pants were too tight. It crossed my mind that she purposely chose a smaller pair of pants as an oblique comment on my lack of performance to date. We found a pair that fitted me better.

When the clerk suggested I take the suit off so that he could wrap them, I declined politely and told him, "We'll be back in about fifteen minutes."

I led a confused Tess out of the store and down to Kincaid's shop.

"Tess," I said. "This gentleman is going to immortalize us by taking our picture."

Micah set us up quickly, posing us in the traditional nineteenth-century manner—the man sitting and the woman standing next to him. I was so pleased to be getting the pictures that I told Micah to take as many as he had plates ready. He ran out with the fifth picture. I was feeling mischievous and, without a lot of thought, asked Tess, "Is this the first time you've ever had your picture taken?"

She gave me a hard look before answering, "No, I've been to the big city. I've had my likeness taken before."

I gave her a smirk I knew would bring consequences later.

Kincaid gave me the second print of the earlier shot of me, and I paid him for all the pictures, leaving my pockets almost empty, considering I still had to cover Tess's purchases. We left and returned to Wright's store.

We left a few minutes later with my new suit wrapped in brown paper and tied with string. We picked up the wagon and started back to the ranch. As we bumped along, I thought about my day, probably as good a day as Tess had. Aside from the unpleasantness with the cowboys, all went well. I'd gotten pictures and videotape of Masterson and Earp; that alone would justify the Project. Although I hadn't viewed the pictures yet, I was sure I had history bouncing around in the back of the wagon.

I looked over at Tess, and smiled at her exuberance. Money couldn't buy happiness, but it could afford a temporary euphoria out of proportion to what the money bought. It was nice to see her so happy.

Ever since I fell in love with her, I watched and savored every little mannerism and her every gesture. Each was precious, a reflection of something beyond her beautiful flesh. Twenty-first-century cynics who asserted that humans were only machines with no soul would have to admit their mistake if they met Tess. She was the ultimate proof of the existence of both God and the human soul. I thought of Darwin's comment at the end of the *Descent of Man*, that "there is grandeur to this view of life." Here, I was feeling a grandeur sitting next to this creature that only a God could have created.

Yes, Tess made me feel bigger, grander than I'd ever felt before. And, to top it off, we were going to get married.

A few minutes out of town, Tess tensed and grabbed my arm. I saw fear on her face as she peered into the distance. Looking up, I saw Indians, the first I'd seen since I arrived. They were far away, but I could count four or five sitting on horseback. The horses moved restlessly, but the Indians didn't seem to move as they watched us.

"Are we in danger?" I asked.

Tess didn't answer at first. She glanced at me, then back at the Indians.

"I don't know," she said unevenly.

"Have there been any incidents lately?" I asked.

"Not recently," she said, still watching the Indians intensely. "But they did find some bodies out beyond the house a few months ago. They blamed the Indians."

As we watched them, the Indians continued to stare at us. I feared they were armed, and I didn't have either a pistol or rifle with me. I cursed myself.

The nearest house was half a mile back. I stopped the wagon to let the Indians make the first move. Every foot we were farther from the ranch houses increased our vulnerability.

My nerves were increasingly on edge as we waited. We only had to wait a couple of minutes before they started moving. At first, they appeared to move toward us, and I felt fear rising from my stomach into my throat. Then, I realized they'd turned their horses and were moving west.

"You okay?" I asked Tess, taking her hand.

"Yes," she said. "I guess so."

I could see she was sweating heavily, and had drops running down her face. She wasn't the only one. I wiped my shirtsleeve across my face and, having nothing better, used my other sleeve to pat the drops off Tess's face.

She blinked and gave me a distracted, uncertain smile.

"The Wild West can be a dangerous place," I said.

She nodded. I flicked the reins on the horse's back, and he plodded forward again.

We were over our scare by the time we reached the ranch. After I unhitched the horse and released him to the pasture, I cleaned up at the pump.

When I entered the house, I knew I'd better ask Tess what she'd bought. She'd already unwrapped the seven or eight packages, and had laid out her purchases on the bed. I acted enthused about her wedding dress, her camisole, and shoes. I even made a fuss about her bonnet.

"Would you try it on?" I asked as enthusiastically as I could.

Wearing it, she looked like Grace Kelly in *High Noon*. Only with a more interesting figure.

Now, it was time for me to open my "packages." I ignored

the suit. My packages were in the form of bits and bytes, very small packages. As they say, good things come in small packages. I hoped.

I removed the digital camera from inside the box camera and ejected the memory card. I delayed my gratification by holding the card up between my thumb and index finger to marvel that such a tiny space held so much information.

Tess watched me with amusement. I almost expected her to say, "Boys and their toys!"

She said nothing, just shook her head.

I'd turned on my laptop, and it booted by the time I finished my musings. I inserted the card into the port and quickly transferred the images. My heart rate accelerated as I loaded *PhotoShop*.

I'd taken 146 pictures, and a glance told me most of them were good—well exposed and seemingly in focus. Of course, the ones I wanted to see were those of Earp and Masterson.

I found them quickly, knowing that they were toward the end, and double-clicked one to fill the screen. It was of Bat Masterson sitting alone. I was ecstatic. I smiled as I looked at it, thinking how that one picture alone would wow the Heisenbergs.

Tess watched me, and I knew she saw the joy on my face.

"Looking at pictures of naked women?" she asked.

I scoffed. "I'm a scientist," I said. "Naked women are of no interest to me."

"Oh, no?" she said, looking askance at me as she started unbuttoning her dress.

"No," I said firmly. "No, don't do that. Okay, I lied. But I need to look at these pictures. If you do that, I'll never get to see them."

Her point made, she re-buttoned her dress.

"Okay, what made you smile?" she asked.

"I have the finest picture of Bat Masterson ever taken," I said. "It captures the setting, the rough wall and chairs, and the

351

mix of his personality. You can see the twinkle in his eyes, but you can also see the toughness underlying it."

Tess came to look, resting her hand on my shoulder.

"That's wonderful," she said, and she seemed to mean it.

I knew how valuable these photos were, and I needed to make a copy of them before I risked losing them. I burned a copy of all hundred-and-forty-six of them onto a DVD. Only then did I inspect the others. Every one of the photos of Masterson and Earp was a magnificent, historical treasure.

I made a duplicate of an image that showed Earp's tough glare and Bat's genial smile, and played with the copy. I converted it briefly to black and white, and found the photo took me back to, well, to 1876.

I was so happy with my work that I wanted to share it with my fellow members, and now hostile former friends, at the Heisenberg Project. Since I dared not travel forward to Washington again, I asked Tess where we could get a sheep that weighed about the same as I. She looked at me as if I were crazy, but she listened as I explained my decision to send the sheep back with data attached to it.

Reluctantly, she told me of a sheep farmer about two miles away. She suggested the price might be high.

"Why?" I asked. "I'll only rent it for, well, 268 or so years roundtrip. For all he'll know, I'll return it in a couple of hours, suffering only from jetlag."

"Jetlag?" she asked.

"Oh, a 20th century term," I said. "It's the fatigue a traveler feels from crossing too many time zones."

She didn't seem to understand.

"Simply put," I restarted, "if you took off from New York at four o'clock and landed in Paris eight hours later, your body would think it was still in New York and would act like it was midnight. In Paris, however, it would be about 6 A.M. and everyone would be getting up. Your whole system would be out of whack with the clock in Paris, and you'd feel jetlag."

"Oh," she said, obviously having difficulty grasping that anyone could travel from New York to Paris in eight hours.

"And the sheep wouldn't really have jetlag, but . . ." It wasn't worth explaining further.

Chapter 64

I had to plant an ad in the *Times* so Joey would know to meet the sheep, but that could wait. He wouldn't see the ad for another 134 years anyway, so I could do that after I sent the sheep. In fact, I could place the ad any time in the next 134 years and Joey would see it before the sheep arrived. Joey would have no trouble finding my ad, since I'd learned only two editions from the 1876 *Dodge City Times* were preserved. I just had to put my ads in those editions.

Despite being the world's most experienced Stripper, I still found aspects of time travel confusing. I didn't bother to think about the paradox that Joey already knew what I hadn't yet written.

I got directions from Tess for the location of the nearest sheep owner, climbed onto the wagon, and visited him. I didn't get a warm welcome. Sheep, and, therefore, sheepherders, weren't welcome in the West because the sheep ravaged the land. Cattle, on the other hand, kept moving around and left the land in better condition after they pastured.

The shepherd, a Ty Billings by name, watched me drive up in the wagon. His face didn't say, "Come on in for a cup of coffee."

I explained who I was and tried to act friendly. It didn't work. I'd have an even harder time explaining why I wanted one of his sheep and, so, decided to skip the explanation and just talk money.

Tess guessed a sheep was worth about fifteen dollars. Using that number, I told Billings that I'd pay him two dollars to rent the sheep for up to forty-eight hours, that I would bring it back in the same condition as I got it, and wouldn't shear its wool (which was already gone anyway). To clinch the deal, I told him that I'd give him fifteen dollars to hold as security for the sheep.

"Twenty," he said, the first words he'd spoken to me.

"But it's only worth fifteen," I bluffed.

"Twenty," he said, thrusting his jaw at me.

I gestured with my hands, went through the motions of being a victim of his shrewd bargaining, but I reluctantly agreed.

"But I'm going to bring that sheep back," I argued. "And I'll need my twenty back."

I handed him two silver dollars and a twenty-dollar gold certificate. He inspected them before turning and walking off.

Billings returned a few minutes later leading a pitiful specimen of an animal. I didn't know anything about sheep, but this wasn't his prize animal. I didn't bother to argue. I tied the animal to the back of the wagon, thanked the man, and drove off slowly.

I was happy again. I liked the haggling, and I especially liked letting these people feel they'd gotten the better of me. I kept in mind, however, that I had to walk a thin line to avoid getting a reputation as a fool.

When I got back to SouthFord, Tess was even less impressed with the sheep than I was. "Joey is going to think that we have wretched sheep in Dodge."

"Yes, he will," I said. "And he'll probably reject him and send him right back."

Tess could see I was pleased, and left me so I could get ready for my launch of 'Dolly' into the future. I staked Dolly away from the house, giving her a lot of rope so she could eat well before she left. Upon returning to the house, I recharged the laptop battery. To do so, I had to yank on the spring-loaded cord. And yank. And yank. All the while, I thanked Joey for saving me from having to crank the tiny handle to charge things.

Including breaks to rest, I pulled on the generator cord for almost twenty minutes. I'd planned to build a small windmill to do the cranking, but hadn't solved the technical problems. The first technical problem was that the crank design I expected had ended up being a pull cord. The second was that the windmill had to be out in the open where it would receive a lot of wind, but the laptop had to be sheltered from rain. I needed to think on it more. The effort needed for the laptop battery gave me a lot of incentive to solve those problems.

When the laptop was ready, I played the video I'd taken of Masterson and Earp, and was pleased. The voices were distant but audible. With small adjustments, the Heisenbergs could listen to the lost voices of the two Western icons. In watching the video, I found myself studying Earp as I never dared in person. The video revealed an even more complex and interesting person. Perhaps it was the presence of Masterson, but the Wyatt Earp on the laptop screen was warmer and more approachable.

The pictures of Dodge appeared, upon casual inspection, to be vivid and accurate depictions of the town I now found familiar. Those pictures didn't thrill me as did the Earp/Masterson photos, but they would be interesting to the Heisenbergs.

I wrote a short letter to the Project explaining my vintage camera, the video holster, and my methods of discretely getting the pictures. Of course, I could've sent a picture of my equipment but I'd do that later. I didn't try to explain or justify my unauthorized return to Dodge.

I typed an equally short note to Joey confirming our plan

for transmitting the data and the letter to the project. I also hinted there would be a very special package coming shortly, and that he needed to be especially attentive to my ads.

I burned a DVD of the pictures, video, and letters for transmittal to Washington. I wrapped the disk in newspaper as I walked to the barn.

I confirmed that the CrossChron had a healthy charge, ripped off a few pieces of duct tape, and marched out to Dolly. She looked at me with suspicion. After soothing her, I taped the DVD to her left rear leg. In doing so, I realized I could never have firmly attached it to Dolly if she still had her wooly coat.

With the DVD on board, I strapped the device to Dolly's right rear leg and turned it on. I led Dolly to the launch site, confident the walk would reveal if the DVD or the device weren't attached securely.

I was nervous when we arrived. I wasn't sure why, maybe because this could be the last I'd see of the device. Dolly sensed my tension and got skittish as I hobbled her. I calmed her as best I could before I told her to say hello to Joey for me.

Just as I patted Dolly and reached for the CrossChron, I caught a movement out of the corner of my eye. When I looked up, I saw a cowboy, on his horse, watching Dolly and me from a hundred feet or so away. He wasn't threatening in any way but his presence startled me—I'd neither seen nor heard him approach.

I stood up and faced him, my posture conveying my curiosity about what he wanted. Not intimidated at all, he smiled and, speaking softly, said, "Hi there." He gently urged his horse forward.

"What can I do for you?" I asked, neither friendly nor unfriendly.

"Nothing," he said. "I was just passing by, and you caught my eye. I don't mean to intrude, but do you mind if I ask what you're up to. Just curious, you understand."

I didn't know what to say. My actions were hard enough to

explain, but I blanched as I considered how much harder it would have been if this guy had seen Dolly disappear right before his eyes.

I had to say something, but nothing came to mind. "I'd rather not say," I mumbled. "I don't mean to be unneighborly but . . ." I gave a gesture that I hoped said I didn't think I had to explain myself.

He got the message and nodded his head, then tipped his hat and turned his horse. I watched him amble off toward the southeast until he was at least a quarter mile out. He never looked back.

Relieved to be rid of my audience, I looked around to make sure no one else was watching. Seeing no one, I pressed the buttons with a small stick to start the device and stepped back. Within seconds, the air popped, and the unsettled sheep was in a twenty-first century Washington cemetery.

If he received the 134-year-old ad and everything went well, Joey would find Dolly eating her dinner somewhere inside the cemetery walls. He'd retrieve the DVD and immediately send Dolly back.

Joey would take the DVD to an Internet café and copy its contents, less my note to him, onto a fresh DVD. He would carefully wipe his fingerprints and any DNA from the disk before wrapping it in a mailing envelope, equally wiped clean, for transmittal to the campus.

The Heisenbergs would suspect, even know, Joey was my link to the twenty-first century, but we didn't want to give them proof they could use. We also hoped the data, and their greed for more of it, would deter them from interfering. Even with that hope, the project would surely follow Joey to learn the arrangements. Joey had to be careful.

I returned to the house, hoping I'd find Dolly back in the field within the hour. I was over my anxiety now, and excited that I'd sent back valuable data. I gave Tess a big hug on entering the house and kissed her on the lips.

"Would you marry me on Saturday?" I asked.

"Maybe," she said.

"And then accompany me on a honeymoon trip to Kansas City?"

"Oh," she said. "How could a girl say no to that?"

That evening, we finalized my plan to deposit a small amount of our money with Wright in Dodge, and arrange for the relationship with a Kansas City bank.

Tess was more interested in the wedding than the bank accounts and wanted to invite a few neighbors. While she planned, I, too, had plans. My plan was to arrange for special witnesses to the wedding. I wanted to stun my detractors at the Project.

I hadn't yet solved how I'd take the wedding pictures without giving away my digital camera and video secrets. With both cameras, I needed to keep people at a distance. I'd have to sleep on that problem.

Before sleeping, however, I checked on Dolly. I sighed with relief when I saw her in the distance. She was happily eating grass, seemingly unaffected by her journey. I became nervous again as I approached her, fearing that, perhaps, she never went to the twenty-first century at all.

My fears were unfounded. I could see a folded sheet of paper where the disk had been. The note was in Joey's handwriting. It confirmed the disk arrived and his arrangements for the "special" package on the 24th, whatever that package might be. There was the paradox again—I hadn't yet decided when I'd send the package, but Joey already knew. Okay, it would be the 24th. I laughed to myself at the thought of not placing the ad. Since Joey already knew, how could he unknow it? The Fity paradox again, but the idea was academic. I wasn't about to test the time-space continuum on this matter.

The next morning, I returned Dolly to the disappointed Ty Billings. He didn't even try to act happy to see me. We both knew he would have preferred to keep the twenty dollars.

I ignored his attitude and made a point of thanking him for his kindness. When I offered my hand, his handshake was weak. It seemed that giving back the twenty-dollars had drained all his strength.

As I drove away, he finally spoke. "Why'd you want that sheep anyway?"

I didn't acknowledge the question.

Chapter 65

My previous encounter with the cowboys didn't dissuade me from returning to the south side of the tracks. It did, however, make me more careful when I did. For one, I kept my distance from drunken cowboys. Earp was right that few of them were looking for trouble, but they were young and couldn't handle alcohol. Some of them were naturally mean, and alcohol brought that meanness to the surface.

One day, I was a couple of blocks below the tracks as dusk settled in. I'd long forgotten the confrontation at Tess's place just after I arrived, when the two vigilantes almost shortened my mission, not to say my life along with it. If they'd shot me, dragged me across the prairie, or hung me, it would have ruined my day. Now, weeks later, my mind was on other things. I'd been taking pictures for most of the day, and was ready to pack up my equipment as the light faded, when that dangerous encounter flashed through my mind.

Intent on gathering my equipment, I didn't notice a man approach me. However, when he cocked his gun inches from my ear as I leaned over my plate case, I froze in place.

"I don't see your lady friend," the man said. It was the cretin, Blaine, the young, high-strung thug who wanted to kill me that day. "Who's going to protect you now?" he asked with a mean laugh.

I stopped breathing, and felt my head get light. My blood pressure soared, but the blood still drained from my head. I didn't move at first. When he pushed the muzzle against my temple, I knew I'd have to respond. Spreading my hands in front of me, I stood up slowly and turned to face him. He kept his pistol pointed, now inches from my eye.

I took a deep breath and tried to stay calm. "I'm not a rustler," I said. "And I didn't come near your camp."

I looked him in the eye, trying to sound reasonable, and unthreatening.

"So you say," he said. He seemed at a loss for anything to say.

"As the lady said, do I look like a cow thief?"

"I'd just as soon shoot you as . . ."

His words were interrupted by the sound of boots approaching loudly on the boardwalk from behind me. The man looked nervously over my shoulder.

"Blaine, put your gun away." It was the voice of Cam, the other vigilante.

"We got him now," said the younger man. There was disappointment in his voice.

"Blaine," Cam said with finality in his voice.

Blaine laughed at me again before withdrawing his pistol. He slowly uncocked the hammer before he put it inside his belt.

"I should have killed you as soon as I saw you," he said, resignation in his voice.

I put on a stern face as I turned to face Cam. Although I was starting to shake, I tried to take control. "I see you're still having trouble with this idiot," I said.

Blaine didn't take kindly to my words. "I can still shoot

you," he said. I didn't bother to acknowledge him.

Cam just looked at me. I couldn't read him just then.

"You should take his gun away," I said.

"Look, Mr. . . .?"

"Barrett."

"Mr. Barrett, Blaine's a little jumpy, but he's not going to shoot anyone," he said. Cam was calmer than I was, but that was understandable, considering that I was the one who'd just looked down the barrel of a forty-five. "If he was inclined to kill you, he would've done it already."

"I don't like guns being pointed at me," I said. "And I don't like people accusing me of being a cattle rustler."

Cam nodded his head before speaking.

"I get you," he said as he turned toward Blaine. "Blaine, I think we treated this man wrong. The lady was right—he's not likely to be a rustler."

To my surprise, Cam offered his hand to me. "Sorry about that. It won't happen again."

I was flustered by the development. I didn't expect it. His hand hung there for a moment before I took it. His grip was firm and sincere.

"Accepted," I said. I looked over at Blaine, who looked as confused as I was.

"You still looking to kill me?" I asked.

Cam gave him an order. "Enough, Blaine. That's it. He ain't the one."

"How can you be sure?" Blaine asked, a squeak in his voice.

"I'm sure. Shake his hand. That's it."

I was relieved and tried to give Blaine what I hoped he'd take to be a winning smile. I knew he might still shoot me if he thought I was mocking him.

Blaine shrunk, as he reluctantly offered his hand. He looked into the street and didn't say anything.

"Blaine, Will's my name," I said as I held onto his hand.

He vaguely nodded his whole body in acknowledgement, still looking past me.

"This the end of it?" I asked him.

He shrugged, enough so I let go of his hand. I put my hand on his shoulder. "You can be a pretty intimidating guy when you're pointing a gun."

I didn't want to sound cloying, but I wanted to pass some easy words with him before moving off.

I took his shrug to mean he took my comment as a compliment. I turned to Cam. "You're a big man to admit your mistake."

He brushed my comment away with his hand before directing Blaine to move on. I watched them walk down the boardwalk together, their gait stiff and awkward as if they knew I was watching them.

Much relieved, I returned to my equipment when I noticed a tall, powerful young cowboy on the other side of the street. Out of pure meanness, he blocked the sidewalk, forcing another cowboy into the street. The target was smart enough to give him the sidewalk and use the street. The punk yelled and cursed at the cowboy as he hurried from the scene.

Disappointed that the previous victim declined to fight, the cowboy looked for another confrontation. He cursed, spit on, or even bumped anyone who happened to pass—anything to intimidate.

I watched him search for new victims. Just when it looked as if he'd go back to drinking, he spied a young, well-dressed woman a half block away. He fixated on her like a cat spying a bird. When he surveyed the street and saw what I saw—an empty street—I sensed trouble. I was under an awning across the street, and the cowboy didn't notice me. He could, and would, do what he pleased.

My chest went empty as the young woman continued

toward the man, oblivious to the danger. She kept walking. For a moment, when she slowed to peer into a saloon, I hoped she'd stay there. But she didn't—she continued sauntering on the boardwalk.

The confrontation happened in slow motion. The girl approached the man without noticing him or sensing her peril. He waited. I looked on—and worried. I watched as I would have watched an auto accident about to happen, unable to do anything to stop it. The cardinal rule of the Project was not to interfere with history and I found myself muttering "This happened already. Stay out of it."

However, this could have been Tess coming down the street, walking guilelessly into danger. Why was this girl in this part of town? Why was she alone in the near dark?

Stay out of it, I repeated.

I wasn't responsible for her safety, as I would be for Tess's. Neither the cowboy nor this woman was my concern. I stooped to pick up my tripod, but stood up again, leaving it where it lay, and returned to watching the events developing across the street.

I wanted to reach for my cell phone and call 911. I wanted to run for help, but I wouldn't know where to run. The marshal's office was too far away and I didn't expect to get help in the saloons. I could've yelled to the girl, but the cowboy would have turned his aggression toward me. I did nothing—just watched.

The cowboy looked over his shoulder toward an alley twenty feet or so behind him. He turned and ambled toward it, the young woman now nearing him from behind. She still didn't see the man and approached without hesitation. He paced himself to reach the alley as the girl came even with him. He stepped toward the street to force the girl to the inside. Now noticing him for the first time, she nodded her thanks and started past him.

In a flash, he grabbed her, covered her mouth, and pushed her into the dark alley. She had no chance to yell. The man surveyed the street, as he pushed her ahead of him and, still not seeing me, thought his crime went unseen.

Should I run for help? Where? I hadn't seen a lawman in hours.

Stay out of it, I said repeatedly. My heart drummed in my chest, and I broke out in a cold sweat.

I stood frozen, looking desperately up and down the street for someone—anyone—to come along. I stood there and did nothing.

Stay out of it. Vaguely, I heard a piano playing in one of the saloons, and the murmur of voices reached me through the fog of my panic. The sounds only made me feel more alone and isolated.

I didn't even yell. I felt like a coward, but justified myself with the Project's mantra and the excuse that I'd be powerless against this man.

They were out of sight in the dark alley now, and she was in terrible danger. Every second increased that danger and reduced her chance of escaping his violent intentions. My lunch rose into my throat. Still, I did nothing.

My mind went blank, and I stood unmoving, seemingly for minutes but, actually, it could only have been seconds. Now, without any thought or plan, still telling myself to stay out of it, I found myself striding across the street. My adrenaline increased when I reached the other side. What was I doing?

Even as I strode, I told myself to stay out of it.

What *was* I doing? I couldn't help this girl—but I also couldn't let him rape her.

I didn't slow until I neared the alley. When I mounted the sidewalk, I peered into the darkness. When I couldn't see them, I thought the cowboy might have dragged her down the alley and out the back. I was about to jump between the buildings when I heard the man speak in a hoarse whisper. He pressed the girl against the wall, not fifteen feet from me.

"Okay, let's see what you've got," he said. He pointed a knife into the soft skin under her chin. He had her pinned against the wall—his leg and hip against her body. His dirty hand crushed her mouth. The girl was quietly crying, her eyes wide with terror. Even in the darkness, I saw she was no more than eighteen years old.

I stood in the alley entrance, no more than three paces from them.

"Oh, Abigail," I said loudly, "there you are."

I startled the man.

My voice was surprisingly calm. I even added a light tone to my words.

The man glowered at me, his eyes as threatening as the knife. He turned and feinted toward me as he worked out how to attack me without losing the girl. I held my ground, forcing him to make a move.

"Abigail," I said, my voice still firm, "Officer Earp was asking about you. He's coming to see you."

I turned to look up the street. The thug froze, his eyes showing uncertainty.

"Here, he comes now," I said. "Officer, officer, over here," I shouted as convincingly as I could. I waved him over. I was waving to an empty street of course, but the man couldn't see that.

"Abigail, come out here now, and say hello to Officer Earp."

The man's eyes darted between the girl and me. Had I overacted? He didn't move for what seemed like seconds but was probably far shorter. If he waited another second or two and called my bluff, I'd become his second victim.

"Hey, officer, over here," I looked up the sidewalk. I spoke as if Earp were nearly to me.

I heard shuffling to my right and, when I looked into the alley again, the thug was running away, already disappearing into the gloom. I took a deep breath and gathered myself before I stepped from the boards toward the girl.

She slid slowly down the wall until she sat in the dirt, tears running down her cheeks. She was sobbing before I reached her, and she flinched when I touched her arm. She cowered from me.

"It's okay," I said as I stepped back. "It's over now."

She covered her face as she sobbed louder. She didn't hear me. I waited a few feet from her.

When she quieted a bit, I suggested, "Come on, we have to leave."

She looked blankly at me before rising to her feet. She recoiled from my offer to help her. She kept her eyes on the ground, and avoided looking at me as she stifled back more sobbing.

"Thank you, thank you," she said between gasps and chokes. "Thank goodness Officer Earp came along."

I let her recover a few seconds.

"Earp's not here," I said.

She looked at me in confusion.

"Just you and me," I said.

She looked toward the dark street, trying to understand.

"We need to get you home," I said.

She took a deep breath and staggered out of the alley with me. I wanted to help her up onto the sidewalk, but I dared not touch her. As we emerged, she looked up the street.

"Officer Earp?" she asked.

I shook my head. "Just you and me."

She gestured toward Front Street, and I ushered her in that direction. She wasn't crying any more, but she walked slowly, as if in a trance, glancing nervously over her shoulder. I hoped she knew where to go. I kept my distance from her as we walked.

We didn't speak except when she said, "My name's not Abigail. It's Susan."

When we reached Front Street, we stopped at the tracks. Susan scanned the dark, empty street across the way.

"Looking for someone?" I asked.

"Yes," she said. I waited with her.

A few minutes later, I sensed her quicken, and I looked across the tracks to see a middle-aged couple. They looked in every direction, visibly desperate, but unable to see us in the darkness.

"Someone you know?" I asked.

"My parents," she said, relief now in her voice. She stepped carefully through the tracks before running to the couple. They saw her when she was halfway to them and rushed to meet her, concern etched in their faces.

Susan fell into her father's arms when they met. I couldn't hear what was said, but the couple surmised that something bad had happened. Her father looked sharply toward me through the darkness, his body tensing. Susan looked over her shoulder at me, as if for the first time. Her father pushed her aside, and started toward me. Just as he leaned to rush me, Susan put her hand on his chest and said something. He stopped in mid-step.

Her father pointed vaguely toward me. She shook her head, and spoke to him again. Even in the dark, I saw the tension in his face—he wanted to strike out. He looked at Susan, then again at me, his face only gradually losing its anger. When she half turned toward me, and spoke to him again, he raised his hand in what I took to be his reluctant thanks.

They turned and disappeared together into the darkness up Bridge Street.

I stood and watched until they were out of sight, not regretting for a moment that I'd altered history. I took a few deep breaths, turned, and headed back down the street. I hoped that my camera would still be where I'd left it.

When I returned to SouthFord, I scribbled a brief account of the incident. I reported it as if I'd observed the incident and described the rescuer—me—only as a 'well-dressed man.'

When Walter printed the piece in the *Times*, he added a line asking that anyone who recognized the attempted rapist should

369

report him to the marshal's office.

A few days after the article appeared, Earp approached me, holding the article out toward me.

"Yes, Marshal?" I said.

"You saw this?" he asked.

I nodded.

"You can identify this character?"

I nodded again.

"What's he look like?"

"Tall, very young," I said. "If you see a mean-looking teenager who looks dumber than that hitching post, you've got him."

"Fits a lot of the cowboys," he said.

"Not many of them are over six feet tall, and none of them look this dumb—or as mean."

"If you see him again, come get me," Earp said and walked off.

Chapter 66

I wore my new suit to my meeting with Bob Wright. He greeted me cordially and invited me to sit at his desk in the back of his store. I looked around at the Spartan office occupied by this powerful man. The store had two employees, Wright and his clerk. Wright didn't really have an office or even an area of his own, but had taken over the back fifteen feet of the store and kept his desk there.

"What can I do for you?" he asked.

"I understand you hold money for people in town, and I'd like you to hold some for me," I said. "But I need some information first." He nodded politely.

"First, I don't see a safe," I said, more as a question than a statement.

Wright assured me there was a very secure safe behind his desk. Seeing my skepticism, he invited me to inspect it. He pointed toward a squat black safe sitting on the floor. It was a cube about two and a half feet on a side. Although I was underwhelmed, I nodded my satisfaction.

"I also need to know whether you have a relationship with

a bank in Kansas City," I said when I returned to my chair.

Wright was confused and looked at me askance.

"I may be doing some business in Kansas City," I explained, "and might need to make transfers between you and a bank there."

Wright wasn't prepared for the question, but he tried to placate me. "That won't be a problem," he said. "We can arrange that with any established bank there. Just choose your bank, advise the officer there that you may instruct me to secure funds for you, and we'll put arrangements in place. I assure you that Bob Wright is well-known in Kansas City."

"I don't doubt that," I said. His answer was vague, but I wasn't going to get anything more specific.

"Next, do you pay any interest on the money you hold?"

Wright took obvious umbrage at that question. "Look, Mr. ah, ah, . . ."

"Barrett," I said, knowing that he faked misplacing my name to put me in my place.

"Yes, Mr. Barrett," he said, "I don't need your money, and I don't charge you to hold it. If you want to leave money with me, fine. If not, I'm just as happy. But I do *not* pay interest on money sitting in a safe on the floor."

"Of course not," I said. "But, as a businessman, I'm sure you would have asked the same question."

His failure to respond told me he agreed with my assessment.

"If you're willing to do me that favor, I'd like to place three thousand dollars with you. With your permission, I'll tell local merchants I have money with you, and that you'll guarantee any charges I make in their stores. I'm sure they'll check with you."

Wright tried to keep his professional face on, but I could tell the size of the deposit impressed him.

"Will you have that money transferred from Kansas City?" Wright asked.

"No," I said. "I'm prepared to make that deposit now."

He raised his eyebrows, now even more impressed.

"You're carrying $3,000 with you?" he asked.

I nodded. As I did so, I could almost see the visible 'Gulp' as it would be shown in a Saturday morning cartoon show.

"Well," said Wright officiously, "we can put that money into the safe right away."

I guessed the accumulated deposits by locals didn't amount to my three thousand dollars. I'd just become a substantial citizen of Dodge.

"Of course," I said, putting a very serious look on my face, "I would prefer no one know about my deposit. You can notify the merchants that my credit is good, but they don't need to know anything more."

This direction was for show. I knew he would respect my privacy for less than ten minutes after I left the store. For that reason, I'd delayed this deposit until just before Tess and I left for Kansas City. The deposit, and the rumor that I might have more, could attract the wrong type of attention. I hoped Tess and I would be safe for the next forty-eight hours.

"Finally," I asked, "I understand that you hold a mortgage on the Christie property. Could you tell me how much she owes?"

My question caught Wright off guard. He flustered and blinked his eyes rapidly.

"Well, Mr. Barrett," he sputtered, "you must understand that Mrs. Christie is entitled to her privacy."

"Of course, you're right," I agreed. "However, I would like to pay it off, and I need to know what my balance will be after it's paid."

This put Wright in a bind. He wanted to preserve the appearance of protecting confidentiality, however illusory that might be, but he was even more interested in getting the mortgage paid.

"Well," he said gravely after checking some papers on his

shelf, "I cannot disclose the amount owed." He paused and did some calculations on a scrap of paper. "However, I can tell you you'd have $2,574 left in my safe if you made the proposed deposit and directed me to retire the mortgage."

I reversed the calculation and determined that Tess owed $426.

Without committing myself, I said, "And you would give me a receipt, deliver a satisfaction to Mrs. Christie, and satisfy the mortgage of record?"

"Of course," Wright said.

"And you would make sure, before you did so, that the property was in Mrs. Christie's name, and that her title was absolutely clear of any other claims."

"We can arrange that," he assured me.

I reached into my inside coat pocket and pulled out my money. I put it on Wright's desk. "Perhaps, you should count it," I suggested.

Of course, he would count it. My suggestion saved him from having to explain. He handled it well.

"If you wish," he said.

He counted the gold certificates into six different piles, with $500 in each. He nodded as he pulled the piles together into one stack.

"Neville," he said to the clerk, "could you prepare a receipt for $3,000 for Mr. Barrett."

"$3,000?" he asked as if he were hearing the figure for the first time. Of course, he'd eavesdropped on our whole conversation, and would probably spread word about it before Wright had the chance.

"Yes," said Wright, "and also a direction from Mr. Barrett that we pay Mrs. Christie's mortgage out of his funds. Then, go over to Kevin Bridges's office and have him prepare the papers to satisfy the mortgage. Got all that?"

"Yes, sir," he responded. He sounded excited about being

involved in such a big transaction. Apparently, I'd made this a big day for Wright's emporium.

When Neville delivered the receipt, Wright signed it and handed it to me. He handed the money to Neville, advising him that he'd open the safe in a few moments. Neville handed Wright a handwritten statement of my instructions on the mortgage and, after reading it, Wright turned it toward me on the desk. I reviewed the instructions, and signed at the bottom.

Our business concluded, I stood and shook Wright's hand. He all but kowtowed to me. Little did he suspect that, money or no money, I was no more than a hijacker from the twenty-first century who was referred to, in kinder moments, as a Stripper. I felt contempt leaking into my attitude toward him. He was suffering from the illusion that money, no matter how gotten, is a proper measure of a man.

I hiked up the hill behind town to the Union Church and arranged for the minister to perform the ceremony on Saturday. That was easy. Next, I had to convince Earp and Masterson to stand up for us. Since it was approaching noon, I had a fair chance of finding one or the other on the street. I hoped I'd find Bat first.

I found neither of them on the north side of the tracks, and received only the usual cover story from the marshal's office— "They should be in any time now."

I wandered across the tracks into the rougher area of town, remembering my recent adventures there. I didn't expect to have further troubles, but I was wary of the dangers of the sin side of sin city.

I tried the Varieties dance hall first, but no one had seen either of the lawmen. The place was almost empty, but the piano player played tune after tune.

After wandering around the streets for half an hour or so, I was discouraged, and headed to the Alhambra on Front Street. Just as I started up the stairs, Masterson came out. He didn't look good. A few more hours sleep might have put a brighter look on his face.

"Officer," I said. "Will Barrett again."

My insistence on re-introducing myself to him didn't improve his mood. He just looked at me.

"I'd like to ask a favor of you," I said.

He continued staring at me.

"I'm getting married to the widow Christie on Saturday," I said speaking a little too fast. "I don't know many people here, and we'd be honored if you'd be one of the witnesses for us."

Masterson's face took on a quizzical look.

"It'll only take about a half hour," I said, now almost pleading.

When he spoke, he spoke slowly, "When's this going to happen?"

"At ten o'clock," I told him.

"Where?"

"In the plaza," I answered.

Bat didn't say no, but his unspoken assent was reluctant at best.

"Could I ask another favor?"

The bland acquiescence now reverted to the earlier scowl.

"We need one more witness," I said, speaking quickly. "Could you ask Officer Earp to do it, too?"

"Oh," he said. "He's gonna to love this."

I cocked my head, seeking his agreement.

Still dyspeptic, Masterson murmured, "I'll make him. If I have to . . ."

He didn't bother finishing his sentence, and he was already looking down the street.

I wasn't delighted by his lack of enthusiasm, but I owed him thanks. I reached out my hand to him.

"We appreciate this very much," I said.

"Yeah," he replied over his shoulder.

"Saturday at ten on the plaza, okay?" I reminded him.

I picked up the wagon at the stable, and headed west to SouthFord. With only two days before the wedding and our honeymoon, I wanted to charge my equipment and pack my scant wardrobe.

Tess was still floating on her own cloud when I returned. I thought my travels were finished for the day, but Tess ended that illusion—she presented me with six handwritten wedding invitations to deliver to the neighbors.

I reluctantly climbed back on the wagon and made my way as directed, hoping I could find the houses. I found them and returned two hours later.

Since July 24 was the day I'd transmit the special package, Tess and I only had four days to make the trip to Kansas City and back. We wouldn't have much of a honeymoon, since the train ride to K.C. would take a full day each way. Tess didn't seem perturbed by the tight schedule. Since she'd traveled so little lately, she'd forgotten how tiring the train ride would be.

She didn't know why we only had two days in Kansas City, and I didn't bother to explain. It would wait until we arrived there.

Chapter 67

With nothing to do but worry, I spent as much time as I could in Dodge. Somehow, I expected that being married might limit my freedom, and I thought I'd better get my picture taking in while I could.

After a hard day of lugging my equipment around and needing some time out of the sun, I sat on the edge of the sidewalk in the shade, my cameras at my side. I squinted at the activity in the street, and lamented that I was again becoming acclimated to Dodge. I'd fought against falling into that familiarity as I would a cold, knowing I needed a fresh eye to report the experience. Every store, every horse, every person could reward my interest—if I paid attention. Even the wagon ruts in the street were worth studying. By the twenty-first century, they'd pave over Front Street, rename it Wyatt Earp Boulevard, and there'd be nothing more interesting than skid marks.

As I thought of his eponymous boulevard, I saw Earp marching down the street, and studied him as he approached. Watching the man is a little like watching paint dry. Nothing much seems to be happening but, the next thing you know, you're looking at a Rembrandt. Earp had that kind of effect. He walked slowly and did nothing to draw attention, but he had a quality that broadcast energy and competence. The Earp I saw in Dodge was like an emerging star in a Grade B movie, like Marilyn Monroe in *Asphalt Jungle*. Hindsight can distort as much as it gives perspective, and I couldn't be sure I wasn't projecting the future onto this 28-year-old.

I returned my attention to the other people who passed me—watching their expressions, the way they walked, and how they interacted. Whenever I could. I listened to them talk. Distracted by Dodge's ordinary citizens, I lost track of Earp and didn't see him moving my way. He was standing above me when he spoke.

"I ran into a friend of yours," he said, not bothering to look at me. He surveyed the street as he spoke.

"Oh?" I said. What was he talking about? I had no friends in Dodge.

"Queer fellow, I thought," Earp said. "Clothes didn't look right. Nothing looked right."

"Said he was a friend of mine?" I asked.

"Not exactly," he said. "He asked for you around town. Didn't seem to like me asking why."

I didn't speak. I figured Earp knew my questions, and would get around to answering them.

"Told him I didn't think I wanted him in Dodge, that he might want to move on." Saying that, Earp spat into the dust.

I looked up at him.

"Said he was a federal officer and had reason to wanna find you," Earp said, now looking at me for a reaction.

I tried to act surprised, but I didn't fool Earp. He'd already drawn his own conclusions.

"Since he didn't seem inclined to leave," he said slowly, "I thought he might need a place to stay. I gave him accommodations at town expense."

"You threw him in jail?" I asked.

"Wanna visit him?" he asked.

"No, no," I said. I didn't want to sound too interested, but I thought I should ask, "What's going to come of him?"

"Come the morning, I'll give him his badge back, and tell him to get out of town. That okay with you?"

When I nodded, Earp turned to leave. After two steps, however, he half turned and said, "Getting married, huh?" He left without waiting for my confirmation.

I continued sitting on the sidewalk, my mind racing. I knew Earp's visit had a dual purpose—to inform me of the danger *and* to get my reaction. I tried to act as if the information was no more than street gossip to me. I desperately wanted to see this guy, but I feared what he might say in Wyatt's presence that would make things worse. I realize, of course, that my lack of interest in confronting him only made Earp more suspicious.

I counted to a hundred before I hurried to the wagon corral with my cameras. I didn't see Wyatt watching me, but I suspected he was.

I told Tess of my conversation with Earp when I returned to SouthFord. She didn't say anything, but her wide eyes begged me to tell her how nervous she should be.

"I doubt he'll leave," I said. "But I don't think he'll want to mess with Wyatt anymore."

"What's going to happen?" she asked.

"Someone'll tell him where I'm staying," I said. "We better be careful."

I stayed put at SouthFord the next day, looking over my shoulder constantly. Every sound made me flinch. I tried to hide my anxiety from Tess, but I didn't fool her. She came to the door of the barn as I was cleaning inside.

"Maybe Earp scared him away," she said.

"No," I answered. "He's from the Heisenbergs. He didn't

come 134 years to go back empty-handed."

She stood there a minute, watching me. When I didn't speak again, she reluctantly walked away.

After Earp's report, I'd purchased a small Smith & Wesson .38. I kept it tucked into the back of my belt as I worked around the barn.

After lunching with Tess behind the house, I was headed back to the barn when I got a feeling things weren't right. I looked around, but couldn't see whatever it was that had spooked me. The chickens were quiet, but the heat of the day could do that. The barn looked like I'd left it.

But I felt jumpy. Since my stomach was full, it shouldn't have had an empty feeling. I approached the barn door slowly, fearing I wasn't going to like what was inside.

There was nothing unusual when I entered it. I was alone. I returned to the door and looked out, but still saw nothing to explain my unease.

"Anything wrong?" Tess asked from beside the house.

I shook my head. She didn't believe me.

I worked around SouthFord the rest of the day, keeping my back to the barn or the house. I watched. I even walked cautiously into the trees a few times to look for unwelcome guests. Earp had only seen one man, but I'd be surprised if Dolan didn't send a pair of agents. There was no one in the woods, but my fears effectively introduced a third person into SouthFord. And, maybe, a fourth. So far, they were there only in my imagination.

Chapter 68

I didn't sleep well, as I spent the night dwelling on the inevitable confrontation. I wished I'd peeked into the jail when Earp invited me. At least, I could have put a face on the "Ghost of SouthFord Woods." I'd given him a name, but I didn't think there was anything funny about the Ghost.

In the morning, I told Tess I had to go to Dodge and face the issue.

"What if they grab you and try to take you back?" she asked.

"Unless they brought a spare device," I said, "they can't transport me without dragging me back here. And I won't let them do that. Besides, maybe I'm wrong, and they don't know where I am. And they can't get my device on me unless they know where they have to bring me for my return jump."

Tess looked uneasy. I saw that hard "Dust Bowl" look returning, the despairing look that first welcomed me to Dodge. I gave her a hug.

"I'll be all right," I said.

She nodded, unconvinced.

"What if they come here while you're gone?"

"They won't hurt you," I said. "They're after me."

I told Tess to signal me if there was danger. It had to be something simple that would mean nothing to them.

"Drop the window shutter on the south side if anyone's here," I suggested. "I'll park the wagon a ways out and walk in to check before I come in."

She nodded again. I was worried about her, but I didn't think Dolan would send someone who'd hurt Tess.

My ride into Dodge was uneventful. For once, the wide-open prairie was an advantage. There were no trees or rocks for anyone to hide behind. The only cover an ambusher could use in Kansas would be a draw, a shallow ravine, and there were none on my route to town. Despite my confidence that no one could accost me, I was tense all the way. I told myself I'd be even safer when I reached Dodge. Besides being around people, Earp seemed willing to protect me.

When I pulled into the corral, I asked Zach if anyone had been asking for me.

"No," he said. "Expecting someone?"

"Got a lot of friends," I said, laughing. "Never know when one might come by."

"If anyone asks, I'll send them up the street looking for you."

"Do that," I said. I didn't mean it.

I spent the morning taking pictures. My fears made me even more attuned to my surroundings than the photography ever had. I knew many of the people in town now, but not all, and I scrutinized every unfamiliar face I encountered. I knew anyone sent by the Heisenbergs would reveal himself by, like me, noticeably searching the faces of people in the street. Because of my frequent appearance with my camera, no one even noticed me anymore, and my constantly darting eyes no longer drew attention.

Everyone was minding his own business that morning and I started to relax. Just before noon, I stowed my equipment inside the Long Branch door and took a table in the rear after ordering lunch from the bartender. I positioned myself in the corner so I could watch the door.

Despite my precautions, I didn't see Bat Masterson until he pulled up a chair at my table. I looked up sharply when he sat down. I knew I didn't look welcoming and apologized to him.

"Wyatt told me to look out for you," he said. "He seems concerned."

"Why?" I asked stupidly.

"Well, you know he ran that stranger out of town," he said. "Told me the guy may not be the only one asking about you."

"Oh?" I said, cutting my steak.

"What's going on?" Bat asked.

I recited what Wyatt had told me when I was last in town. Bat interrupted me.

"Wyatt told me all that," he said. "Why is someone looking for you?"

I paused with my knife and fork in the air, and looked at Bat.

"I don't know," I said without conviction. "I haven't committed any crimes. I'm not an escaped criminal. I don't have a wife and family back East that need support."

I shrugged as if that was all the possibilities.

"Why didn't you want to face the guy he threw in jail?" Bat asked.

I had no plausible explanation for that. I tried.

"If someone's looking for me," I said, "I didn't want to put a face on my name. Whoever these people are, knowing what I look like would only make it easier."

Bat scratched his forehead while he digested my explanation.

"Didn't you want to ask why he was looking for you?"

"I was hoping Wyatt would do that for me," I said. "He told me the guy resented his interest, but he was pretty much at Wyatt's whim since he was in jail. He might've talked."

Bat searched my face.

"Did Wyatt question him?" I asked.

"Not that I know of," Bat said.

"Has Wyatt seen him again?"

He shrugged, either signaling Wyatt hadn't seen the man or that he didn't know.

Masterson was clearly dissatisfied with my answers, but decided to let it go. Looking down at the table, he nodded his head a few times before he pushed his chair back and got up. He gave me a small salute before walking out.

I didn't resume eating right away, while I reflected on our conversation. Did I know more now than I did before? Did I still have Wyatt's support? Did Wyatt get information from the guy after we spoke?

I needed to find out what I was facing, but, without 'fessing up, I couldn't expect help from Wyatt, Bat, or anyone else.

Chapter 69

I stopped the wagon a few hundred yards from SouthFord after crossing the river, and cautiously approached the house on foot. I was still behind a rise when the house came into view. I breathed easier—the window shutter was still braced up. Although intruders could have stopped Tess from setting the signal, I thought that unlikely.

When I pulled in, Tess was out of the house immediately. Neither of us had to say anything. Our faces told each other that everything was okay. We hugged when I dismounted from the wagon.

"No problems in town?" she asked.

"Only Masterson questioning me," I said.

"And?"

"He knows something's up, but I didn't tell him anything," I said. "I don't know if Earp got anything from the agent before he released him but, if he did, it wasn't enough to expose me. Bat didn't have a clue."

Tess shook her head. I could see the uncertainty was putting her on edge and turning her inward. I didn't want to see the "Dust Bowl" look come back again. However, I didn't know how to bring this to a head.

For lack of anything better to do, I pulled out my computer to download my pictures from the cameras. As it booted, I looked around Tess's modest home and reflected on the incongruity of using a twenty-first century computer in a nineteenth-century sod house with spider webs hanging from the tin roof, and smelling of earth, mold, and mildew. I was glad that the wonder of it all hadn't disappeared. I was so lucky to have gotten this mission.

I scrutinized my pictures, studying the faces just as I had when I watched the people walking the streets of Dodge. Every person was the potential agent, and I was now so obsessed that I didn't exclude the women, even though it wasn't likely Dolan would send a woman into this era. Frontier women had considerable authority in the home, but none on the street.

At first, I saw nothing suspicious and was about to turn my computer off when something nagged at me, something in one of the earlier photos. I searched out the picture and looked at it again. Nothing jumped off the screen at first but, then, I noticed a figure standing in an alleyway where he didn't belong.

I zoomed in on the figure, but couldn't see much. Since he was such a small image, slightly out of focus, and darkened by a shadow, the detail wasn't good. I could tell little beyond that he was a lean male in dark clothes and a gray-looking hat. I backed off the zoom more to reduce the grain, and he returned to looking like a man again instead of clumps of pixels, but it didn't help me see his features.

I switched pictures, hoping I had another shot of the scene. My heart rate increased when I found that the next shot was of the same scene but framed tighter. The man was still inside the right edge. He'd turned his head to his left and was looking out of the frame. His right hand was up, and he seemed to be pointing at me.

That told me three things I didn't want to know. First, he

probably was looking for me. Second, he knew what I looked like.
And, third, he wasn't alone. Aside from that, all I could tell was
that he had a mustache. Not much to go on.

Tess came into the house and hesitated in her tasks.

"What's wrong?" she asked.

"I think I see someone in a couple of the pictures," I said.

I showed her the figure, and could see her trying to make
sense of the pixilated, zoomed-in image.

"Yes," she said slowly, "it does look like he's pointing at
you. Can you show that to Wyatt?"

"No, I have no way of printing it out."

"Couldn't you have the photographer in town do it for
you?"

She didn't understand digital photography and I didn't
bother explaining. There were only two ways to show Earp—by
showing him the image on the laptop screen or by having Micah
Kincaid take a picture of the screen image. I couldn't risk either.

I had another fitful night, deciding whether to hide out at
SouthFord, or to go back to Dodge and seek out my pursuers. By
the morning, I had a plan, however thin it was.

I kissed a worried Tess goodbye and flicked the reins on
the horse. I worked on my plan along the way. I had half of it in
place, but the second, the harder half needed work.

I visited Kincaid as soon as I parked the wagon, leaving my
cameras under a tarp with Zach.

"Can I hire you to take some pictures for me?" I asked
Micah.

"Sure," he agreed. "What do you need?"

I explained that I didn't yet know, but that I might need
him to come at my beckoning and set up quickly for several
pictures.

"Can you have some plates ready?" I asked.

"Why do you need me?" he asked.

"Oh," I said, "just want to compare shots to see how well

I'm doing. I'll pay you well for your time and the prints."

We agreed I'd have a street kid summon him when I needed him.

I walked back to the wagon corral, scanning every shadow and alley for my mustachioed stalker. I felt eyes on me constantly, but didn't know where they were.

Since I was certain someone was watching me, I intended to take zoomed-in shots of every angle from my camera. Even if I didn't actually see the stalker, the camera would and he'd be in a shot. That was plan B. The first half of my plan required me to see him so that I could put Micah's camera to use.

Assuming that Micah got a good picture of the man, one that I could show Earp, what story would I tell Earp to get his help? The story had to be a good one to get him to continue ignoring a federal badge and help me, a newcomer to town, evade arrest, no matter how suspicious the stalker seemed. I'd have to think some more about that. It would have been easy if Earp were just a dumb flatfoot. He wasn't. However, he was independent and courageous and, I hoped, looking for any reasonable basis for helping me. I just had to give him a reasonable story.

I was in Dodge an hour or so when my paranoia intensified. The hairs on the back of my neck raised a little, and I trusted their wisdom. I didn't know what set them off, but it was time to take my zoomed-in panorama. I quickly set up my camera, turned on the video, and slowly turned it in a slow circle so that it faced, however briefly, in every direction. I had a picture of every person on the street.

As soon as I finished, I called a kid over, handed him a couple of pennies and sent him to fetch Micah Kincaid. While I waited, I fiddled with my camera to cover my careful scanning of the scene. Finally, I saw him. He was hiding in the shade of an awning, leaning against a saloon. I avoided making eye contact.

When I saw Kincaid turn the corner, struggling under the weight of his equipment, I left my camera and ran to meet him.

"Look at my camera as I say this," I said. "There's a man against the wall to your right." I pointed toward my camera to pull Kincaid's attention away from the man.

"He's leaning against the wall there, even with us now," I said, still gesturing toward my camera. "Can you set up as if you're going to shoot the saloon door or something but get him in the picture?"

Nervously looking at me, Kincaid said he could.

"Overexpose a couple of stops to make sure we can see him clearly."

I returned to my camera and made a show of talking to Kincaid as he worked. He was no more than twenty feet from the man and, so far, hadn't spooked him. I watched as he took two pictures, never once looking directly at the man. He then looked over at me, gave a small nod, and left.

I, too, moved on, following Micah back toward his studio. I set up a couple of times along the way to slow the Heisenberg down. I stowed my equipment in the wagon, asked Zach to keep an eye on it, and took a back route to Kincaid's.

"What do you have?" I yelled into the dark room.

"Just coming up now," he yelled back.

In a minute, he came out with a wet print.

"Great shot," I said as I looked at the print.

"Someone you know?"

"No," I said. "But he's been asking about me, and I want to show the picture to Officer Earp."

I gave Micah five dollars for his help. That stifled any further questions. I carried the picture away from my body to get it to dry before I reached the marshal's office.

I found Earp there for a change.

"This the guy you jailed?" I asked.

Earp looked at the photo.

"No," he said. "Not him."

Chapter 70

My anxiety increased as our wedding day approached. I felt the world closing in on me, and I feared I'd never reach Saturday without something bad happening. Unfortunately, I was right.

After helping Tess with her laundry, I left her behind the house to clean the barn. As I crossed the yard, my senses sharpened. Something wasn't the same—the chickens weren't dancing around, and the place seemed unusually quiet. The barn door seemed to be open more than I'd left it. I took a deep breath and told myself it was all my imagination. Despite my reassurances to myself, I hesitated a few feet from the barn. I stopped and listened.

"Come on in," said a disembodied voice from the dark of the barn. I didn't recognize the voice, but I knew I wasn't going to like this guy. I stepped forward but stopped again at the door, waiting for my eyes to adjust to the darkness.

In time, I made out a man sitting on a bale of hay to the left of the doorway.

"Come in," he said again. It was an order. I stepped in and

moved to the right. In the tight confines of the barn, we were only about six or seven feet apart.

"Who're you?" I asked.

"Your travel agent," he said.

Since federal agents don't generally have a sense of humor, I surmised the Heisenbergs had sent the twenty-first century equivalent of a bounty hunter.

"I wasn't planning to go anywhere," I said, looking him over. He looked to be in his late thirties, and, to my now-experienced eye, wearing a cowboy costume. This is how I must have looked to Tess when I first arrived. I'd only been in the West for a couple of weeks, but I could see why Earp thought that he looked out of place.

"Someone's already made plans for you," he said. "Where's your CrossChron?"

"Don't know," I said.

That stopped him for a second.

"Does the lady know about your flights of fancy?"

I nodded.

"Then, she'll understand its flight time."

He acted sure of himself, but it was the kind of confidence that betrayed itself.

"Earp told you to move on," I said.

"When the President tells me to do something," he said, "I don't answer to a deputy marshal in a backwater like Dodge City. Earp doesn't tell me what to do."

I'd been right—I didn't like this guy. It was his move and I didn't say anything. My silence made him nervous.

"How about if you go find your plane ticket, and we'll get seats together," he said, gesturing toward the house.

"And if I don't?"

"I don't think you want to fly with a broken leg, do you?"

He stood to make his point. He was bigger than I thought, a good two inches taller than me, and thirty or forty pounds heavier.

I reached into my belt in the back and pulled out the pistol.

"I'm afraid I'm carrying a gun, and guns aren't allowed on flights," I said, pointing it generally at his belly. I stepped back against the far wall to make sure that he couldn't disarm me with a quick movement.

His face showed a flicker of alarm, but he tried to cover it.

"Aha," he said with a false laugh, "you've become a regular gunslinger, huh."

I didn't answer him.

He took a step toward me, but I stopped him with sudden movement of my head.

"Now, Mr. Barrett," he said with his hands out. "I studied you before I jumped, and I talked to a few people about you. You're not a violent man. You didn't fight as a kid, and you never hunted. You're not about to start shooting people just because you're in the Wild West."

Saying that, he started moving toward me. Suddenly, the whole barn erupted with an explosion of noise, light, dust, and smoke. I was so frightened that I almost pulled the trigger of my gun. The bounty hunter fell backwards over the bale of hay he'd been sitting on.

My pulse rate had to be over 200 as I coughed uncontrollably from the dust filling the room. My ears rang, my eyes watered, and my lungs hacked as I tried to see what happened.

Silhouetted in the doorway, I saw a figure pointing a pistol at the bounty hunter. Still behind the hay bale, the intruder got onto his knees, raised his hands, and looked at the gun with terror on his face. His mouth and eyes were wide open.

I could barely hear Tess when she spoke.

"Mr. Barrett may not be about to shoot you," she said softly, "but I'm just dying to kill someone."

She let her words sink in. The bounty hunter said nothing, his eyes full of fear.

Tess continued, "You're a trespasser on my property, and I have every right to kill you. No one would even ask a question."

I could see the man's hands shaking. Mine were none too firm either. In fact, my knees began to shake when Tess spoke again. Her voice was completely under control, and she spoke deliberately and slowly.

"Now, you have three choices as I see it. One, you call my bluff, and I blow a hole through your chest as big as my fist. That's the easiest one for me. Mr. Barrett would help me bury you out on the prairie.

"Two, you could try to leave and tell Officer Earp about all of this. I'm sure he'd be very helpful. But, to save him the trouble, I'd probably put a bullet through your heart before you left the property.

"Finally, you could press some buttons on your toy, return to Washington, and tell your masters you couldn't find Mr. Barrett. If you decided to do that, but changed your mind after you got back, we'd see someone else coming back for Mr. Barrett. So, we'd know. If that happened, I'd kill your replacement, strap his device onto my leg, and find you in Washington. And I would kill you."

She stepped up closer to him, pressed the barrel of the Colt into his eye, and asked him, "Any questions?"

He shook his head.

"Now, decide," she said. She was again the hard woman I first encountered.

The bounty hunter didn't speak for a moment.

"Now," Tess bellowed, causing me and the bounty hunter to jump.

His voice was shaking and barely audible, "I'll go."

"You'll go now," she said. "Stand up."

She pushed him into the yard with the barrel of the gun. The man tottered into the bright sunlight, his legs shaking uncontrollably. His pants were soiled and, for the first time, I noticed the barn smelled of more than horse droppings.

I edged to the door as Tess and the bounty hunter moved away from the barn.

"Go," she said with force, not as loud as she yelled in the barn, but with the authority of a .45 caliber gun backed by a woman who'd use it.

Not taking his eyes off Tess, the man leaned down, raised his pants cuff, and tried to punch the buttons. He failed the first time.

"I'm trying," he said. He was sweating and shaking. He could barely get his words out.

Tess gave him a look that would have stopped a cattle drive.

The man looked down at his device and tried again. I've never seen anyone's hands shake so badly.

This time, he got it right, and he disappeared with a soothing pop. Tess stared for a second or two at the spot where he'd just been, then she dropped the gun, and collapsed to the ground. She was crying uncontrollably by the time I reached her.

I held her. It took five minutes for her to stop wailing. When she did, I helped her up, and half carried her into the house.

When I got her into her bed, I kissed her forehead and said, "My hero."

She hugged my neck but started crying again.

"It's over," I said. "It's over."

I left Tess in bed and went back out into the yard to pick up her pistol. I told her that it was over, but I knew better. The man she'd intimidated back to the twenty-first century wasn't the man in the photograph, which, to me, meant one down and one to go.

I'm generally a good judge of people, and I thought about what happened in the barn and what my reactions were. I was never worried that the man had an accomplice nearby. Everything the man said, and did, indicated he was alone. Even when Tess pushed him out into the yard, he never looked around for help.

I took my usual seat against the barn, rested the Colt in my lap, and thought about what this meant. Since this guy expected me to get my device and leave immediately, that meant he'd leave his accomplice in Dodge with no knowledge of what had occurred at SouthFord. It made no sense that, if the Heisenbergs sent two men, they wouldn't have been at SouthFord together. And, certainly, this guy would never leave his partner in the nineteenth century with no idea I was already gone.

The only conclusion I could reach was that the man spying on me in Dodge was not from the Heisenbergs. He had to be from this century. Since Earp didn't recognize him, he wasn't from Dodge, and he was still in Dodge despite Earp's warning. And he was still looking for me. I didn't know if he was dangerous. I figured I'd find out.

Chapter 71

"Have you ever seen this guy?" I asked, showing Earp one of Kincaid's pictures.

Wyatt gave me his distant look. I waited him out. When he saw he wasn't going to intimidate me into explaining myself, he looked out the window as if something distracted him in the street. We were sitting in the marshal's office, just south of the tracks, and Earp could watch everyone passing on Front Street.

"Maybe," he said.

I took that to be a "yes."

"Know who he is?"

"Said he was just passing through," he said. "On his way to Ellsworth."

I cocked my head in expectancy. Earp spat on the floor.

"Asked him when he planned on leaving," he continued.

He kept looking out the window. Even though I was asking politely, he made it clear he didn't like me interrogating him. I thought I'd better defer to him if I wanted to know more.

"And?"

"Said in a couple of days," Earp said. Every word carried

reluctance, and I feared he was about to stop answering my questions. It was my turn to update him.

"Tess and I ran into some trouble out at SouthFord," I said.

He tilted his head and questioned me with his eyes.

"A guy, not this guy, accosted me in the barn and implied he was going to take me away. I pulled a gun on him, but Tess really did him in. Told him she was itching to kill someone. I think it was the guy you threw in the tank."

I had Earp's attention.

"He left after that, and Tess told him he'd better not come back. If he did, she'd kill him."

"She scared him?" Earp asked, clearly skeptical of what I was telling him.

"Well, she kind of got him focused when she came up behind him and fired her gun by his ear." I paused for effect. "Then, she got firm with him. Maybe you haven't seen that side of Tess, but she's good at it."

"What came of it?"

"He left," I said. "I'm thinking he won't be back."

"So who's the Ellsworth guy?" he asked.

"I'm hoping he was just a hired lookout, looking for me."

Earp got quiet before he addressed the core issue.

"You still haven't told me why anyone's after you."

He turned toward me. He wasn't going to take "I dunno" for an answer.

"He didn't tell me anything, but I owe some money to a bookie in Baltimore. Could be that."

"How much you owe?"

"Wasn't much. It's the principle rather than the money. They want to make an example of me."

"All the way out to Kansas?"

I shrugged. I didn't think I should add too many details.

"Did you offer to repay the money?"

"We didn't really discuss much before Tess intervened," I

said.

"If he came all the way from Baltimore," Earp said, thinking as he spoke, "I doubt that he's going to quit so easily."

"I'd sure like to know what he told the Ellsworth fellow," I suggested. "That might give me a better idea what I'm facing."

"Gambling debt, huh?" Earp asked before walking out.

While Earp and I were exchanging half-truths, Tess was doing some thinking back at SouthFord.

"Will, I've got an idea," she said even before I dismounted from the wagon.

"And your idea is?"

"That man thought he could make you put on the device and return with him."

"Yeah, that was his plan."

"Suppose you couldn't get to the device?"

Her idea was that she would turn over the device to someone with instructions that he or she would relay it on to someone else, until three or four people separated it from me. Then, it would be impossible for any future bounty hunter to make a quick snatch.

"What if someone along the chain asks what the device is or why you're asking them to do this? Or, worse, suppose someone misplaces it?"

Those questions stumped Tess.

"We've got to make sure they can't just take you," she said.

The idea had merit, but I didn't trust the details. Tess returned to her chores, and I thought about her plan as I took care of the horse and wagon.

By the time I finished, I had two possible ideas.

"What do you think of these ideas?" I said. "I could box it up and ask Bob Wright to keep it in his safe."

Tess seemed receptive to that possibility.

"But you have another idea?" she asked.

"Who's our security blanket here?" I asked.

The term confused her.

"How about giving it to our protector—Wyatt Earp?"

"I don't think that's a good idea," she said. "It would only make him ask more questions."

She was right. Both Earp and Masterson already found me a little too strange, and my entrustment of a mysterious package would make it worse.

"What would you think of merging the two ideas, but not letting Earp know he's part of it? I could have Wright place it in the safe with written instructions that he's not give it back to me unless Earp authorized it."

Tess mulled that over, but I could see she was looking for arguments against it.

"That'd mean you could never go back without letting Earp in on the secret," she finally said. "That doesn't seem like a good idea."

We sat in silence for a few moments.

"Come on, Will," Tess said. "You're good at ideas."

"The reason I'm considering involving Earp is to make sure that no bounty hunter could blackmail me into cooperating. If he threatened you, I'd do anything he asked."

"As long as he thought you could get the device, that would work," she said, thinking aloud. "But it wouldn't work if we arranged it so it appeared you were powerless."

Oh, what a tangled web we came up with. We decided I'd entrust the CrossChron to Wright with two sealed envelopes. If both Tess and I asked for it back, he would open envelope one and it would authorize him to return it; if I asked for it without Tess present, he would open up envelope two and find that he couldn't release the package without authorization from Wyatt Earp. Presumably, the bounty hunter wouldn't want Earp involved and would back off when told of the need for his participation.

The only hole that I saw in the plan was that the bounty

hunter could bring a spare CrossChron with him and transport me back without me needing my original device.

Tess grew despondent when I pointed out that possibility.

Chapter 72

For a time, I thought we'd make it to the wedding without further distractions. Not to be, it turned out, although we made it to Friday evening before Dolan injected himself again.

The sun was getting low in the western sky when I heard someone approaching on horseback. I told Tess to stay inside, grabbed my Smith & Wesson, and stepped out the door. The rider cantered slowly into the yard until he was about thirty feet away from me. He was husky and rough looking.

"What do you want?" I said.

He pulled up his horse, and studied me with a smile on his face before speaking. "Now, Mr. Barrett, you know exactly what I want. Why don't we make it easy?"

I held my pistol across my stomach. The man didn't display a gun, but I assumed he had one. Despite the heat, he wore a jacket that would hide any weapon.

"I don't much care what you want," I said. "You're not welcome here. Get off our property."

"Your property?" he asked sardonically. "You've made yourself right at home, haven't you?"

I turned the pistol outward without directly pointing it. The man glanced at the gun, but didn't show any concern.

"Look," he continued when I didn't respond, "I've come a long way—a long time might be more accurate—to get you. I don't intend to return without you. Let's make it easy."

"Another Dolan henchman, huh?"

He shrugged acceptance of my characterization.

I continued, "The last one we sent back with an earache. Maybe, we won't be so soft with you."

"Yeah, he wasn't real pleased about how he was treated. Where is the little lady, by the way?"

"You're dealing with me, not her."

The man sat in the saddle, leaning forward onto the horn. Although his clothes weren't quite right, he looked comfortable on the horse and seemed to think he was in control.

"I'm just here to take you back," he repeated, implying the result was inevitable, and only the manner was in doubt. "If it's not me, it'll be someone else. Dolan's not going to let you stay here and jeopardize the whole project."

I pointed the pistol at him. "Get off our property."

"If I leave, I'll come back or I'll find you somewhere else," he said with tenuous patience. "I'm not going back without you."

CLICK!

We both looked left to the edge of the house. Tess was standing there with a shotgun in her hand. She had just cocked one of the barrels and pointed it at our trespasser. At first, she didn't speak.

Tess got the man's attention, but he tried to regain his control of the situation.

"You're pretty good at—" he started before Tess interrupted.

"You're right," she said. "You're not going back without Will." She stopped, but there was more to come, "You're not going back at all." She walked forward slowly until she was five or six feet away from the man. She pointed the shotgun at his chest the whole time.

"Will, disarm him," she said. I didn't need to imagine how intimidated the man was. She wasn't pointing the gun at me, but she had me scared. As I edged forward, she gave me another order. "Stay on the other side of the horse. If it lurches or he makes any move, I'm going to unload. So duck."

I did as I was told and, with a gesture, indicated for the man to show me where he packed his gun. Without looking away from Tess and the shotgun barrel, the man slowly, very slowly, opened the lapel of his jacket to expose a shoulder holster. I reached up to retrieve the pistol, keeping the horse between the shotgun and me.

When I had the man's pistol, Tess told me to check his ankle for another weapon.

"Nothing, just the CrossChron," I reported. "I can't reach the other side."

"Unstrap the saddlebags and throw them down," Tess instructed me.

"The CrossChron's next," she said. "Unstrap it."

When I had it in my hand, Tess told me to throw it in front of the horse and step away. As soon as I did so, she spun quickly and blasted the device into small pieces, leaving nothing in the dust except a crater. As quickly as she destroyed the CrossChron, she spun back to the man and cocked the remaining hammer. Still wide-eyed and even more frightened, the man fought to keep the horse in place.

"Now, mister," she said evenly, "that settles the return issue. And don't think you're going to get Will's device 'cause we've put it in a safe place where even we can't get it. Will's staying here and, it appears, so are you."

The man didn't say anything. He understood there was nothing to gain challenging an angry woman eager to shoot again.

"I'm inclined to blow your foot off to make sure you don't give us any more trouble," Tess said. She stopped as if she were considering whether to do it or not. "Will, what do you think?"

I was on edge and jumpy from the confrontation and the loud blast. The adrenaline in my blood almost made me tell her to do it but, as the bounty hunters knew, I'm not a violent man.

"If you do that Tess, you're going to hurt the horse," I said after thinking long enough to make an impression on the man. "Maybe I should just get a knife and cut his Achilles tendon."

"We've got to show him we're serious," Tess said. "Or he'll be back."

The man spoke for the first time, "No, Ma'am," he said with a quavering voice, "I won't be back. I promise."

Neither Tess nor I reacted to his promise except to exchange looks. I didn't want to maim the guy, but I thought he could be an ongoing annoyance.

Tess broke the silence, "What's your name?"

"Dave Webb," he said.

"Get off your horse," Tess said.

Webb didn't move.

"*Get* off your horse," she repeated, emphasizing the first word and sharpening her eyes to show she meant it.

I stood back farther, so I wouldn't be caught in the blast if Webb made a false move. Tess moved around in front of the horse to keep the gun on Webb as he dismounted.

Webb held his hands out, his face white with fear.

"Will, check him again to be sure there's no other gun." I pocketed the gun I already held and patted him down.

"That's it," I said.

"On your face," she said. When Webb hesitated, Tess tilted her head and gave him a stern look. He got on his knees and slowly lay down. He was shaking all over now, and I actually felt sorry for him. I wasn't handling the situation much better. If Tess killed or even maimed a helpless man . . .

"Pull off his boots," she directed me. She had moved up closer now and held the gun only a couple of feet from the back of the man's head. She kicked his hat aside.

"Now, take off your pants," she said to Webb.

Moving slowly, he did so. Tess looked at me when she saw the Jockey shorts she'd first seen on me. When she stifled a smile, I knew she wasn't going to shoot him.

Tess moved the barrel to get him on his belly again. She looked at me and bounced her head back and forth, which I took to mean she was just letting time pass.

"Now, Mr. Webb," Tess said after twenty seconds or so, "you've threatened my husband, and I don't take kindly to that. A big part of me says that an accidental twitch of my finger would end this whole matter. You're just an irritating piece of dung to me, and I wouldn't lose any sleep over shooting you."

She let that hang in the air for a while. Despite the life-and-death urgency of what was happening, I found myself smiling about Tess referring to me as her "husband." I quickly replaced the smile with my game face when Tess gestured toward me with the shotgun.

"Will might feel differently, however. He seems to think I should let you go."

Webb seemed to breathe for the first time since he returned to the ground.

"Am I right?" she asked me with a wink.

"Tess," I said, "I don't like the idea of killing, but I don't want to be looking over my shoulder the rest of my life. It might be easier to just . . . you know."

Webb stopped breathing again.

"What do you think, Webb?" she asked.

"I won't be back," he whined. "I promise."

With his face in the dust, Webb couldn't see either one of us. Tess gestured for me to pipe in.

"How about this, Tess—if he really means it and leaves Dodge for good, we could let him go. If he ever bothers us again or if he's even seen around here again, we kill him?"

Tess softened. "I guess we could have Officer Earp keep an eye open for him." I smiled slightly at Tess's words. It was the first time I noticed her pronounce Wyatt's name correctly.

We exchanged looks while we let Webb get his hopes up. After a time, Tess said, "Aw, he's not worth worrying about. I'm just going to kill him."

Webb started sobbing. I felt sorry for him, but I reminded myself that he was a bounty hunter who wanted to destroy my life. I let him sweat for a time before rescuing him. "Tess, let him go this time. I promise that if he's around or bothers us, I won't stop you next time. Is that okay, Webb?"

"Yes," he sobbed.

"But if you make a fool out of me in front of my wife, I might just kill you myself," I said. "Are we clear?"

"Yes," he said, his voice sounding like the dust he was eating.

"Back off, Tess," I said softly. She did. "Now, Webb, I want you to get up very slowly so Tess doesn't get nervous. Okay, now, get on your horse, ride west, and don't stop until you get to the next town. Just follow the railroad track. You understand?"

He stood next to his horse now. He nodded.

"Get on your horse," I said, as if to a child.

"My stuff?" he said, pointing at his boots, clothes, and saddlebags.

I shook my head and pointed toward his saddle. He cast me a pleading look. I pointed at the saddle again. He climbed up and gave me a final pleading look. I pointed toward the west.

"Next town," I said again. "Then, keep going after that. We don't like your kind living close. You understand?"

He was over his gratitude now and glared at me.

"Aw, Tess, maybe you should shoot him," I said.

Webb raised his hand to placate me. "I'm leaving," he said, "and I'll keep going."

I shook my head and pointed west again. Webb kicked his

horse with his stocking feet and set his horse cantering out of the yard. He looked back once to find that Tess still pointed the shotgun at him. He passed around the trees and left our lives.

Tess lowered the shotgun and broke it before releasing the hammer. We were both calm. We were getting better at this.

"I hope this isn't a regular thing," she said.

I shrugged. "I'm not sure Dolan's going to stop. If it happens again, maybe we kill the guy and send the body back to the twenty-first century."

Tess smiled and took a deep breath. "You're all talk, Will Barrett."

Chapter 73

Tess and I awoke early on Saturday morning, our wedding day, to a dark, dreary dawn. Heavy gray clouds hung low in the sky. When Tess looked at me in dismay, I wished I could offer her encouragement, but I had none. We had no choice but to go forward, since we had to be on the train to Kansas City.

Instead of donning our wedding clothes, we packed them into bags, wrapped them with oiled canvas, and stowed them under the wagon seat. I put on work clothes and Tess appeared in her drab calico dress. The look on her face pained me. I wanted this to be a beautiful day, but I was powerless to make it happen.

After loading our bags and my equipment onto the wagon, I stretched an oil slick over them, and we set out for Dodge. I scanned the sky, hoping the rain would hold off until after the ceremony. I winked encouragement to Tess. Her dazzling skin, usually so alive, appeared pale and green in the gloomy light. Even this beacon of my life couldn't overcome the murky background.

We rode in silence, rumbling toward Dodge in the midst of the gray fog, surrounded by one hundred percent humidity. Both of us occasionally glanced to the north where the darkest clouds, sodden with torrential rain, lurked above the invisible horizon.

I could smell the rain as we entered Dodge. Were it not so dark or the mist so thick, we could have seen sheets of rain falling in the low hills to the north. The clock in the plaza showed 9:30. Would it hold off for another forty-five minutes?

We changed into our wedding clothes in stalls in the corral. Tess and I met in the corner of the plaza and made our way to the center. I carried my cameras and Tess had the plate box strap over her shoulder. We both wore long coats over our finery and looked less like the wedding couple than a pair of newly arrived immigrants.

I searched the empty plaza for a solution to my photography problem. I was looking for a kid who knew nothing about cameras to stand next to the camera and trip the shutter when I signaled. My ruse would be exposed if anyone noticed that no one was changing plates.

I set up my cameras as the neighbors started arriving. Tess greeted them warmly and they reciprocated. Everyone ignored the ominous weather, and acted as if they were happy to be standing in the open while a monsoon impended. I shook a few hands, but, for the most part, stood off to the side. I searched in vain for Bat and Wyatt—so far, no sign of them.

Even as I worried about my witnesses, I found my photographer. I saw a little boy, probably nine or ten years old, walking with his parents. I asked the mother if he could trip the camera for me. Her hesitation evaporated when I suggested that he would be "paid" for his labor. I gave her a wink, and she smiled at our conspiracy. She probably expected me to give him a dime, one of those precious "Seated Liberty" silver coins kids saw rarely.

In reply to my question, the boy told me that his name was Teddy.

"Good, Teddy," I said. "All you have to do is push that button whenever I signal you. Want to try it?"

I had the camera aimed and a blank plate in the back. I didn't want anyone to look inside and see the digital camera.

I showed Teddy how to hold the plunger and I stepped into place where the wedding would occur. He waited for my signal, seriousness all over his face. I pushed my left thumb down just as I wanted him to do.

"Get it?" I asked.

He nodded his head vigorously. From what I saw, he seemed to do it perfectly. The only problem I saw was that I'd positioned him on the right side of the camera and the cable release or his hand might block the video camera. I moved him to the left, telling him to make sure that the cable didn't block the lens. He took his position like a soldier. His parents beamed as I encouraged him.

I was satisfied. However, despite the chilled air, I began to sweat as the clock edged, minute-by-minute, closer to ten and there was no sign of my Western legends. In the saturated air, while everyone else was at least "glowing," I was dripping. The minister was, too. He glanced at me for assurance that my witnesses were on their way. I made a face that didn't hearten him.

However, with less than a minute to spare, Masterson and Earp turned the corner onto Front Street and headed toward us. Both were dressed in black over white shirts and wore grim looks. They didn't seem unpleasant, but they left the impression they'd rather be elsewhere. Despite being just the two of them, their march reminded me of the movie depictions of the Earps and Holliday marching toward the Gunfight at the O.K. Corral.

I stepped forward to greet them.

"Thank you for doing this, Officer," I said to Earp, shaking his hand. "And, Bat, thank you for arranging it."

Earp nodded his head, not unkindly, but he looked awkwardly at Masterson as I thanked him.

The minister, mopping his face with his handkerchief, was all pleasantness compared to Bat and Wyatt. He gathered us together, glancing at the sky over our shoulders. We were facing him at a forty-five degree angle to the camera. Suddenly, I remembered the video and ran over to turn it on. I masked what I was doing by fiddling with the large camera's lens as if it needed adjustment.

"Ready, Teddy?" I asked. He nodded.

As I stepped back into position, I noted how truly dazzling Tess looked. Every time I saw this magnificent woman in a different circumstance, she presented a new, and more fascinating, aspect. Today, although so young, she had the look and manner of an English Lady. She stood regally, so self-possessed, so clearly above everyone else. Yet, she deigned me with a modest smile, almost as if I were her equal. I wondered if she could ever see herself as others, and particularly I, saw her.

The ceremony took no more than ten minutes. During that time, I signaled Teddy to take about two dozen pictures. Every time I moved my thumb, he clicked. He was so good that I winked at him, distracting the minister until he saw the object of my approval. I wondered if Teddy got a picture of my face when I learned during the ceremony that Tess's real name was Contessa.

When the minister declared us man and wife, I kissed Tess with passion and whispered in her ear, "I can't wait to get to Kansas City."

The sparkle in her eyes told me she understood.

As we broke our embrace, driving rain crashed against the buildings behind us, drowning out the congratulations of our guests. The rain was only fifty or so yards away. I thanked the minister, shook Bat and Wyatt's hands, and ran for the cameras. I handed Teddy a silver dollar, along with my thanks, as I gathered the equipment together.

Tess and I made it into Mueller's shop as the rain hit. Everyone else had already scurried from the plaza and it was completely empty when I peered out the store window. Tess and I glanced at each other as the rain roared in. The noise was deafening, as the large raindrops crashed down onto the metal rooftop, sounding more like hail than rain.

The plaza was a huge mud puddle within seconds. Small patches of slick, dark mud punctuated the large puddles that reflected the gray sky. Raindrops splashed into the puddles with ferocity, breaking up the reflections. During the height of the storm, we couldn't see the railroad tracks fifteen yards away. The visible world ended less than twenty feet from the store window.

Lightning flashed overhead as the walls and windows vibrated in tune with the thunder. When a lightning bolt flashed to earth close to us, its Ka-Bang and bright flash overwhelmed us. The intensity frightened me to such a level that I hugged Tess so that we might die together. I couldn't imagine the spindly shacks of Dodge surviving the driving wind, the rain, and the lightning. My heart beat as loudly as the thunder while the storm continued to assault us.

Holding Tess was my salvation—she gave me comfort. I leaned over and shouted into her ear.

"If this storm kills me," I said into Tess's ear, "I'll die a happy man, because you're my wife."

Tess actually blushed. It encouraged me, "I'm proud that you're Mrs. Williamson Barrett."

Apparently, Tess couldn't endure the pride and happiness on my face. She blinked her eyes a couple of times before looking down in embarrassment. I wasn't embarrassed. This was the happiest day of my life, and the second Great Flood wasn't going to ruin it. I gave Tess a squeeze and decided dying today wouldn't be the worst thing that could happen.

Of course, we didn't die. And Dodge wasn't blown away or set afire by lightning. Abruptly, the storm passed, as had hundreds before it, and the sun came out.

However, even the brutal Kansas sun couldn't resurrect the plaza before we had to board our train. I told Tess to stay in the store while I got our bags from the wagon.

I returned in ten minutes, my arms and hands burdened with our luggage. My pants were splattered, and my shoes caked, with wet mud. I laid the bags down and planned how I'd stage them, and the camera equipment, to the train platform. I wasn't concerned since we still had forty-five minutes.

We were surveying the plaza when I saw Earp making his way toward us. His head was down, his face blocked by his black sombrero, as he tried to avoid the biggest puddles with little success.

We were, by then, in high spirits—that is, until he spoke to us.

"Someone's been asking about you," he said.

"Asking what?" I asked.

"Don't know," he said. "Someone just told me two strangers asked for you."

Damn that Dolan.

"What'd they look like?" I asked.

"Don't know," he said. "Only heard one seemed dumb, and the other wasn't dressed right."

My heart seized. My only thought was that Dolan was escalating his war against me. Why'd he have to do it on our wedding day?

Seeing my distress, Tess took on her own look of concern. She looked to Earp, seeking assurance from him, but he offered none.

"Still think this is that Baltimore thing?" he asked.

"No," I said, my voice shaking a little. "We're carrying a lot of cash to Kansas City, and word might have gotten out."

"Cash, huh?" he repeated.

His look and words were questions.

I didn't want to dignify his skepticism with a response. Instead, I said, "I want to put it in a safe bank. Wright's safe's okay, but he doesn't pay interest."

He nodded, feigning satisfaction. He left the store,

declaring without turning, "I'll make sure you get on the train."

I had faith in Earp, but suddenly the train platform looked very, very far away.

Chapter 74

After Earp left, Tess turned toward me. "What should we do?" she asked, tension filling her voice.

"We go to Kansas City," I said.

"Maybe, we're better off staying here where the marshal can protect us," she said.

I thought about that.

"Maybe," I said, "but I don't think so. We're pretty isolated out at SouthFord."

Tess watched me with wide-open, unblinking eyes.

"Whoever it is probably doesn't know anything about us getting on the train," I said, thinking aloud. "We'll probably be safe once we've boarded."

"Dolan again?" she asked.

I nodded, but I had an uneasy feeling that the dumb pursuer was Blaine. I couldn't shake the feeling and wondered, if I was right, how Dolan was able to identify my one enemy in Dodge.

Tess and I waited in silence, which gave me time, too much time, to think. I was discouraged that Dolan kept sending people. Maybe Dave Webb was right, that Dolan wasn't going to give up on me. So far, I'd escaped being dragged back to the twenty-first century only because of Tess—and that rankled me. Like any man, I thought of myself as the protector. Instead, Tess had to rescue me—not once but twice. Then, I remembered the vigilante incident when I'd first arrived. She'd saved me three times, not twice.

I was well into working myself into a bad mood when Tess snuggled against me, squeezing my arm and leaning her head against my shoulder. Somehow, despite our history, her gesture made me feel like I could protect her. How could she trust me after twice seeing me intimidated by bounty hunters?

I felt like an imposter, and even the bright sun couldn't lift the clouds of my mood. Tess must have sensed my feelings because she rubbed my arm again and looked up at me.

"We're going to be fine," she said. "You and the marshal can handle them if you have to."

"You think so?" I asked.

"I think so."

What the sun couldn't do, this wonder at my side could. I smiled and rubbed her hand.

Even as I rubbed her hand, I accepted, for the first time, that I would ultimately have to do battle with Dolan. Webb, bless his naked little heart, was right after all. At this moment, considering that we were more than a thousand miles and a hundred-and-thirty-four years apart, I couldn't imagine how the confrontation would be resolved. I patted Tess's hand and returned my thoughts to the present—get on the train safely and fight Armageddon another day.

Chapter 75

Earp's assurance that he'd get us on the train further bolstered my spirits. As we waited, I repeated to Tess what I'd said to myself many times: "I'd rather have Earp as a friend than an enemy."

She nodded, but her face betrayed her agitation. She waited a few minutes before asking me, "When will it end?"

"I don't know," was all I could say.

"Now, he's sending two men," she said, despair in her tone.

"Or Webb again with backup."

"Well," she argued. "They can't make you go back."

She was right about that, but she hadn't seen the obvious. I decided to remind her.

"Yeah," I said. "Earp won't let them drag me away. But the money's really theirs."

"Oh," she said but added hopefully, "but Wyatt wouldn't believe them, would he?"

The lurking predators made the wait agonizing. Instead of looking forward to our honeymoon, Tess and I cowered in a darkened store, left alone with our private demons.

My ongoing fear of project goons now joined with concern for our money. Either way, the cancer of my fears was the cache of money packed under our clothes in the suitcase. We didn't speak much, but our eyes gravitated toward the bag containing the money.

I planned to wait until I heard the train coming before we moved to the platform. I was aware, however, that trains from the east and west met in Dodge at noon. Since they were rarely on time, I might move us out into the open for the wrong train. The late rush to the train wasn't a perfect plan—but it was the best I had.

I heard a train whistle in the distance, and I immediately jumped into action and hefted the bags, hoping it was the right train. I slopped through the hardening mud to the platform. I glanced down the tracks to the west as I mounted the steps. We lucked out—I could see the locomotive chugging brashly toward me, spewing dark smoke from its stack. I retreated across the plaza to get Tess and my camera equipment. As I danced around the puddles, I glanced nervously over my shoulder at the bag, with so much money in it, sitting unattended on the platform. Maybe, I shouldn't have left it there.

Fortunately, the bag was still there when Tess and I returned. As we stepped up onto the platform, I saw Earp watching us from under the awning of the Alhambra. To the right, in front of the Dodge House, Bat seemed to be leisurely walking toward us, only he carried a shotgun instead of his usual cane. His eyes missed nothing.

I wished I'd asked Earp more about the strangers. I couldn't have done anything with the information, but I'd have felt better knowing whether it was Webb and whether his accomplice was Blaine.

As the train slowed into the station, belching steam from under the engine and black smoke from the stack, someone came up behind me.

"Mr. Barrett?"

My heart stopped. I looked at Tess before turning around. Her face paled, her eyes opening with fright.

"You'll need these," the ticket man said, handing me our tickets. I'd paid for them, but hadn't picked them up.

I started breathing again as I took the tickets. I was glad I didn't have my hand on my gun or I might have shot the man.

With the help of a porter, we loaded our bags and camera equipment onto the train and, with one last glance up and down the platform, climbed aboard. My last act before following Tess into the car was to catch Wyatt's eye and salute him. I did the same to Bat as the train started out of the station and chugged past him.

We still weren't safe, but I felt safer than I had in Dodge. For one thing, if the strangers knew I was boarding the train, they wouldn't have been asking about me in town. I patted Tess's leg, and winked at her to reassure her.

The ride to Kansas City was long and tiring. It seemed longer, since, after my patting of Tess's leg, I started thinking about what awaited me when we arrived. Although we hoped to see some of the town, we both had more important things to attend to.

I had no high expectations for Kansas City. I knew, in 1876, the Kansas side was almost non-existent, no more than a ferry port for crossing the Missouri or Kansas rivers. Even Kansas City, Missouri, the only Kansas City of the time, had only about 2400 people, three times the size of Dodge. Of course, its location on the river made it more of a commercial center than Dodge could ever be.

After 14 stops and more than ten hours on the train, we crossed the river on the high trestle spanning the narrow part near Kaw Point. It was almost completely dark, and we could see little of the city as we approached.

We chugged into a more formal train station, a step up from Dodge's platform. After the porter gathered our luggage on his trolley, I asked where we should stay. He suggested the Dixie Hotel as he loaded our bags onto a carriage.

We tried to see as much of K.C. as the faint light permitted. The city had taller buildings and looked more cosmopolitan than Dodge. We found the Dixie to be a surprisingly attractive hotel, and Tess seemed pleased. I hoped it wasn't just because of the hotel.

I advised the desk clerk we'd both need baths. His resistance, after a glancing at the clock, melted when I placed a couple of gold coins on the counter.

Our room was well decorated and roomy. As soon as the door closed, I suggested to Tess she should take advantage of the bath first. She didn't fight me. When a knock came at our door and an announcement that the bath was ready, she reached into her purse and handed me the mystery packets she found at the ranch.

"You might need these," she said before grabbing her robe and following the bellhop down the hallway to the bath. I stepped out the door to watch as the bellhop showed her the room and handed her a key. I returned to our room when I heard the click of Tess locking herself in.

My pulse was elevated and my blood pressure high when Tess returned to our room. She seemed shy as she handed me the key, and I left to take my bath. My state was less anticipation than it was anxiety. Now that the big moment had arrived, I feared that I might not be up to it. I owed Tess more than that.

My anxiety only increased as I bathed, and I found myself drawing out the bath more than it required. My fingertips were shriveling by the time I summoned enough courage to finish my bath and return to the room. I walked down the hallway slowly, trying to be quiet. When I reached our room, I knocked lightly. I heard Tess bound out of bed, unlock the door, and race back to bed. As I reached for the doorknob, I smiled at the thought of Tess bounding and racing—that just wasn't Tess.

When I opened the door, however, I found the same Tess

I'd fallen in love with—my Tess, my beautiful, self-assured Tess. I felt my courage rising when I saw her in bed faintly illuminated by the oil lamp. She was smiling brightly, but she was also blushing, and her eyes and hands were fluttering. She was as nervous as I was! Where was the bold, brazen woman I knew at SouthFord? Where were those wise and knowing looks? Where was that soaring spirit that had so exhilarated me for these past several months?

I found myself standing in the open doorway, beaming with joy at her. The brazen woman, the exhilarating spirit was there, under the covers waiting for me. And it was time for me to get under the covers with her. I closed and locked the door, and took one last look at her before turning down the lamp wick until it flickered and died. I lifted the covers, climbed onto the high bed, touched my hand to the side of Tess's flawless face, and kissed her softly.

Chapter 76

The whistle blew twice, and the train jolted to a start. We were on our way back to Dodge. Although Kansas City was more Paris, Idaho than Paris, France, neither Tess nor I were disappointed. We succeeded in our objectives for coming to the city—I'd deposited the money, and we repeatedly met our other objectives. Although we were both worn out, neither of us left Missouri dispirited.

I studied Tess to confirm she'd enjoyed our honeymoon as much as I did. She looked tired, but she continued to wear a blush and a smile that only comes from experience. And we both had quite an experience.

I wanted to tell Tess about her next trip, but decided to wait until we were home. She was exhausted and needed rest. If I told her now, it might stir her up so she couldn't rest on the way back. It could wait.

A return journey always seems longer, but enduring seven or eight hours on an air-conditioned jet from Europe is different from suffering ten hours on a hot, noisy train crossing Kansas. Even with short naps, the trip back to Dodge seemed far longer than the 134-year trip from Washington to the same Dodge City.

As we crossed the characterless landscape of Kansas, I experienced anxiety attacks. Not performance anxiety as I had in the Dixie, but fear of the unknown. We didn't talk about it, but I knew Tess was as worried as I was about what awaited us in Dodge. I calmed myself with the thoughts that the money was now safe, and that Earp would help to thwart any kidnap attempt. If I knew who the men were, I wouldn't have worried as much. But I didn't know.

We pulled into Dodge just after dark. I imagined assailants lurking in every shadow. Unfortunately, virtually the whole town was in shadows as I stepped off the train first and looked around. The only light oozed reluctantly, along with loud noises, from the dance halls and saloons.

I helped Tess down from the train and glanced around nervously. There was nothing to scare me except my own demons. I left our things with a porter and hurried, with Tess at my side, to retrieve our wagon. Once back at the station, we loaded up the wagon quickly and headed for SouthFord.

The slow trek to the ranch was excruciating. In the dark and with our occasional drowsing, we might have gotten lost. Fortunately, the horse knew the way and kept his steady slow pace in the right direction.

When we arrived at SouthFord, I had barely enough energy to unload the wagon and release the horse. Neither of us had the strength for talk, and I didn't get to tell Tess about her next trip. It could wait until morning.

Chapter 77

Presumably, the sun rose, crisp and bright, at its usual time, and, I surmise, the rooster trumpeted its greetings to the dawn, but neither of us was awake to witness any of that. We slept past ten o'clock and, even then, it took some effort to get up.

The long sleep had rejuvenated me enough to consider asking Tess to join me back in bed. I restrained myself with the thought that we should take baths first, then do it, bathe again, do it again, bathe . . . Well, that's how my thoughts went.

As we ate lunch, I suggested to Tess that she would be taking another trip soon.

"How soon?" she asked wearily.

"Tomorrow," I said apologetically.

"Why?" She slumped as she asked, "I haven't recovered from this one."

I had to dress it up to make it attractive to this tired woman.

"It'll be a short trip," I said. "Well, maybe not short but very brief. Not exactly, but it won't take long. You'll be there in no time."

None of that was exactly correct, and Tess studied me

skeptically.

"What's going on? Why don't you tell me where I'm going?" she asked, adding, "*If* I'm going anywhere."

The last statement was a threat. Wife or no wife, she would make her own decision.

"How would you like to go to Washington?" I asked disingenuously.

"Washington?" she said loudly. "That would take days, and I'm frazzled from a one-day trip to Missouri."

"Twenty-first century Washington," I said.

Her eyes opened wide. She studied my face.

"You'll take the express train," I continued. "Be there before you know it."

"Is that possible?" she asked. Now she was interested.

"There's no reason why you can't go if Dolly and I did it safely. I'll place an ad for Joey to meet you, and he'll care for you while you're there.

"How long would I stay? And what would I do?"

Her excitement confirmed she'd go.

I refrained from telling her that the reason I was sending her was to get her out of the danger in Dodge. I'd had enough of Tess rescuing me, but, more importantly, each incident had put her in mortal danger. I didn't want to risk her life again because of my petty squabbling with Dolan. My guess was she'd be safer in Washington, under Dolan's nose, than in Dodge.

"You need to see certain things," I said. "Like jet planes, movies, television, and just what it's like in 2010. I think you'll need three days. Any longer than that might be overwhelming."

She sat there speechless.

"There's some risk, though," I said. "You might be captured."

Her excitement quickly evaporated. Now, her face showed distress.

"I might never see you again," she said.

I nodded.

"But I wouldn't send you, and risk not seeing you again, if I thought Joey wasn't being very careful."

"Is it painful?" she asked.

"Not at all," I said. "There's almost no feeling at all."

I explained to Tess that she had to go on the twenty-fourth because, although I hadn't yet placed the ad, Joey had seen it and expected her on that date.

"But, if you haven't placed it yet, you could make it any date you want?"

"You would think so," I agreed, "but, for reasons I don't completely understand . . . "

I stopped explaining because I was so at a loss that I couldn't find a way even to state the issue.

"You have to leave on the twenty-fourth," I said.

"That's tomorrow," she said. "Don't I have to pack?"

"No packing," I said. "You go as you are. Joey will get you everything. The only thing you'll carry is a letter from me."

I worried the whole night about Tess's trip, worrying that she'd have a breakdown from the cultural shock. I worried she'd be hurt while in the twenty-first century. I worried the Heisenbergs would seize her. I worried they'd seize the device. I worried.

Unable to sleep, I arose and wrote my letter to Joey. Foregoing the tools of the nineteenth century, I wrote the letter on my laptop for later transfer to a CD.

I suggested the experiences he should give Tess. He wouldn't have to expose her to cars or traffic—she would see them as soon as she arrived. I made a list for him to consider:

- Television, especially instant news from anywhere on the planet

- The airport and, if she could handle it, a flight on a modern jetliner
- A DVD of old Western TV shows, especially *Wyatt Earp*, *Bat Masterson*, and *Gunsmoke*
- A supermarket
- The monuments to Lincoln, Washington, and Jefferson
- A large cruise ship, if he could find one, or an aircraft carrier
- The National Aeronautics and Space Museum
- New York City, probably a good destination for her jet flight
- A major league sports stadium
- The Internet, especially to let her see the *Dodge City Times* archives

There were hundreds of other novelties she'd unavoidably experience—modern bathrooms, microwave food, cell phones, paved highways, and the subway. I mentioned them anyway. I also suggested he take her to a movie.

I didn't know how Joey would get her on a plane without a driver's license or other picture ID, but that was his problem.

All the while I typed, I worried that the hyper stimulation of the modern world would frighten Tess. I wrote to Joey of my concerns, and asked him to protect her and to be sensitive to her emotional state. I knew he would be, but I had to write it anyway.

I suggested he return her on the twenty-seventh and, without wanting to alarm him, wrote that my life would be destroyed if she didn't return safely.

I asked him to report whatever information he had about STRP, although I couldn't imagine he'd have any—unless they'd been in contact with him.

My final words were, "Beware of the Germans." He'd understand.

As I burned the CD, I felt I hadn't said what needed to be

said. I had confidence in my brother, but my dread about sending Tess consumed me. Risking my life was one thing. Risking Dolly, a small issue. But risking the life of this precious woman wasn't, perhaps, reasonable. I consoled myself with the thought that the *possible* dangers of Washington were better than the *certain* dangers of her staying in Dodge.

I returned to bed and spent the next several hours dwelling on how to prepare Tess for the culture shock. For all my fears, I suspected she was more capable of dealing with the experience than I was in sending her into it.

Tess awoke in buoyant spirits, quite in contrast to my nervous fog. While we ate breakfast, I gave her a litany of warnings and advice. The most pressing, aside from interference from STRP, was that the fast pace and crowds would overstress her. If that happened, she might be in no condition for Joey to restore her to 1876. I pictured myself going out to the field day after day for the rest of my life, waiting like the French Lieutenant's woman.

Tess endured my worry without allowing it to quench her excitement.

"I'll be fine," she said, stroking my hand.

"I hope so," I said. "But I don't know how to prepare you for how fast-paced everything is—people rushing about, cars speeding past and blowing their horns, planes thundering overhead.

"The noise will be more than you've ever heard before," I said. "You'll constantly be hearing the equivalent of a train engine blowing off its steam."

"I'll be fine," she repeated.

She understood my biggest fear. "And I'll be back on Wednesday."

"I hope so."

Chapter 78

My arm sore from recharging the CrossChron, Tess and I walked to the field together. We were both uneasy and didn't talk on the way out. Tess was as worried about me as I was about her, but she didn't know how to reassure me. Nothing she said could have helped.

When we arrived at the launch spot, I greeted my rodent friends, trying to sound relaxed. Tess wasn't fooled. I attached the device to her leg, giving her calf a caress after I did so. I turned the device on and pointed out the sequence of buttons she needed to press to activate the CrossChron.

"Nothing will happen for a few seconds. When it activates, you'll feel almost nothing. One second, you'll be looking at me and the next, you'll be in a cemetery in Washington in 2010.

"Are you ready?" I asked, my voice cracking.

She nodded and wiped a tear from my eye before hugging and kissing me.

"I'll be fine," she said.

I looked into her eyes, but couldn't see her clearly through my tears.

I knelt down, appropriate for my adoration of her, but I was there just to trigger the device.

"Goodbye, Tess," I said. "God speed."

I pressed the buttons with a stick, and stepped back.

We looked at each other, grim-faced and silent.

She started to raise her hand to wave, but, before she could finish, she was gone.

The farewell exhausted me and left me too weak to return to the ranch. I laboriously lowered myself to the ground and lay back. I looked up at the sky, the same sky that Tess, I hoped, was seeing in Washington. I tried to think, but I couldn't focus. I felt tired, numb, and very, very alone.

I fell asleep and, the next thing I remember, I stared up at a darkening sky. Night was already approaching, and I had to get back to the ranch before it got dark.

I crawled into bed as soon as I stumbled into the house and didn't wake up until dawn. I felt better, but the house was unbearably quiet, and I was at a loss about what to do. I'd made no plans for my time while Tess was away.

After eating some dry biscuits and a cup of water, I decided to go to Dodge. I needed to get away from the terrible loneliness.

As I hitched up the horse and loaded my camera equipment into the back of the wagon, I felt as if I were eighty years old. I had no energy—I was depressed. The experience was especially difficult for me because I'd always been an upbeat person and rarely suffered down periods. In short, I'd been spoiled. I was soft, and now I'd have to toughen up.

I told myself to act like an adult, but saying it and doing it were two different things. Nonetheless, I got everything ready and flicked the reins at the horse to send him on his way.

The ride to Dodge added to my low spirits. The exciting American West no longer seemed exciting, as I bounced through the bland plain looking at the tail end of a horse. With no help from me, the horse eventually brought us onto Front Street.

The town's activity temporarily revitalized me. The noise, the smell, the horses and wagons in motion, and, especially, the people all reminded me that life went on. Not one of the people I saw walking the streets would have the slightest sympathy about my plight. They would probably have thought there was no reason to be depressed just because my new bride had taken a trip to the future without me.

Zach greeted me as I pulled into the corral.

"You okay?" he asked.

"Just tired," I said. "The trip to Kansas City took a lot out of me."

He gave me a knowing glance, but he looked away to avoid embarrassing me.

I loaded my equipment onto my shoulders, and headed across the tracks to the south side. Although my experiences there hadn't been all been good, I wanted to document it better. If I were killed in the process, that wouldn't have bothered me.

As I walked through the dusty streets, avoiding the freshest horse droppings, I realized I was preparing myself for the possibility I'd never see Tess again. Even though I'd lived my entire life in the twenty-first century, its dangers seemed far more formidable now that Tess was there. The expected dangers of Dodge—the lurking bounty hunters and the possibilities of an armed confrontation—no longer seemed to justify the risk of sending Tess to Washington. I feared Tess would be injured, seized, or even killed. It didn't bother me that I'd be forever trapped in the nineteenth century. I could make do in frontier Kansas, but I couldn't go on without Tess.

I wished I'd committed her to only twenty-four hours in Washington. I wished I hadn't sent her at all. I wished she were with me.

I must have been talking aloud, because people were staring at me and giving me a wide path. I needed to get to work and let Tess enjoy her holiday. I also needed to turn my attention to protecting myself.

So far, I'd documented the buildings of Dodge pretty thoroughly. However, aside from my precious shots of Earp and Masterson, I had few photos of the people. I needed to capture the life of the city—the looks of its people, the movement in the streets, the horses and wagons, the dust they raised.

Just as important, I needed to document the cowboys, and how they acted in town. I had been avoiding them for fear of another incident like the one Earp rescued me from. Now, in my morbid mood, I was less cautious.

I started small, recording the street scenes, trying to see them as I'd seen them the first day I stepped into town. I was far more at ease now, but I still was a twenty-first-century city kid. I had to force myself to focus and renew the freshness of Dodge, to see its foreignness.

I photographed horses at hitching posts, and riders ambling through the streets. I approached cowboys walking on the plank sidewalks and asked them to pose. In every instance, they cooperated.

I set up in locations where there was a lot of traffic and, without asking permission, shot the faces, clothes, and manner of Texans and locals alike. I got pictures of the occasional women who hurried through with their children. I got shots of the other women, too, as they made their way to the saloons.

I went into those same saloons and, more bold than before, I told the bartender my intentions and went about taking pictures as if he couldn't stop me. Unlike Las Vegas casinos, no one in a Dodge saloon cared that I was photographing them, regardless of what they were doing. Of course, most of it was harmless and only mildly shameful—drinking and gambling—but I also managed to get many pictures of men and women doing things in public that would never occur in the twenty-first century. I canvassed the saloons and dancehalls and shot priceless images that showed the different characters each had—characters in the sense of the patrons, and characters in the sense of the mood, ambiance, and furnishings.

In a shabby dancehall just south of the Lady Gay, I came close to dying a hundred years before I was born. I was focusing my camera on a table, with the girls dancing in the background, when I felt a sudden rustling to my left. As chairs crashed to floor, I turned to see two men scrambling to their feet and pulling guns out of their waistbands. My stomach knotted as the fight erupted before me. Standing no more than eight feet apart, the men raised their pistols. Before I could get frightened, they started shooting at each other. I lunged to the floor, landing on someone who was quicker than me. I crawled off him, and tried to press myself into the filth on the floor as the room filled with smoke and the deafening noise of the gunfire, of chairs falling, of women screaming, and of me cursing. I was afraid of getting shot, but I also feared being steps away from a dead man. And one or both of those men would be dead in seconds. Four, five, six shots, maybe more, and their loud reports overwhelmed my thoughts. I lost count in the noise and smoke, and chairs scattering, and women and men screaming.

Oblivious to the shouts around them, the men cursed each other and shuffled noisily around the table, cocking and shooting while keeping the table between them. Bam! Bam! Bam! Everyone else in the room was scattering and diving onto the floor while the two combatants danced around each other, jabbing their guns at each other. Gun smoke filled the room quickly and made it difficult to see what was happening, especially from my vantage point—on my belly and peering through table legs and overturned chairs. I heard the bullets slamming into the walls and shattering windows. I was so close that one of the men stepped on my arm as he circled the table.

To my amazement, neither of the men fell and, when men braver than I yanked their pistols from their hands, neither of them had been hit. Once the shooters were gunless and restrained, I cautiously raised my head and looked around. In my fog of diminishing fear, I saw everyone was getting up from the floor—the bullets had struck *no one.*

The exchange took no more than four or five seconds but seemed far longer than a TV commercial. In that short time, I went from standing upright to lying flat on my stomach and fighting to control my bowels and bladder. Now, in the sudden silence, I took a few deep breaths, breathing in the filth of the floor, and tried to squelch my breakfast from charging out of my mouth. I didn't want to look like the coward I was. I'd heard that men firing wildly rarely hit anything, but I was astonished that these guys, barely a broom's length apart could miss each other with all those bullets.

When the guns were safely away from the duelists, the shooters were released. Instead of being dragged out and turned over to the marshal, they were left standing awkwardly in the middle of the room. The bartender ambled over to them, picking up chairs along the way, took possession of the pistols, and stuck his fist in the face of one of the men. To my further astonishment, he only lectured the men.

"If you ever do that again, Dick," he said, "I'll banish you for the rest of the season. Now, sit down and act like you have brains in your head." Looking to Dick's adversary, the barman shook his head and said, "You can pick up your guns when you leave." He shoved Dick toward his chair. Dick righted the chair timidly and sat down.

Just like that, the incident was over, and the card game resumed as if they'd been hurling insults instead of bullets. The two men didn't look at each other, but kept their eyes down, looking small and stupid. I surveyed the room and, while there was resentment on faces about the shootout, no one left or seemed inclined to get the authorities. As the bartender returned to his place behind the bar, the music and dancing resumed, and the normal rumble of voices picked up.

I blinked a few times, asking myself if this was Hollywood. Did the guns fire blanks? How could two men fire so many shots and not hit each other, or anyone else? As soon as my shaking hands and legs permitted, I gathered my equipment, which was undamaged, and left the dancehall. If I was going to throw up, I wanted to do it outside.

It was hot outside, but it felt cool to me. My clothes were sweat-soaked and I felt alternately hot and cold.

It took me a while to recover. I sat on the edge of the boardwalk a hundred feet or so from the saloon and put my head between my legs. My legs started shaking again as my head cleared, and my breakfast stayed where it belonged. I glanced around, but passersby didn't seem to see my condition or, if any did, they didn't care. I considered loading up and heading back to SouthFord, but I still needed to be around people. Not gun-slinging people maybe, but people.

I also had to stay in Dodge to bait my pursuers into the open before Tess returned. SouthFord was no longer a place of safety but, rather, a convenient place for the bounty hunters to ambush me and take me into custody.

Scanning the street for strangers, and seeing none, I went back to work with my camera.

Chapter 79

Although I was constantly looking over my shoulder, I convinced myself the shootout in the saloon was the biggest excitement I'd face in Dodge that day. I took dozens of pictures of people and details, but I found myself reviewing the incident over and over again. As I got further away from it, I became increasingly pleased that, finally and unexpectedly, I'd witnessed a classic Western gun battle—I had a story to tell my grandchildren (that is, after I told them about my time traveling).

I stopped for lunch in Beatty & Kelley's on North Front Street and found a table near the front. As I ate my steak and potatoes, I made notes about the shootout—the setting, the people in the room, and the jumble I remembered of what happened. If I was to get it right, I had to write the facts down right away, because, in hours, they would be forgotten or distorted. As with photographs of colors, there are the actual colors, the perceived colors, the remembered colors, and the ones that appeared on the film—and all of them are different. My perception of what occurred would surely be different from everyone else's in the room, and it might not reflect the events as they happened, but they were mine, and I wanted to make sure I got them on paper.

I didn't notice B & K's door open and two men walk in. Scribbling my notes, I wasn't aware of them until they stood at my table, one on each side of me. My chest tightened when I looked up and saw them staring down at me.

I looked from one to the other. "Blaine," I blurted out. "What're you doing here?"

One of the men was the cretin vigilante from the incident at SouthFord and the later street encounter. He had a look of satisfaction on his face. Unfortunately, the other man wasn't Cam, his brighter, and more reasonable, partner. Instead, he was a man of medium height, shorter than me but heavier. He also looked pasty, clearly a twenty-first century softy.

Blaine didn't answer me, but the other man spoke in a low voice. "Barrett, it's time to go. Don't make a fuss. Just get up, and walk out with us."

I turned back to Blaine. "I thought we agreed this was over," I said. "You know I didn't steal any cows from you."

In my panic, I was talking nonsense. This had nothing to do with cattle rustling or vigilantism. Blaine didn't respond—he just kept staring at me as he moved his hand toward the gun in his belt. He wasn't about to draw it, but he wanted to make it clear that he was heeled.

"Time to move," the other man said, still speaking quietly.

Despite the quiet discussion, the other patrons in the room could feel the tension, and were watching us. I glanced at them, and saw them as my allies. I also noted the front door was still open as I raised my voice a little.

"Why are you men trying to take me?" I said, my voice a little too high-pitched. "I'm a law-abiding citizen of Dodge, and we have marshals to protect us."

"Move," the heavier man said again.

"Look," I argued, "if you've got any beef with me, let's get Marshal Earp over here and settle it."

"Move," he said. "Move *now*."

Blaine roughly grabbed me under the arm to lift me out of my chair.

"Hey, get your hands off me," I said, almost shouting now. I rose to my feet so I wouldn't be looking up at them.

Kelley, one of the owners of the restaurant, started over.

"What's going on here?" he asked. I didn't get the impression he was out to protect me—he just didn't want his lunch trade disturbed. I turned to him.

"These thugs," I said, gesturing at Blaine and the bounty hunter, "are trying to force me to go with them. Would you get Marshal Earp for me?"

Kelley hesitated a moment. I repeated myself more forcefully, "Get Earp, I said."

He moved away from our table and hurried out the door. Immediately, Blaine and the man grabbed me, kicked my chair out of the way, and started dragging me out. Although I resisted, I was no match for them as they held firm to my upper arms and forced me forward. But I wasn't going to make it easy. I collapsed my legs and made myself a dead weight.

"Help," I shouted. "Someone help me."

Dead weight or not, I was moving inexorably out of the restaurant. In desperation, I reached for Blaine's gun and, in the shuffling and grabbing, managed to pull it from his belt. I couldn't get a grip on it, however, and among the grappling and struggling, it fell to the floor.

Blaine was now punching me at the same time he was trying to retrieve his pistol. As a result, he no longer had a grip on my arm, and I slipped out of the bounty hunter's grip and fell to the floor. It was a melee now—kicking, shuffling, punching—and I was at the bottom of it. As I tried to protect my face, I found the pistol had been kicked in between my knees and chest. Twisting and dodging, kicking out and ducking, I kept control of the gun with my legs and finally managed to get it near my hand.

Although I couldn't get my hand on the grip, I got my thumb on the hammer and managed to cock it.

KA-BAM!! The pistol went off. Somehow, I'd found the trigger and fired. The gun wasn't aimed at anyone, and I have no idea where the bullet flew, but the discharge changed the balance of power.

Blaine stopped kicking and punching me, and stepped back. I don't know what the other man was doing—he was behind me. He was probably kicking at me—but I was momentarily free. I grasped the pistol in my hand and, lying on my back, pointed it generally toward Blaine. He dove out of the way as I recocked the gun and fired again. The bullet put a hole in the ceiling as the restaurant patrons scrambled out of harm's way.

Recocking again, I turned the pistol toward the bounty hunter, but he was nowhere to be seen. Checking nervously for Blaine, I scrambled to my feet, waving the pistol in all directions. When I couldn't find either of my targets, I rushed out the door, lurching sideways and pointing the gun wildly back into the room. In my desperation, I wasn't looking ahead and didn't see it coming—however, just outside the door, I was body-blocked onto the wooden sidewalk. The breath was knocked out of me, and the pistol clattered to the planking.

KA-BAMM!! The pistol discharged as it bounced on the sidewalk, but I only vaguely heard it, as the bounty hunter, who'd apparently exited the restaurant before me, kicked me hard in my shoulder and started pummeling me. I cocooned into a fetal position, covering my head and face as best I could, as the punching and kicking continued.

"Hey, stop that!" someone yelled.

The hunter paused for a moment before one last kick.

"I said stop!" It was Earp's voice, much closer now. I could hear him, and others, running toward us through the dusty street. Horses were neighing and snorting in fear as they pulled at their reins, which were tied to the hitching posts.

By the time Earp arrived, the bounty hunter had run off. Pistol in his hand, Earp leaned down over me, "You okay?"

Still in a fetal position, I nodded my head. Without hesitation, he was upright,\ and ran off in pursuit of the bounty hunter. Kelley rushed over to me and re-asked the question, "You okay?"

I started unfurling when I heard a gunshot down Front Street to the east. Bleeding from my nose and mouth, as well as from cuts on my forehead, I lay back on the boardwalk. People had poured out of the restaurant, and gathered from the street as I fought to catch my breath. I was opening and closing my fingers to see if any were broken when a huge shape rushed out of the restaurant, shoving men and women aside, and barreled into Kelley, sending him sprawling.

Ignoring me, Blaine lunged for his pistol, still lying just a couple of feet from me. Seeing his intentions, which probably included shooting me, I grabbed his booted foot and tried to roll onto it to push him off balance. He'd grabbed his gun while I did that, and I heard the hammer cock. I had just enough time to think I'm dead! I clenched my eyes tightly shut, as I awaited the bullet to my brain.

Still hugging Blaine's boot, I felt him lurch away from me, dragging me as I refused to give up my hold. In the midst of this, the pistol fired, seemingly just feet from my face. The blast deafened me and, I thought, made my heart stop, but I realized I was still alive when I smelled the burnt gunpowder mixed with the leather of Blaine's boot.

I only released Blaine's foot when I felt him being beaten and subdued by Kelley and a couple of other men. I fell back away from them and lay on my back until I started vomiting. After all that had happened, I felt embarrassed to be messing up Kelley's front walk.

I was a mess of vomit, blood, and sweat by the time I finished. I kneeled up to move away from the disgusting puddle on the boards, and crawled over to the wall and leaned my back against it. I spit out the residual vomit from my mouth and wiped my lips with my shirtsleeve. For the first time since the incident started, I surveyed the scene. Blaine lay on his side on the sidewalk, not moving, with three men kneeling on him. The sidewalk and the street were crowded with onlookers, most of them looking back at me.

As things quieted, the gossiping started.

"Isn't that Tess's beau?" someone said.

"They had a fight over the check in the restaurant," someone else added.

"No, I was there," a third man added. "The cowboy and another guy tried to push this guy around."

"Isn't he the photographer?"

"Yeah, that's him. His equipment's still inside."

"Someone should take a picture of him."

All the while, I leaned against the front wall of the restaurant, still breathing hard and starting to feel the pain from the beating. My legs splayed and hands hanging loosely on my thighs, I took deep breaths to compose myself. My eyes were closed, only partially from the punches and kicks.

"Okay, Will, it's time to start talking."

I opened my eyes to see Earp standing over me.

Between panting, I asked, "Did the other guy get away?"

"Not hardly," said Earp.

"You kill him?"

"Didn't need to," Earp explained calmly. "He made it as far as the Dodge House before he decided to shoot it out."

"I only heard one shot," I said, rolling my head.

"Ahh, he fired at me from a mile away," Earp said. "I just kept walking at him, and that was enough. He dropped his gun, and raised his hands."

"You got him in custody?"

"Yeah, I gave him a shot across his head to teach him a

442

lesson."

"Buffaloed him?"

"Yeah, if you want to call it that," Earp said. "Not too hard, you understand. I didn't want to have to drag him to jail. Just enough to knock him down."

"And?" I asked.

"And what?"

"What'd he say? Why was he after me?"

"I'm figuring you're going to tell me that," he said. "Be in my office in five minutes."

With that, Earp headed across the tracks to the jail. Now, what was I going to do?

Chapter 80

I didn't have much time to come up with a story. My five minutes were almost gone by the time Earp closed the door to his office behind him.

I considered skipping the meeting and leaving town. I could claim the tussle so traumatized me that I forgot to go. Yeah, and that would buy me about twenty-four hours, and whatever story I gave then would be even more suspect.

Reluctantly, I got up from the sidewalk and began my death walk to meet with Earp. I had no choice but to tell him the truth. He had no choice but to disbelieve me, and we'd end in a stalemate.

As I approached the jail, I could hear the bounty hunter shouting, but I couldn't hear what he said. When I opened the door, his braying filled the small building. Earp sat at the desk, his feet up on the desktop, and a look of utter fatigue on his face.

"Listen to me, you idiot," the bounty hunter yelled. "I'm Jacob Deacon, and I'm a deputized federal marshal sent by the President of the United States. You are a backwater deputy marshal, and you have no authority to hold me. You will go to federal prison for this. Mark my words. . . ."

Earp gave me a look that said it all—he'd already had enough of Deacon. While I stood at the door, Deacon continued his shouting and threats, making it hard for Earp and me to hear each other.

"He says he's from the future," Earp said, trying to keep his voice even. "Claims you're a time traveler from the twenty-first century, and the President of the United States wants you back."

Earp, understandably, was buying none of it. "I asked him if he'd ever met with President Grant, but he didn't even know who Grant was."

This was my chance. "Now you know what I've been facing. This is the third crazy to come after me—all of them spouting preposterous stories."

Earp shook his head. I thought he was signaling he needed a better explanation from me, until he added, "This guy's certifiable."

"What're you going to do with him?"

"Send him to the loony bin, I guess," he said. "The judge won't pause a minute before sending him on to Topeka. In the meantime, I've got to listen to him. No, I don't. Let's get out of here."

"What about Blaine?" I asked once we were outside.

"Blaine?" he asked.

"The other guy, the dimwitted one."

"He doesn't sound crazy like the other," Earp said. "Just a hired hand, I guess."

"Blaine's had it out for me since he accused me of cattle rustling," I said. "Wanted to shoot me."

"Wonder how Deacon found him," Earp said.

"It's a small town, Marshal. What'll happen to him?"

Earp shrugged. "He's claiming self-defense. Says you reached for his gun and tried to shoot him. Says he had to fight to protect himself."

"Not surprising," I said.

"I'll charge him with assault and battery," Earp said. "He'll get ten days."

"Do you think I'm safe now?" I asked.

"Wouldn't know," he said. "You sure do attract flies. There might be more out there, so you better watch your back. If you need help, call me."

I shook Earp's hand, thanked him, and took my leave.

As I made my way back across the tracks, Earp yelled after me, "Better have Mrs. Christie take care of those cuts."

"Will do," I yelled back. I was going to correct him, that it was Mrs. *Barrett* now, but ah . . .

Chapter 81

Greatly relieved by not having to explain events to Earp, I returned to Beatty & Kelley's restaurant to retrieve my equipment. Only when I entered the restaurant did my heart clutch at the thought that someone might have inspected it while I was away—and discovered my dirty little secret.

Kelley's face showed only concern for me—no hint of either suspicion or curiosity.

"Are you okay, Mr. . . ?" he asked.

"Barrett," I said. "This stuff happens to me all the time."

Kelley didn't know how to take my answer.

Better to aw-shucks him than to joke about the fight. "I'm just sorry about the disturbance. If I'd known this was going to happen, I would have stayed out of your place."

"Friends of yours?" he asked.

"Nah, the tall guy's got it in for me. I've never seen the other guy before."

"Can I get you anything?" he asked. "On the house."

"Thanks, but I don't have much of an appetite."

I left but, content for the time being that no one else was

likely to be stalking me, I returned to my picture taking. I took many close-ups of people. I found every face I focused on to be fascinating, and I had to resist the urge to interview each of them. They all had a story to tell, an interesting story, and no two of them would be the same.

I forced myself to keep shooting pictures, and left the interviewing until another time. It reminded me how desperately I wanted to pin Earp down for an in-depth interview. I wanted Bat, too, but he would be easy. He loved talking and telling stories. I could get him any time. Earp would be a challenge, but, braver now, I was willing to meet that challenge.

I smiled to myself at what I'd probably get from him if he ever agreed— "Yup," "nope," "don't know," "don't remember," and, probably an occasional, "that's none of your business." I laughed because I wasn't being cynical—that was the man and that was his manner. I'd have to draw him out.

Before I left town, I witnessed the arrival of a stagecoach. Because of the railroad, stagecoaches arrived in Dodge only once a day. When the Abilene coach came in, it caused a bigger stir than the train. Everyone stopped and watched. They stared at the passengers as if they were celebrities. Few of the gawkers would ever ride in a stagecoach, and they assumed the passengers had to be wealthy to ride in such high style.

Just as the stage left and before the dust even settled, a dray wagon pulled in from the east. It stopped in front of the Long Branch, and the teamster started lugging boxes into Wright's and Hoover's stores. While he did that, the bartender came out from the Long Branch and started unloading his boxes. After some money changed hands, the teamster moved on to other businesses and saloons until his wagon was empty. He spent some time in one of the saloons, re-boarded his wagon, snapped his reins at the two oxen, and sent them slowly back out of town from where they came.

I took dozens of photos of the stage and supply wagon

before they were gone. When the wagon pulled out, leaving a cloud of dust in the air, I felt it was another part of the Old West disappearing into the past.

Even as I worked, Tess's safety weighed heavily on my mind. I thought about her while I was dragging my equipment over the deadline into the south side of town. I thought about her when I photographed cowboys on the street and drunks in the saloons. I thought of her as I framed prostitutes returning from their cribs with their satisfied clients. I even thought about her when bullets were flying by my ears.

I thought of her as I made my way back to Zach's corral and dropped my equipment off with Zach.

"Watch this for a while, would you?" I asked. I left, still thinking about Tess.

I made my way to the *Dodge City Times*. I found Lloyd there, my preferred owner/editor, hard at work. Although he'd hired me, it'd been a few weeks and I didn't expect him to recognize me. I re-introduced myself and reminded him of his willingness to have me do occasional pieces for him.

"Need a filler?" I asked.

"Always need fillers," he said. "What do you have for me?"

I had nothing but my imagination and the benefit of 134 years of hindsight. I almost asked to use a typewriter again, forgetting again that he'd have no idea what it was.

"Can I borrow a pencil and some paper?"

He reached behind himself and handed me both. I pointed the paper toward a small table.

"Sure," he said. "You can use that."

He seemed skeptical of my apparent intention to sit down and write my piece. I thought it best to ignore his look—better to answer it with a creditable essay.

That was the hard part. I didn't have anything in mind. Now, I would have to write something.

"How long a piece do you want?" I asked, knowing the weekly paper was slim, perhaps comprising no more than 4,000 words total, and half of that came in by the train with canned stories many of the frontier newspapers used to fill their editions. The *Times* produced only two pages locally.

"A couple of hundred words would work just fine," Lloyd answered.

The American Myth

Through clouds of dust, prosperity and history are driving toward Dodge. With each herd reaching us from Texas, our city gains greater importance in the cattle trade. The stage arrives daily and the supply wagon several times a week. Trains arrive and depart from the East and the West. However, it is the cattle that make Dodge what it is.

Our fair city is only four years old, but it has already had an impact. The cattle drives that formerly poured into the eastern part of our state now are all headed for Dodge. Unless the legislature extends its quarantine of Texas cattle to the whole state, Dodge will be the queen of the cattle for years to come.

Of course, the railroad will eventually extend its tentacles into Texas and, when it does, the cattle drives will stop. Dodge will have to find a new industry. Just as the buffalo trade dried up a couple of years ago, the cattle now in, around, and on their way to Dodge will disappear. They will head east directly from Texas, riding in the comfort of rail cars all the way. We will no longer have Texans dropping their loose change in our noble establishments.

Before that occurs, however, Dodge will handle millions (yes, millions) of head of cattle and our town will prosper. Enjoy it while it's here.

When the cattle are gone, when foreign cowboys no longer invade Front Street, and when our saloons and dancehalls no longer are open 24 hours a day, Dodge will lose its prosperity. However, it will still have its legacy. It will be the legacy of The Queen of Cow Towns and Sin City. It will also be the legacy of an era, an era that will come to represent America. History books, and legends, will remember Dodge City, as a central part of the American Epic, a period of hardy settlers, rowdy cowboys, and of almost mythical lawmen. Yes, Larry Deger, Bat Masterson, and Wyatt Earp will be remembered for keeping order in these disorderly times. Likewise, every reader of this column will leave his/her mark, for the pioneering spirit civilized the American West. Maybe not by name, but their legacy will endure.

Lloyd looked it over. Before he was halfway through, I could see he wasn't impressed.

"Legacy? Mythical lawmen?" he snorted, trying to be polite. "Dodge City is just a place for ugly, smelly cattle to leave their droppings. I doubt anyone east of Ellsworth's even heard of us, or ever will. If the Texans get the railroad, we're back to being a watering hole for the Fort, and that'll support only one or two saloons at best."

"You don't think your readers will like it?" I asked. I thought I'd done a good job of imitating the purple prose typical of the Victorian age.

Lloyd was a gentleman by nature, but he was certainly questioning his wisdom in allowing me to write for him. He tried to let me down easily.

"Everyone likes to think he's important," he said. "I understand more than a few residents will puff out their chests and be convinced, despite all evidence, that they, and Dodge, are important. Most will snicker at the idea that Dodge is anything but a backwater, and I'm afraid they may laugh me out of town."

"Will you give it a chance?"

He reluctantly agreed, adding only that he might cut it back a little.

"How much you paying me for it?" I asked.

"Penny a word," he said.

"Is that before or after you cut it?"

My question surprised him, and he looked at me with surprise. I smiled at him and didn't back down.

"That's why you wrote so many words," he laughed. "I'll pay you for the whole piece this time. Next time, you only get what's printed. Deal?"

"Deal," I said. "Give me the pencil back, and I'll give you a news item." I leaned over the table and wrote quickly:

The midday quiet was broken today when two out-of-towners assaulted a patron at Beatty & Kelley's restaurant. After they tried to drag him from his seat, the man resisted and managed to get a pistol from one of the men. The victim got off a shot, but missed his target. When he tried to leave the restaurant, a heavy-set man named Jacob Deacon knocked him to the sidewalk. He escaped further harm when Marshal Wyatt Earp arrived on the scene. After pursuing Deacon to the Dodge House, and being fired upon by the man, Earp buffaloed him, and dragged him to the jail. Returning to the restaurant, Earp collared the other man, a Texas cowboy named Blaine, and locked him up next to Deacon.

In an interview with this reporter, Marshal Earp indicated he would charge Blaine with assault and battery, and seek to have Deacon moved to Topeka, and locked up as insane. In explaining why he thought Deacon needed to be locked up, he said that the man was out of touch with reality and couldn't be released to endanger other citizens of Dodge.

The victim, whose name is not known, suffered minor injuries and refused medical treatment. Kelley, who witnessed the assault, said only that he was glad that no one was more seriously injured.

Lloyd read it over quickly. "Did you just make this up?" he asked.

"No, happened just that way. I saw it myself. Earp or Kelley can verify it." They couldn't comment on Earp's arrest of Blaine, but a little wishful thinking only adds to a good story.

"No charge?" Lloyd asked.

"No charge."

We shook hands. He quickly looked over my essay, estimated its length, and asked me, "Three fifty do it for the fiction part?"

I started out the door with the coins in my pocket, but I turned back before I closed the door.

"Want to bet this three-fifty Dodge won't be famous in a hundred years?"

"Get out of here," he roared good-naturedly.

My few moments of writing and bantering with Lloyd Shinn had briefly distracted me from Tess. Now, my heart was heavy again, as I contemplated what I'd do for the next several days without her. And what I'd do with the rest of my life, too. I was almost in tears by the time I reached Zach's.

"You okay?" he asked again. I was asked that a lot.

I nodded, trying to hide my red eyes.

"Your lovely bride okay?"

Zach was no fool. He knew what mattered to me, and he had to know what was causing my distress.

I tried to laugh it off. "She's fine. Unless she's run off with some cowboy since I left this morning."

Zach studied me before reluctantly accepting my answer.

Chapter 82

I frittered away the next couple of days—I slept a lot, but not well; I took pictures around SouthFord, but not good ones; I ate, but not much. I felt sorry for myself, and I did a very good job of that.

By the time I woke up on Wednesday, the day of Tess's scheduled return, I'd switched back from self-pity to worrying about Tess. I could survive in Dodge and, aside from losing Tess, I could prosper and be happy. I wasn't confident Tess would endure the twenty-first century as well. Even if no calamity befell her, she'd face the challenges of "modern" life every day. In addition, unlike me, she wouldn't have a hefty bank account of borrowed money.

As I raced out to the launch spot, Ground Zero, I beat myself up for sending her. How selfish of me to use the CrossChron to show her what a big man I was. How foolish to risk her, and her safety, because I lacked the ability to protect her in Dodge.

I arrived an hour early, and had time to talk to the prairie dogs and, more importantly, to think. With no trees to shade me and the only wind more a furnace-like blast than a breeze, I shriveled in the heat. I sought relief from the sun by lying down in the tall grass. It offered a degree of shade and a respite from the convection heat. I gazed at the sky and the sometimes elephantine, sometimes dog-like, clouds as they evolved over the plains.

In time, I fell asleep, and I awoke with a start to find the sun off to the west and the winds down. The prairie dogs had grown accustomed to me and were going about their business as if I weren't there. In horror, I realized Tess's arrival time had come and gone. I jumped to my feet and scanned the fields for her—nothing. She must have arrived, failed to see me, and found her way back to SouthFord. I hoped.

Despite the considerable heat, I ran all the way back to the ranch. I yelled expectantly when I was still hundreds of yards away. I yelled louder as I approached the barn, and louder still when I neared the house. I expected to find Tess, radiant as ever, lounging in the bathtub, washing off the Washington grime.

However, she wasn't in the yard. And she wasn't in the house. And she certainly wasn't in the tub. Silence answered my efforts. Echoing silence.

I looked around in panic, my mind not focusing. I ran out to see if the horse and wagon were still there. They were. I looked in the dusty yard for signs of her footprints. Nothing.

I ran into the barn. Not there. I walked back out. And stopped.

This was my worst fear. I tried all kinds of comforting thoughts. I entertained the idea that Joey was late getting her to the cemetery. Or that a fender bender delayed their arrival. Or that Tess begged to stay another day. Or . . . . Or . . . .

I sagged to the ground, splaying my legs, and hanging my head and arms. What had happened to her? Was she safe? Was she hurt? Had the device malfunctioned and sent her to another time or place? Had it killed her?

I had no answers. I also had no Tess. Nevertheless, I

would gladly give her up if I only knew she was safe and happy.

Acceptance takes time, and I wasn't yet ready to let Tess go. I walked out to Ground Zero every day for two weeks. Every day, I waited. To no avail. Each day, my hopes grew dimmer. After two weeks, all hope was gone. As long as she was safe and happy, I was happy, too. But was she safe? Was she happy?

I didn't believe that. Not that I didn't want Tess safe and happy. I did, more than anything else, but I wasn't happy. I wasn't happy without her, and I wasn't happy without knowing her fate.

I lay awake at night, thinking about how I'd imposed myself into her quiet life, turning it upside down. From the beginning, I was a disruption, but I convinced myself I'd make her life better. Now, I knew better. No part of me believed she was better now than before I arrived.

I took inventory of my situation. I lived on a remote ranch that produced no support. I didn't even own the ranch and would never be able to explain where Tess went. I might have to leave SouthFord very soon.

I had a wagon and a five-year-old horse, both in good condition. I had a few chickens and some marginal crops behind the house. I had furniture in the house worth less than the chickens.

Of course, I had resources, both in Dodge and Kansas City. However, maybe, I wouldn't have them for long. If I became a suspect in Tess's disappearance, it might be hard to get to the money.

As my situation became clear, I had to make a plan. I weighed several options, but they all came down to two basic ideas: one, I ride it out at SouthFord and invent a plausible explanation for Tess's disappearance, or, two, disappear myself after retrieving my money. Certainly, the second would convict me of Tess's disappearance, unless it appeared we'd left together. Now, there was an idea worth pursuing.

Over the next week, with nothing better to do, I spent a lot of time thinking. Eventually, my plan came to this—I'd sneak into Dodge late one evening, and find a prostitute that looked vaguely like Tess. Of course, 'vaguely' was the best I could expect. I would pay her enough for her to leave Dodge. She would leave with me, heading east. If I could subtly spread the word that Tess and I were thinking of leaving Dodge for a while, dress my imposter in Tess's clothes, and manage to whisk her onto a train without anyone seeing us, I might get away with it. Then, when I returned several weeks later without Tess, I could confide in a few people that Tess and I had a falling out, and she declined to return to SouthFord with me.

Of course, the plan had holes. First, the whisking onto the train without being exposed would be near impossible. Second, Tess's dedication to the schoolchildren of Dodge was so well known that few would believe she'd let a scoundrel like me make her abandon them. Those were only the obvious holes. The many other defects came to me as I lay awake in the middle of the night, sweating far beyond the call of the summer heat.

My worst fear about the plan, and my greatest hope, would be that Tess would return one day. I'd have to explain her reappearance. However, I'd look forward to that contrivance.

If, instead, I fled with my bank accounts, and then Tess returned, she'd find me gone, and her life ruined again. She'd have a mortgage-free SouthFord, and she'd have her children to teach, but she'd also have the bitter memory of the snake who stole her life, pitched her into the twenty-first century, and then abandoned her without money or means.

No, I couldn't leave. And, no, I dared not try the masquerade. I was running out of ideas. In the end, without a workable plan, I did nothing. I stayed.

To fill my time, I frequented Dodge more. In my despair, I applied myself increasingly to my responsibilities as a STRPer, studying the town as a scientist and not as a tourist. I became even more adept at masking my digital equipment, and at presenting myself as an itinerant photographer.

With my increased presence, it was inevitable I'd encounter Micah Kincaid, and he'd challenge me on my promise to advertise his photo shop on my camera. When the reckoning came, Micah was understandably displeased with me.

"I know about your visits to Dodge while I was away, and I've had a couple of friends watching for you. They told me when you were here."

"A couple of friends?" I asked. That was reassuring— apparently, not all the stalkers were sent by Dolan.

"Yes," he said. "And they reported you were in town one day and took off on the train."

"Oh, yes," I admitted, "but I wasn't trying to avoid you. I'd just gotten married, and my bride and I were leaving for Kansas City for our honeymoon."

Was it possible some of the men Earp had seen were only Kincaid's friends? Hearing that, I was inclined to be magnanimous.

"Micah," I said, "you're right, and I'm wrong. Although I've taken no business from you, and haven't sold a single picture, I did promise to advertise for you on my camera. Here's what I propose: I'll pay you an additional two dollars for breaking my promise, and, in addition, I'll take this camera right over to the sign man and, while you and I wait, pay him to paint anything you like onto the camera."

My response so flustered Micah, he didn't answer. His look evolved into one of skepticism, but I kept a conciliatory smile on my face, even when I realized the foolishness of my offer— Micah was sure to notice the modifications I'd made to the front panel, and would know that any holes in the box would destroy the usefulness of the camera. My hands began to sweat, and I moved away from the camera, hoping to draw his attention from the modifications.

"Well, look," he said, "I don't mean to start a feud with you. You're a good man, I think, and I'm sure you can be trusted. How about if you pay me two dollars, and just make sure the sign's there the next time you come to town?"

To avoid having to shake his hand with my sweaty palm, I reached out and put my arm around his shoulder, wiping the sweat onto his shirt.

"That's very generous of you," I said. "I'm pleased to do business with you."

I paid him the two dollars on the spot and, true to my word and glad to get away, I hauled my equipment to the sign shop. The sign man asked no questions about the unusual condition of the camera, charged me a dollar, and told me not to touch the paint for a couple of hours. I returned to the streets in better spirits with my integrity redeemed—and my imposturing unrevealed. I felt good about myself, even though I was the biggest fraud in the American West. It was the first time in my life that I'd been the biggest anything.

That incident aside, my life passed uneventfully, week after week. Four weeks had elapsed since Tess left and August was giving way to September when the big question came. I didn't expect the question to come from Bat.

"I haven't seen your lovely bride in a while," he said.

"She's fine," I said expansively. "She just got tired of me taking pictures all the time, and is taking care of SouthFord while I disturb the citizens of Dodge."

Bat wasn't convinced, but seemed to want to believe me.

"I passed out that way a couple of weeks ago," he said, "and didn't see her around."

"While I was in town?" I asked. He nodded.

I retorted, "I'll just have to ask her where she goes while the rooster's away."

Bat smiled, and wanted to end the awkward conversation as much as I did, but he didn't believe me. I watched him walk away, knowing this wasn't going to be the end of questions. Bat's problem was that we were friends, and he didn't want to cause me any problem. However, he was also an assistant marshal. I wished I could relieve him of his concerns, but I couldn't.

I accumulated a huge collection of photographs of Dodge. Since I had so much free time, I kept extensive notes about the exact locations of the pictures, the nature of the building, and the names of the owners. I even asked and recorded the names of the individuals I photographed on the street.

My problem was that my well-documented data accumulated in my computer and on backup DVD's. I had no way to transmit the information, except, of course, the linear way—archive it where people of the future would inevitably find it. However, those people had to be twenty-first century people, ones who'd have the technology to access it.

After considerable thought, I recognized that my inability to transmit it "now" was only my problem. The linear transmission would, if planned right, have the disks arrive at the same time as if I had used the device. My problem was that I'd receive no immediate satisfaction that Joey and the Heisenbergs were receiving it. My problem, as I say, not theirs.

As I worked on the problem of sending the data forward a hundred and thirty four years, I hadn't been able to communicate my concerns to Joey, since none of the early August editions of the *Times* survived into the twenty-first century. Now, with the one August edition that did survive about to be published, I had to write him. He might not be able to respond, but he'd know of my situation and my concerns about my beloved wife.

I returned to Dodge and visited Lloyd Shinn.

"Ready to write more inspiring tripe about our Paris on the Arkansas?" he asked, a twinkle in his eye.

461

"No, not today," I said. "I need to place an ad in your next edition. Think of it this way, I'm still writing for you, but this time I'm paying you to publish it."

I passed him my carefully worded communication:

Shipment long overdue. Convey desperate concerns. Please advise situation if possible. Hope you and family are well. Many photos on hand, if anyone interested. My stay here very productive. Missing package my only true concern. Will.

Only Joey would look for my ads, and only he could decipher my message. I placed the ad with little hope, knowing he or the project would have made contact before this, if possible. Something was wrong, and I harbored no hope the ad would make any difference, but I placed it anyway.

Lloyd counted the words. "Thirty-five cents," he said. I reached into my pocket. "Forget it," he said. "I'll take it off your next story."

I thanked him and left.

Chapter 83

After I placed the ad, I visited Ground Zero every day, just in case. I didn't believe I'd hear from Washington, but I couldn't give up hope. Every day, the same result—nothing.

Until one day, a week later, I found the prairie dog village strangely quiet—not one of the rodents was in sight. Then, I saw why—there was a dark dog in the distance. It was a hundred yards away, and barely visible in the tall pale grass. Were he not so dark, I'd never have noticed him. However, he saw me, and watched me intently. Obviously, the prairie dogs knew he was nearby.

I approached the animal, moving slowly to avoid spooking him. My caution was unnecessary, since he didn't seem afraid of me. He was a large dog and, when I got closer, I saw what seemed to be a collar on him. If it was a collar, this dog was from the twenty-first century.

I got within about twenty feet before he grew uneasy. He backed up a little and stepped from side to side. I got down on my haunches, and called to him. He watched me. When I called again, he paused, smelled the ground, and looked at me again. He took two steps toward me and stopped, his ears and eyes alert.

In time, he approached me and I could see, for the first time, that he wore a CrossChron, and that he had something taped to his back. I petted him when he got within range. From the look of him, he'd been in Kansas for a while. He looked scrawny and thirsty. He was as glad to see me as I was to see him.

I was exhilarated. At last, word from the twenty-first century! But I had mixed feelings. My plan had failed—something had happened, and it was more likely something bad than something good.

I removed the device from the dog's leg first and carefully folded it up inside my shirt. Then, I turned my attention to the parcel. It was a hard square envelope taped to his haunch, apparently a CD. I couldn't remove it, since I didn't have a knife to cut the tape away from his hair. It wouldn't do to just yank if off. I had to lead him back to SouthFord with the package attached.

Fortunately, he was friendly and followed me as I started walking. He stayed close all the way back. When we arrived, I led him to the water trough and started pumping water. He didn't need any encouragement and jumped in to drink. I ran into the house and found a knife.

When I returned, he acknowledged me briefly and ignored me as I cut the packet off him. I clasped the CD, knowing it held my fate. Before I could look at it, however, I had to feed Fido. My hands were shaking as I put food next to the trough.

My heart raced as I booted up my laptop. I slipped the disk in before it finished. Just as the computer was fully up, however, I got a warning screen that the battery was almost exhausted. "Battery Critical!! Close all programs and recharge battery immediately!" Just what I needed.

I located my hand generator and yanked it hard and fast.

It'd take at least twenty minutes to charge the battery fully, but I didn't need a full charge. I stopped after ten minutes and booted up again. This time, it was ready.

I clicked on the D: drive and tapped my fingers on the edges of the machine as the CD started spinning. Finally, the drive came up, and displayed two files and a folder. I clicked on the smaller file. Right choice. It was a short message from Joey.

Dear Will,

Sorry about the long delay. Things have gotten complicated here. I'm writing this with the permission of the project.

The short version is the project people followed me to the cemetery and were present when Tess showed up. [She's a gorgeous girl, by the way.] They seized us, but we're both okay. Tess was terrified at first, as was I, but no one mistreated us. They took us into custody and questioned us. We told them what we knew, explaining who Tess is and your efforts to accumulate the data for them. John Dolan was the only one who showed any hostility, explaining that we were both guilty of many violations of federal law.

In general, while not happy with your action (or my part, for that matter), they wanted to reach a resolution. It's taken this long for them to make a proposal. It's set out in one of the other files on the CD. The other CD is a set of photos and videos so that you can see we're all right.

Tess misses you badly and looks

forward to seeing you soon. I hope that
you like "SaTRaP," a dog the Project
picked up from the pound. He's friendly;
we hope he'll eventually find you. If you
are reading this, he did.

I'm sorry about messing things
up. I'm confident we can work
everything out.

Your loyal and loving brother,

Joey

P.S. Tess sends her love.

I was crying as I finished reading the note. It put my
biggest fears to rest—Joey was okay and Tess was safe. Nothing
else mattered.

I switched CDs, and opened the photos and videos. I pored
over each of the dozen or so pictures, zooming in to fill the screen
with Tess's glorious face. She looked content, although I saw, or
hoped I saw, a longing in her eyes. Whether it was longing to
return to Dodge or to return to me, I didn't know.

The video was even better. I heard her voice and felt the
love in her words. It gave me shivers as I listened to her. We
would be together again. I had to keep wiping my eyes as they
filled with tears. I was so happy that I started saying lines that
would make a B-movie director blush, like "God may be in his
heaven, but my Goddess is in Washington, and she'll return to me.
Or I to her."

I didn't bother to read the proposal. Exhausted from my
fears and anxiety, I fell asleep without even turning the laptop off.

I awoke to the crow of the rooster. It was barely light, and
I was stiff and sore from spending the whole night with my head
resting on the table. I'd crushed my arm beneath my head, and it
was so asleep and painful I feared it wouldn't wake up for hours.

Seeing the computer, I remembered the events of yesterday. I came alert, but I was powerless. Literally. The laptop had run down, and the dark gray screen reflected my face with no chance of access until I wore out my still nerve-dead right arm yanking in the electrons. Despite the shooting pain in my arm, I went right to work on the recharging.

I gave it a full twenty minutes of charge before booting up. It came on, but the battery was only thirty percent charged—my session would be short.

I accessed the CD and pulled up the proposal. It was short and business-like:

Mr. Barrett:

In pursuit of your selfish motives, you have done a grave disservice to the project and your country. We have invested billions of dollars and hundreds of thousands of man-hours in the Space Time Research Project with the aim of providing mankind with a valuable storehouse of verified historical data. Your unauthorized use of the only operational device has set the project back many months.

Through dedicated investigation, STRP has broken your unlawful ring and we have taken your co-conspirators into custody. Your brother, Joseph, will undoubtedly be treated very harshly since he, like you, violated the trust of everyone who is committed to this important work. Among the charges he is facing are: grand theft, criminal conspiracy, unauthorized use of a government vehicle, trespass upon a secure government facility, burglary, false personation, misuse of governmental access, electronic interception of classified material, and other serious charges. His potential penalties exceed two hundred years, fines exceeding $500,000, as well as confiscation of his home and bank accounts.

Mrs. Christie, or Mrs. Barrett, as she seems to want to be called, is certainly less culpable in the matter. Nonetheless, she is a prisoner in a federal facility and is facing some of the same charges as your brother. Her exposure is approximately seventy-five years in federal prison.

You may, or may not, be out of our reach. Without wishing to make a pun, time will tell.

As you know, however, we are reasonable men. We are prepared to make some concessions in exchange for your return to Washington, your surrender to federal authorities, and your submission to the charges you will face. As you must understand, you would face essentially the same charges as your brother, but you are likely to be punished more harshly for obvious reasons.

The federal prosecutor handling these cases, as well as the President, has authorized me to make the following proposal to you:

    a. You must return immediately to Washington.

    b. You will surrender immediately upon arrival to the federal marshals who will be present when you arrive.

    c. You will waive counsel and answer all questions asked of

you concerning this matter.

d. You will plead guilty to four (4) federal felonies.

e. You will stipulate to a cumulative sentence in federal prison for a period of 40 years with a minimum period to be served of 35 years.

f. You will make no contact with the press or any other media.

g. You will not disclose the circumstances of your crimes, or of this plea bargain, to any person under penalty of being further charged on the otherwise-waived charges. You would have already admitted all of the facts and circumstances supporting those charges and your admissions would assure your conviction on the re-instated charges.

h. You will forfeit all of your assets.

Considering your age, it is likely that these terms would enable you to look forward to a release during your lifetime and return to a normal life.

In exchange for your compliance, the following would apply:

a. Your brother would plead guilty to one charge of criminal conspiracy and would be sentenced to no more than five years in federal prison.

b. He would pay a fine of $100,000.

c. Mrs. Christie, or, if you wish, Mrs. Barrett, would plead guilty to a misdemeanor of unauthorized possession of governmental property and be released.

d. She would be returned to 1876 Dodge City and be subject to the same non-disclosure that you and your brother would agree to.

e. If either your brother or Mrs. Christie violated the non-disclosure agreement, your brother would face additional charges and you would be treated the same as if you had made the disclosures.

You may signal your acceptance of these terms by transporting yourself immediately back to Washington or by transmitting your acquiescence using the dog now in your possession.

Although a specification of a time deadline is problematic in this matter, your prompt agreement is required if only for the reason that your brother and Mrs. Christie will remain in our custody until we have your satisfactory answer in hand.

Very truly yours,
John Dolan

That son-of-a-bitch. My low opinion of Dolan never included that he'd use blackmail and hostage taking to get his way. If I weren't 134 years away from him, I'd kill him, and take my chances a jury would find the homicide justified.

Even though, as Dolan said, time was an ambiguous issue under the circumstances, I felt pressure to act right away. Layered heavily onto my anger was my anguish over Tess's plight and, to a lesser extent, Joey's. I felt, unreasonably, that every minute I delayed meant another minute in custody, in doubt, and in jeopardy.

I found myself sweating, and my head was a muddle of racing thoughts. I was unable to think clearly. I fought to keep myself under control, but I lost the battle. I was in no condition to make decisions. I'd have to take my time.

I summoned all of my self-control, and turned the computer off. I got up from the table quickly, too quickly, and got dizzy. I leaned down, hands on my knees to keep from passing out. I breathed deeply, and felt a cold sweat taking me over.

When I recovered sufficiently to walk, I left the house to see if Fido, no, I now knew his name to be Satrap, was all right. I found him lying in the yard, but his head came up as soon as I left the house. I checked the trough and found it dry. I ran the pump until there was a few inches of water. Satrap jumped into the trough again and eagerly lapped it up. I concluded that he wasn't the smartest dog since he needed to walk only thirty feet or so to drink from the river.

I returned to the house to get some food for him.

I knew I had all the time I needed to come up with a plan, but the urgency I felt was fogging my mind. I decided to go to Dodge to force myself to deliberate on my next step.

I charged my cameras, loaded them and the rest of my equipment into the wagon, and ambled onto town. Thinking as I drove, my stomach was in a knot, and my mind continued to race with regret about putting Tess in danger. Despite the reassuring pictures Joey sent, I envisioned her in a stark, concrete woman's prison, frightened out of any rational thought. I realized that, although I wasn't in prison, I remained too angry to think clearly. I tried to rid my mind of the disturbing thoughts.

When I reached Dodge, I shouldered my load, and headed down Front Street. I was surprised to find myself approaching

Wyatt Earp. Although I was increasingly at ease with him, I hadn't yet reached the point where he didn't raise my blood pressure. I tried to cover my tension, but felt, as I always felt, that Wyatt sensed my fear, and took some perverse pleasure in it.

I greeted him warmly. He eyed me before replying.

"You're looking better," he said.

"Thanks, feeling better, too," I said. "Did you send Deacon on to Topeka?"

"He's with his own kind now," he said. "By the way, there's talk about your *Times* ad."

"Oh?" I said, buying time to come up with a plausible explanation.

"Shipment?" he asked. "Desperate concerns?"

I shrugged as if there were no story to tell. He gazed at me, but didn't voice a further question.

"I've ordered some camera supplies," I said. "I'm running out, and getting pretty desperate."

I smiled to imply 'that's all there is.'

"You order them in Dodge?" he asked.

"No," I said. "I ordered them from Washington."

"Oh," he said, nodding his head. "Someone in Washington's going to read the *Dodge City Times*, huh?"

Uh-oh, I thought. *Now, that was a stupid lie.*

"Well, yes, as a matter of fact," I said. "Lloyd sends copies east, and I've got someone in Washington who sees it as soon as it arrives. It's an easy way for me to get his attention."

He still didn't believe me, but he left it at that.

"I'd like to get some more pictures of you," I said to change the subject.

This renewed his skepticism. He looked down at his boots, and screwed up his mouth before replying.

"In case *anyone's interested*?" he asked.

I was taken aback again about his scrutiny of my ad. I should've been more careful when writing it. I had only thought in terms of Joey reading it, and ignored the local readership.

"I think you're going to be my fortune," I said. "You're going to be more important than just an assistant marshal in Dodge City. I want to have the pictures of you when you're famous."

"Yeah," he said. He was at a loss for words. He turned, spit on the ground, and walked off.

I needed more pictures of him, but I didn't want to face any further questioning. He was too smart to believe my thin explanations.

As I recovered from my interrogation, I thought about whether Shinn did send some copies east. I knew Earp would ask. However, I turned my thoughts to my immediate problems and the longer term.

I came up with a plan, one that could save Tess and Joey. Not to mention me.

I immersed myself in photo work and spent the rest of my time in Dodge taking pictures and making extensive notes about everything I saw, and everyone I met. Some of the best data I could collect wouldn't be in images.

I also spent hours just absorbing the atmosphere of Dodge. I inhaled deeply, and made mental notes of the smells—the horses, their manure and urine, the alkaline dust, and the people. Oh, the people. I listened to the boots clomping on the wooden sidewalks and shuffling through the deep dust on the streets. I heard the calupping of horse hoofs in the street, and the snorting and whinnying of the impatient horses hitched to the posts. I watched people and saw in their faces a naivety, an innocence of not knowing the future.

I touched the horses and their sleek leather saddles. I looked into the horses' eyes and saw the same innocence I saw in the people. I fingered the boards of the buildings, feeling their rough-sawn texture and primitive paint. I put my hands on the smooth metal doorknobs and latches. I ran my hands over the bars and countertops, tested the texture of the cloth and the clothing in the stores, and I ran my hands through the grain in the barrels. I sat down in the Long Branch, and ate a 25-cent lunch of steak and potatoes, finding myself sensitive to the difference from modern foods. As I sat there, I listened and watched as no man had before. My crisis had focused my senses. Knowing how history would view this period, I had the unique opportunity to swim in its flow and texture, seeing it as it truly was, as well as how we would mythicize it.

I left Dodge in mid-afternoon. I'd had a good day—many photos, pages of notes, and, best of all, I had a plan. Satrap was heading back to Washington.

Chapter 84

Back at SouthFord, I enjoyed the rare luxury of a bath, a treat I felt I'd earned. It made me think of Tess and how much she enjoyed the bathtub, especially when I took pictures of her.

After drying off, I downloaded the day's pictures and video, and transcribed my notes into a long memo. Careful documentation of my work was part of the plan.

I opened up a new Word file and began to write.

Dear Mr. Dolan,

I was disappointed to receive your recent letter. I am sure that I unfairly understood it to constitute an attempt to extort my cooperation. Since you are certainly too honorable to do that, I must have misconstrued your intentions.

With it understood that extortion is not a gentlemanly thing to use, I would like to explain the situation to you. First, I journeyed to 1876 Dodge City on an expensive governmental program with the objective of testing the platform and obtaining data of tremendous historical importance. As we know, I returned to Washington prematurely and had to travel again to Dodge to assure the Project realized the benefit of the tremendous effort and cost already invested in the mission. As you will see from the accompanying material, I have assiduously applied myself to the mission. The data is, I believe, far more detailed and more valuable than we expected. The Project has been justified by this one mission.

Despite my faithful application to my duties, including transporting a person from 1876 to your time for the purposes of providing further data, you have perverted the aims of the Project to your own ambitions. You have deprived the Project's investigators of access to Mrs. Barrett and prevented them from collecting the wealth of information she possesses.

You may think you're immune from disclosure of your corruption. That, fortunately, is not the case. I have, in this eighth month of 1876, established a perpetual trust and funded it with five hundred dollars. The object of this Trust is to preserve history for future generations. Because of my concern that the history is accurate, I carried back with me full documentation of your mendacity, some of it in your own voice. I have placed into the hands of the Trustee a long and detailed account of the Project, its funding, my mission, and, of course, documented your corrupt and vile activities. The trust will endure, through a financial institution that remains in operation in the twenty-first century, through a succession of well-paid Trustees. Right now, in your time, at an institution very close to your office, there is the tenth or eleventh successor Trustee, gathering the material together.

Under the directions I provided, the Trustee will transmit copies of all of my material, including all data and reports, to four major news outlets for dissemination on September 1, 2010. Upon publication of the material and the authentication of the contents, you and I will be major figures in history. If I have been persuasive in my account of events, it will show you to be a malfeasant, corrupt, and self-serving administrator, who has done all in his power to advance his own interests at the expense of the American taxpayer. I, on the other hand, appear as among the handful of American pioneers who, at great personal risk and without any expectation of financial benefit, took on a perilous and uncertain mission. It will accurately report that I carried out my mission under the most trying circumstances to ensure that the American taxpayer received the benefits of the billions of dollars expended on this secret program. I can assure you that everything I assert will be (1) true, (2) well-documented, and (3) verifiable.

The story will be in the upper right corner of every major newspaper in the world, will lead the evening news programs in every nation, and will be fully documented on the Internet.

There is, however, an alternative to this scenario. Under the Trust, I am the only person who can change the directions to the twenty-first century Trustee. If I alter the directions before September 1, we could publish a different story. In that version, you would resign after having led the Project to this momentous first mission. The President would issue full and unconditional pardons to Tess, Joey, and me. The country would honor my brother as one of the essential contributors to the success of my mission. It would fete and honor my wife for her courage in traveling to the twenty-first century. I would be the paladin of the successful mission and given the honors and recognition that my status justifies. You would assure that I retained an honorary position with the Project and be paid adequately for my services.

As a condition of the second scenario, you must apologize in writing to both my brother and my wife. It had better be good.

Finally, I think you should recognize Satrap for his role.

I will look forward to your prompt reply.

Sincerely, your humble servant,
Will Barrett

I reviewed the letter, understanding the risks I was facing. If Dolan chose to call my bluff, he would have a few days to set up a re-emptive strike to undermine the impact of the disclosures. My defense against his strike would be to include, in the escrowed material, copies of his undercover plunder program, including the taped meeting, as well as our letters, his blackmail to me, and my equally extortionery letter to him. Such disclosures wouldn't put me in the best of lights, but it would expose Dolan's corruption. He had more to lose than I did, especially since I would be dead for eighty or so years.

Of course, the biggest losers in a Mexican standoff could be Tess and Joey. They might be the collateral damage in the war. Even with the exposure of Dolan's misconduct, Joey could still face charges for assisting me in returning to 1876. Although the penalties would be nothing like Dolan threatened, he might end up with a conviction and a few years in prison.

Tess certainly wouldn't be prosecuted, but she'd never return to 1876, or, more importantly, to me. I would remain marooned in 1876 and she in 2010. Probably, she'd do fine in any era, and she'd get over me. At her age and with her unlimited beauty and personality, she might do better in 2010 than in 1876. I, in contrast, would never recover from her loss. On the positive side, I had resources, and I could travel the West following the sweep of historical events.

Accepting my fate, I actually planned my itinerary. Certainly, there was enough history to follow. I regretted that I'd already missed the August 2 shooting of Wild Bill Hickok in Deadwood, Dakota Territory. I'd also missed Custer's massacre in Montana Territory, which occurred in late June, just before my arrival, and was the main topic of conversation on the streets of Dodge when I arrived. I'd have plenty of time to be nearby when

Billy the Kid murderously escaped in Mesilla, New Mexico, in April 1881, only to be killed by Pat Garrett in a dark bedroom a few months later.

Of course, I couldn't miss the October 1881 Gunfight at the O.K. Corral in Tombstone, Arizona, or the violent retributions that followed. I would be renewing my acquaintance with Earp when I arrived.

I wasn't oblivious to the moral issues my presence presented. If I went to Deadwood, would I have had a duty to warn Hickok that Jack McCall was gunning for him? Certainly, I had no responsibility to protect Billy the Kid, but should I warn the Sheriff of Mesilla that Billy had a gun stashed in the latrine? Billy got what he deserved from Garrett, but the two men he killed in escaping custody in Mesilla didn't deserve to die. However, although my friend, Wyatt Earp, escaped uninjured from the Tombstone shootings, his life immediately thereafter was chaos. He faced murder charges (acquitted), lost his brother Morgan to an assassin, had his older brother Virgil maimed in another assassination attempt, and was himself banished from the Arizona Territory after his yearlong vendetta to kill the assassins. I knew the events leading up to the Gunfight, and could probably nudge history to avoid it ever happening. I'd have to think about that, and consider the possibility an alternative history I might create could end up with Wyatt in worse circumstances, perhaps even dying at the hands of the cowboys.

I read and re-read my letter to Dolan. I decided to sleep on it to give me time to reflect on any weaknesses in the plan. I slept well that night, a good sign. Nevertheless, I reviewed the letter again in the morning.

The letter wasn't perfect, and I could edit it forever. It might end up in every newspaper in the world, but I could become afflicted with paralysis by analysis and, with time, lose confidence. I was in that middle ground of feeling impulsively aggressive while still having enough reflective restraint to make me cautious.

I decided to take five more minutes to reconsider. Tick-tock, tick-tock—three hundred seconds ticked away as I stared at my computer screen. When they were gone, I had no further reservations. I burned a CD, and wrapped it in paper.

I found Satrap easily, gave him some more water, and fed him some scraps. I'd grown fond of him, and felt guilty sending him back into the hands of Dolan and his henchmen. Nonetheless, I led him out to Ground Zero, hobbled him, attached the device, and taped the CD to his side. I gave him one last pet, pressed the buttons, and stepped back.

My fate, and the fates of Tess and Joey, was now on its way to noisy, complex, and corrupt Washington. I took a deep breath, and walked back to SouthFord.

I assumed my letter would take a day or two to bring a response, if there were to be one. Dolan would have an arrangement in place that assured he'd read my response before anyone else. After he read my letter, he'd never let anyone else see it. He could, after private ruminations, frame a position he would present to the Project and, perhaps, to the President, without disclosing my proposal in detail.

I felt I was in a position of strength, but I knew I'd acted in isolation, with no opportunity to hear a dissenting opinion. I could've missed something. On the other hand, I didn't see I had other options. Either this worked, or I'd have to accept the nineteenth century as my home.

I couldn't know what course Dolan would take. Increasingly paranoid, I considered the possibility he'd send a team of assassins to kill me. Of course, they could kill me only after I told them the location of the incriminating data I'd placed in Trust. That would undermine my plan, assuming they could take out the Trustee and gain control of his entrustment.

Now, suddenly, my plan didn't look so solid. I needed to implement the Trust plan immediately and do more thinking about how to assure a death squad couldn't compromise its effectiveness. I had a lot of thinking—and worrying—to do in the next day or so.

Chapter 85

I again visited Ground Zero every day, and my anxiety increased when Satrap wasn't there on each of the next three days. I worried about Tess most of all, but Joey as well. Of course, I worried too that my foolproof plan had a huge hole in it. That is, beyond the obvious one that I might be taken prisoner, interrogated, and killed.

I'd already established the Trust and did so at two different banks in Kansas City. I wanted to go to the banks myself and personally make the arrangements, but I dared not leave SouthFord. Instead, I sent the Trust instruments, the accounts, and the data by train. I wired the banks about the arrival of the packages, and requested confirmation of their receipt. By the third day, I had confirmation from both banks of delivery, and of their willingness to take on the responsibilities.

Now, with two Trusts in place, I could give in to any torture and disclose one of the banks, but I would never disclose both. While I doubted the banks would compromise their fiduciary responsibilities, I didn't want to have too much faith in fallible human beings.

When I visited Ground Zero on the third day, I found that the food and water I'd left for Satrap hadn't been touched. I was out of ideas. I'd fired my round, and its effect was out of my control.

As I started my walk back to SouthFord, I heard a bark behind me. It was Satrap, and I ran back to greet him. I led him to the water and food, and relieved him of the envelope attached to his haunch while he ate.

The letter was hand-written by Dolan. He didn't disappoint me. He was as smarmy as ever. He wrote:

Dear Will,

It is clear that you have misunderstood me. My letter merely sought to bring to your attention how serious are the matters we're facing. While you and I have often disagreed, we have always found common ground on which to resolve our differences. That will certainly be the case here.

Much of what you have proposed is agreeable. In order to implement your suggestions, however, it will be necessary for you to return to Washington and finalize the details with me and with other officials having more authority than I have.

I will have men at the cemetery and will direct them to convey you directly to my office upon your arrival. I look forward to seeing you.

Sincerely,
John Dolan

Of course, I was gratified to learn that I'd misread his previous letter. And I was most relieved to see he'd agreed to my terms. I had no doubts he'd already released Tess and Joey, and had delivered his personal apologies to them. And I believed that Santa Claus would pick me up in his sleigh and carry me back to Washington.

I ripped off a piece of his letter. I wrote:

Dear Mr. Dolan,

September 1st is impending. I will not be returning until I have written confirmation from you accepting all my terms without conditions. An "official with more authority than [you]" must sign that confirmation.

Your humble servant,
Will Barrett

I re-taped the letter to Satrap, apologized to him for having to return him so quickly, and pressed the buttons to send him on his way.

I felt good heading back to SouthFord. Dolan had delayed the three days to put pressure on me to return without a deal. I felt the pressure, but my confidence in the plan returned. If he didn't cave in, the damning material would be published, and, presumably, Tess and I would be reunited anyway. I believed I had the winning hand. But, then again, Wild Bill Hickok believed his aces-and-eights was a winning hand, too.

With just two days left, I checked Ground Zero twice a day. The difficult walks out there wouldn't be as stressful as being back at SouthFord worrying—worrying about Washington, worrying about Tess, or worse, worrying that Satrap had returned, enjoyed his water and food, and headed out in the wrong direction onto the prairie.

I visited Ground Zero just after 8:00 A.M. on the 30th. Nothing. No evidence that Satrap had been there. I had a nagging worry that some other animals would eat the food and give me a false indication of Satrap's return. So far, that hadn't happened.

I returned to SouthFord and spent the next several hours trying to fill the time. Not very successfully. I gave up and revisited the site at noon. Nothing.

The afternoon didn't pass any better. I was exhausted and unsuccessfully tried to nap. I sweated terribly from both the heat and the anxiety. I couldn't eat and could barely keep water down. I had diarrhea constantly, and was weak from dehydration. I knew my symptoms were stress-related, and I repeatedly dragged myself out of the house, alternately to the outhouse and to the pump.

As the afternoon waned, I marshaled what energy I had to make one last trip to Ground Zero. I drank as much water as I could in preparation for the trek. I filled a canteen, but, just as I started out, I started vomiting and had to retreat to the outhouse. I was getting sicker and weaker by the hour. I feared that, if this trip were again fruitless, I might not have the strength to make it the next day.

I drank some more water and started out.

I laboriously approached Ground Zero, moving like a mountain climber at very high altitude—two steps, rest; two steps, rest, and so on. It made for slow going, but I dared not sit down, for fear that I wouldn't be able to get up

I reached the site as the sun was setting. I squinted from a hundred yards, but saw nothing. I tried again at fifty yards, but my vision was deteriorating along with the rest of my body, and I no longer saw clearly. As I got closer, I grew increasingly depressed. Nothing. No Satrap. No evidence he'd been there. Nothing but disappointment.

I collapsed on the ground and started crying. Crying for me, crying for Tess, crying for Joey, and crying for being such a fool. My body was so frail and weak, I couldn't sustain a good cry. I stopped abruptly and just lay on my back. With neither the strength nor the will to get up, I considered cutting myself to attract wolves to the smell of my blood. I felt even more a failure when I realized I didn't have a knife with me. With no knife or any sharp stones, I couldn't even kill myself.

Another failure. My whole life a failure. A failure to me. A failure to Tess. A failure to Joey and my whole family. Moreover, if the truth be known, a failed mutineer. I finally admitted to myself that I had no right to hijack the device and return to Dodge. It was a selfish act that jeopardized the project and all of my friends there.

I cried again, but no tears came. I still had the canteen, and it was half-full, but it went to waste, because I couldn't raise my arm to pull it to me.

The only benefit of my collapse was that I no longer entertained any hopes of winning my contest with Dolan. I felt no anxiety, because I no longer believed there was a contest. I was beaten, and I was going to die in the middle of nowhere. I fell asleep expecting never to wake up again.

But I did awake, several times during the night. Each time, I fell back to sleep quickly when I remembered my plight. My mouth was pasted together from dehydration. I couldn't swallow, and had trouble breathing. The merciful end wasn't far off.

In my dreams, I remembered the vultures that greeted me when I first arrived in Kansas. They'd be circling in the morning and, when they saw no movement, they'd descend and start pecking me to pieces. My eyes first, then the soft flesh of my face. Eventually, I would cease to exist, only a pile of bones. I didn't care.

However, I didn't die so quickly. The night and my pathetic existence endured. At dawn, I wasn't yet dead, and I heard the rustlings of prairie dogs scraping through the grasses in search of breakfast. I also heard a larger animal not far off, undoubtedly the first wolf to smell death. He would attract others. When they came, I wouldn't fight back.

I heard him come closer. When he reached me, I didn't even bother to look at him. I could sense him a few feet away, and pictured him lurking, his eyes and ears alert, ready to attack. Even in my despair, even though I wanted to die, I cringed when he came up and smelled me. I felt his hot breath on my face and waited for his rapacious teeth to tear at my cheeks and neck.

He made noises, almost whimpers. I tired of waiting for

him to strike. "Do it, dammit," I screamed to myself.

And, then, he did. His breath inches from my nose, he licked me. Licked me! I'd clenched my muscles in anticipation of a vicious battle and a slow and grisly death. Now, I froze, my mind not processing what just happened. I opened my eyes and, even with everything blurred, I saw Satrap! No wolves in sight. Satrap had returned.

I was elated, but it took me a few moments to recall the significance of Satrap being back in Kansas. I petted him as I put the pieces together. I now had the energy to reach for the canteen. My lips were cracked and covered with dust, and they didn't work very well but, with great effort, I was able to spill some water onto and, eventually, into my mouth.

But Satrap was back!

I struggled onto my knees and pulled Satrap around to locate his cargo. Again, it was an envelope, larger this time. I pulled it off, sent Satrap over to his water and food, and sat up to rip the envelope open. It was Dolan's handwriting again.

Dear Will,

It's time to let bygones be bygones. I am hurt and disappointed that you would question my good faith, but I understand that circumstances might be influencing your judgment. Therefore, I have carried out your wishes and have obtained the pardons you requested. I enclose copies. I also enclose a copy of my resignation, which the President said he would accept.

I agree to all of your terms. You have my word for that, as well as this letter confirming my agreement.

We've already released Mrs. Barrett and Joseph, and they have my written apologies for the misunderstandings.

Please transport yourself back to Washington immediately, and we will put the arrangement into operation. I will look forward to seeing you shortly.

Sincerely,
John Dolan

I looked at the photocopies of the pardons. They looked authentic, and the President's signatures looked real.

Aha, I thought. It's over, and we've won. Dolan was out. Tess was free, and we'd be reunited. I fell back on the grass again, this time full of energy. It was time to go back.

I called Satrap over, and switched the device from his leg to mine.

"I'm sorry I have to leave you like this," I said, petting him on the nose. "I can't take you with me."

Chapter 86

One hundred and thirty-four years later, I arrived in a cemetery in the middle of noisy, hot, and claustrophobic Washington. As soon as I appeared, two men jumped out of a car and rushed to me, their dark suits bulging with guns. The guns never came out, but determination was apparent on their faces. They didn't have to tell me they were there to take me into custody at all costs.

I signaled them to relax by snapping my finger at them, smiling, and nodding. They got the message that I had no intention of bolting. Nonetheless, they continued toward me as fast as they could walk, never taking their eyes from me.

"Mr. Barrett, I presume?" the shorter, gray-haired one asked.

"Of course," I said.

"You need to come with us," he said. The men took positions on both sides of me, and gestured toward their car. Neither one of them touched me, but the implied threat of physical force was present.

We walked to the car together. They weren't into small talk and never identified themselves. The taller, younger agent (I decided his name was Bret) opened the back door of the black Town Car and waved me in. As I stooped and slid in, the older agent hurried to the other side and climbed in next to me. Of course, the door didn't open from the inside.

Bret got behind the wheel and reported to someone that we were "onboard." He was wearing an earpiece, and spoke into a mike hidden somewhere on his suit.

They carried me to the Washington Plaza Hotel, and escorted me up to the fourth floor on the elevator. They opened room 4475, and signaled me in. Although they hadn't commented on my frontier clothes, Bret told me there were appropriate clothes in the closet, and that I should take a shower.

"Twenty minutes," the older agent said brusquely. (I decided he was "Jake.") He closed the door and probably took positions on either side of the door in case anyone was foolish enough to try to rescue me. Jake didn't tell me what I had twenty minutes to do. I really didn't care—I doubted he'd come in and drag me from the shower if I tarried too long. They'd simply have to wait for me.

I looked at myself in one of the several mirrors in the room. I was unimpressive: gaunt, sunburned, and sunken eyed, and sporting a three-day beard. Besides that, I was dusty, dirty, and undoubtedly smelled of the nineteenth century. Altogether, with my shabby, drab clothes, I looked like a man out of his time.

"Clothes do make the man," I said to myself. Despite the stern demeanors of Jake and Bret, I remained in good spirits, looking forward to seeing Tess.

I took my time in the shower, and was toweling myself, when there was a knock on the door. Without waiting for me, Bret opened the door and told me, when I peeked out of the bathroom, that I had guests.

Was it Dolan and his henchmen? Was it Joey and Tess? I opted for friends and hurried my toilet. I shaved quickly, and put on the white shirt and blue suit I found hanging in the closet.

When I was fully presentable, I went to the door.

To my timeless joy, Tess stood right outside the door, looking nervous and impatient. Her face changed as soon as she saw me. She leapt at me. I hugged her as if I hadn't seen her for more than a century.

"Oh, my darling," she said, sounding as if she were in the nineteenth century. I kissed and held her. Then, I noticed Joey standing to the side, and reached out my hand to him.

"I'm sorry I put you through this," I said.

He seemed glad to see me, and showed no ill humor toward me. I invited them in. Jake and Bret held the door open, allowing the reunion to continue, but unmistakably indicating we weren't to take long.

"Where do we go from here?" I asked Joey.

He shrugged theatrically. "Damned if I know. A couple of goons came and got us from our rooms and dragged us here."

"Are you ready?" Jake asked.

"Where are we going?" I asked.

He gestured with his head that we were to leave the room. When we didn't immediately do so, he said, "Let's go."

"I'm afraid I'm not going anywhere until I meet with a friend of mine," I said.

Jake glared at me for a moment before stepping out into the hall. I could hear him speaking into his high-tech, government-issued microphone, but I couldn't hear what he said. He stuck his head back in.

"Bill Brohawn, State Department," I said. "He'll take my call."

I went to the sofa and spoke with Brohawn. He agreed to come to my room immediately.

Bill arrived within twenty minutes, and was immediately admitted. I asked Joey and Tess to wait outside while we spoke. They didn't have to wait long. Brohawn and I emerged within two minutes, and I gestured toward the elevators. The six of us made our way out of the hotel. The black Town Car remained where we'd left it, with a smaller, black Cadillac parked behind it.

Joey," I said. "Why don't you ride with Bill."

Jake touched Joey's arm. "Get in," he said, pointing to the Town Car. Joey got in.

I told Brohawn to follow us.

Bret didn't immediately put the car in gear.

"Mr. Barrett," he said without looking back, "we were told to drive you to a bank. Can you tell us which one?"

After I paused just long enough to annoy him, I told him, "First National on K Street NorthWest."

We drove off.

Brohawn's car pulled in behind us as we parked illegally in front of the bank.

Of course, I'd never met the Trustee, but found him to be an affable, professional man. When I told him who I was, he went to a vault outside our sight. He returned a few minutes, accompanies by two bank guards.

He ushered us into a small conference room, and placed a folder and a metal box on the table. He looked uneasily at Jake and Bret.

"Now, what can I do for you?" he asked.

I explained that the Trust provided I could change the directions for his action set for September 1, and that I wished to do so.

"Yes," he acknowledged. "It also requires that I obtain identification from you, and that you give me a password."

I showed him my driver's license, my passport, and my STRP badge, all of which were in the hotel room when I arrived. He looked them over, sent them for copying, and turned back to me.

"And the password?" he asked.

I wrote 'Tess made me do it' and passed it to him.

As he was reading it, Tess leaned across the table and read it upside down.

"Tess?" Tess asked laughing. "You're blaming me?"

The Trustee acknowledged the password, returned the scrap to me, and pushed a single sheet of paper across the desk to me. I read it, added some words, and confirmed that it carried out my new directions. I signed, and had Brohawn and Joey witness it. A woman notarized my signature. The Trustee directed the woman to take a digital photo of me, and attach the photo and the copies of the identifications to the new directive.

I directed the Trustee to provide a copy to Jake. He did so. He also handed the contents of the file to me; I, in turn, handed them to Jake.

I shook the Trustee's hand and left. Our feelings of freedom and exhilaration increased—we'd finished one more step toward completion of our part of the bargain.

As we walked out into the sunlight, we paused for just a moment. As we did so, however, Jake and Bret walked away and got in the Town Car. Within seconds, three men walked up to me. They, too, wore dark glasses and suits. They must have used the same costume department as Bret and Jake. They crowded around me before I could say anything.

"Mr. Barrett," the huskiest one said. "You'll have to come with us."

He nodded at the others. They handcuffed Tess, Joey, and me in seconds. Brohawn stepped away from us. I turned and looked at him. He nodded and left.

They corralled us into three separate black cars and, without further explanation, drove to the same federal holding facility that had previously held Tess and Joey. They locked us in adjacent jail cells, still without any explanation.

As soon as the jailers left, Tess came over to our common wall and, in tears, said, "Will?"

I winked at her to reassure her. Her beautiful face showed so much strain. I wished I could tell her that everything was going to be all right.

Just then, the door down the hall loudly clanked open, and Dolan strutted in, accompanied by a couple of more dark suits.

"You're scum," I said mildly.

"You didn't think I was going to let you get away with your little game, did you?" he asked arrogantly.

"We had a deal and presidential pardons," I said evenly.

"Mere paperwork," he said. "The pardons were defective, it turns out. And, by the way, your Trustee is in custody as a material witness. He'll cooperate, I'm sure."

He had it all covered.

Just then, the hallway door clanked open again. The jailer led two more dark suits in. The jailer walked over to my cell and unlocked it.

"Just a minute," sputtered Dolan. "What are you doing?"

The jailer unlocked Joey and Tess's cells in turn. The jailer stepped back and turned to the men he'd led in. They moved over to a bewildered Dolan and took his arms. One of them looked up at me, and signaled for me to leave my cell. When I did, he pushed Dolan in.

"What's the meaning of this?" he demanded.

They didn't answer, but gestured for Joey and Tess to exit their cells also.

The jailer told us to pick up our belongings at the front desk. "You're free to go," he said.

When we got back outside into the sunlight again, Tess turned to me.

"What just happened?" she demanded. Despite her tone, she was visibly relieved to be back on the street.

I looked at Joey. He shrugged. He was along for the ride, and was letting things happen as they happened.

"You remember I insisted on Brohawn being there with us.

Well, I didn't tell you he's Under Secretary of State and has been a close friend of mine since college. He also happens to be a close friend of the President's Chief of Staff.

"When I met privately with him, I told him where to find a second complete copy of the incriminating evidence and a summary of what had occurred, including our negotiations and settlement. Knowing Dolan, I expected something like this. I told Bill that if something went wrong, he should bring the evidence to the Chief of Staff with a request that he show it to the President immediately. I guess he did.

Just then, my cell phone rang. It was Bill.

"Yes," I said into the phone. "We're fine. Thanks for all your help."

I hung up and confirmed to Joey and Tess what Brohawn had told me. "The President was meeting with the Prime Minister of Israel, but he'd interrupted the meeting to read the summary. I guess he had Dolan's number, too, because he directed our immediate release, Dolan's arrest, and preparation of authentic pardons. We're all invited to the State dinner tonight."

Tess was in tears again. "I guess," she said, "you're smarter than you look."

We hugged each other.

I shook Joey's hand and tears came into both of our eyes.

He spoke first. "It's always interesting with you, Will, always interesting."

I smiled through my tears. We hugged.

I didn't bother telling them about the duplicate Trust still in place right across the street in the Bank of America. I found it ironic that I had planted these trusts more than 130 years ago and they ended up across the street from each other, one at 1800 K Street NW and one at 1801.

My material revealed to the President the existence of the second Trust and the fact that the Trustee would release the information to the media on September 1 as directed. He apparently had no objections, and I wasn't going to cancel it unless he instructed me to. Dolan deserved the public humiliation.

Chapter 87

I caught Joey looking at me during the State dinner. He made a face at me, trying to get me to laugh aloud. We both looked ridiculous in black tie. In contrast, Tess stole the show in her designer dress. I never thought I'd attend a State dinner, and I certainly never expected my wife to steal the attention from the President of the United States.

The President met with me after the dinner. He asked a few details, and nodded his head when I confirmed what he seemed to know already. He then gave me some information, including that there was going to be a ticker tape parade to celebrate my mission, that he would name me, if I accepted, to be head of STRP, and that Tess and I would have lifetime passes to visit Dodge, or any other place on earth and at any time in history, whenever we wanted.

I thanked the President, but indicated I'd have to speak with Tess about where, and when, we would live. He smiled knowingly. "I understand," he said.

"There is one thing, sir," I said.

He cocked his eyebrow at me.

"There's this dog still back in 1876 . . ."

"We'll get him back," he said, smiling.

As I left, the President told me he'd directed the preparation of the real presidential pardons. He would issue them privately at the White House before the public celebration.

I told Tess immediately of the President's proposal, and explained that, if I accepted, we'd have to live in Washington. Although Washington and the twenty-first century still bewildered her, she saw my excitement that the President would appoint me head of the *Space Time Research Project*. With a smile, she agreed to live in Washington for at least a year. That was good enough for me and, in turn, I agreed that, if she wanted out, I'd return to Dodge and SouthFord forever.

Chapter 88

I sat uneasily on the platform behind the Capitol as I looked out at hundreds of thousands of people, knowing they were all there to see and honor me. Although it had taken me 134 years to reach this point, I felt like my life had changed overnight.

As the President finished introducing me, Tess leaned over to me and patted my arm. She whispered in my ear, "We'll do just fine on a government salary." She patted my arm again, and smiled as brightly as she could. In the short time since the dinner, and the President's offer to appoint me to head STRP, Tess had done some considerable research, on the Internet of all things, and she now had a firm grasp of the measure of money in the twenty-first century and in Washington. She was no longer thinking in terms of what my salary would mean in 1876.

I took a paper out of my pocket and handed it to her.

She looked at it with a confused look on her face. The President had turned toward me, gesturing with his hand for me to come to the podium.

"Twenty-seven thousand dollars?" she asked, bouncing her head a little to show she was confused.

It was a current brokerage statement for Tess and me.

"Look again," I said as I stood to join the President.

She looked again, and her eyes opened wide.

"Twenty-seven million dollars," she mouthed. I was still next to her.

"I invested the Dodge City money and, somehow, I avoided the big crashes and recessions," I said with a wink. "The President has waived any government claim to the money."

"Twenty seven million dollars!" she said, a little too loud. Now it was me patting her arm as I stepped toward the President.

"Ladies and gentlemen," the President repeated. "I am proud to present the Presidential Medal of Freedom to Williamson Barrett, the first time traveler in the history of man, and the new head of the *Space Time Research Project*."

Three hundred thousand people stood and cheered for me. I turned and looked at Tess. Hers was the only approval I needed. She was standing and smiling. She cupped her right hand up next to her eye, and pushed her index finger down as if she were taking a picture of me.

- The End -

ABOUT THE AUTHOR

Gerald B. Keane is the author of *Florida Law: A Layman's Guide* and *Florida Divorce Handbook*, both published by Pineapple Press of Sarasota Florida. He holds a degree in Mechanical Engineering and worked on ICBMs, high-powered lasers, and the Apollo Moon Program. He is currently an attorney and lives with his wife of 46 years on the west coast of Florida. Both of his children are also attorneys.

Gerald B. Keane

ACKNOWLEDGMENT

This book would not have been possible without the generous help provided by **Fred Young**, the world's greatest expert on the history of Dodge City, and by **Dave Webb** at the Kansas Heritage Center. In addition, while many members of the Sarasota Fiction Writers and Fiction Writers Forum have provided helpful insights and support, I am especially grateful to **Pat Gray** and **Amy Ratcliffe** for their invaluable suggestions, and to **Bill Carrigan** for his many lessons on writing mechanics.

JFK's Last Motorcade

The sequel to SomeWhere SomeTime will soon be available. An excerpt follows.

Dallas, Texas
November 22, 1963

No man could be comfortable waiting to shoot the President of the United States. And so it was for Lee Oswald as he sat with a high-powered rifle overlooking Dealey Plaza. A cool breeze wafted through the open window in front of him, but the twenty-four-year-old man was sweating, sweating so badly he had to wipe his brow to keep drops from running into his eyes.

The day had started cloudy and unpromising, but the sun had won out in the last hour, leaving the day crisp and clear. The sun was so bright that Oswald had to squint to see the crowd lining the street six floors below.

Earlier in the day, he'd built a fort four- and five-boxes high around the sixth floor window. At the window itself, he'd carefully arranged three more boxes as a rest for his rifle. Now, holding his mail-order Mannlicher-Carcano on his lap, he pumped his knee to quell his nerves.

He lifted each of his hands off the rifle in turn and wiped it on his pants. When he rewiped his forehead, however, his palms were wet again, so he leaned the rifle against the wall of boxes and ran both palms down his thighs to dry them. While he did so, he took a couple of deep breaths, and said to himself, barely audibly, "It's okay to be nervous."

Oswald had sat alone on the sixth floor in his mini-fort for almost fifteen minutes. His fellow workers were either eating lunch below or were out on the street to see the President. When Oswald had slipped into his hideout just before noon, he took his dismantled rifle from the brown paper wrapper he'd used to carry it into the Texas School Book Depository that morning. Now, it took him only ninety seconds to reassemble the gun. Then, he removed high-velocity military bullets from his right-hand pocket and inserted them, one by one, into the rifle until he had four cartridges pushed down into the magazine. He listened for any sound to be sure no one was nearby before he thrust the bolt forward and down to chamber a round. Now that he was ready, he again leaned the rifle against the wall of cardboard boxes.

He was sitting back from the window to keep out of sight, but he leaned forward briefly to look down at the crowd again. People lined the sidewalks on both Houston Street, almost straight-ahead of him, and Elm Street, which passed below his window. Before retrieving his rifle, Oswald extended his empty left hand, palm up, onto the boxes in front of him, and hoisted his right hand up near his cheek. He closed his left eye and sighted down Elm over an imaginary rifle. Because of how the street snaked away from the building, Oswald was able to aim directly down the roadway. His heartbeats accelerated as he curled his right index finger three times. "Pow, pow, pow," he said in a voice just above a whisper.

He was about to reach for the real rifle when a sharp sound caused him to freeze. His attention sharpened, he listened to hear if someone else were on the sixth floor. When he heard no further sound, he let out a breath of relief. It must have been from below.

Oswald wiped his hands on his pants again before picking up the rifle. He rested the butt on the floor, closed his eyes, and reviewed what the Marines had taught him. "Deep breath, hold it, sque-e-e-eze the trigger," he said to himself. He bit his tongue slightly, just as he did when he was a Marine, to remind himself to hold his breath as he fired. "Let the rifle fire itself."

As he reviewed those instructions, he was breathing so hard, almost panting, and he worried he might not be able to hold his breath long enough to get off the three shots. His stomach felt hollow and his hands tingled. He'd been never been so nervous before.

"You can do this," he muttered to himself. "Calm, calm. Take a breath. They trained you to kill. Now it's time to put it into practice."

Oswald glanced out the window again, looking up Houston toward the corner of Main Street, where the motorcade would emerge and turn toward him onto Houston. Nothing had changed—the people still milled aimlessly.

"Come on, you son of a bitch," he mouthed. "Where are you?"

After saying that, he momentarily felt sorry for Kennedy and his wife. He didn't hate them. This was just something he had to do. The brightness outside made his eyes water, and he blinked to both clear the tears from his eyes and his mind of any further sympathy.

"Don't screw this up, Oswald," he said. "You've done this before. You know how to do it."

He was referring to the time he'd fired through a window at that crazy right-winger, General Edwin Walker a few weeks earlier. Oswald just barely missed his single shot, and he escaped without being caught. He dismissed the idea that he'd fail again. The attempt on Walker was just a training mission, he thought—just preparation for this.

Come on, come on. His hands were tingling worse, and his palms were again dripping with sweat. He wiped his brow once more, and dried his hand on his thigh. He shifted the rifle to that hand and dried his other hand the same way. Come on, come on, he thought, as his legs chattered up and down. He needed to get up and walk—heck, he needed to take a leak—but he couldn't leave his perch. Kennedy was due any minute.

Oswald's attention sharpened. He heard motorcycles—or had he? He leaned toward the window, and cocked his ear. There it was again—yes, they were coming. He wiped his hands again and gripped the rifle to steel himself. He stopped pumping his legs as he got ready. His stomach and bladder still jumped around on him, and his heart pounded in his chest. He quickly blinked several times. He was ready.

The sound of the motorcycles was louder now. Their thumping increased in pitch as they approached the corner of Main and Houston, and the spectators on Houston jostled for positions nearer the curb. Although buildings still blocked his view of the motorcade, Oswald could almost picture it coming up the street. The people lining Houston Street craned their heads toward Main, waiting for the first motorcycled officer to reach the corner. Everyone, and everything, was suddenly in motion.

Oswald was still sitting back from the window on the box of books while he watched intently for the lead car to turn onto Houston. First, however, came a number of motorcycles, then the pilot car, the car sent ahead to clear the roadway. Just as he was about to get in position to shoot, there was nothing turning onto Houston. There were no more cars after the pilot car. Oswald's eyes jumped around in panic, but then, as the lead motorcycles and pilot car were almost turning onto Elm, another group of motorcycles, and then a car and more motorcycles reached the corner of Houston and Main.

Finally, Oswald saw the Presidential limousine. Flags on the front fenders flapped wildly in the wind, and he could almost hear them over the thunder of the motorcycles. Jackie, in a bright pink hat and outfit, caught his eye. Then, to her right, he saw Kennedy. Oswald was briefly filled with awe—he was looking at the President of the United States.

But he had a job to do. The Presidential car slowly covered the seventy or so yards from Main to Elm and, for a moment, Oswald considered firing a shot as the car approached. It would have been so easy, but he restrained himself. Take your time. Follow your plan. Besides, with the boxes stacked in front of him as they were, he couldn't easily get a shot up Houston.

So, instead, Oswald raised the rifle onto the boxes and pointed it to the right, down Elm. He kept the barrel inside the window for now, looking left as Kennedy come closer. The car was now almost directly below him, and he could see Kennedy smiling as he waved to bystanders. Oh, he was so close. The thumping of ten motorcycles shook the windows as Oswald took a deep breath.

As the limousine made the turn, and crept under the oak tree and onto Elm, Oswald slid off the box and onto his left knee. He inched the rifle forward until the muzzle was just outside the window and leaned forward so his eye was on the telescopic sight. He aimed over the tree and onto the middle of Elm, as the lead car slipped into his view. Oswald briefly aimed at the driver as he hooked his finger onto the trigger. He waited, seemingly forever, for Kennedy to emerge from the tree. Then, he was there, and Oswald move to adjust his aim to put the crosshairs on his target.

As he moved the rifle, he flinched and yanked off a shot without intending to. It flew off to who knows where.

"Oh, Oswald, you dick," he muttered as he gulped two

shallow breaths and quickly worked the bolt. "Don't screw this up. Aim. Take . . . your . . . time. Hit the bastard. You can't miss."

Now he had the crosshairs on Kennedy's head. Remember your Marine training, he told himself. This time he aimed before firing . . .

www.ingramcontent.com/pod-product-compliance
Lightning Source LLC
Chambersburg PA
CBHW070825260626
47170CB00007B/2267